Praise for *The Miseducation of Cameron Post:*

"*The Miseducation of Cameron Post* is indeed an important book—especially for teens growing up today in communities that don't accept them for who they are. But it is also a skillfully and beautifully written story that does what the best books do: It invites us to find ourselves in the lives of others."   **—Malinda Lo, NPR.org**

"For LGBT youth and outsiders everywhere, Cameron's story will take on epic resonance."   **—*Entertainment Weekly***

". . . Danforth has crafted a story that's likely to be remembered long after readers of any sexual orientation have put it down."
            —*Los Angeles Times*

"You'll love it if you've ever struggled to come to terms with a part of yourself that you fear others might not accept. *Miseducation* is incredibly well-written, and stays lighthearted throughout, even as Cam faces serious social prejudices and her own internal dilemmas."   **—Seventeen.com**

"The story is riveting, beautiful, and full of the kind of detail that brings to life a place (rural Montana), a time (the early 1990s), and a questioning teenage girl."   **—*Publishers Weekly*** (starred review)

"Rich with detail and emotion, a sophisticated read for teens and adults alike."   **—*Kirkus Reviews*** (starred review)

"There is nothing superficial or simplistic here, and Danforth carefully and deliberately fleshes out Cam's character and that of her family and friends. Even the eastern Montana setting is vividly realized and provides a wonderfully apposite background for the story of Cam's miseducation."   **—ALA *Booklist*** (starred review)

"This finely crafted, sophisticated coming-of-age debut novel is multilayered, finessing such issues as loss, first love, and friendship. An excellent read for both teens and adults."
—*School Library Journal* (starred review)

"If Holden Caulfield had been a gay girl from Montana, this is the story he might have told—it's funny, heartbreaking, and beautifully rendered. Emily Danforth remembers exactly what it's like to be a teenager, and she has written a new classic."
—**Curtis Sittenfeld**, bestselling author of *Prep* and *American Wife*

"A beautifully told story that is at once engaging and thoughtful. *The Miseducation of Cameron Post* is an important book—one that can change lives." —**Jacqueline Woodson**, award-winning author of *After Tupac and D Foster* and *Hush*

"This novel is a joy—one of the best and most honest portraits of a young lesbian I've read in years. Cameron Post is a bright, brash, funny main character who leaps off the page and into your heart."
—**Nancy Garden**, award-winning author of *Annie on My Mind*

"A story of love, desire, pain, loss—and, above all, of survival. An inspiring read." —**Sarah Waters**, author of *Tipping the Velvet* and *The Little Stranger*

USA Today New Voices pick
Publishers Weekly Flying Start
Boston Globe Best Young Adult Book
ALA *Booklist* Editors' Choice
Kirkus Reviews Best Teen Book
School Library Journal Best Book
Winner of the Montana Book Award
LAMBDA Literary Award Finalist
AfterEllen.com Visibility Awards: Best Book

The MISEDUCATION of CAMERON POST

emily m. danforth

BALZER + BRAY

An Imprint of HarperCollinsPublishers

Balzer + Bray is an imprint of HarperCollins Publishers.

An altered version of the first chapter of this novel was previously published in *Dogwood: A Journal of Poetry and Prose.*

The Miseducation of Cameron Post
Copyright © 2012 by Emily M. Danforth
Art on pages 188, 251, 286, and 296 copyright © 2012 by Marcus Tegtmeier
All rights reserved. Printed in the United States of America.
No part of this book may be used or reproduced in any manner whatsoever without written permission except in the case of brief quotations embodied in critical articles and reviews. For information address HarperCollins Children's Books, a division of HarperCollins Publishers, 195 Broadway, New York, NY 10007.
www.epicreads.com

Library of Congress Cataloging-in-Publication Data
Danforth, Emily M.
    The miseducation of Cameron Post / Emily M. Danforth. — 1st ed.
        p.   cm.
    Summary: In the early 1990s, when gay teenager Cameron Post rebels against her conservative Montana ranch town and her family decides she needs to change her ways, she is sent to a gay conversion therapy center.
    ISBN 978-0-06-202057-4 — ISBN 978-0-06-288449-7 (special edition)
    1. Lesbians—Fiction.   2. Gays—Fiction.   3. Orphans—Fiction.   4. Montana—Fiction.]   I. Title.   II. Title: Mis-education of Cameron Post.
PZ7.D2136Mi   2012   2011001947
[Fic]—dc22   CIP
                                                                                     AC

Typography by Erich Nagler
18   19   20   21   22   PC/LSCH   30   29   28   27   26   25   24   23   22   21
❖
First paperback edition, 2013

For my parents, Duane and Sylvia Danforth,
who filled our home with books and stories

Part One

Summer 1989

CHAPTER ONE

The afternoon my parents died, I was out shoplifting with Irene Klauson.

Mom and Dad had left for their annual summer camping trip to Quake Lake the day before, and Grandma Post was down from Billings *minding me*, so it only took a little convincing to get her to let me have Irene spend the night. "It's too hot for shenanigans, Cameron," Grandma had told me, right after she said yes. "But we gals can still have us a time."

Miles City had been cooking in the high nineties for days, and it was only the end of June, hot even for eastern Montana. It was the kind of heat where a breeze feels like someone's venting a dryer out over the town, whipping dust and making the cottonseeds from the big cottonwoods float across a wide blue sky and collect in soft tufts on neighborhood lawns. Irene and I called it summer snow, and sometimes we'd squint into the dry glare and try to catch cotton on our tongues.

My bedroom was the converted attic of our house on Wibaux Street, with peaking rafters and weird angles, and it just baked during the summer. I had a grimy window fan, but all it did was blow in wave after wave of hot air and dust and, every once in a while, early in the morning, the smell of fresh-cut grass.

Irene's parents had a big cattle ranch out toward Broadus, and even all the way out there—once you turned off MT 59 and it was rutted roads through clumps of gray sagebrush and pink sandstone hills that sizzled and crisped in the sun—the Klausons had central air. Mr. Klauson was that big of a cattle guy. When I stayed at Irene's house, I woke with the tip of my nose cold to the touch. And they had an ice maker in the door of their fridge, so we had crushed ice in our orange juice and ginger ale, a drink we mixed up all the time and called "cocktail hour."

My solution to the lack of air conditioning at my own house was to run our T-shirts under the cold, cold tap water in the bathroom sink. Then wring them out. Then soak the shirts again before Irene and I shivered into them, like putting on a new layer of icy, wet skin before we got into bed. Our sleep shirts crusted over during the night, drying and hardening with the hot air and dust like they had been lightly starched, the way Grandma did the collars of my dad's dress shirts.

By seven that morning it was already in the eighties, and our bangs stuck to our foreheads, our faces red and dented with pillow marks, gray crud in the corners of our eyes. Grandma Post let us have leftover peanut-butter pie for breakfast while she played solitaire, occasionally looking up through her thick glasses at the *Perry Mason* rerun she had on, the volume blasting. Grandma Post loved her detective stories. A little before eleven she drove us to Scanlan Lake in her maroon Chevy Bel Air. Usually I rode my bike to swim team, but Irene didn't have one in town. We'd left the windows down, but the Bel Air was still all filled up with the kind of heat that can only trap itself in a car. Irene and I fought over shotgun when my mom was driving, or her mom was driving, but when we were riding in the Bel Air, we sat in the backseat and pretended to be in the Grey Poupon commercials, with Grandma as our chauffeur, her tenaciously black hair in a newly set permanent just visible to us over the seat back.

The ride took maybe a minute and a half down Main Street (including the stop sign and two stop lights): past Kip's Minute Market, which had Wilcoxin's hardpack ice cream and served scoops almost too big for the cones; past the funeral homes, which stood kitty-corner from one another; through the underpass beneath the train tracks; past the banks where they gave us Dum-Dum Pops when our parents deposited paychecks, the library, the movie theater, a strip of bars, a park—these places the stuff of all small towns, I guess, but they were our places, and back then I liked knowing that.

"Now you come home right after you're done," Grandma said, pulling up in front of the blocky cement lifeguard shack and changing rooms that everybody called the bathhouse. "I don't want you two monkeying around downtown. I'm cuttin' up a watermelon, and we can have Ritz and cheddar for lunch."

She *toot-toot*ed at us as she rolled away toward Ben Franklin, where she was planning to buy even more yarn for her ever-expanding crocheting projects. I remember her honking like that, a little *pep-in-her-step*, she would have said, because it was the last time for a long time that I saw her in just that sort of mood.

"Your grandma is crazy," Irene told me, extending the word *crazy* and rolling her heavy brown eyes.

"How's she crazy?" I asked, but I didn't let her answer. "You don't seem to mind her when she's giving you pie for breakfast. Two pieces."

"That still doesn't mean she's not a nutter," Irene said, yanking hard on one end of the beach towel I had snaked over my shoulders. It slapped against my bare legs before thwacking the concrete.

"Two pieces," I said again, gripping the towel, Irene laughing. "Second-helping Sally."

Irene kept on giggling, dancing away from my reach. "She's completely crazy, totally, totally nuts—mental-patient nuts."

This is how things usually went with Irene and me. It was best friends or sworn enemies with no filler in between. We tied for top grades in first through sixth. On the Presidential Fitness Tests she beat me at chin-ups and the long jump and I killed her on push-ups, sit-ups, and the fifty-yard dash. She'd win the spelling bee. I'd win the science fair.

Irene once dared me to dive from the old Milwaukee Railroad bridge. I did, and split my head against a car engine sunk into the black mud of the river. Fourteen stitches—the big ones. I dared her to saw down the yield sign on Strevell Avenue, one of the last street signs in town with a wooden base. She did. Then she had to let me keep it, because there was no way of getting it back to her ranch.

"My grandma's just old," I said, circling my wrist and lassoing the towel down by my feet. I was trying to twist it thick enough to use it as a whip, but Irene had that figured out.

She jumped backward, away from me, colliding with a just-finished swim-lesson kid still wearing his goggles. She partially lost a flip-flop in the process. It slid forward and hung from a couple of toes. "Sorry," she said, not looking at the dripping kid or his mom but kicking the flip-flop ahead of her so she could stay out of my reach.

"You girls need to watch out for these little guys," the mom told me, because I was closest to her and I had a towel-whip dangling, and because it was always me who got the talking-to when it came to Irene and me. Then the mom grabbed the goggle boy's hand as though he was seriously hurt. "You shouldn't be playing around in the parking lot anyway," she said, and pulled her son away, walking faster than his little sandaled feet could quite keep up.

I put the towel back around my shoulders and Irene came over to me, both of us watching the mom load swim-lesson kid into their minivan. "She's nasty," Irene said. "You should run over and pretend to get hit by her car when she backs up."

"But do you dare me to?" I asked her, and Irene, for once, didn't have anything to say. And even though I was the one who said it, once the words were out there, between us, I was embarrassed too, unsure of what I should say next, both of us remembering what we'd done the day before, right after my parents had left for Quake Lake, this thing that had been buzzing between us all morning, neither of us saying a word about it.

Irene had dared me to kiss her. We were out at the ranch, up in the hayloft, sweaty from helping Mr. Klauson mend a fence, and we were sharing a bottle of root beer. We'd spent the better part of the day trying to one-up each other: Irene spit farther than I could, so I jumped from the loft into the hay below, so she did a flip off a stack of crates, so I did a forty-five-second handstand with my T-shirt all bunched down over my face and shoulders and the top half of me naked. My roller-rink necklace—both of us wore them, half of a heart each, with our initials—dangled across my face, a cheap-metal itch. Those necklaces left green marks around our necks where they rubbed, but our tans mostly covered them up.

My handstand would have lasted longer if Irene hadn't poked at my belly button, hard.

"Knock it off," I managed, before crumpling over on top of her.

She laughed. "You're all pasty white where your swim-suit covers you up," she said, her head close to mine and her mouth huge and hollow, and begging for me to stuff hay into it, so I did.

Irene coughed and spit for a good thirty seconds, always dramatic. She had to pluck a couple of pieces out of her braces, which had new purple and pink bands on them. Then she sat up straight, all business. "Show me your swimsuit lines again," she said.

"Why?" I asked, even though I was already stretching my shirt to show her the bright stripe of white that fell between the dark skin on my neck and my shoulder.

"It looks like a bra strap," she said, and slowly ran her pointer finger along the stripe. It made my arms and legs goose-bump. Irene looked at me and grinned. "Are you gonna wear a bra this year?"

"Probably," I told her, even though she had just seen first-hand how little need I had for one. "Are you?"

"Yeah," she said, retracing the line, "it's junior high."

"It's not like they check you at the door," I said, liking the feel of that finger but afraid of what it meant. I grabbed another handful of hay and stuffed this one down the front of her T-shirt, a purple one from Jump Rope for Life. She shrieked and attempted retaliation, which lasted only a few minutes, both of us sweating and weakened by the thick heat that filled the loft.

We leaned up against the crates and passed the now-warm root beer back and forth. "But we are supposed to be older," Irene said. "I mean, to act older. It is junior high school." Then she took a long swallow, her seriousness reminding me of an after-school special.

"Why do you keep saying that?" I asked.

"Just 'cause we'll both turn thirteen and that means we'll be teenagers," she said, trailing off, pushing her foot around in the hay. Then she muttered into the pop bottle, "You're gonna be a teenager and you won't even know how to kiss anybody." She fake giggled as she sipped, the root beer fizzing out of her mouth a little.

"You neither, Irene," I said. "You think you're such a Sexy-Lexy?" I meant this as an insult. When we played Clue, which we did often, Irene and I refused to even take the Miss Scarlet marker from the box. We had the edition where the cover featured photographs of people in weird old outfits, posed in a room with antiques, each of them supposedly one of the characters. On that version the busty Miss Scarlet lounged on a fainting couch like a panther in a red dress, smoking a cigarette from a long black holder. We nicknamed her Sexy-Lexy and made up stories about her inappropriate relationships with the paunchy Mr. Green and nerdy Colonel Mustard.

"You don't have to be a Lexy to kiss someone, dorkus," Irene said.

"Who's there to kiss, anyway?" I asked, knowing exactly how she could respond, and holding my breath a little, waiting for her answer. She didn't say anything. Instead she finished the root beer in one swallow and set the bottle on its side, then gently pushed it, sending it rolling away from us. We both watched it move toward the opening over the hay pile, the steady noise of glass over and over and over soft barn wood, a hollow sort of noise. The floor of the loft had a slight downward slope. The bottle reached the edge and slipped from our view, made an almost inaudible swish as it hit the hay below.

I looked at Irene. "Your dad's gonna be pissed when he finds that."

She looked back at me, dead on, our faces close again. "I bet you wouldn't try to kiss me," she said, not moving her stare for a second.

"Is that a real dare?" I asked.

She put on her "duh" face and nodded.

So I did it right then, before we had to talk about it anymore or Irene's mom called out to us to get ourselves washed up for dinner. There's nothing to know about a kiss like that before you do it. It was all action and reaction, the way her lips were salty and she tasted like root beer. The way I felt sort of dizzy the whole time. If it had been that one kiss, then it would have been just the dare, and that would have been no different than anything we'd done before. But after that kiss, as we leaned against the crates, a yellow jacket swooping and arcing over some spilled pop, Irene kissed me again. And I hadn't dared her to do it, but I was glad that she did.

And then her mom did call us in for dinner, and we were shy with each other while we washed at the big sink on the back porch, and after hot dogs from the grill the way we liked them (burned and doused in ketchup) and two helpings of strawberry pretzel salad, her dad drove us into town, the three of us sharing the bench seat of his truck, the ride quiet save for KATL, the AM radio station, staticky all the way to Cemetery Road at the far edge of Miles City.

At my house we watched a little *Matlock* with Grandma Post and then made our way to the backyard and the still-damp-from-the-sprinklers grass beneath the catalpa tree, which was heavy with white bell-shaped blooms that sweetened the hot air with a thick fog of scent. We watched the Big Sky do twilight proud: deep pinks and bright purples giving way to the inky blue-black of night.

The first stars flickered on like the lights over the movie marquee downtown. Irene asked me, "Do you think we'd get in trouble if anyone found out?"

"Yeah," I said right away, because even though no one

had ever told me, specifically, not to kiss a girl before, nobody had to. It was guys and girls who kissed—in our grade, on TV, in the movies, in the world; and that's how it worked: guys and girls. Anything else was something weird. And even though I'd seen girls our age hold hands or walk arm in arm, and probably some of those girls had practiced kissing on each other, I knew that what we had done in the barn was something different. Something more serious, grown-up, like Irene had said. We hadn't kissed each other just to practice. Not really. At least I didn't think so. But I didn't tell any of that to Irene. She knew it too.

"We're good at secrets," I finally said. "It's not like we ever have to tell anybody." Irene didn't answer, and in the dark I couldn't quite make out what face she had on. Everything hung there in that hot, sweet smell while I waited for her to say something back.

"Okay. But—" Irene started when the back porch light flicked on, Grandma Post's squat frame silhouetted in the screen door.

"About time to come in, gals," she told us. "We can have ice cream before bed."

We watched that silhouette move from the door, back toward the kitchen.

"But what, Irene?" I whispered, though I knew Grandma probably couldn't have heard me even if she was standing in the backyard.

Irene took in a breath. I heard it. Just a little. "But do you think we can do it again, though, Cam?"

"If we're careful," I said. I'm guessing she could see me blush even in that much darkness, but it's not like Irene needed to see it anyway: She knew. She always knew.

• • •

Scanlan Lake was a man-made sort of lake-pond that was Miles City's best stab at a municipal pool. It had two wooden docks set fifty yards apart, which was a regulation distance according to federation swim rules. Half of Scanlan was bordered by a gravelly beach of brown sand, and they used that same hard sand to coat the bottom, at least part of the way out, so our feet didn't sink in pond muck. Every May the city released a flow tube and filled the then-empty lakebed with diverted water from the Yellowstone River—water and whatever else might fit through the metal grate: baby catfish, flukes, minnows, snakes, and tiny, iridescent snails that fed on duck poop and caused the red rash of bumps known as swimmer's itch, the rash that covered the backs of my legs and burned, especially in the soft skin behind my knees.

Irene watched me practice from up on the beach. Right after our moment in the parking lot, Coach Ted had arrived, and there was no time for any more *shenanigans*, and maybe we were both a little glad about that. While we were doing our warm-ups, I kept hanging on the docks to scan for her. Irene wasn't a swimmer. Not at all. She could barely thrash her way through a few strokes, forget passing the deepwater test necessary to go off the diving boards that towered at the end of the right dock. While I was learning to swim, Irene had spent her summers building fences, moving cattle, branding, and helping the neighbors who bordered her parents' ranch, and their neighbors. But because everything with us was a challenge, and so often there was no clear winner, I clung to my title as the better swimmer, always showing off when we were at Scanlan together, proving my superiority again and again by launching into a lap of butterfly or jack-knifing off the high dive.

But this practice I wasn't just showing off. I kept looking for Irene on the beach, relieved, somehow, to see her there, her face shaded by a white baseball cap, her hands busy building something in the thick sand. A couple of times she noticed me hanging on the dock, and she waved, and I waved back, and it was this secret between us that thrilled me.

Coach Ted noticed the waving. He was in a mood, pacing back and forth, up onto the low dive, around the guard chair, chewing on a liverwurst-and-onion sandwich, whacking our butts with a hard yellow kickboard if we weren't off the starting blocks fast enough after the whistle. He was home from the University of Montana for the summer, all tan and oiled up and smelling like vanilla extract and onion. The Scanlan lifeguards doused themselves in pure vanilla to keep the gnats at bay.

Most of the girls on my team had a crush on Ted. I wanted to be like him, to drink icy beers after meets and to pull myself into the guard stand without using the ladder, to own a Jeep without a roll-bar and be the gap-toothed ringleader of all the lifeguards.

"You bring a friend to practice and you forget what you're doing here?" Ted asked me after we swam a hundred-yard free and he didn't like the time staring back at him on his stopwatch. "I don't know what you wanna call what you just did off the walls, but they sure as shit weren't flip turns. Use your dolphin kick to whip your legs over your head, and I want at least three strokes before you breathe. Three."

I'd been swim teaming it since I was seven, but I'd come into my own the summer before. I finally put together the breathing—how to blow out all my air while under the surface, just how much to roll my head—and I'd stopped slapping the water with every stroke. I'd found my rhythm, Ted said. I'd placed at state in all my events, and now Ted was expecting something from me, and that was sort of a scary place to be: in the scope of his expectation. He walked me off the dock and up the beach after practice. His arm was hot and heavy around my lake-cold body, and my bare shoulder wedged up into his armpit hair, which felt gross, like animal fur. Irene and I laughed about that later.

"Tomorrow no friends, right?" he said loud enough for Irene to hear. "For two hours a day it's just about swimming."

"Okay," I told him, embarrassed that Irene saw me get a talking-to, even a small one.

He grinned a Coach Ted grin, small and sly, like a cartoon fox on a cereal box. Then he rattled me back and forth a little with that heavy arm. "Okay what?"

"Tomorrow will be all about swimming," I said.

"Good girl," he told me, squeezing me in a bit, a coach's hug, then swaggering off toward the bathhouse.

It had seemed such an easy promise to make at the time, to spend a couple hours the following summer day focused on swimming—on flip turns and pull-outs and tucking my chin during the butterfly. Piece of cake.

• • •

Grandma put on a *Murder, She Wrote* rerun after lunch, but she always dozed during those, and Irene and I had already seen it, so we quietly left her asleep in the recliner. She made tiny whistling noises as she breathed, like the last seconds of a Screaming Jenny firecracker.

Outside we climbed the cottonwood next to the garage and then swung over to its roof, something my parents had told me again and again not to do. The surface was black tar and it was sticky and melted; our flip-flops sank in as we stepped. At one point Irene couldn't pull her foot out and she fell forward, the melted roof burning her hands.

Back on the ground, the soles of our flip-flops gummy with tar, we prowled the yard, the alley, stopping to examine a wasp nest, to jump from the top porch step to the sidewalk below, to drink well water from the hose. Anything at all, so long as it didn't involve talking about what we had done the day before in the barn, what we both knew we wanted to do again. I was waiting for Irene to say something, to make a move. And I knew that she was waiting for the same thing. We were good at this game: We could make it go on for days.

"Tell me your mom's Quake Lake story again," Irene said, plopping herself into a lawn chair and letting her long legs hang limp over the plastic arm, those tarry flip-flops heavy and dangling from her toes.

I was attempting to sit Indian style in front of her, the brick patio hot, hot from the sun, burning my bare legs enough for me to change positions and pull my knees into my chest, wrap my arms around them. I had to squint up at Irene to see her, and even then it was just a hazy-dark outline of Irene, the sun a white gob of glare behind her head. "My mom should have died in 1959, in an earthquake," I said, putting my hand flat on the brick, right in the path of a black ant carrying something.

"That's not how you start it," Irene said, letting one of her dangling flip-flops fall to the patio. Then she let the other flip-flop go, which startled the ant, causing it to try a different route entirely.

"Then you tell it," I said, trying to make the ant climb onto just one of my fingers. It kept stopping. Freezing in place. And then eventually going around.

"C'mon," she said. "Don't be such an ass-head. Just tell it like you usually do."

"It was August, and my mom was camping with my grandma and grandpa Wynton, and my aunt Ruth," I said, making my voice as monotonous as I could, dragging out each word like Mr. Oben, a much-despised fifth-grade teacher.

"Forget it if you're gonna suck." Irene tried to scoop her toe along the patio and hook one of her flip-flops.

I pushed them both out of the way so she couldn't. "Okay, big baby, I'll tell you, I'll tell you. They'd been camping sort of by Yellowstone for a week and were supposed to set up at Rock Creek. They even pulled in there that afternoon."

"What afternoon?" Irene asked.

"In August," I said. "I should remember which day but I don't. My grandma Wynton was setting out lunch, and Mom and Aunt Ruth were helping, and my grandpa was getting his stuff ready to fish."

"Tell the part about the pole," Irene said.

"I'm going to if you let me," I said. "The way my mom always tells it is that if Grandpa had even just dipped his fishing pole into the water, they would have stayed. They never would have gotten him to leave. Even if he'd just made one cast, that would have been that."

"That part still gives me goose bumps," she said, offering her arm as proof, but when I grabbed her hand to look, we both felt a little current of electricity between us, remembering what it was we weren't talking about, and I dropped it fast.

"Yeah, but before my grandpa could get down to the creek, these people they knew from Billings pulled in. My mom was really good friends with the daughter, Margot. They're still friends. She's cool. And then everybody decided to eat lunch together, and then Margot's parents convinced my grandma and grandpa that it would be worth it to drive up to Virginia

16

City and camp up there for a night so they could see the variety show at the old-timey theater up there, because they had just come from there."

"And to eat at that buffet thing," Irene said.

"A smorgasbord. Yeah, my mom says what really convinced my grandpa was when he heard about the smorgasbord, all the pies and Swedish meatballs and stuff. 'Cause Grandpa Wynton had a *helluva sweet tooth*, is what my dad says."

"Didn't someone in that family they had lunch with die?" Irene asked, her voice one shade quieter than before.

"Margot's brother did. The rest of them got out," I said, the whole thing making me shiver a little, the way it always had.

"When did it happen?" Irene swung her legs back over the arm and put her feet on the ground, leaned over her lap toward me.

"Late that night, close to midnight. The whole Rock Creek campground was flooded with water from Hebgen Lake, and then the water couldn't get back out because this entire mountaintop fell down and dammed it."

"And made Quake Lake," Irene finished for me.

I nodded. "All these people got buried at the bottom of it. They're still down there, plus cars and campers and everything that had been in the campground."

"That's so creepy," Irene said. "It has to be haunted. I don't know why your parents want to go there every year."

"They just do. Lots of people still camp around there." I wasn't sure why they went, either. But they'd been doing it every summer, for as long as I'd been alive.

"How old was your mom?" Irene asked, toe-nabbing her flip-flops and standing up, stretching her arms far above her so I could just see a thin line of her stomach.

That feeling that being with Irene kept giving me when I least expected it again floated up in me like a hot-air balloon and I looked away. "She was twelve," I said. "Just like us."

. . .

Eventually we wandered away from my house, no plan, just the two of us meandering through shady neighborhoods. It was late enough in June that the firework stands were open, and already there were kids in their backyards blowing things up, *ka-boom*s and smoke curls from behind tall fences. At a yellow house on Tipperary I stepped on a couple of those white snap-pops that somebody had scattered all over the sidewalk. I had barely shrieked at the tiny explosions beneath my thin soles before a gaggle of boys with skinned-up knees and red Kool-Aid grins charged us from their tree fort.

"We won't let you pass unless you show us your boobies," one of them yelled, a tubby one with a plastic pirate patch over one eye. The other boys cheered and laughed, and Irene grabbed my hand, which didn't feel all awkward in that moment, and we ran with them chasing us, all of us screaming and crazy for maybe two blocks, until eventually the added weight of their plastic guns and the small strides of their eight-year-old legs slowed them down. Even in the heat, that running felt good—hand in hand, all out, a group of shirtless monsters just behind us.

Out of breath and sweaty, we wandered into the cracked lot in front of Kip's Minute Market, tightroping the cement parking blocks one after another, until Irene said, "I want strawberry Bubblicious."

"We can get it," I told her, hopping from one block to another. "My dad gave me a ten before they left and told me not to tell my mom."

"It's just a pack of gum," she said. "Can't you steal it?"

I'd shoplifted at Kip's maybe a dozen times, but I'd always had something of a plan. I had always set out to do it, Irene sometimes giving me a list, making it a challenge—like a licorice rope, which was both long and loud, the cellophane on those things a dead giveaway; or a tube of Pringles, which bulged pretty much no matter where you stuffed it. I didn't do the whole *put it in your backpack* thing. Too obvious. A kid in a candy aisle with a big bag? No way. I crammed things beneath my clothes, usually in my pants. But I hadn't been in for a while, not since school let out, and I'd been wearing a lot more the last time—a big sweatshirt, jeans. And Irene had never come inside with me. Never once.

"Yeah, but you have to buy something anyway," I told her. "So you don't just walk in there and hang around and walk out. And gum's already cheap." Usually I bought a couple of Laffy Taffys or a can of pop, the real loot hidden from view.

"Then let's both steal gum," Irene said, trying to pass me on a block, our bare legs tangled up while she did it, me perfectly still or we both would have fallen.

"I have money," I said. "I can just buy us both gum."

"Buy us a root beer," she said, finally all the way around me.

"I could buy us ten root beers," I said, missing the point.

"We shared one yesterday," she said, and then I got it. The whole thing again fizzling around us both, around our closeness, like a just-lit sparkler, and I didn't know what to say back. Irene was studying her bare toes, pretending like she hadn't said anything important.

"We have to be fast," I said. "My grandma doesn't even know we left the house."

• • •

After the scorched cement of that parking lot, Kip's was almost too cold. Angie with the big brown bangs and long nails was behind the counter, sorting packs of cigarettes.

"You girls getting ice cream?" she asked, sliding a stack of Pall Malls into its place on the shelf.

"No," we answered together.

"Twins, huh?" she said, marking something on a tally sheet.

Irene and I were both in shorts and flip-flops. Me in a tank top, Irene in a T-shirt, not exactly concealing clothing choices. While Irene pretended to study the label of an Idaho Spud candy bar, taking her time, I grabbed two packs of the Bubblicious and tucked them just inside the band of my shorts. The waxy gum wrappers were cold against my skin. Irene put the candy bar back and looked at me.

"Will you get us a root beer, Cam?" she asked, all loud and obvious.

"Yeah," I said, rolling my eyes at her, mouthing *Just do it* before I headed to the refrigerated section along the back wall.

I could see Angie in one of those big circular mirrors Kip's had in the far back corners, and she was still stacking and sorting cigarettes, not paying any attention to us at all. As I grabbed the root beer, the door beeped and this guy my parents knew came in. He was dressed in business clothes, a suit and tie, like he was maybe just getting off work, even though it was too early in the afternoon for that.

He *hey*ed Angie and headed straight for the beer section, the big cooler next to where I was standing. I tried to pass him in the chip aisle.

"Hey there, Cameron Post," he said. "You stayin' out of trouble this summer?"

"Trying to," I said. I could feel one of the packs of gum slipping a little. If it slid too far, it would drop right out the bottom of my shorts, maybe bounce off of suit guy's shoe. I wanted to keep walking but he kept talking, his back now to me, the top half of him behind the glass door to the beer case.

"Your parents are up at Quake Lake, aren't they?" he asked, grabbing six-packs, the bottles clanging around. The back of his suit was wrinkled from where he'd sat in it all day.

"Yeah, they just left yesterday," I said as Irene joined me in the aisle, a big grin stretched across her face.

"I got one," she told me through her teeth, but still kind of loud. Loud enough for this guy to have heard if he'd wanted to. I gave her a face.

"They didn't take you along, huh? You a style cramper?" The suit guy backed out of the case, turned, and pinched a bag of tortilla chips against one of the six-packs he was carrying. Then he winked at me.

"Yeah, I guess," I said, faking a smile, wanting him to scoot along, stop talking.

"Well, I'll tell your mom that I only saw you hitting the root beer and not the hard stuff." He raised up one of his six-packs, grinned again, too many teeth, and headed toward the front of the store. We followed behind him, pausing for a few seconds here and there, pretending to consider other possible purchases that we had no intention of making.

The suit guy was putting bills in his wallet when we reached the counter. "That all you two are getting?" he asked, and lifted his chin toward the sweating bottle of root beer tight in my hand.

I nodded.

"Just one for both of you?"

"Yeah," I said. "We're sharing."

"It's on me," he told Angie, handing her back one of the dollars she'd just given him as change. "A root beer to celebrate summer vacation. They have no idea how good they have it."

"No kidding," Angie said, sort of scowling at us, Irene practically hiding behind me.

The suit guy whistled "Brown Eyed Girl" as he walked out, those six-packs rattling.

"Thanks," we called after him, a little too late for him to hear, probably.

In the alley behind Kip's we shoved piece after piece of gum into our mouths and chewed, those first, hard chews, the gum thick with sugar, our jaws aching, trying to thin it and soften it for bubble blowing. The sun felt good after the cold of the store, both of us still hopped up on what we had done.

"I can't believe that guy bought us the root beer," Irene said, chewing hard, attempting a bubble; but it was too early, and she barely made one the size of a quarter. "We didn't pay for anything."

"That's because we've got it so good," I told her, trying on his deep voice. We impersonated him all the way home, laughing and blowing bubbles, both of us knowing that he was right. We did have it so good.

• • •

Irene and I were wedged down beneath the covers on her big bed, the room cold and dark, the sheets warm, just how I liked it. We were supposed to be sleeping; we were supposed to have been sleeping for maybe an hour, but we weren't at all. We were recounting the day. We were making up the future. We heard the phone ring, and knew it was kind of late for a call, but this was the Klausons; they were ranchers and it was summer, sometimes the phone rang late.

"It's probably a fire," Irene said. "'Member how bad last summer was for fires? The Hempnels lost like forty acres.

And Ernest, he was their black Lab."

I was supposed to be at my own house with Grandma, but when Mrs. Klauson came to pick up Irene that afternoon, after Kip's and the gum, we met her in the driveway, Irene already asking for me to spend the night before Mrs. Klauson had even finished rolling down her window. And she was so easy that way, Mrs. Klauson, always with a smile, her small hand through her dark curls, *Whatever you want, girls.* She even convinced Grandma Post, who had been planning tuna salad on toast, had already mixed a dessert for the two of us—pistachio pudding. It was chilling in glass sundae cups in the fridge, Cool Whip, half a maraschino cherry, and a few crushed walnuts on top of each serving, just like on the cover of her old *Betty Crocker Cookbook*.

"I'll drive Cam in for her swim practice," Mrs. Klauson had said, standing just inside the front door, me already halfway up the stairs, mentally packing my bag—toothbrush, sleep shirt, some of what was left of our stolen Bubblicious. "It's no trouble at all. We love having the girls at our place." I didn't listen for Grandma's response. I knew I'd get to go.

It was as perfect a summer night as the one before it. We watched the stars from our place in the barn loft. We blew stolen pink bubbles bigger than our heads. We kissed again. Irene leaned toward me and I knew exactly what she was doing, and we didn't even have to talk about it. Irene silently daring me to keep going every time I came up for air. I wanted to. The last time it had been just our mouths. This time we remembered that we had hands, though neither of us was sure what to do with them. We came inside for the night, drunk on our day together, our secrets. We were still telling those secrets when we heard Irene's parents in the kitchen, maybe ten minutes after the phone rang. Mrs. Klauson was crying, her husband saying something over and over in a calm, steady voice. I couldn't quite catch it.

"Shhhh," Irene told me, even though I wasn't making noise beyond the rustle of the covers. "I can't tell what's going on."

And then from the kitchen, Mrs. Klauson, her voice like I'd never heard it, like it was broken, like it wasn't even hers. I couldn't hear enough to make any sense. Something about *taking her in the morning. Telling her then.*

There were heavy footsteps in the hallway, Mr. Klauson's boots. This time we both heard him perfectly, his soft reply to his wife. "Her grandmother wants me to bring her home. It's not up to us, honey."

"It's something really bad," Irene said to me, her voice not even quite a whisper.

I didn't know what to say back. I didn't say anything.

We both knew the knock was coming. We heard the footsteps stop outside Irene's door, but there was empty time between the end of those steps and the heavy rap of his knuckles: ghost time. Mr. Klauson standing there, waiting, maybe holding his breath, just like me. I think about him on the other side of that door all the time, even now. How I still had parents before that knock, and how I didn't after. Mr. Klauson knew that too; how he had to lift his calloused hand and take them away from me at eleven p.m. one hot night at the end of June—summer vacation, root beer and stolen bubble gum, stolen kisses—the very good life for a twelve-year-old, when I still had mostly everything figured out, and the stuff I didn't know seemed like it would come easy enough if I could just wait for it, and anyway there'd always be Irene with me, waiting too.

CHAPTER TWO

Aunt Ruth was my mother's only sibling and my only close relative save Grandma Post. She made her entrance the day after my parents' car crashed through a guard rail on the skinny road that climbed the ravine over Quake Lake. Grandma and I were sitting in the living room with the shades drawn, with a sweaty pitcher of too-sweet sun tea between us, with a *Cagney & Lacey* rerun filling up our silence in gunshots and sass.

I was in this big leather club chair that my dad usually read the paper in. I had my legs pulled up to my chest and my arms wrapped around in front of them and my head resting on the dark dry skin of my bare knees. I had been in this position for hours, one rerun after another. I used my fingernails to dig half moons into my calves, my thighs, one white indentation for each finger, and when the creases faded away I did ten more.

Grandma jumped when we heard the front door open and shut. She did her fast walk toward the entryway to head off whoever it was. People had been stopping by all day with food, but they had all rung the doorbell, and Grandma had kept them on the front porch, away from me, even if they were classmates' parents or whatever. I was glad for that. She'd say some version of three or four of the same lines to them—*It's just been a terrible, terrible shock. Cameron is home safe with me; she's resting. Joanie's sister, Ruth, is on her way. Well, there are no words. There are no words.*

Then she'd thank them for coming by, and bring back to the kitchen another casserole dish of broccoli-and-cheese bake, another strawberry-rhubarb pie, another Tupperware bowl of Cool Whip–rich fruit salad, another something neither of us would eat, even though Grandma kept fixing us both heaping plates of the stuff and letting them pile on the coffee table, fat black houseflies buzzing over them, landing, landing, buzzing again.

I waited to see what she'd haul to the kitchen this time, but Grandma didn't seem to be getting rid of whoever was at the door. Their voices in the entryway mixed with the voices on TV—Grandma saying *accident*, Cagney saying *double homicide*, the other voice in the entryway saying *Where is she*—I let them blend, didn't try to sort them out. It was easier to pretend that it was all from the TV. Cagney was telling some detective that Lacey had "a black belt in karate-mouth" right as Aunt Ruth walked into the room.

"Oh sweetheart," she said. "You poor girl."

Ruth was a stewardess for Winner's Airlines. She served on 757s that did daily Orlando-to-Vegas trips for retirees looking to strike it rich. I'd never seen her before in her uniform, but her normal clothes were always so put together, so Ruth. This person crying in the doorway and calling me *poor girl* looked like a clown made up like *Sad Ruth*. The skirt and shirt of her uniform—which were the exact same shade of green as the felt of a casino card table—were travel rumpled and creased. She had a brooch on her lapel that looked like a spread of poker chips, with WINNER'S in shiny gold across the arch, but it was pinned crooked. Her blond curls were messy and squashed on one side, her eyes pink and the skin around them puffed up like mascara-stained marshmallows.

I didn't really know Aunt Ruth, not like I knew Grandma Post. We saw each other usually just once a year, maybe twice, and it was always fine, nice enough: She'd give me clothes I probably wouldn't end up wearing; she'd tell us funny stories about unruly passengers. She was just my mom's sister who lived in Florida and who had fairly recently been *born again*, something I understood only vaguely as a reference to the particular way she practiced Christianity, and something my parents rolled their eyes at when they spoke of—but not in front of her, of course. She was more a stranger to me than Mrs. Klauson, but we were related, and here she was, and I was glad, I think. I think I was glad to see her. Or at least it felt, just then, like it was the right thing, the correct thing to have happen, for her to walk into the room.

She wrapped up both me and part of the chair I was in in a tight hug that filled my lungs with Chanel No. 5. Ruth had always, always since I could remember her, smelled like Chanel No. 5. In fact I only knew of that perfume, its name and spicy scent, because of Ruth.

"I'm so sorry, Cammie," she whispered, her tears wet on my face and neck.

I'd always hated when she called me Cammie, but it didn't feel okay hating her for it right then.

"You poor thing. You poor, sweet girl. We just have to trust God in this. We have to trust him, Cammie, and ask him to help us make sense. There's nothing else to do. That's what we'll do. That's all we can do right now." She told me this over and over and over, and I tried to hug her back, but I couldn't match her tears, and I couldn't believe her. Not one word. She had no idea how guilty I was.

• • •

After Mr. Klauson knocked on Irene's bedroom door and ended my final sleepover with his daughter, telling me, as he scooped up my bag and my pillow, that I needed to go home, and then taking my hand and walking me out of the house, past Mrs. Klauson as she stood crying over the brown kitchen stove, and away from Irene's unanswered shouts of *Why does she have to go? But why, Dad?*—I knew that all of this meant something probably more terrible than anything had ever been in my life, ever.

At first I thought that Grandma had fallen, or that maybe they'd found out about the shoplifting. But then, as he drove me, still in my pajamas, the forty miles back to my house, the whole trip telling me nothing more than that *my grandma needed to speak with me* and that I needed to be there with her, I convinced myself beyond a doubt that Irene and I were found out.

It was Mr. Klauson's silence during that endless trip, silence filled only with the thick roll of tires over cracked highway and his occasional sighs in my direction, plus the way he shook his head to himself, that convinced me: He was disgusted with me, with what he somehow knew that Irene and I had done, and he didn't want me in his house for one more second. I sat all the way against the hard door of his truck, trying to will myself into something small and distant from him. I wondered what Grandma would say to me, what my parents would say when they got home. Maybe they'd come home early. Some park ranger had tracked them down to tell them about their weirdo daughter. I tried out various scenes in my head, none of them good. *It was only a couple of kisses,* I would tell them. *We were just practicing on each other. We were just goofing around.*

So when Grandma met us on the front steps in her purple

housecoat, and hugged a stiff Mr. Klauson beneath the orange glow of the porch light, the millers swooping around their awkward embrace, and then sat me on the couch, and gave me the mug of now lukewarm, too-sweet tea she had been drinking, and wrapped my hands in hers and told me that she was just sitting down to watch TV when the doorbell rang, and it was a state trooper, and there had been an accident, and Mom and Dad, *my* mom and dad, had died, the first thing I thought, the very first thing, was: *She doesn't know about Irene and me at all. Nobody knows.* And even right after she said it, and I guess I knew then that my parents were gone, or at least I had to have heard her, it still didn't register right. I mean, I had to have known this big thing, this massive news about my whole entire world, but I just kept thinking, *Mom and Dad don't know about us. They don't know, so we're safe—* even though there was no more Mom and Dad to know about anything.

I had been bracing myself that whole pickup ride to hear how ashamed Grandma was of me, and instead she was crying, and I'd never seen Grandma Post cry like this, I'd never seen anyone cry like this. And she was making no sense, talking about some far-off car accident, and a news broadcast, and my dead parents, and calling me a brave girl and stroking my hair and hugging me to her soft chest, her talcum powder and Aqua Net smell. I felt a wave of heat prickle across me, and then the nausea, all-consuming, as if I was taking it in with every breath, like my body was reacting since my head wasn't doing it right. How, if my parents were dead, could there still be some part of me that felt relief at not being found out?

Grandma clutched me tighter, heaving with sobs, and I had to turn my head away from her sweet smell, the smother of that flannel housecoat, and pull myself out of her reach, run with my hand over my mouth to the bathroom, and even then there was no time to lift the lid on the toilet. I threw up into the sink, onto the counter, and then slid down to the floor, let the blue and white tiles cool my cheeks.

I didn't know it then, but the sickness, the prickly flush of heat, and the feeling of swimming in a kind of blackness I couldn't have ever imagined, all the things I had done since I'd last seen my parents bobbing around me, lit up against the dark—the kisses, the gum, Irene, Irene, Irene—all of that was guilt: real, crushing guilt. From that tile floor I let myself sink down into it, down and down until my lungs burned, like when I was in the deep wells beneath the diving boards at the lake.

Grandma came to help me to bed and I wouldn't budge.

"Oh honey-girl," she said when she saw the mess in the sink. "You need to get into bed now, sweetheart. You'll feel better if you do. I'll get you some water."

I wouldn't answer her back and I stayed completely still, willing her to just leave me alone. She left but came back with a glass of water, which she set on the floor next to me because I wouldn't take it from her. Then she left again and this time returned with a can of Comet, a rag. After all that had happened Grandma was going to clean the sink, clean up after me, another mess, and it was this moment that somehow made what she had told me take hold. Seeing her there in the doorway with that green can, her pink eyes, the hem of her nightgown peeking from beneath her housecoat, Grandma stooped over with a yellow rag, sprinkling out the cleanser, that chemical-mint smell puffing around us, her son dead and her daughter-in-law dead and her only grandchild a now-orphaned shoplifter, a girl who kissed girls, and she didn't even know, and now she was cleaning up my vomit, feeling even worse because of me: That's what made me cry.

And when she heard me crying, finally saw me with actual tears, she got down on the floor, which was painful for her, I knew, her bad knees, and held my head in her lap and cried with me, stroked my hair, and I was too weak to tell her that I didn't deserve any of it.

• • •

In the days before the funeral, Irene stopped by the house with her mom, and she called to speak with me a few times after that, and all those times I asked Aunt Ruth to tell Irene that I was napping. People kept sending me all sorts of things, so I knew that even if I ignored her, it was only a matter of time before she sent me something too. It came the same day the swim team sent a big bouquet of sunflowers, a box of cookies, and a card that everyone signed. Coach Ted must have passed it around right after practice, because there were all these water spots where wet swimmers had handled it, smudged the ink. Most of the kids just signed their names. Some wrote *I'm sorry*. I wondered what I would have signed if I'd just been one of those wet swimmers, practice over, my towel around my waist, chewing on a granola bar and waiting for my turn to sign the card for the teammate who'd lost both of her parents. I decided I'd probably have been one of the ones who just signed her name too.

Aunt Ruth had been putting everything on the dining-room table, but even with both of the extra leaves in, we were running out of room, and she started just setting stuff anywhere there was free space. The whole of the main floor smelled like a flower shop, and with the heat, the shades drawn on all the windows, that scent of roses and irises and carnations and on and on was almost cloudy, like a gas. It made me hold my breath. I found the bouquet of pink baby roses and an envelope with *Cam* written on it over on the oak buffet my dad had refinished. I could tell they were from Irene without even opening the card. I just could. So I peeled the card from the vase, took it up to my room. Alone on my bed with the door shut, the thick heat all around me, the card on my lap weighing almost nothing but seeming full of weight, I felt as criminal as I would have had it been Irene herself there with me.

The card had a night sky on the outside, dozens of stars spread across it, and on the inside something about stars being like memories in the *darkness of sorrow*. I knew right away that her mom had picked it out. But below that was Irene's cramped cursive, and she had written:

Cam, I wish you would have seen me or answered the phone when I called. I wish I could just talk to you and not write in this card. I wish I didn't even have a reason to send this card at all. I'm sorry and I love you.

She didn't sign her name, but I liked that.

I felt flushed when I read what she'd written, and then I read it again and again until I was dizzy with it. I traced my finger over and over the ballpoint *I love you*, and the whole time I felt ashamed, some sicko who just couldn't stop, even after her parents died. I buried that card deep beneath a pile of already-spoiled death casseroles in the metal trash can in the alley. I burned my thumb just taking the lid off, the whole can oven hot and reeking. That act of burial felt good, like it meant something, but by that point I had memorized every word she had written me anyway.

Grandma and Ruth were out getting things done that

needed to be done, going to the funeral parlor, the church. They'd asked me if I'd wanted to go with them, but I'd said no, though I did spend the rest of that afternoon making my own kinds of funeral arrangements. First I hauled the TV and VCR from my parents' bedroom, where Ruth had been sleeping, up the steep stairs to my own. I hadn't asked anyone's permission to do this. Who was gonna tell me no, or yes, even? It was hard work, moving that TV, more activity than I'd done for days, and I almost dropped the thing once, my sweaty fingers slipping on its film of dust, its sharp edges poking into my stomach, into my hip bones, while I steadied it against myself, staggered up another stair, rested, then did another.

Once I'd situated the TV and VCR on top of my dresser and got everything wired together, plugged in, I went back to my parents' bedroom and straight to the bottom drawer of the dresser, where Dad kept neat rows of white cotton briefs and black socks with gold toes. He had a roll of tens and twenties hidden in the back, and I took it; and even though I was alone in the house, I stuck it in the waistband of my shorts, to hide it. And then I took one more thing. An important thing. A photograph housed in a pewter frame and sitting on their dresser top, which was cluttered mostly with snapshots of me.

In the picture my mother is twelve, her hair a stylish pageboy, her smile wide and toothy, her knees knobby in shorts, and she is surrounded by trees, the sunlight filtered around her just so, lighting her up. I'd known the story of that photo for as long as I'd known that photo. Grandpa Wynton snapped it August 17th of 1959, and in less than twenty-four hours the place where it was taken, Rock Creek Campground, would be torn apart by the worst earthquake in Montana history, and then that place would be flooded by water sloshing over an upriver dam, and it would become Quake Lake.

I put the picture right on top of the TV, so I couldn't miss it. Then I put all that cash into the hollowed-out base of the high-point trophy I'd won at the divisional meet the summer before. All that cash except for one ten, which I stuck in the inside band of a sweat-stained Miles City Mavericks cap I'd had forever. Dad and I had liked to go to their ball games together and eat Polish sausages and laugh at the old guys who swore at the umps. That cap in my hand, its rim of crusty salt stain against the dark-blue background, made me almost lose it for a second, but I didn't let myself. I squashed it down over my dirty hair, and then I was off.

Save my burial at the trash can, I hadn't been outside since the night Mr. Klauson had driven me home. The glare of the sun felt good, even while it was almost immediately uncomfortable. I felt like I deserved it. My bike had been leaned up against the garage for days in that sun bake, and the metal scorched my legs when they brushed against it. I pedaled as fast as I could, let the sweat from my forehead sting my eyes, blur my vision for a few seconds. I took the alleys and concentrated on the sound of my tires over the loose gravel, on the whir of the gear chain. I came out onto Haynes Avenue and pulled into the parking lot of the Video 'n' Go.

It was July 2, and there was a swarm of cars and bicycles in front of the Golden Dragon fireworks stand in the corner of the lot. The Elks club ran that stand, and my dad always worked a shift or two. I wondered who was covering for him as I wove my way through the pileup and toward the store, hoping my cap would keep me invisible—I felt like a ghost anyway.

I knew just what I was looking for: *Beaches*, over with the new releases. I'd gone to see it at the Montana Theatre with my mom the year before. We cried and cried. We bought the soundtrack the next day. Then I went back to the Montana and I saw it with Irene. We argued over who, between the two of us, was Bette Midler and who was Barbara Hershey. We both wanted to be Bette.

Barbara Hershey's character dies near the end of the movie. Her daughter, Victoria, is left behind, like me. She wears a black velvet dress and white tights and gets to hold Bette Midler's hand during the funeral. She was maybe four years too young to be my equal, and had only really lost one parent (because her dad, while absent, was at least still alive) and she was just an actor, I knew, playing a part; but still it was something to go by. I felt like I needed something official to show me how all of this should feel, how I should be acting, what I should be saying—even if it was just some dumb movie that wasn't really official at all.

It was Mrs. Carvell, formerly Miss Hauser, at the register. She taught fourth grade during the school year and worked the video store in the summer—her parents owned it. I'd had her the first year she'd ever taught, but I wasn't one of her favorites because I didn't take the after-school tap classes she held in the gymnasium, and also maybe because I didn't giggle and ask stupid questions about weddings and dating when she'd brought her then-fiancé, Mr. Carvell, to class one day in the spring and had him do dorky science experiments with us. In the end-of-year comments on my report card she had written, *Cameron is very bright. She'll do well, I'm sure.* My parents thought this was a riot.

Mrs. Carvell took the case from me and found the video to put in it without much seeing me, but when I had to say "Post" for her to look up our account, she did a double take, peered close beneath the brim of my cap, and flinched.

"Oh my God, honey," she said to me, just standing there

sort of gaping, the video stiff in her hand. "What are you doing in here? I'm so sorry about . . . "

I filled it in for her in my head—*about how your parents swerved off a mountain road and drowned in a lake that shouldn't even exist, shouldn't even be there, all of this while you stayed home and kissed a girl, stole some gum.*

"I'm so sorry, just—well, I'm sorry about everything, honey," she finished. There was a high counter between us, and I was glad she couldn't easily get around it to hug me.

"It's okay," I mumbled. "I just really need to rent that right now. I've got to get back home."

She looked more carefully at the title, her wide face scrunched up a little, confused, like she was trying to figure this out, like she could really make sense of it. "Well, you just go on and take this then, okay, hon?" she told me, handing it back without ringing it up. "And you can just call me, even, to come and pick it back up when you're finished. You keep it for as long as you want."

"Are you sure?" I asked, unaware that this was the first official time of so many to come when I'd receive the pro-rated orphan discount. I didn't like it. I didn't want Mrs. Carvell "taking care" of me.

"Of course, Cameron. It's nothing at all." She smiled her big smile at me, one I'd never been granted personally but had seen, on occasion, when she'd trotted it out for the whole class to share—like the time our room won the school-wide pop-top-collecting contest.

"But I have money," I said, feeling like I would cry just any second and keeping my eyes away from hers. "I'm gonna want to rent something else soon, anyway."

"You can rent as many as you like," she said. "You come see me. I'll be here all summer."

I couldn't let her do this thing for me. It made me twist up inside. "I'll just leave this and then rent more later," I mumbled, my head down, putting the ten on the counter and walking as quickly as I could, without technically running, to the door.

"Cameron, this is too much," she called after me, but then I was out of the store, back on the sidewalk, free from her generosity or pity or kindness, all of it.

• • •

Aunt Ruth was waiting for me in my room, her back to the door, new clothes, funeral wear, hung crisp from cheap hangers, in either hand. She was just standing and staring at my new entertainment center and didn't turn when I first came in. I shoved the movie into the waistband of my shorts, just above my butt. I blushed even as I did it, a flash of the bubble gum, Irene.

"I do already own clothes, you know," I said.

She turned, did a tired smile. "I didn't know what to get you, hon, and you didn't want to come with me. I just brought you a few choices from Penney's. We can take back whatever you don't end up wearing. I just hope it all fits—I had to guess." She put everything on my bed, gently, like laying a baby down to change her diaper.

"Thanks," I said, because I knew that I should. "I'll try them on tonight, when it's cooler." I didn't look at her. I focused, instead, on the navy dress, the black skirt and top, the clothes now on my bed that looked nothing like any clothes that had ever been on my bed before, at least not since I could dress myself.

"It must have been hard work getting this thing up here," she said, patting the TV like she sometimes did me. "I would have been happy to help you."

"I got it okay," I said, "but thanks, though." I kept my back pressed up against the open door.

"You doing okay, kiddo?" she asked me, stepping closer, the requisite arm around me, her signature hug. "Do you want to pray with me a little, maybe? Or I could read you some passages that I've been thinking about a lot. They might give you a little peace."

"I just want to be alone right now," I told her. If I could have, I'd've recorded that line on one of those handheld machines with the minitapes and then worn the whole thing on a chain around my neck, just hit Play maybe eight or nine times a day.

"Okay, sweetie. I can sure help you with that. We'll talk when you're ready, whenever you are; it doesn't matter when—I'll be here." She kissed my cheek and was two stairs down when she turned back. "You know you can talk to God best alone anyway. You can just close your eyes and be with him, Cammie—ask him anything you want."

I nodded, but only because she seemed to be waiting for me to say something.

"There's a whole world beyond this one," she said. "And sometimes it helps even just to remember that. It helps me a lot."

I stayed with my back to the door until she was well down the stairs. I was afraid she'd see the outline of the movie, or that it might slip from my waistband and clatter hard on the wide planks of the floor. I didn't want to have to explain anything about *Beaches* to her. I wasn't sure it made sense even to me.

I shut the door to my room and put the tape in the VCR and settled back on my bed, right on top of the new clothes. My twelve-year-old mother grinned down at me from another world, one beneath the shady pines and cedars, one where she was giddily unaware that she was just hours away from escaping a tragedy—and a lifetime away from a day that tragedy would find her anyway.

The navy dress was bunched weird beneath my neck. I shifted, shifted again. I couldn't get comfortable. I kept hearing Ruth's advice about talking to God. I didn't want to hear it but I did. It wasn't like I'd never prayed before, I had: at the Presbyterian church sometimes, and when my goldfish, four of them, had died—one after the next—and other times, too. Those times I had tried to talk to something greater, something out there in the world bigger than me. But all those times, no matter what the occasion, it had eventually ended up feeling sort of phony, like I was playing at a relationship with God, just like any little kid playing house or grocery store or anything else, but not like it was real. I knew that this is where the faith part was supposed to come in, and that faith, real faith, that's what was supposed to keep the whole thing from just being make-believe. But I didn't have any of that faith, and I didn't know where to get it, how to get it, or even if I wanted it right then. I felt like it could be that God had made this happen, had killed my parents, because I was living my life so wrong that I had to be punished, that I had to be made to understand how I must change, and that Ruth was right, that I had to change through God. But I also thought, at the exact same time I was thinking the other stuff, that maybe what all this meant was that there was no God, but instead only fate and the chain of events that is, for each of us, predetermined—and that maybe there was some lesson in my mom drowning at Quake Lake thirty years later. But it wasn't a lesson from God; it was something else, something more like putting together a puzzle, making the pieces fit to form an image. I didn't want to have those thoughts running simultaneously and constantly, constantly. What I wanted to do was to hide from all of it, to be small and unseen and just to get along. It might have comforted Ruth to talk to God, but it made me feel like I couldn't breathe, like drowning, the diving wells again.

I lifted the remote control, pushed the Play button, and started the video. I guess, in that moment, I also started my new life as *Cameron-the-girl-with-no-parents*. Ruth was sort of right, I would learn: A relationship with a higher power is often best practiced alone. For me it was practiced in hour-and-a-half or two-hour increments, and paused when necessary. I don't think it's overstating it to say that my religion of choice became VHS rentals, and that its messages came in Technicolor and musical montages and fades and jump cuts and silver-screen legends and B-movie nobodies and villains to root for and good guys to hate. But Ruth was wrong, too. There was more than just one other world beyond ours; there were hundreds and hundreds of them, and at 99 cents apiece I could rent them all.

CHAPTER THREE

The first semester of seventh grade they had me in the counseling center for one period a day—the orphan in residence. On my schedule that period was listed officially as study hall, but Aunt Ruth, my new legal guardian, had spoken with the administrators, and everyone but me had decided that it would be best for me to spend that hour sitting on one of the center's sea-green vinyl couches, talking with Nancy the counselor about one of her many pamphlets on loss: "Teens and Grief." "All Alone with My Troubles." "Understanding Death and Letting Go."

Mostly I spent my time in the counseling center fiddling at homework or reading a paperback, maybe eating the little thises and thats the secretaries would sneak me from the teachers' lounge—a couple of brownies folded up in a napkin, a plate of somebody's seven-layer dip with Triscuits—gifts they'd present to me with kind smiles and soft pats on my shoulder. These small offerings of food, of *looking out for the kid*, somehow made me feel more alone than when the secretaries didn't remember to include me at all.

• • •

They'd gotten used to me over at Video 'n' Go, and now that school was back in session, Mrs. Carvell was gone and it was almost always Nate Bovee behind the register, and he let me rent whatever the hell I wanted—no questions, just a wink and a grin creeping from behind that scraggly goatee he was always trying to grow but never quite did. I just had to hide the cases from Ruth, keep the volume semilow.

"Whatcha pickin' up today, sweetheart?" Nate would ask me, his squinty blue-gray eyes hawking me as I wandered the aisles. I always got a couple of new releases and then kept working my way through the older stuff.

"I don't know yet," I'd tell him, trying to stay behind the shelves farthest from the register, which didn't help much, 'cause he could just watch me in the big shoplifter mirror hung above the door to the back room. When I went in the afternoons, right after school let out, it was usually just the two of us in the store. Video 'n' Go always smelled too strongly of some carpet cleaner they used, like chemical roses, and I began to associate that smell with Nate—as if it radiated from him.

I tried to like him because he let me rent the R-rated videos and because sometimes he'd offer me a free pop from the cooler up front, but I didn't like that he knew every movie I took out of that store, watching me, watching me pick them up and bring them back. It felt like in knowing that, he knew more about me than anyone else right then, definitely more than Nancy the counselor, and more than Aunt Ruth, too.

• • •

Sometime in late September Irene Klauson came to school with the kind of smile kids wear in peanut-butter commercials. She and her dad had been out building onto their new corral and branding area. Irene said she was the one working the shovel when they first found it. A bone. A fossil. Something big.

"My dad's already called some professor he knows at Montana State," she told a few of us who were clustered around her locker. "They're sending out a whole team."

Within weeks scientists, "paleontologists," Irene would remind us, sounding like our fucking science book, had swarmed all over the Klausons' cattle ranch. The paper called it *a hotbed for specimen recovery. A gold mine. A treasure trove.*

Irene and I hadn't seen each other much since our robot-hug at my parents' funeral in June. Mrs. Klauson kept trying to arrange sleepovers and day trips to the mall in Billings, to a rodeo in Glendive, but I would back out at the last minute.

"We understand, sweetheart," Mrs. Klauson would tell me over the phone. I guess the "we" she was speaking of included Irene, but maybe she meant Mr. Klauson. "We're not going to stop trying though, okay, Cam?"

When, in late August, I had finally agreed to go with them to the Custer County Fair, I spent the whole evening wishing that I hadn't. Irene and I had done up the fair before—we'd done it up big. We'd buy the wristbands that let you ride all the rides you wanted. We'd eat graveyard snow cones—lime, orange, grape, cherry mixed together—and pacos from the Crystal Pistol booth—seasoned beef in a cocoon of hot fry bread, the orange grease squirting and burning the insides of our cheeks. We'd wash everything down with lemonade from that stand with the wasps buzzing all around it. Then we'd make fun of the blue-ribbon craft projects and dance a wild jitterbug to whatever lame-o band they'd brought in. In years before, we thought we owned the fair.

But that August we haunted the midway like ghosts—stopping in front of the Tilt-A-Whirl, then the fishbowl game, watching like we'd already seen everything there was to see but couldn't quite pull ourselves away. We didn't talk about my parents, the accident. We didn't say much of anything at all. Everything was painted in ringing noises and flashing lights and shouting and screaming, crazy laughter, little kids crying, the smell of popcorn and fry bread and cotton candy thick in the air, but it all just sort of floated around me like smoke. Irene bought us tickets for the Ferris wheel, a ride we'd deemed too boring the year before, but it seemed like we should be doing something.

We sat in that metal car, our bare knees just touching. Even when we'd jerk them apart, they'd wind up magnetized again some moments later. We were closer together than we had been since the night her father knocked on her bedroom door. We were lifted up into the hot embrace of the ever-blackening Montana sky, the lights from the midway sluicing us in their fluorescent glow, a tinny kind of ragtime music plinking out from somewhere deep in the center of the wheel. Up on top we could see the whole of the fair: the tractor pull, the dance pavilion, cowboys in Wranglers leaning cowgirls built like sticks of gum up against pickups out in the parking lot. Up on top the air smelled less like grease and sugar, more like just-baled hay and the muddy waters of the Yellowstone as it lazed its way around the fairgrounds. Up on top it was quiet, everything squashed down below us, the loudest noise the squeak of the bolts as the wind shifted our car just so. Then we had to float back down into all of it, the whole midway pressed up against us, and I held my breath until we were back on top again.

Our third time up there Irene grabbed my hand. We stayed like that for one full rotation, saying nothing, fingers wound together, and for that forty seconds or so I pretended like things were just as they always were: me and Irene at the fair.

When we got back to the top again, Irene was crying, and

she said, "I'm really sorry, Cam. I'm sorry. I don't know what else to say."

Irene's face was bright against the dark of the sky, her eyes all shimmery wet, pieces of her hair blown free from her ponytail. She was beautiful. Everything in me wanted to kiss her, and at the same time it felt like everything in me was sick. I pulled my hand away from hers and looked out over my side of the car, dizzy with nausea. I closed my eyes to keep from throwing up, and even then I could taste it. I heard Irene next to me saying my name, but she sounded like she was saying it from beneath a pile of sand. They had stopped the ride to let people off and on down below. We shifted in the wind. We started up again, moved a few clicks, stopped. Now I wanted to be back on the midway and in the rush of all that noise. Irene was still crying beside me.

"We can't be friends like we were before, Irene," I told her, keeping my eyes fixed on a couple all twined up in the parking lot.

"Why?" she asked.

The ride started up again. Our car jerked and we were lowered a few clicks. We stopped. Now we hovered half in the sky and half in the midway—level with the bright canvas tops of the game booths. I didn't say anything. I let the music plink. I remembered the feel of her mouth that day in the hayloft, the taste of her gum and the root beer we'd been drinking. The day she dared me to kiss her. And the very next day my parents' car had veered through the guardrail.

I didn't say anything. If Irene hadn't connected those dots herself, then it wasn't my place to do it for her, to explain that everybody knows how things happen for a reason, and that we had made a reason and bad, bad, unthinkable things had happened.

"Why can't we just be friends like we were?"

"Because we're too old for that stuff," I told her, tasting the lie on my tongue even as I said it, thick as a wad of cotton candy, but not nearly so easy to make shrink into sugar crystals and disappear.

She wouldn't let me off that easy. "Too old for it how?"

"Just too old," I said. "Too old for all of that kind of stuff."

They started the ride again, and since there was no one in the car below us, we were back on the ground just like that. Everything that had just happened left up on top.

Mr. and Mrs. Klauson found us by the Zipper just after that. They fed us thick-crusted pie and corn on the cob and took Polaroids of us with Smokey the Bear, with balloon hats on. The two of us played along pretty well, I thought.

We kept playing along once school started. We sat together in World History. We went down to the Ben Franklin lunch counter sometimes and ordered chocolate milks and grilled cheeses. But whatever we once were we weren't anymore. Irene started hanging out with Steph Schlett and Amy Fino. I started hanging out even more with my VCR. I watched from the bleachers as Irene kissed Michael "Bozo" Fitz after a wrestling match. I watched Mariel Hemingway kiss Patrice Donnelly in *Personal Best*. I watched them do more than kiss. I rewound that scene and watched it again and again until I was afraid the tape might break, and handing a broken tape of that movie to Nate Bovee, trying to explain it while he smiled his smile, would have been unbearable. He'd already given me shit when I'd checked it out.

"You gettin' this one today, huh?" he'd asked. "You know what goes on in this movie, sweetie?"

"Yeah, she's a runner, right?" I wasn't playing dumb, not really. The tape case read: *When you run into yourself, you run into feelings you never thought you had.* On the back there was a picture of Mariel and Patrice standing close to each other in dim light. The synopsis mentioned *more than friendship.* I had picked it up mainly because it was a story about runners, and I was planning on going out for track. I guess somewhere there was a part of me that had figured out how to read those codes for gay content, but it wasn't something I could name.

Nate had held on to that tape for a long time before giving it back, just sorta studying the picture of tussled-up Mariel Hemingway on the cover. "You let me know what you think about this one, huh, kiddo? These gals sure can run together." He'd done a little *hoo-wee* whistle after that, licked his lips.

I took that tape back when the store was closed and put it through the drop box. Nate didn't say anything about it the next time that I rented, so I was hopeful that he'd forgotten about it. I was hopeful, but I wasn't stupid enough to try renting it again, even though I wanted to. Sometimes I dreamed that scene from the movie but with Irene and me instead. But I couldn't ever make that dream happen. It just came on its own, the way dreams do.

• • •

Grandma and Ruth didn't involve me much in the way they settled things between them—things like who would be in charge of me and where I would live and how I would be paid for. I could have asked more questions. I could have asked all of them, the big questions, but if I had then I would have just been reminding everyone, including me, that I needed to be taken care of because I was now an orphan, which made me think about why I was now an orphan, and I didn't need one more reason to think about that. So I went to school and I stayed in my room and I watched everything, everything, without any discretion—*Little Shop of Horrors* and *9½ Weeks* and *Teen Wolf* and *Reform School Girls*—usually keeping the volume low, the remote control in my hand just in case I had to hit the Stop button fast, Ruth on the stairs; and I let every decision being made at that kitchen table just settle around me like plastic snow in a snow globe and me frozen in there too, just a part of the scene, trying not to get in the way. And for the most part, that seemed to work.

Grandma officially moved out of her apartment in Billings and into our basement, which my dad had put a bathroom in but never got around to completely finishing. So some of the guys who used to work for him did, fast, within a month or so—they put up drywall and made Grandma a bedroom and a living room, soft blue carpet and a new La-Z-Boy recliner, and it was pretty nice down there.

Obviously Ruth couldn't still be a stewardess for Winner's Airlines and live in Miles Shitty, Montana. We did have an airport the size of a double-wide trailer, but it only served private planes and Big Sky Airlines—which people called Big Scare because of its reputation for flights so bumpy they practically guaranteed the need for extra puke bags—and Big Sky flights ran only between Miles City and other Montana towns, anyway: tiny planes with few passengers and no need for a lady in a uniform serving ginger ale and bags of peanuts.

"This is a new phase of my life," Ruth said all the time in those first months after the accident. "I never planned to be a flight attendant forever. This is a new phase in my life."

This new phase included doing secretarial work for my dad's contracting company. My mom used to do most of that kind of bookkeeping stuff at night, for free, after she'd gotten home from her job at the Tongue River Museum; but Greg Comstock, who took over Dad's business but kept the name, made Ruth an official employee of Solid Post Projects—one with a desk and a name plate and a twice-monthly paycheck.

That fall Ruth had to fly back to Florida to sell her condo, pack her belongings, and wrap things up in general to prepare for this *new phase* in her life. She had to have some surgery, too.

"Minor," she'd told us. "Routine business for my NF. They've got to scrape me off, clean me up."

NF stood for Ruth's neurofibromatosis. She'd had it since birth, when Grandma and Grandpa Wynton noticed this lump, about the size of a peanut, in the middle of her back, along with a flat, tan mark like a puddle of milky coffee (appropriately and officially called a café au lait spot) on her shoulder, another spill on her thigh. The doctors told them not to worry; but as she got older there were more growths, some of them the size of walnuts, of babies' fists, some of them in places where a pretty girl like Ruth didn't want them growing, not during bikini season, not during prom. So they'd had her diagnosed, had the benign tumors removed, save the one on her back, which never changed much. It had done a little growing, then stopped, but the surgeons feared its close proximity to her spinal cord, so they left that one be.

I thought it was weird that she, shiny, perfect, glowy Ruth, was so glib about having a bunch of tumors hacked off her nerves (this batch was on her right thigh, apparently, and also one behind her knee); but she'd had it done enough now that it was just what she did, I guess, every half decade or so: one more piece of the beauty routine with a little more effort involved. With the surgery and everything else, she was gone for over a month, and Grandma and I had the house to ourselves again. It was nice. The big thing that happened while Ruth was away was that my mom's friend Margot Keenan paid us a visit. Actually, she paid me a visit. Margot Keenan was tall and long limbed and was a semipro tennis player for a while after college before going to work for some big-deal sportswear manufacturer. I remember that the few times she came to visit when my parents were alive, she gave me tennis lessons, letting me use her fancy racket, and once, in the summer, she came to Scanlan to swim with me, and she always brought great presents from Spain, from China, from wherever. My parents stocked gin and tonic for her visits, bought limes just so they could make her drink the way she liked it. She had been friends with my mom since grade school. And more important than that, they had Quake Lake in common. It was Margot's family who had convinced my grandparents to drive up to Virginia City the day of the earthquake while they stayed behind, and so it was her family who'd lost a son, Margot's brother.

She was now living in Germany and hadn't even heard about my parents' accident until a month after the fact, and then she'd sent a huge bouquet to me. Not to all of us: to me. That thing was gigantic, with flowers that I didn't even know the names of, and in the card she promised that she'd come to visit as soon as she was back in the States. Some weeks later she'd called while I was at school and talked with Grandma and told her when she'd be arriving and that she'd like to take me to dinner, and Grandma said yes for me, which was what I'd have said anyway.

She pulled up on a Friday evening in a dust-skinned blue rental car from the Billings airport. I watched out the window as she walked up the front steps. She seemed even taller than I remembered, and she was now wearing her shiny black hair short and asymmetrical, with one side tucked behind her ear. Grandma opened the door, but I was right there too, and even though I didn't really know Margot well, when she leaned down a bit to hug me, I didn't freeze my shoulders the way I had been doing for months when on the receiving end of such hugs. I hugged her back, and I think it surprised us both. Her perfume, if that's what it was, smelled like grape-fruit and peppermint, fresh and clean.

We all had Cokes in the living room while Margot talked a little about Berlin, about the various business things she was doing while back in the U.S. Then she looked at this nice silver watch she had on, a big watch with a blue face, like a man's watch, maybe, and she said that we should get a move on if we were to make our reservation at the Cattleman's. That was kind of funny, because even though it was Miles City's nicest steakhouse, tucked between the bars, a place with lots of dark wood paneling and stuffed and mounted animals, it still wasn't a reservations kind of restaurant. But apparently she had made them just the same.

I could tell Margot was nervous when she opened my car door for me and then told me to pick any radio station I wanted for the sixty seconds it would take us to get down Main Street; and when I didn't make a move for the dial, she did it for me, cycling through the three stations that came in, making a face, and then just turning the radio off entirely. But I was nervous too, and that made me feel like we were on a date, which we sort of were, I guess. The couple of worn-in ranchers who were ponied up to the Cattleman's bar gave Margot, in her black pants and black boots and her non–Miles City haircut, the once-over as we passed them for our table; but things seemed decidedly calmer once our drinks arrived: the requisite gin and tonic, and for me, a Shirley Temple, double the cherries, light on the ice.

"Well, I'll go ahead and say that this is strange, isn't it? Awkward is probably the best word." Margot took a long swallow from her drink, letting the ice cubes collide with the lime wedge. "But I am very glad we're doing it."

I liked how she said *we*, and made this dinner something the both of us were doing and not something she had done wholly *for* me. It made me feel like an adult.

"Me too," I said, drinking from my mocktail, hoping that I looked as sophisticated doing it as Margot looked to me.

She smiled, and I'm sure that I blushed in response.

"I brought pictures," she said, digging in this nice brown leather bag she had, more like a satchel than a purse. "I don't know how many of these you've seen before, but I want you to have whichever you'd like." She handed me an envelope.

I wiped my hands on my napkin before removing the photos. I wanted her to notice how seriously I was taking all of this. I hadn't seen most of the shots before. The first dozen or so were from my parents' wedding. Aunt Ruth might have been the maid of honor, but Margot was a bridesmaid. I thought she looked pretty but uncomfortable in her gown and long gloves, much how I imagined I might have looked in the same getup.

"Oh, your mother and that peach monstrosity," she said, reaching across the table and bending the picture in my hand toward her so that she could shake her head at it. "I had every intention of changing into blue jeans before the reception, but she bribed me with champagne."

"Looks like it worked," I said, coming across a picture of her drinking straight from a champagne bottle, my grandpa Wynton in the corner of the frame, laughing a big laugh. I showed it to her and she nodded.

"You didn't get a chance to know your mom's parents, did you?"

"Except for Grandma Post, none of my grandparents ever

even met me," I said.

"You would have liked your grandpa Wynton. And he would have liked you. He was very much a rapscallion."

· I liked that Margot had decided, reflecting on the small collection of times she had "known" me, that I would have been appealing to my grandfather. My mother had told me that before too, but it was different coming from Margot.

"Do you know what a rapscallion is?" she asked, waving at the waitress to bring her another drink.

"Yeah," I said. "A trickster."

"Very nice," she said, chuckling. "I like that—a trickster."

The pictures at the back of the stack were older, from my mom's high school days and before: a picnic, a football game, a Christmas pageant, Margot towering over the girls in each shot, and as she and my mother grew younger, photo by photo, Margot towering over many of the boys as well.

"You were always really tall," I said, and then was embarrassed about having said it.

"At school they called me MoM for years and years—it stood for Miles of Margot," she said, looking not at me but at a table of diners who had started their cross-restaurant trek to the salad bar.

"That's sort of clever," I said.

She smiled. "I think so too. Well, now I do. Not so much then."

The waitress came back to take our order and bring Margot her second drink. We hadn't even looked in the maroon menu folders with their gold tassels, but I knew that I wanted chicken-fried steak and hash browns, and Margot apparently knew that she wanted prime rib, because that's what she ordered, with a baked potato, as well as another Shirley Temple for me. She ordered it without even asking me if I wanted it. It was nice.

I pulled three photos from the stack—one of my mom and dad dancing at their wedding, one of my mom on the shoulders of some unknown boy with a chipped front tooth, and one of Mom and Margot, maybe nine or ten, in shorts and T-shirts, arms around each other's waists, handkerchiefs on their heads— that one reminded me of a picture I had of Irene and me. I held up my choices in front of her and shrugged my shoulders.

"So you've made your selections, then." She nodded at the pictures in my hand. "The one with both of us was taken at a Campfire Girls jamboree. I was looking for something the other day and came across my old handbook. I'll try to remember to send it to you; you'll get a kick out of it."

"Okay," I said.

Then we looked at each other, or the table, or the salt and pepper shakers, for what seemed like a very long time. I concentrated on tying one of my cherry stems into a knot with my tongue.

Margot must have noticed my mouth working, because she said, "My brother, David, used to do that too. He could do two knots on a single stem, which he told us meant that he was a very fine kisser."

I blushed, as usual. "How old was he?" I asked, without finishing the question with *when he died*, but Margot understood me all the same.

"He had just turned fourteen the weekend before the earthquake," she said, stirring her drink. "I don't think he had actually kissed very many girls before he died. Maybe none except for your mother."

"Your brother kissed my mom?"

"Absolutely," she said. "In the pantry of the First Presbyterian Church."

"So much for romance," I said.

Margot laughed. "It was very innocent," she said. She picked up the salt shaker and tapped its glass base against the tablecloth a few times. "I haven't been back to the Rock Creek area since it happened, but I'm going straight there after I leave Miles City tomorrow. I feel like I need to."

I didn't know what to say to that.

"I wanted to go back anyway; I've been wanting to for several years," she said.

"I don't ever want to go there."

"I don't think there's anything wrong with that." Margot reached her hand across the table like she was maybe going to take my hand, or just touch it, but I moved it fast to my lap.

She smiled a tight smile at me and said, "I'm going to level with you here, Cameron, because you seem adult enough to handle it. Grief is not my strong suit, but I did want to see you and tell you that if you need anything from me, you can always ask and I'll do my best." She seemed like she was done, but then she added, "I loved your mom since I met her."

Margot wasn't crying and I couldn't read on her face the potential for it, but I knew that if I looked at her long enough, I could definitely get all weepy, and maybe even eventually tell her about me and Irene and what we had done, what I had wanted to do and still did want to do. And I knew, somehow, that she would make me feel better about it. I could just tell that Margot would assure me that what I had done hadn't caused the accident, and that while I wouldn't believe anybody else telling me that exact same thing, I might actually believe her. But I didn't want to believe her right then, so I didn't keep looking at her face but instead drained the rest of my Shirley Temple, which took several swallows; but I finished every last sweet pink-red carbonated drop until the ice clacked against my teeth.

Then I said, "Thanks, Margot. I'm really glad you came."

"Me too," she said, and then she put her napkin back on the table and said, "I'm ready for that salad bar. How about you?"

I nodded, and then she asked me if I knew the German word for *bathroom* and I said no and she said *das Bad*, and it seemed funny so we both smiled, and then she stood and told me that she was just going to *pop into das Bad* for a minute before we ate. And while she did that, I took her photos back out of the envelope and found that wedding shot of her drinking straight from the champagne bottle and I slipped it up under my shirt and just inside the waistband of my pants, its surface cool and tacky against my stomach.

• • •

After Ruth came back, a moving van followed close behind; we had to make room for some of her stuff. This meant tackling the garage, closets, the storage shed in the backyard. During one of these clearing sessions we unearthed a dollhouse my father had made for my fifth birthday. As dollhouses go, it was amazing. It was a built-to-scale reproduction of some big old Victorian in San Francisco—according to my dad, it was a famous one on a famous street.

The version he built for me was three feet high and a couple of feet wide. It took both Ruth and me, working together, to get it out of the narrow opening of the cluttered storage shed.

"Should we put this in the car, take it to St. Vincent's?" Ruth asked after we'd made it through the cobwebbed doorway and were standing together on the lawn, both of us sweating. "It would make some little girl awfully happy."

We'd taken carload after carload to that thrift store. "It's mine," I told her, though I wasn't planning on keeping it until right that minute. "My dad made it for me, and I'm not giving it to some stranger." I hoisted it up by its peaked roof and took it into the house, up the stairs to my room, and shut the door.

Dad had painted it a blue he called cerulean, and I thought that name was so pretty that I named the first doll to live in the house Sarah Cerulean. The windows had white trim, and real glass panes, and flower boxes with tiny fake flowers in them. There was a fence made to look like ornate wrought iron around the little platform yard, which was done up with synthetic turf scraps left over from the indoor soccer field in Billings. I don't know how Dad even wound up with those. He'd cut up scraps from real shingles to do the roof. The outside was entirely finished, every detail, but the inside was another story.

The whole dollhouse was hinged, so you could close it and see it from all four sides, or open it and have access to each of the individual rooms, like a diorama. He'd done the framing for all of the rooms, and put in a staircase and a fireplace, but that was it as far as it got, no other decorations or finishes. He'd wanted to have it ready for my birthday, and he'd promised that we could finish it later, together, which we never did. Not that I minded. Even unfinished it was a better dollhouse than any I had ever seen.

My mom and I had picked out a few pieces of furniture for it at the crafts display counter at Ben Franklin. Irene and I used to spend hours with that thing, until sometime after my tenth birthday, when I had decided that I was too old for dolls, and therefore, dollhouses.

While Ruth continued her decluttering, I moved the dollhouse over to the corner of my already cramped room and put it on my desk, which was another thing—a monstrous thing—Dad had built for me, with cubbyholes and all sizes of drawers, a wide top for art projects. But the dollhouse was monstrous, too, and it left me only one small corner of free desktop. Still, I liked having it there, despite its bulk, but for a few weeks that's all it was: there, hulking and waiting.

• • •

The Klausons had hit it big with their dinosaur farm. "Raising dinosaurs beats the hell outta raising cattle," I heard Mr. Klauson say more than once. Mrs. Klauson bought a slippery teal convertible even though it was fall in Montana. Irene came to school with all kinds of new stuff. By Halloween it was settled: She was off to Maybrook Academy in Connecticut. Boarding school. I had seen the movies. I knew all about it: plaid skirts and rolling green lawns and trips to some seaside town on the weekends.

"Where are all the boys?" Steph Schlett had asked Irene, a bunch of us crammed in a booth at Ben Franklin, some of the girls *oooh*ing and *aaaah*ing over a glossy brochure.

"Maybrook's a girls' academy," Irene said, taking a slow drink from her Perrier. You couldn't buy Perrier at the Ben Franklin lunch counter, or anywhere else in Miles City; but Mrs. Klauson had taken to buying it in bulk in Billings, and Irene had taken to carrying a bottle with her practically everywhere.

"Bor-ring," Steph giggled in this high whinny thing she was known for.

"Hardly," Irene said, careful not to catch my eye. "Our brother school, River Vale, is right across the lake, and we have socials and dances and whatever with them all the time. Almost every other weekend."

I watched as Steph trailed a french fry through a pool of ketchup, and then into a big plastic vat of the good ranch dressing Ben Franklin made gallons of, before popping the fry into her mouth and starting on another. "But why are you going now?" she asked, the chew of mealy potato thick in her braces. "Why not wait until next fall, or until spring semester at least."

I had wanted to ask the same thing, but was glad that Steph did it for me. I didn't want Irene to notice how jealous I was. I could see part of that brochure from where I sat: fresh-faced girls playing lacrosse, or cuddled in thick wool cardigans sipping cocoa in rooms filled with leather-bound books. It really was just like the movies.

Irene took another drink of her Perrier. Then she screwed on the cap really slowly, sort of puzzling her forehead, as though what Steph had asked was just incredibly thought-provoking or something. Finally she said, "My parents think it's best that I start my education at Maybrook as soon as possible. No offense, you guys," she said, looking right at me, "but it's not like Miles City is known for its outstanding school system."

Most of the girls around me nodded their heads in agreement, as if they weren't insulting the next five years of their own education but somebody else's.

"They looked at my grades and are gonna let me do independent studies in the classes I was taking here, just to finish fall term," she said, emphasizing *term*, somehow giving a snobby ring to it. It so wasn't how we said things in Miles City. None of us would have even said *fall term* at all. Well, not before this.

• • •

The next weekend Irene had me out to the ranch. She was leaving that coming Monday. It was incredibly warm for

Montana in November, even early November—just freezing at night but midsixties during the day. We walked side by side without coats on. I tried to breathe in that ranch smell of pine and earth, but it wasn't anymore the place it had once been to me. There were white tents set up everywhere, a circus of scientists and also some earthy, dirty, long-haired types picking in giant trenches, treating the dirt as if it was fragile, like it wasn't the same dirt Irene and I used to kick at, spit on, pee on behind the barn.

Now Irene talked like the movies too. "They've never found a hadrosaur in this area before," she said. "Not one this complete."

"Wow," I said. I wanted to tell her that I had thought a lot about that ride on the Ferris wheel. I wanted to tell her that maybe I was wrong about what I had said to her that night. I didn't do it, though.

"My parents are building a visitors' center and museum. And a gift shop." She actually swept her hand out over the land. "Can you believe that? They might even name something after me."

"The Ireneosaur?" I asked.

She rolled her eyes. "They'll make it sound more professional than that. You don't really understand any of this."

"My mom ran a museum," I said. "I get it."

"It's not the same thing," she said. "That's a local history museum that's been around forever. This is a brand-new thing. Don't try to make it the same." She turned away from me and walked fast in the direction of the barn.

I thought that maybe she would lead me up to the hayloft. And if she had started up that ladder, I would have followed. But she didn't. She stopped just outside the entrance. There were tables set up there, and they were covered with various clumps of that rust-colored mud so greasy it's mostly just clay, and poking from some of those clumps were the fossils. Irene pretended to examine them closely, but I could tell that's all it was—pretending.

"Do you know who your roommate is yet?" I asked.

"Alison Caldwell," Irene said, her head all leaned down over some specimen. "She's from Boston," she added with that new tone of hers.

I tried on my best Henry Higgins. "Oh, the Boston Caldwells. Good show, old girl."

Irene smiled, and for half a second she seemed to forget how important she was supposed to be now. "I'm just glad I know how to ride. At least I know I can ride as well as any of them."

"Probably better," I said. I meant it.

"Different, though—western, not English." She turned from the fossils completely, grinned right at me. "They have scholarships to Maybrook, you know. You could apply for one for next fall. I bet you'd get it, because of—" Irene let what she was gonna say drop off.

"Because of my dead parents," I said, a little meaner than I felt.

Irene took a step toward me, put her hand on my arm, a little of that greasy mud smearing my shirt. "Yeah, but not only. Also because you're smart as hell and you live way out in the middle of nowhere Montana."

"Way out in the middle of nowhere Montana is where I'm from, Irene. You too."

"There's no rule that says you have to stay in the place that you're born," she said. "It's not like it makes you a bad person if you want to try something new."

"I know that," I said, and I tried to picture me cropped into one of those glossy brochure photos, me on a green lawn recently covered in an Oriental carpet of fall leaves, me in my pajamas reading one of those leather-bound books in the common room. But all I could see were versions of those pictures with both of us in them, the two of us, Irene and me, together in the boathouse, in the chapel, on a flannel blanket on that thick lawn, as roommates . . .

Irene could read my thinking, just like old times. She moved her hand from my arm, grabbed my hand. "It would be totally awesome, Cam. I would go first and get used to the run of the whole place, and then you'd come next fall." Her voice had the kind of excitement it got when we used to dare each other, something we hadn't done in what seemed like forever.

"Maybe," I said, thinking that it did sound so easy, in that moment, the almost-winter sun hot on the tops of our heads, the clink of the tools from the digging paleontologists, the feel of Irene's hand in mine.

"Why maybe? Just yes. Let's go ask my mom to get you an application." Irene pulled me with her toward the house. Mrs. Klauson smiled at our plan, everything so easy, as always. She said she'd be sure to have someone at Maybrook send me an application. She drove us back to town just after that. She had the top down, of course, and we made wind snakes off the sides, our arms rising and dipping with the rush of air. The weeds alongside the highway were partially gilded in death from the frosts at night—parts of them gold and ochre, dried and curled, but the rest of the weeds still green, hanging on, trying to keep growing. If you squinted your eyes, the wind snakes looked almost like they were swimming through those weeds. We did them for miles, until we were off the highway, back on town streets. And then Mrs. Klauson dropped me off in front of my house. And then Irene was gone.

CHAPTER FOUR

M y parents had been half-lapsed Presbyterians. We were a church-on-Easter-and-Christmas Eve kind of family, with a few years of Sunday school thrown in for good measure. Grandma Post said she was too old for churchgoing and could get to heaven just fine without it. Aunt Ruth was not either of these kinds of Christian. We had been attending services at First Presbyterian practically every Sunday since the funeral, because it had been the "family church," but Ruth made it clear during the car rides home that the mostly elderly congregation and dry sermons were not to her liking. For my part I liked them well enough. I liked, at least, that I knew the people in the pews around us, and that I knew when to stand and sit, how most of the hymns went. I liked the stained glass in the sanctuary, even though crucified Jesus was really bloody, too bloody for stained glass, I thought, all those red and magenta pieces filtering sunlight. I didn't feel close to God at the Presbyterian church, but some Sundays I felt really close to my memories of being at church, at this place, with my parents. And I liked that feeling.

Ruth held on through the holidays, but when we were taking down the Christmas tree, she told me that she'd been thinking that the First Presbyterian just wasn't *quite right for us anymore*. She embedded this deep in another conversation we were having about how just because I didn't have mandated sessions with gooey Nancy the counselor during the spring semester, that didn't mean that I wouldn't need to continue to talk with someone.

"You know, Greg Comstock and his family go to Gates of Praise, and the Martensons, and the Hoffsteaders," she told me. "And they all seem to just love it. First Presbyterian doesn't have the kind of fellowship we need right now. There's not even a youth group."

"What the heck is a youth group, anyway?" Grandma asked from behind the *Outrageous Detective Stories* magazine she was reading on the couch. "I thought children go to Sunday school until they're old enough to behave during the service. Can't you behave yourself, Cameron?"

Ruth laughed the way she did when she wasn't sure just how much Grandma was teasing and how much she was serious. "Gates of Praise has a group just for teenagers, Eleanor," she said. "According to Greg Comstock, they do all kinds of community service projects. It might also be nice for Cammie to hang out with some Christian teens."

As far as I knew, everybody I "hung out with" was a Christian teen, and even if some of them maybe weren't so convinced, not a one of them was talking about their doubts. I knew what Ruth was getting at, though; she wanted me to hang around with the kids who carried their Bibles class to class. She wanted me to wear the T-shirts of Christian rock bands and to go to the summer camps, the rallies, to talk the talk and walk the walk.

She was kneeling on the hardwood in the living room, plucking pine needles one after another from the tree skirt, an antique lace one that my mother had loved. She was putting each one she retrieved with her right hand into the cup of her left hand, like picking blueberries. Her blond curls—she'd taken to spending a lot of time in the mornings smoothing a special cream into them and then blow-drying them just so—hung in front of her face as she did this, making her look young, cherubic even.

"Why are you doing that?" I asked her. "We always just take the tree skirt outside and shake it."

Ruth ignored my question and kept plucking. "You must know lots of kids from school who go there, don't you, Cammie?"

Now I ignored her question. The real, live, bought-from-the-VFW-booth Christmas tree was a concession of Ruth's. My mother had been a big proponent of live Christmas trees. Every year she'd put up several at the Tongue River Museum, themed, of course, and we always had one at home, too. We used to go get them all in one trip, just the two of us, load them up into the back of my dad's pickup, and then maybe stop off at Kip's Minute Mart for ice cream. My mother had also been a big proponent of winter ice-cream cones.

"Well, we don't have to worry about these melting," she used to say, holding a cone in her elegant, leather-gloved hand, her breath visible in the air even as she took a bite.

The question of Christmas trees had come up at Thanksgiving. Ruth mentioned that she had been eyeing some very nice synthetic trees in a couple of the advertising inserts in the paper, and I had thrown a little fit at the table, Grandma backing me up the whole time. *It's her first year without them, Ruth. Let her keep her traditions.* And she *had* let me keep those traditions. She had gone out of her way, in fact, to ask me about the exact recipes I wanted for Christmas dinner, and where to hang certain decorations, and we'd gone together to the downtown Christmas Stroll. She'd baked batch after batch of sugar cookies and peanut-butter blossoms, and Ruth really had done everything that was supposed to be Christmasy even more perfectly than my parents had ever quite managed. And instead of making me feel better, Ruth's perfect imitation of a Post Family Christmas had just made me feel worse.

I'd been *cranky*, Grandma said, for weeks, and now Ruth's continued plucking made me grit my teeth. "It's just gonna spill more needles when we try to take it out of here, Ruth," I said. Sometime that December I had started dropping the "Aunt" out of her name, mostly because I knew that it annoyed her. "It's stupid to try to pick them up by hand. That's what they invented vacuum cleaners for."

This stopped her. She sat back on her feet and brushed her hair to one side with her non-needled hand. "Maybe that's what they invented artificial trees for," she said in that crispy-sweet voice she was so good at. "Which is why we'll be getting one next year." It was near impossible to get her to go beyond that hard-edged sweetness, but that didn't stop me from trying.

"Whatever," I said, flopping on the couch next to Grandma and purposefully knocking a box of lights and tinsel off the corner of the coffee table with my foot. "Let's just not get one at all. Why don't we just skip Christmas altogether?"

Grandma put her hand inside the magazine, marking the page she was reading, and swatted my arm with it, hard, a definite smack—like the one you'd use to kill a big spider. "Cameron, you pick those up," she said. She turned to Ruth. "I'm not sure this one is yet ready for one of your youth groups. First she'd best learn to act like a teenager and not a two-year-old."

She was right, for sure, but it made me flinch to have her side with Ruth.

"Sorry," I said, untangling strands of tinsel and not looking at either of them.

"So I think we'll try Gates of Praise next Sunday," Ruth said in that Ruth way, everything better. "Something new. I think it might be fun."

. . .

Gates of Praise (GOP) was one of those industrial-size churches that look more like a giant feed shed than a house of worship. It was a one-story metal building on a hill just outside the city limits, surrounded on three sides by a cement parking lot and on the only remaining side by a very small, very square patch of grass.

After the stained glass and worn mahogany pews of the First Presbyterian, GOP felt something like an office building, or even a factory. And it was, kind of. This was especially true in the main chapel, which was large enough to comfortably hold the congregation of over four hundred, and then some; it was all echoes, with bulky black speakers here and there, fluorescent lighting hanging from high above, and about an acre of blue office-building carpet spread out over the floor.

Services were rarely less than two hours, ten to noon. Aunt Ruth and I went every Sunday. Ruth joined the choir, and then the women's Bible study. As promised, Ruth had me join Firepower, the teen group.

What I remember from Sunday school at First Presbyterian was kind Mrs. Ness teaching us to sing "Jesus Loves Me," her silver hair in a bun, a guitar in her lap. I also remember the children's Bible they gave us, with its bright-colored pictures of pairs of animals boarding the ark, and Moses parting a very red sea, and a long-haired Jesus walking across water, his arms stretched wide, somehow reminding me of Shaggy from *Scooby-Doo*. And I remember that during the services it was just row after row of old people repeating some verses, painful organ music, a lengthy sermon that was hard for me to follow. Right from the start, Gates of Praise was different.

It wasn't enough to accept that Jesus had died for my sins, and to try and not break any of the Ten Commandments, to be kind to people. Things at GOP were much more specific than that. Evil, I learned, was all around me, constantly needing to be battled. Being a true believer meant helping others, lots of others, to believe just like me. *To be an agent of God for evangelizing the world.* Rather than convincing me of the righteousness of this kind of believing, rather than making me certain of its correctness, it made me question, and doubt, all the more. I knew it wasn't how my parents had thought about the world, about God. I guess we hadn't discussed it specifically all that many times, but this, I knew, wasn't their version.

At my first Firepower meeting our adviser, Maureen Beacon, who looked weirdly, weirdly like Kathy Bates, gave me my very own *Extreme Teen Bible*. We were in the big meeting room at the back of the church, and there were dozens of kids my age and older filling plastic cups with Sunny Delight and milling around the snack table, plucking grapes from bunches and tossing them at each other, and each and every one of them had a copy. The *Extreme Teen Bible* had a black cover with hot-blue writing and these laser-type neon bolts everywhere, symbolizing what, I don't know. I don't remember our group-discussion concerns from that first meeting—maybe Christian Teens and Anorexia, maybe Christian Teens and TV Watching; but no matter what the topic, from Acne to Dating, our *Extreme Teen Bible* had it covered.

I hadn't ever known exactly what the Bible said about the way that I felt about Irene, the way that I knew I could let myself feel about other girls. I had some vague idea that it wasn't too favorable, but I had never sought out the hard evidence. That night of the first Firepower, after I got home, I went to my room, put on *Fatal Attraction* as my background movie, and searched out homosexuality under the handy Topics to Consider contents inside the front cover. I underlined passages from Romans and Corinthians. I read all about Sodom and Gomorrah, had questions about the nature of brimstone. Though what seemed to me the most specifically damning passage, Leviticus 18:22, only mentioned male homosexuality (*when a man lies with a man, this is an abomination*), this didn't actually make me feel any better. My *Extreme Teen Bible* had explicit notes in the margins: *"Man with a man" can be expressly understood to mean any and all forms of same-sex attraction and same-sex acts.* I read that line probably ten times. Things seemed clear enough.

I was all sprawled out on my stomach, my feet on my pillows, my face so close to the TV screen, I could feel the static electricity pulling my hair toward it. I closed the Bible, let it slide off the mattress and *thunk* on the floor. My twelve-year-old mom, as always, watched me from the Quake Lake photo.

"I'm not gonna be ignored!" Glenn Close was telling Michael Douglas, her own hair that unraveled kind of messy that showed just how crazy she was about to get. I shoved my hands into the pockets of my jeans so that I was lying on my arms, all of me one long mass. The knuckles of my right hand jammed against something I hadn't remembered was there: a jagged piece of bright-purple fluorite that I'd nicked from the Earth Science room during mineral lab.

I took it out and rolled it against my fingers. It was warm

from my pocket and glassy smooth along some of its sides, sandpaper rough on others. I put it in my mouth for a moment to feel the weight of it against my tongue, to hear it click along my teeth. It tasted like the Earth Science room smelled—like metal and dirt. I was still holding it against the roof of my mouth, half watching the movie, half not, when I glanced at the dollhouse, lurking, lurking, as always. I decided that piece of fluorite would look nice, would even look right, somehow, hanging above the fireplace in the room I thought of as the library. So instead of waiting and thinking about it more, or wondering about doing it, I got up, scavenged around in my desk until I found a tiny tube of Super Glue, and then stuck it there, just above the fireplace, with Glenn Close boiling a bunny in the background.

I'd been keeping a little collection of things that I'd taken from various places. I had it in the back of one of my desk drawers. I spread it all out on top of my quilt and knelt at the side of the bed to look at it all there, my plunder. It didn't add up to much, just small things: an authentic Nixon campaign button from Mr. Hutton's bulletin board; a thermometer magnet of praying Jesus from the fridge in the kitchen at GOP; a tiny glass frog from counselor Nancy Huntley's desk; an aluminum ashtray from the bowling alley, the disposable kind, with BOWL-N-FUN on it in red; a Swiss Army knife keychain a kid in my World History class had hanging from his backpack; a beautiful all-color origami flower one of the Japanese exchange students had made; one of those cut-apart school portraits of a kid I had babysat for once or twice; and also that picture of Champagne Margot I'd grabbed while she was *in das Bad*; an airplane-size bottle of vodka that I'd found during Mom's office cleanout; and finally, a pack of Bubblicious that I'd taken from Kip's Minute Mart just because I was thinking of Irene.

I started gluing more of my little treasures to that doll-house. I made a gum-wrapper rug for the kitchen. I hung the Nixon button on the wall in what I imagined to be the oldest boy's room. I put the frog in the garden and took the lampshade off a piece of my old dollhouse furniture to make a vodka-bottle floor lamp for the living room. The movie played on and then finished and then ran its credits, went to black screen, clicked off, rewound, started playing automatically again; I kept on gluing. It felt really good to do something that made no sense at all.

Part Two

High School
1991–1992

CHAPTER FIVE

The summer before freshman year I came home from swim team and there's Aunt Ruth in the dining room with all these pink cartons spread around on the floor, on the table, and pink Styrofoam peanuts everywhere. She had her back to me, singing a little something, maybe it was Lesley Gore, maybe not, but definitely somebody from her high school days.

I dropped my backpack on the floor because I knew it'd startle her, and even though there were only the next fifty-some summer days between me and high school, I wasn't above these immaturities.

She overdid the *you startled me* jump and turned around, a pink-handled hammer in hand. "Cameron, you startled me," she said as if she was on a soap opera and had been caught rifling through someone else's desk.

I nodded at the hammer. "What's with the pink hammer?"

Her eyes flashed bright like when you first light a smoke bomb, all sulfur and heat. "It's my Sally-Q Busy Lady Hammer. Meet Miles City's first official Sally-Q Tool distributor." She was doing her pageant smile; she was every infomercial I'd ever seen, with me as the studio audience.

She flittered around some peanuts in the carton nearest her and pulled out a small, pink cordless drill, pressed the On lever. It buzzed the way you'd expect a drill like that to buzz.

Just exactly that way, like a mechanical hummingbird might: high-pitched and fast but without much presence.

"Actually, I'm the only Sally-Q Tool sales representative in eastern Montana. I'm a hub!" She let the drill buzz for a few seconds more and then clicked it off.

Already I could see the Sally-Q parties in the living room: a little spinach quiche, lemonade with mint sprigs, and then the pitch: *Practical can still be pretty. This isn't your husband's socket wrench.*

She handed over the drill for me to marvel at. "They're made in Ohio," she said. "It's all been researched and tested. These tools are built specifically for women." She saw my face, which said back, *I didn't know other tools were built only for men.* "It's things like making the handles smaller and the grips closer together," she said. "Even you have small hands, Cammie. Long fingers, but dainty hands."

"They're bony," I told her, handing it back.

"They're just like mine," she said, but I barely had time to smirk at her immaculate manicure before she added, "and just like your mother's, too."

I remembered that we did have the same hands, my mother and I. I remembered pressing my palms to hers, waiting for my fingers to grow, to catch up, and how she'd use both of her hands to smooth cherry-almond lotion over one of mine, her skin warm, the lotion cool.

"You're right," I told Ruth, and it was a nice moment between us, this memory of my mother, her sister; but those pink boxes were everywhere, the sad confetti of pink packing peanuts, and I didn't let the moment linger very long.

I went to the kitchen, got a granola bar. Ruth kept on with her unpacking, checking her inventory against an order form, again humming her song, or another one just like it. From the doorway, as I chewed, I took in all the tools, so many of them. They were stupid, but still, I was glad Ruth had this thing, because it would keep her busy, and I wanted her busy. I had plans for my summer break, for how I wanted to spend it. Or how I thought I did, anyway. And Ruth being occupied would help out with that, because what I had planned definitely wasn't something Ruth would okay.

• • •

In May they had finished building the big medical center over on what had once been grazing land, and they left the carcass of the old hospital in the center of town. Though pretty much every kid in Miles City had been born there, and had visited the pediatrician Dr. Davies there, and had our broken bones set in pink and green casts, our ears tubed, our heads sewn with stitches there, once empty, Holy Rosary Hospital took on the eerie and irresistible aura of any massive and abandoned place.

There were nine empty stories of exam rooms, operating rooms, extended-care rooms, and offices, plus a cafeteria and kitchen still glinting with stainless-steel counters and shelves, all connected by a labyrinth of seemingly endless hallways— more than enough to occupy any mildly adventurous kid with a couple of friends game to go along.

But it was the older section of the hospital, the 1800s original dark brick building that was added onto in the 1920s and then again in the 1950s, that became the ultimate destination for dare fulfillment. It was creepy enough from the outside, the Spanish-style architecture crumbling from age, broken windows, a weathered stone cross at the top, all the classic dark-and-stormy-night elements. Any teenager could tell you that a place like that just had to be worse on the inside.

My first time, getting in was easy. Jamie Lowry had somehow stolen the bolt cutter from the janitor's room at school. He had also brought a massive plastic bottle of Dr. McGillicuddy's Peppermint Schnapps and one thin flashlight, both items buried beneath sweaty shorts and a jockstrap in his track practice bag. Since, as usual, I was the only girl invited along, I didn't say anything about how gross peppermint schnapps is, even before it rides around with a sweaty jockstrap for a few hours.

Five of us from the team had skipped out early on the end-of-the-year pizza party, even before Hobbs did his signature move of eating all the remaining slices and crusts, the stuff left in the cardboard boxes sitting sad and abandoned in pools of orange grease. He would cram it all down, follow it with Mountain Dew, and then do jumping jacks until he puked. I'd seen it the year before, anyway.

Jamie had already broken into Holy Rosary once, with his older brother, so that plus the bolt cutter gave him authority, and he was loving it. "We didn't get very far," he told us on the way. "It's really dark once you get inside, and we started out too late—the sun went down. But what we did see—the place is unreal."

"But like how?" somebody had asked him, probably Michael, who didn't really want to go anyway but would do things like this every so often, just so nobody stopped asking him altogether.

"Just wait, dude," Jamie had said. "I'm serious. It's fucking hard-core." Since Jamie described everything from zombie movies to his parents' fights to the new enchilada platter at Taco John's as "fucking hard-core," none of us could gauge much by it.

Once we were within the cover of the old hospital

courtyard, its overgrown vines and shady trees, each of us took turns downing as much of the schnapps as we could. We did pretty well, considering the lukewarm temperature of the liquor and the piles of cheap pizza it was following after.

"Let's rock this shit," Jamie said, pulling out the cutter. "My bro and I busted in a window on the other side, but they boarded that up already." He led us to a hatch just a couple of feet off the ground. "Used to be for deliveries," he told us. "Goes straight into the basement."

The padlock snipped off surprisingly easy, Jamie working one handle and Michael pushing the other. But once the wood panel was raised, the narrow steps offered up, Michael had done his part and said he had to get going.

"Fucking pussy," Jamie said, and then he took a drink of the schnapps, all serious-like, trying to make it look tough and John Wayne, as if it was the code of the West or something: *You curse a man, you take a swig.* But he didn't say it until Michael was already well out of the courtyard and probably feeling pretty good about his stint as the bad-ass.

I skipped my turn as the bottle was again passed around.

"You wanna leave too, Cameron?" Jamie asked me, and it pissed me off that he didn't ask it the way he would have one of the guys. Instead it was in a mocking sort of baby-talk tone, all whiney. He asked it as sincerely as Jamie Lowry could, like it would be okay if I wanted to go, since I was just a girl and should be expected to be scared.

"I just don't want to drink any more of that shit. It's foul. Let's do this already."

"The lady has spoken," Jamie said, and started down.

That flashlight was a joke. Even when it was working, it was just a skinny strip of light, and it was dead by maybe four minutes in, anyway. It had been such a rainy May, and the basement felt appropriately cryptlike: cobwebs around the doorframe ghosting our faces, that smell of dirt and rot and trapped air, and it was dark, totally dark. I mean, there was a patch of light from a window on the far side, just like one square of light, but it didn't do anything to help us see where we were going. I could feel hot schnapps breath on my neck, probably from Murphy, maybe Paul, and I didn't mind whoever it was being that close. His breath even smelled kind of good, pepperminty but rotten, somehow. I liked knowing someone was right behind me, though.

We were four of the stars of the junior-high track team, but we moved through that basement a few timid steps at a time. Even with all that pizza to sop it up, the liquor seeped its way through my arms, my legs, everything heightened and muffled at once. My mind kept replaying clips from all those slasher flicks I'd rented.

Paul was our mutterer. "I don't like nuns," he said. "Never liked 'em. Nuns are fuckin' creepy as shit. They're creepy. Married to God? What is that? That's fuckin' psycho." Maybe he was talking to us, but nobody answered him.

Every so often my hand swiped in front of me for Jamie, almost an involuntary move, like my palm had Tourette's, me gripping a handful of the damp cotton T-shirt and twisting it, pulling it tighter and tighter, stretching the fabric taut across his skin, same as I did to my own pant leg when I rode the Tilt-A-Whirl at a parking-lot carnival. Jamie didn't say a thing about it, and he didn't laugh but instead let me cling to him like that as we fumbled and tripped our way to the door leading the hell out of there.

Though the old stairs sagged beneath us, the stairwell was draped in a filmy light from the open doorway to the floor above. Jamie "Fuck-yeahed!" as he reached the top and Paul and Murphy echoed something similar, all of us wrapped in the giddy elation that comes with escape.

It was still soon enough after the shutdown that some electricity remained on in the building (upstairs, anyway), and even though it seemed too modern for its surroundings, the fact that, at the end of the hallway, an EXIT sign glowed its appropriate Christmas-light red, gave me comfort, somehow, a sense of normalcy. Because nothing else about that hospital was normal.

That day we only had time for the old wing, and that was plenty. It was all tall archways and gold foil wallpaper, too decadent to resemble the stark hospital rooms we knew from our checkups. There were green couches, definitely antiques, and in one corner there was even a piano, a baby grand. As soon as he saw it, Murphy charged the bench and clanked out a pause-filled "Heart and Soul" while Jamie and Paul tackled each other the way boys do when they're pumped up with excitement and thrown together in a place where you're supposed to behave—or at least were once supposed to behave. Above us, stern nuns in crisp whites watched our intrusion from the strokes of a massive oil painting housed in a gilt frame.

When Jamie proposed a toast to the "broads of God," I raised the bottle to the painting and drank a swig, same as the guys. This time the schnapps burned hard all across the roof of my mouth, the back of my throat, and I coughed some of it out, embarrassed.

Then the wrestling started up again, this time with Murphy included, and I watched from the arm of one of the couches and wondered what it was I should be feeling. It wasn't a performance for my benefit, like the way male tigers show off for the female, courting her with manly prowess and antics, though I had seen these guys do that shit before around Andrea Harris, around Sue Knox. What they were doing was what they did all the time when we were together. It was some sort of freedom guys allowed themselves around each other, and I envied every moment of it. It was something louder, and harder, than anything I'd ever been part of with a group of girls. Not that I was really a part of it with these guys. It all seemed to come so easily to them, and I could only get so close to any of that.

"Hey Camster," Jamie shouted at me from the bottom of a dog pile, "come rescue me."

"Fuck off," I yelled back.

"You said you wanna jerk me off?"

"Yep. You heard me exactly right."

Jamie's mom went to Gates of Praise. His dad didn't come along. Jamie only got out of it once in a while. We'd started hanging around the year before, during track practice warm-ups and cooldowns. I'd seen even more movies than Jamie had, which made me some sort of authority to him. The other guys just followed along.

"C'mon, Cameron," Jamie tried again, untangling himself from the pile and jogging over to the baby grand. "Let's act out the piano scene from *Pretty Woman*."

Murphy and Paul laughed pretty hard at this.

"Okay," I said. "You want Paul to play Julia, or Murphy? 'Cause he's got the red hair."

The light from outside was cut into strange strips, weird angles, by the cheap lumber somebody had used to do a half-assed board-up job of the windows. Those strips of light illuminated the thick dust that the boys had stirred in their play, and its slow descent back to the ground, like glitter, like snowflakes, made everything just a little dreamy and unreal.

And the schnapps helped. It felt like we'd entered a world that wasn't supposed to be found this way. I liked it.

• • •

That summer Lindsey Lloyd and I traded off for high point in the Intermediate Girls Division at each of the Eastern Montana Federation swim meets. She would beat me by half a stroke on the hundred free, I'd out-touch her on the IM, and then it would come down to the timers comparing their stopwatches each and every hundred butterfly we swam. Lindsey spent her summers with her father—he was working some construction thing near Roundup—and the school year with her mother and stepfather in Seattle. We'd been each other's competition since even before my parents had died, with Lindsey always at an advantage, because her school in Seattle had an indoor pool and I had only June, July, and August at Scanlan Lake.

We'd always been friendly—we made small talk while sitting on the heat benches and sometimes stood in line together at the concession stand, waiting for our haystacks, a swim meet favorite of seasoned hamburger, cheese, sour cream, tomatoes, and olives all served with a personal-size bag of Fritos corn chips, the fork sticking out of the top. Lindsey loved those things. She ate them maybe twenty minutes before a race and could still win, a kind of "fuck you" to the stupid *wait two hours before you swim* rule.

Lindsey Lloyd had just always been there, part of the summer swim team experience. I remember that my first meet back after my parents' funeral, she didn't try for one of the weird hugs some of the other girls I competed against went for. Instead, she mouthed "I'm sorry" when we caught eyes during the crackly "Star-Spangled Banner" that they insisted on playing over the PA before every meet—all of us still dripping from warm-ups and gathered around the pool deck, hands on our hearts, nobody quite sure where the flag was hanging at this particular pool. That "I'm sorry" seemed the right way to handle things.

But this summer Lindsey had come back a lot taller, and she'd changed other things, too. She'd chopped off the pony-tail that she used to tuck up into her swim cap and she'd bleached what was left of her hair a bright white. She soaked it in conditioner before meets to keep the chlorine from turning it green. She also had an eyebrow ring, a little silver thing that the stroke judges made her remove before she could compete. Coach Ted said she had a butterflier's shoulders, and that there was nothing I could do about my own non-butterflier shoulders but train harder.

Between races Linds and I sat together on beach towels, playing Uno and eating icy red grapes from the bottom of a pink Sally-Q cooler Aunt Ruth had already been awarded for her commitment to the company. Lindsey told stories about Seattle, where everything sounded edgy and cool, stories about the concerts and parties she had been to, all the crazy friends she said she had. I told her about the hospital, the secret world we'd discovered by breaking in. From our beach towels in eastern Montana we listened to mix tapes of bands I'd never heard of, our heads close together, each of us with one ear pressed to one side of Lindsey's black headphones.

A couple of weekends in we were at the Roundup meet, Lindsey's home water for the summer, and I was rubbing suntan lotion on her back, those butterflier shoulders—her skin soft and warm from the sun. She used the oily stuff that smelled like coconuts, like Coach Ted, even though she didn't need it, as tan as all of us were; *little natives*, Grandma liked to say. All of us practiced for hours a day in summer sun, and there wasn't anything all that special about putting lotion on each other, but there was when I did it to Lindsey. It made me jittery, anxious, but I couldn't wait for her to ask me, each and every meet.

My hands were all gooped up with stuff and I was trying to do under the straps of her suit when she said, "If I was back in Seattle, I would be at Pride this weekend. Now that's supposed to be a fucking blast. Not that I would know." She tried to sound all nonchalant while she was saying this, but I noticed her trying.

Lindsey was always talking about these Seattle events and concerts that I'd never heard of before, so not knowing what kind of Pride she was talking about didn't necessarily mean anything to me right at that moment.

I kept on rubbing, working that soft area at her lower back, where the required team racing suit just allowed for a window of skin, a couple of knobs of vertebrae. "What do you mean *not that you'd know*?" I asked.

"Because June is always Pride month, and I'm always in Montana in June," she said, moving her shoulder straps so I could reach better. "It's not like Roundup-fucking-Montana has a Pride."

"Yeah, no kidding," I said, still working the lotion.

She shifted herself around at this so she could look at me, trying, not very well, to keep the smirk on her face from stretching wider. "You don't know what I'm talking about, do you? Like at all."

I could tell by her face, her tone, that I had somehow missed something important in what she'd said, and had again revealed myself as the small-town hick I often felt like around her. My answer to this was to feign indifference. "I'm not an idiot. You're talking about some festival you miss every year."

"Yeah, but what kind?" She leaned closer, her face so close to mine.

"I don't know," I said, but then, even as I said it, I think part of me did know, sort of, like it washed over me and I knew. I could even feel my stupid blush, my body's way of telling me that I knew. But there was no way I was gonna say it out loud. So what I said was "German Pride?"

"You're adorable, Cam," she said, her face still close enough for me to smell the Fruit Punch Gatorade on her breath.

I didn't want to be adorable the way she meant it. "You don't always have to work so hard to convince me how cool you are," I said, standing up, grabbing my goggles and cap. "I get it. You're very, very cool. You're the coolest girl I've ever met."

A couple of my teammates walked by and told us that they'd just called the hundred free. I started after them, not waiting for Lindsey, even though this was her event too, like always.

She caught up with me over behind the concession stand, where they'd set out the gallon jugs they used to make sun tea—a neat row of fifteen or so, the water inside now various shades of brown. We stepped over them together and she grabbed my arm, just above the elbow, and pulled me to her, her mouth at my ear.

"Don't be mad at me," she said, her voice quiet and much less Lindsey than usual. "It's Gay Pride. That's what it is."

It felt like a declaration when it wasn't. At least not completely. "I kind of got that," I said. "I mean, I figured it out." We were weaving through groups of parents, of swimmers, the lawns crowded and loud; and even though we had a kind of anonymity in that, I worried about where this was going, what she'd say next, what I might say if I wasn't careful.

"If I could take you to Pride, like in a perfect world, if I could private-plane us to Seattle, would you want to go with me?" Lindsey asked, still holding my arm tight.

"Well, is there cotton candy?" I asked, because we were there, the heat benches, and it felt like the right time for a nonanswer.

But that's not what Lindsey wanted. "Whatever," she said, taking her card from the lady who was always in charge of time cards at the Roundup meet, the one with red hair in two ponytails and a white safari hat she kept on for the entire day. "Forget it."

The heat benches were clumped up with nervous swimmers, some stretching, others pulling their tight silicone caps over a heap of hair, leaving a tumorlike protrusion encased in neon purple or metallic silver at the back or top of their heads. A group of girls waved us over, girls we'd been competing against for years, forever. Lindsey was in the heat ahead of mine, but we still had maybe five heats before that.

We found a place at a back bench, close together like you always had to sit on those benches. When our bare knees touched, the way they had to in order to even fit back there, I couldn't help but remember Irene and the Ferris wheel, just like an allergic reaction. I jerked away, let my other knee collide, instead, with that of the girl on the other side of me.

Lindsey couldn't not notice this. "God—I didn't mean to upset you so much," she said, too loud for me, for where we were.

"I'm not upset. I just don't want to talk about this two minutes before we have to swim." I had lowered my voice and was looking around, though there was really no need. Everyone was in their own conversation or prerace zone.

"But you do want to talk about this sometime later?" she

asked, sticking her face right up close to mine again, another blast of Gatorade and something else, cinnamon, maybe. Gum.

"You have to spit your gum out before you swim," I said, thinking again of Irene.

"Ms. Lloyd, did I just hear that you have gum?" Always vigilant, Safari Hat took a couple steps toward us with an outstretched arm, her palm faceup and cupped.

"You want me to spit it in your hand?" Lindsey asked her, though it was obvious that yes, that was exactly what was expected.

"Otherwise I'll just find it stuck under the heat benches when we put them away. C'mon." Safari Hat snapped the fingers of her palm before making it a little cup, again. "Whatever you have isn't going to kill me."

"Don't be so sure about that," I said, right as Lindsey spit.

"I'll take my chances." Safari Hat examined the little hunk of chew-marked red before turning to find the trash.

"What exactly is she gonna catch from me?" Lindsey asked me. She tried to look pissed, but I winked at her and she cracked up.

"I can think of a few things," I said.

Lindsey let that sit there for a little while, but then she asked again, and with complete seriousness, "But you'd go to Pride with me, wouldn't you? You'd want to go to it. Just say yes."

I knew that my answer meant more than just the words I was saying, but I nodded and said, "Yeah, I'd go. I'd go with you."

She smiled big but didn't ask anything more. They called her heat pretty soon after that, and I was just left there on the bench, waiting to be called up too.

• • •

We only ever had two days to get reacquainted, prelims Saturday and finals on Sunday, and then there was the matter of being there to compete. I had to be caught up fast. Lindsey had kissed five girls before, and had done other, mysterious, *serious stuff* with three of those. Lindsey's mom knew a guy, Chuck, who was a drag queen, Chastity St. Claire, and Lindsey had seen him perform at a charity thing. Lindsey was gonna join the GLBU group at her high school. *U* stood for *undecided*. I hadn't known, before Lindsey, that it was an actual category.

"*Personal Best* is good, but you need to rent *Desert Hearts*," she told me.

"I'm pretty sure they won't have that at Video 'n' Go," I told her back after she explained the plot.

When Coach Ted passed out sign-up slips to house swimmers for our own meet, I didn't even put the paper in my bag but rode my bike home with it pressed against my handlebars. Even though Ruth said we could sleep four comfortably if we used the pullout couch, I returned the little white slip to Ted with an X in the box next to: *We can provide lodging and dinner for 1 swimmer.* Lindsey sometimes got housed at meets and sometimes her dad came with his camper. I had a fifty-fifty shot. I tried to ask her about it casually, at the heat benches the next weekend, but it felt somehow like a big step.

"You're coming to our meet, right?" I kept pulling at the straps on my goggles. I'd already spit in them twice, rubbed it around with my pointer finger, but I did it again.

"Yeah, why wouldn't I?" she asked, noticing my busy hands, my obvious need to be doing something other than looking at her and having this conversation.

"I don't know," I said, still fiddling. "Because the lake is gross and nobody ever comes to our meets." The heat co-ordinator moved us to the next bench forward and I stubbed my bare toe, hard, on the edge of the cement lip of the pool deck, watched a blood blister form almost instantly under the nail.

Lindsey saw me wince and touched the top of my knee, left her hand there for a second longer than it took to ask if I was okay. "I like your lake," she said. "It's something different than all the other meets."

"Yeah," I said, and then didn't know where to go from there, or why this was so hard, exactly. Then Lindsey started messing with her goggles, and we both sat like that, silent, on the benches some idiot had painted a glossy blue, the kind of paint that heats up like a car hood, toasts the back of your thighs the minute you sit on it in your swimsuit.

I waited until the walk to the starting blocks—when Ted said we should be visualizing the race ahead, focusing on our stroke length, our kick rhythms, picturing turns and pull-outs over and over in our minds—to finish asking her. "Your dad isn't coming, is he?"

She had already put on her thick silicone cap, and she pulled one side out and away from her ear, looked at me like she was glad I had said something, even if she wasn't sure what it was.

"I mean, to Miles City," I said. "Is he coming to the meet? Do you need to stay somewhere?"

"I'm staying with you, right?" She said it so easily that I felt like I'd walked into a trap, into something I wouldn't be able to handle once it arrived. It was "Swimmers take your marks" maybe fifteen seconds after that, and it was the worst race I swam all season.

· · ·

Dave Hammond was back from his mom's in Texas, and he was even crazier than Jamie—up for anything. In the summer he lived in a camper out behind his dad's fruit stand, and for the last week of June and first week of July, he got to man the red, white, and blue booth they set up next to the long tables of watermelon and corn—Dave's Fireworks. You can't be much more popular the first week of July than to be the fourteen-year-old with access to an entire stand of cheap shit made specifically for blowing up. And the best part was that even after the Fourth, when it was illegal to continue selling them, the Hammonds kept the remainder of their stock in a storage shed over by the Dairy Queen. So it was a Butterfinger Blizzard and then a stop at the shed for bottle rockets, for roman candles, for Black Cat crackers and cherry bombs. I smelled like sulfur smoke and sunscreen for days on end.

I wanted to share this summer world with Lindsey when she came, all of what was best about Miles City in July spread out before us like a picnic table heaped with pies. The meet seemed like a formality, and no home meet had ever felt that way before. In our prelim heats, on Saturday, I beat Lindsey's time in every event, even the freestyle. Other teams weren't used to the thickness of the water, the feeling of lake weed tickling their legs, their toes slipping off the algae coating on our homemade turn boards, costing them precious seconds. Most embarrassing, but probably effective at giving us an advantage, were our starting blocks. We stored them in the musty shed across the parking lot from Scanlan, stacked atop one another from September through May, nesting grounds for spiders and the occasional rat or garter snake. They were heavy constructions of plywood, a sanded dowel for backstroke starts, puke-green carpet torn from somebody's basement stapled into the sloping tops for traction, and lane numbers spray-painted in orange on the backs. Team dads had made them for us one summer, mine included.

Before the free relay, Ruth brought Lindsey and me plates of lime and orange Jell-O cut with a star-shaped cookie cutter. It was cold and sweet and we both agreed it was the best Jell-O either of us had ever tasted, so when Lindsey dropped hers in the sand, I gave her the rest of mine, but as usual, I blushed as I did so. Lindsey didn't blush at all.

Grandma was there too, in a big weird sunhat and those dark plastic inserts you wear behind your glasses if you're a certain kind of old lady and want to block the sun. She sat in a lawn chair under the team tarp and ate her sugar wafer cookies and read her detective stories magazine until it was time for my races, and then she walked down to the edge of the dock and watched me. She gave me a big hug when I got out of the water even though it soaked her.

"Your grandma's a trip," Lindsey told me after Grandma said something about my having mermaid blood, or at least guppy blood. Lindsey saying that reminded me again of Irene, always Irene, and I got even more nervous than I already was about what might happen, what felt like it just had to happen.

The meet ended by three and that meant maybe six good hours of daylight left, six and a half if we counted twilight, which seemed far darker from inside the hospital. We rushed through taco pizza at the Pizza Pit, Ruth telling me to slow down, to chew like a lady, to stop popping my knuckles and gnawing on my straw. Lindsey rolled her eyes and made faces every time Ruth looked away, and that was enough to get me through the meal. We were scooched together in one of those red vinyl booths and were both in shorts, the seats icy on our sun-hot legs. Our bare arms touched as we ate, our thighs, and it felt like heat lighting, it felt like a quick brush against the electric fence at Klauson's Ranch, like the promise of something more.

"We're gonna go meet Dave at his stand and get some ice cream and then go to the six-thirty show," I told Ruth as soon as she had the last bite of her second piece in her mouth. I surprised myself by grabbing Lindsey's hand and pulling her from the booth. I think I surprised Lindsey, too.

"What's playing? It has to be PG. Those PG-13 movies might as well be R-rated, and I don't want you girls seeing that junk." Ruth was dabbing at her mouth with her paper napkin, ever dainty, ever refined, even as the slot machines clanged and beeped one room over.

"It is PG," I lied, knowing that Ruth could (and in fact did) check the marquee as she drove past the theater on her way home. But by then she'd think we were already inside and watching the very R-rated *Thelma & Louise*, and would talk with me about that lie later, which was a talk I deserved, I suppose, because even though Lindsey and I didn't go to see *Thelma & Louise* that night, it was a movie I rented and rented and rented once it came out.

• • •

Dave and Jamie met us in the hospital courtyard with a backpack full of smoke bombs and sparklers. Dave eyed Lindsey for a long time, like he knew her type, or like he wanted to. I thought his skull earring looked stupid with the beaded rattail he had cultivated—like he was trying too hard to be a pirate or something.

They were already drinking from a thermos, the one Dave said his father had carried in Vietnam. It was half full of a mixture of Sunny Delight and Beefeater gin. It tasted the way children's medicine tastes when they try to give it orange flavoring.

I had in my backpack some tools that had been my dad's—a handsaw and a little ax—and for a while we slashed at the rotted wood frame of a basement window before eventually giving up and just bashing it in, each of us dropping down inside after the shattered glass. Lindsey cut the top of her shoulder on the way down, and it bled through her white T-shirt, formed a little map of some unknown continent.

"You gonna be okay?" I asked her, worried that this could make the whole thing seem too dangerous to continue with, worried that she'd want to just go to the movie we were supposed to be at, or worse, back to my house and Aunt Ruth undoubtedly waiting with popcorn and board games.

But that wouldn't have been like Lindsey at all. "Yeah. It's just a stupid cut," she said, but she pulled back the hand that was pressing it and her fingertips were sticky red. She put them in her mouth and I blushed in the dark of the hallway, embarrassed even as I did so.

"Pour some of the gin on it. That'll clean it out." Dave wedged himself between the two of us, offering up the thermos.

"Don't be an asshole," she said, taking it from him. "I'm not gonna waste our liquor supply on my arm." She swallowed hard and passed it to me, and I did the same, thinking as I did that her lips were just pressed to the same place, and wondering if she was thinking that too.

We spent maybe thirty minutes just fucking around in the 1800s section, trying to impress our guests, which wasn't hard. Back when it was first shut down, and they moved the patients—at least the serious ICU types—it was in a real hurry. That was in the *Miles City Star*, how they went about the transports and everything. It's serious procedural stuff, moving sick people across town. But what remained in those rooms, what was left behind, made no sense to teenagers who weren't supposed to be seeing any of it.

On the top floor, in what we guessed was originally the nuns' quarters, we found a trunk full of dolls, old, old dolls, with leathery skin that was broken and creased from wear or age. The stuffing in one doll was something like black sand, spilling out as we lifted it. Each doll had a tag carefully sewn to it, and on it was the name of a child in elegant black script, old names—Vivienne and Lillianne and Marjorie, Eunice— and the child's illness. On most it was something simple, like fever or influenza, and the final line on each tag had a date and then read: *Met her Father in Heaven.*

"This is insane," Lindsey said, reaching for one, half of it collapsing as she gripped it. The doll's torso burst open, a pile of the black sand stuff left in Lindsey's hand. "Fuck!" She dropped the whole thing; its head came off in the box.

"You scared?" Dave asked, gripping her shoulder and sort of leering, but he sounded a little creeped out himself.

"Whatever," she said, shaking him off. "I want to see something else." She took my hand, pulled me to her. "Show me the new part, the room with the keys."

The 1800s section and the 1950s high-rise were connected by sort of a tunnel, maybe six yards wide and probably half a football field in length, or it seemed that way. It was all cement and linoleum, walls and ceiling and floors, and it echoed just like you'd guess it would. When we reached the opposite end, Jamie and Dave announced that they were gonna shoot rockets back down the tunnel—rockets Dave had conveniently forgotten to show us outside in the courtyard.

"It'll be too loud, Dave," I said. "The police are driving by here like ten times an hour now."

"They're not gonna be able to hear us from outside," he said, removing the thin fireworks, yellow tubes with red heads and red writing, Moonstrikers and A-11s. He studied them and then handed one to Jamie, who was saying something to Linds, something she did a half smile back at.

"They don't always just stay outside," I said. "Let's just leave if you want to fucking shoot fireworks. We can do that somewhere not in a building."

"The whole point is to do it in a building," he said. "You guys should stay here, just in case we do have to run. We shouldn't split up." He said it like he was somehow the authority and I was the one trying to crash the party. He held out a rocket toward Lindsey like it was settled. "You want this one?"

"No," she said. "I want Cam to show me the room with the keys. We'll meet you back here."

"It's a dumb fuck of an idea to split up," Dave said again.

But Lindsey took my hand again, pulled me away even though she had no idea where she was going. And I let her. And I was glad when she didn't drop my hand, even when the boys were six floors beneath us, the muffled sound of rockets as they glanced off cement echoing up to the key room like it had been piped in for us, the stuff of mushy movies when the main characters first kiss—rockets and starbursts.

We'd found this room before, Jamie and I—the key room. It had boxes and boxes and boxes stacked in sloppy, leaning, sometimes crashing towers, and in all of those boxes were keys, some on rings thick like a janitor's, the keys threaded together tightly, little pointy clumps of metal that hurt when Jamie winged them at you. There were so many keys, like maybe it could have been every key, ever, to the building, the keys somebody had made all the doctors and nurses and staff people turn in before they left. And there they were in damp cardboard boxes all strewn around some random room on the sixth floor.

"This is it," I said when we got there. "It's crazy, right?"

"Yeah," she said. "It is."

We were still holding hands, but it felt like the moment could slip away at any time if we didn't just go for it, just finally do it.

Lindsey did. "I want to kiss you now," she said.

"Yeah," I said.

So that, and the gin, and the dark, were enough for us to act on what had been there all summer. Lindsey was the expert, and I let her lead me, her mouth hot and her lips frosted with sparkly orange-flavored lip gloss. She pulled off my tank top in a couple of jerky moves and took off her own T-shirt even faster. Her skin was warm and smooth on mine. Her hands pulling me into her until there was no space between us at all. She had me pressed up against the wall, a light switch indenting my back, her wet mouth everywhere, when she pulled away.

"I've never really done anything more than this," she said.

"What?" I was breathing hard, my body wanting in a way that it never had before, in a way that I didn't know it could.

"I mean, I've done this lying down or whatever, but this is it," she said.

"Okay," I said, reaching out to pull her back.

"Is that okay?" she asked.

"Yeah," I told her, because it was. It was plenty.

CHAPTER SIX

If I'd learned anything from repeated viewings of *Grease*, besides the obvious—that wholesome and beskirted, pre-transformation Olivia Newton-John is ten times hotter than posttransformation, permed and leather-panted Olivia Newton-John—it was that the start of the school year can effectively end even the most passionate of summer relationships. Especially if the other half of said relationship went to school just shy of a thousand miles away from me in a city on the Pacific Ocean that she painted as chock-full of flannel-clad, Doc Martens–wearing, out and proud lesbians.

The seven-hour car ride across Montana to the state swim meet in Cut Bank—Ruth playing one oldies tape after another, the two of us eating Red Vines, watching for out-of-state license plates—gave me plenty of time to think about Lindsey and me. This meet was our big good-bye, and also the end of my last summer before high school, and all that had made me prematurely nostalgic.

What had seemed at first a revelation to me was that despite our ever-expanding make-out repertoire—hands up each other's shirts while hidden within the blue tunnel slide on the playground next to Malta's pool; Lindsey's tongue in my mouth behind the Snack Shack not five minutes after I won the Scobey meet's Intermediate Girls High Point; pressed together, our swimsuit tops pulled down and the straps dangling from our waists like slack suspenders while we were supposed to be drying off and staying warm in Lindsey's dad's camper during a thunderstorm that stalled the divisional meet at Glasgow for the better part of an hour—I hadn't really fallen in love with Lindsey, and she hadn't with me; but we were okay with that, and liked each other maybe more for it.

What I'd been doing with Lindsey all summer somehow didn't seem as intense as whatever Irene and I had shared, even though we had been younger. With Irene nothing we were doing or feeling was named as part of anything bigger than just the two of us. With Lindsey, everything was. She started me in on the language of gay; she sometimes talked about how liking girls is *political* and *revolutionary* and *counter-cultural*, all these names and terms that I didn't even know that I was supposed to know, and a bunch of other things I didn't really understand and I'm not sure that she did then, either—though she'd never have let on. I hadn't ever really thought about any of that stuff. I just liked girls because I couldn't help not to. I'd certainly never considered that some-day my feelings might grant me access to a community of like-minded women. If anything, weekly services at Gates of Praise had assured me of exactly the opposite. How could I possibly believe Lindsey when she told me that two women could live together like man and wife, and even be accepted, when Pastor Crawford spoke with such authority about the wicked perversion of homosexuality? Not that he ever really said the word *sex*, even when it was burritoed inside another word; it came out more like "homo-sesh-oo-ality" and even more often simply as "sickness" and "sin."

"God is very clear about this," he would tell us some Sunday morning when something happening with gay rights, something undoubtedly happening on one of the coasts, had worked its way to the *Billings Gazette*. "Don't be fooled by what you might see on television, the kinds of sick movements happening in parts of this country. Time and again, in Leviticus, in Romans, the Bible is exact and unwavering about homo-sesh-oo-al acts as clear abominations upon the Lord." He would then go on to explain that people lured into this sort of unhealthy lifestyle were those in most desperate need of Christ's love: junkies, prostitutes, the mentally ill, and teenage runaways like the kind actors portrayed in tattered denim jackets and with dirty-looking hair in those Boys Town National Hotline commercials they played during late-night TV. Why not throw orphans into the mix?

During these sermons I would try to melt into the gray seat cushions of our wooden pew. Ruth would be next to me, her Sunday shiniest, somehow pious but also sexy in that Ruth way, her delicate cross necklace glinting from the freckled patch of skin showing at her neck, her perfect manicure, her smart little church suits in navy or plum. I would hope and hope that she wouldn't look at me during those moments, my face hot and my skin itchy, not turn to nod at me or even offer me one of the Brach's Ice Blue mints she kept in a baggie in her purse.

A couple of times, because I was already there in church and it seemed like I should at least be attempting to save myself, even if it was halfhearted, I tried to imagine Lindsey as the pervert who had corrupted the otherwise innocent me. But even though it did make me feel less guilty, for just a moment, not entirely to blame, I knew that I wasn't hiding anything from God, if there was one. How could I pretend to be a victim when I was so willing to sin?

• • •

After our butterfly final Lindsey and I made out hard behind a dirty curtain in a changing stall at the Cut Bank municipal pool, a thick steam of chlorine and fruity shampoos clogging up the air. When we were finished, she wrote my address in the front cover of her journal in sparkly purple pen.

"You gotta get the fuck out of eastern Montana," she said, sitting on the little wooden bench in there and pulling me toward her as she lifted up my tank top and used that pen to start a sparkly purple heart on my stomach. "Seattle's boss for girls who like girls."

"I know, you've said that like sixty-two times—you wanna take me with you?" I asked, not totally kidding.

"I wish. I'll write you all the time, though." She was now coloring in the heart, which tickled in a way I liked.

"Just don't send postcards if you don't want Ruth reading them," I said as she finished my new and thankfully tempo-rary tattoo, signed her name just below it.

Lindsey pulled out this camera her dad had given her and held it in front of the two of us, judging how best to fit us both in the frame. She took a couple with me looking straight on as she kissed my cheek, like in the old-timey photo-booth strips, but then she said, "Are you gonna kiss me back or what?"

So I did, and the flash lit up our stall and now there was photographic evidence of me with a girl. Lindsey packed the camera in her duffel while I contemplated the film inside it, how it was pregnant with our secret, its birth inevitable.

"How are you gonna feel when you go to get your pictures at the store?" I asked her. I tried to imagine me getting those prints, facing bearded Jim Fishman at Fishman's Photo-Hut, him behind the desk, handing me my envelope, making change, his big forehead all pink, trying to pretend like he hadn't just seen me kissing a girl on a four-by-six in his quivering hand.

"Are you cereal? There's like a dozen photo places I could go to where they'd probably give me a round of applause.

Tell me 'Way to go, baby dyke.'" Lindsey was back to doing the big-talking lesbo act she had maybe convinced me of at the start of the summer, but I knew all the little cracks in it now. (She'd also been replacing *serious* with *cereal* for a while, which was totally stupid but weirdly infectious.)

When we came out of the stall, a cluster of girls in the Senior Division were standing by the sinks, watching us, arms folded, a few still in their dripping swimsuits. None were from my team, but a couple were from Lindsey's. Their faces were masks of disapproval, sneering mouths and squinty eyes. My first reaction was to try to believe that they must have been looking beyond us, or were going to fill us in as to just what was so disgusting. Linds and I were high pointers, top-scoring swimmers, and that had always afforded us some status. It only took one glance behind me to realize my mistake.

"It's not like I'm gonna change out of my suit now," one of Lindsey's teammates, squawky MaryAnne Something-or-other, said to the group. "Like I want to be eye-raped again this summer."

The others sniffed in agreement and looked away, as if they couldn't bear to take us in any longer, whispering loud enough for us to make out *dykes* and *sick*.

Lindsey stepped toward them and said something that began with *Yeah right, bitch*, but I couldn't tell you how it ended, because I headed straight out the door and onto the pool deck, my flip-flops slapping the wet concrete as I went. The sun was white-bright outside after the dark cloister of those cement changing rooms, and while I tried to make sense of the hazy outlines in front of me, I squinted back a kind of shame—I hadn't ever felt quite that way before. Before that moment it had somehow been sort of easy for me to pretend like nobody else had noticed anything about me, about us. That if we just didn't say anything out loud about us to anyone but each other, then that would be enough to keep what we were hidden from everyone but us and God and maybe, depending on the day and how I was thinking of them, my all-seeing parents.

It was probably only twenty seconds later that Lindsey was out on the pool deck too. She tried to grab my arm, but I jerked it away and looked around to see who might have noticed. No one. The deck was in the rush of the usual postmeet cleanup. Oily lifeguards were winding up the lane ropes for open swim and a gaggle of coaches crowded around the awards table, sorting nine colors of ribbons into thick manila envelopes. Nine colors because just that summer the federation had added ribbons for seventh, eighth, and ninth place: Pearly Pink, Royal Purple, and, as we swimmers called it, Shit Brown, respectively.

Coach Ted saw me standing there and he waved me over. Lindsey walked just behind me, her voice low.

"It's not worth being all pissed. They're stupid bitches, anyway."

"It's pretty easy to say that when you're getting on a plane tomorrow, huh?" I was trying to be mean and feeling bad about it all at once.

"Oh, like Seattle doesn't have homophobes?"

"Not the way you talk about it."

"Grow up," she said. "It's not like it's San Francisco; it's just better than here."

"Exactly," I said under my breath, just as we reached the table. In that moment I was as jealous of her getting to leave Montana as I'd ever been of anything or anyone in my life.

Ted was grinning his winning grin, his mirrored lifeguard sunglasses reflecting tousled-hair, butterfly-finals-and-make-out-session me back to me. He did the heavy, hairy arm around each of us, pulled us into an embrace that smelled of sweat and beer, which he was coolly drinking from a big plastic cup, despite the NO ALCOHOLIC BEVERAGES signs posted every ten feet. "None of these brown ones for you girls, huh?'

"Nope," we said exactly together.

"You almost caught her, Seattle," Ted said, jostling Linds back and forth a little under that arm. "She only pulled out of your reach on the last turn. It was all that practice racing mud puppies back at the lake."

"Yeah, I guess," Linds said, sort of shrugging out from under his embrace some without seeming too obvious about it.

"Lindsey would kick my butt if we swam a fifty, not a hundred," I said, trying it out as something like an *I'm sorry*.

Ted shrugged. "Probably. Good thing you don't."

Lindsey's coach asked Ted something about relay tabulations and I stood there under the heavy, hot weight of his arm, feeling a strange kind of protection, like I was safe from whatever those girls might have said, might still be saying, so long as Ted had hold of me. I was also stalling because I didn't want to go off again alone with Lindsey, because that would just mean it was time to say good-bye.

I could see Aunt Ruth on the grass on the other side of the chain link, under our blue team tarp. She had all my swim team shit—the towels, my backpack, our blanket and lawn chairs—packed up neat and tight, and was sitting atop the pink Sally-Q cooler, waiting for me, patient, sipping on a lemonade from the concession stand. My mom was never, as I remembered her, patient. Just the opposite, really. Seeing Ruth there, alone under the tarp, waiting, just sort of staring out at the bustle on the deck, made me feel really sad for her. How she'd taken me to all these meets, every weekend, all summer long, and how I had nothing much to say to her, ever, and when I did it was never the truth.

"You coming back next summer, Seattle?" Ted asked Lindsey as a now-dressed MaryAnne and another of the girls from the changing room walked up to the table.

"Probably. My dad might spend next summer in Alaska, though, so I don't know," Lindsey said, eyeing MaryAnne as she pretended that she had something to say to her coach, some reason for coming over.

"Alaska?" Ted said, shaking his head. "You have to dodge icebergs if you're gonna swim in Alaska."

MaryAnne turned to us at this, as if she had been part of the conversation all along. "Are you serious, Lindsey? That would really suck for you and Cameron. I mean, you two are best, best friends, right?"

"It would suck a helluva lot more for your team," Ted added, which was better than anything Linds or I could have said right then, and was enough to make a couple of the coaches standing around chuckle. He went on, pushing me out and away from him to look me in the face. "I don't know though, Cam. You think you can keep your speed without Lindsey one lane over?"

It seemed like the whole of the ribbons tent was waiting for me to answer, Ted and MaryAnne and coaches I didn't even really know, and even Lindsey. And probably it was just me reading Ted's question that way but it made me sort of nervous.

"I'll just remember what Patrick Swayze taught me and be nice until it's time not to be nice," I said.

Ted mock-punched me on the shoulder, laughing along with most of the coaches. "That's Dalton talking, not Swayze. Dalton's a bad-ass. Swayze's a chump. I'm pretty sure you're not supposed to be watching *Road House*, are you?"

"You'd be surprised," I said, and MaryAnne rolled her eyes, but it was enough to get her to take her ribbons and move on.

. . .

Out in the pool parking lot Lindsey gave her bag to her dad and then helped Ruth and me load the white Ford Bronco Ruth had chosen at the beginning of June to help her haul all her Sally-Q stuff *with ease*. Jamie had promptly christened Ruth's new ride the Fetus Mobile, or the FM for short, after she neatly situated a couple of antiabortion stickers on the rear bumper—ANOTHER FORMER FETUS FOR LIFE and PRO-CHOICE IS NO CHOICE FOR SOMEONE. Ruth suggested that it would make more sense for us to call it the LM (the Life Mobile), but there was no fun in that.

"Keep me posted on any additions to the bumper art gallery," Lindsey said, close to my ear, as Ruth took a couple of Shastas from the cooler and slammed down the hatch.

"Well, honey," she said to Lindsey, "I hope you have just a super school year. You call Cammie collect if you need to."

"I'm sure I'll call her all the time," Lindsey said, double raising her eyebrows at me as Ruth pulled her in for a hug. Linds was mostly bare skin in her spaghetti-strap tank, and she yelped as one of the cold pops mashed against the top of her back.

"Oh, lookit me," Ruth said, pulling back and giggling like she sometimes did. "I didn't mean to send you back to Seattle an icicle." Ruth was always her most embarrassing when she was being her nicest. "You take care, kiddo, okay? Cammie, remind me to stop at the gas station before we get on the road. You know I'll just drive right past." She opened her door and fiddled with her seat, the pops, the sweater she liked to drive in, and finally, finally climbed in and left us alone.

Now Aunt Ruth was waiting, probably watching the rearview, and Lindsey's dad was waiting, leaned up against his pickup smoking the tail end of a cigarette, and we had used up all our time just like that.

It was one of those August afternoons that Montana does just right, with heavy gray thunderheads crowding out the movie-blue sky and the feeling of a guaranteed downpour just beginning to change the touch of the air, the color of the sunlight. We were right in the middle of the maybe twenty minutes before the storm would hit, when it was only just promised, and every single thing in its path—from the strings of multicolored turn flags over the pool to the sheen of the oily puddles in the parking lot to the smell of fried foods wafting over from the Burger Box on the corner—was somehow more alive within that promise.

We stood there in that world for what felt like a long time. The second that I started to say something, Lindsey did too, so then we laughed weirdly and stood there some more.

"I hope you really do write to me," I finally said as I hugged Lindsey all fast and awkward like I used to hug teachers on the last day of class when I was little and there would be a whole line of students behind me also waiting to get a hug, and we were all shy and embarrassed about the whole thing.

Thankfully Lindsey was back doing her lesbian bravado, and she said, "I'm making you a mix tape like the second I get home," and pulled me in for another hug, a real one. "You can come visit me in Seattle. It would be awesome."

"Yeah," I said, "maybe."

And then she was jogging off toward her dad. I watched her spiky white-blond head bounce with the slap of her flip-flops, the clouds already that much closer together, the parking lot a shade or two darker than it had been a minute ago.

CHAPTER SEVEN

By the end of the Gates of Praise Labor Day picnic, Ray Eisler was officially dating Aunt Ruth. It was Jamie Lowry, staying with his mom that weekend and thereby forced to attend the picnic, who saw Ray do his little courtship ritual. Most of us kids in Firepower were busy hauling folding chairs back into the church or cleaning up the sticky plastic cups that dotted the little square of grass where we'd spent most of the afternoon. But Jamie had given up helping and instead was breaking thick hunks of crust off the disheveled pies still hanging around the dessert table. He'd bend back a chunk in such a way that it was still dripping with just enough of the blueberry or cherry or apple filling to give all that flaky lard and flour a little sweetness, and then he'd throw that into his mouth and start in on another.

He'd been at this for maybe ten minutes when I walked in front of him with the big electric coffee urn, and he said, his mouth full and his words all gummed up with pie filling and good church-lady crust, "Looks like somebody wants to stock Ruth's freezer."

I wasn't sure if I'd heard him right. "What in the hell are you talking about?" I asked, balancing the coffee urn on the edge of the table.

Jamie was working a wedge of coconut cream, and he didn't take his eyes off the pie but jerked his chin in the general direction of the dwindling crowd around the dwindling fellowship fire. "Ray's been pulling out his *Top Gun* moves all afternoon."

The weird glow of the campfire made Ray and Ruth look like silhouettes of themselves, but there they were, side by side on a log bench small enough for one, each totally absorbed in the other. Ray was one of those middle-aged Miles City guys who wasn't a rancher but still wore the jeans-and-buckle getup sometimes—skinny guys with close-cropped dark hair and big eyebrows and not too tall, maybe only five nine in cowboy boots, their voices soft and their pickups spotless, inside and out. Ray was a guy I didn't really notice at all unless he was still in his blue pants, blue shirt, blue baseball cap work getup, which he sometimes sported to GOP functions when he'd come straight from work, which was not the case today.

"Hey, if Ray starts banging her, maybe you can score us some of them orange push-pops. Those are the shit," Jamie said, catching the stern eye of his mother, who was gathering her casserole dishes close by.

He was referencing Ray's job as a Schwan's man, delivering frozen foods across the plains of eastern Montana. Irene's parents used to have a big freezer in their basement stocked full of Schwan's stuff: pizzas and egg rolls and chicken nuggets, ice-crystaled foods, hard and blue white, frozen in time, waiting for you to unwrap them from their plastic sheaths and toss them into the oven, make them real again. I'd been sentimental about frozen foods since I'd rented and rewatched (for the first time since probably second grade) the movie *The Care Bears Battle the Freeze Machine*, wherein evil Professor Coldheart and his sidekick Frostbite attempt to freeze all the children in town and succeed at ice-blocking a couple of the bears, who, when melted by the warmth of one's heart, become entirely normal again. Creating an actual, edible dinner out of a sidewalk-hard, so-cold-it-burned-your-hand box of chicken legs or a potpie began to seem a little bit magical.

"I don't think I've ever even seen Ruth talk to him before," I said, watching Jamie's careful maneuver of a particularly messy chunk of strawberry-rhubarb as he attempted to dunk it into what was left of a tub of Cool Whip.

"Well, she made up for it today. She wants him bad."

He got most of the final wedge into his mouth in two bites, took one of the baked-on dishes from his mom, and managed a chewy "Five thirty in the a.m., JJK" before doing his long stride off to their car.

He'd been calling me JJK, short for Jackie Joyner-Kersee, since we'd started the Custer High cross-country season a few weeks previous. I hadn't planned on going out for cross-country, but Jamie had talked me into it, and now that the swim season was over, and Lindsey was over, it gave me something to be a part of besides Firepower, and it helped make high school feel less like foreign ground. Some of the team had been running all summer, but me being in swim shape, with what Coach Rosset called *swim lungs*, helped out enough to keep me with the pack, anyway.

I put the coffee urn in the church kitchen, which was filled with ladies doing dishes in the cavernous metal sinks, everybody full of food and laughing about nothing. This was the way I liked Gates of Praise best, after services, *after* prayer circles or Bible studies or Firepower meetings, when everybody was filled up with the spirit and maybe a little sugar high, when we were all done talking about wickedness and sin and shame and all manner of things that made my face burn when they were brought up, which they almost always were.

The urn went on this shelf way in the back of the pantry, and after I'd found its spot I hid back there for a minute, listening to the ladies, the way the pots and pans clattered together and sloshed the water as the dishrag was passed over them. I liked being a ghost in this place, unseen. Part of it might have been that story Margot had told me—the one about her brother and my mom kissing in a church pantry. But it was also that the neat stacks of dishes on the high shelves and the smell of Pine-Sol made me feel weirdly safe, or warm, or just normal, I guess. They kept a List of Events calendar on a little bulletin board just inside the pantry, and every single day of September had at least one event listed: Kinder-Care, Moms' Circle, SonLights, Just-4-Dads, and on and on. Next to the calendar somebody had stuck a button with a picture of a loaf of bread on it, and the question THE BREAD OF LIFE—ARE YOU FULL?

Just a few months before the accident my dad had finally bought this $350 Hitachi bread machine he'd seen in a catalog and had been wanting and that my mom thought was *unnecessary* and *ridiculous*. They'd argued about spending the money on it for a while, and then my dad just did it anyway. And then he made bread in it a bunch of times, all in one week, like just to prove that he was actually gonna use this thing. He made a crusty sourdough and a thick wheat one too, and the whole house had smelled amazing, and my dad was so proud of himself, and we sat on the front porch with a tub of butter and a plastic bear of honey and ate and ate warm bread, and my mom wouldn't join us and as far as I could tell she never ate any of it. But then my dad made cinnamon bread, which smelled the best of all of them, but he made it just for my mom and brought it to her at the museum, which I guess was like an apology. And it worked, I think, because

111

then he didn't feel like he had to use the machine all the time and they'd put it in one of the cupboards, had to make room for it, and though I hadn't thought of it since before their funeral, I guessed that it was still there.

I reached up and grabbed the BREAD OF LIFE button, clicked the sharp pin into its holder, and slipped it into the back pocket of my jean shorts. I had a place for it in the attic of the dollhouse. And then I was crying, there in the pantry, unsure of why, exactly, but missing my parents in a way that I had made myself pretty good at avoiding most of the time.

Somebody dropped a glass in the kitchen. I heard the shards break and scatter. Everybody was laughing, shouting *Nice one* and *Way to go, fumblehands* and *You sure you haven't been in there drinking the communion wine?* I took that as my cue and used the hem of my T-shirt to wipe my face, get my shit together.

Ruth met me at the now-empty dessert table, red eyed from all that time by the fire, her hair tousled. She looked younger than I'd seen her in a long time, maybe since before the accident.

Ray was standing behind her just a bit, holding the wheat-colored stone bowl we'd brought potato salad in. I remembered my parents buying it at a little gallery in Colorado when we were on vacation once. It felt weird to see him holding it; not bad necessarily, just weird, out of place.

• • •

True to her word, even before midterms Lindsey had already sent me maybe twenty handwritten notebook pages filled with her observations and current love interests, always in sparkly pen, as well as a busted-up copy of *Rubyfruit Jungle*, a couple of random issues of *The Advocate*, and maybe a dozen mix tapes with each song written in a different color on the cardboard liner inside. Everything but the tapes I hid under my mattress, which is what I knew that teenage boys, including Jamie, did with their porn-mag stashes. The tapes I wore threadbare on my Walkman during cross-country practices.

We ran three routes, one right through the downtown, past bars and banks and the Presbyterian church and then on out past the fast-food and motels and past Gates of Praise around the cemetery, back to the school. Another circled the fairgrounds and Spotted Eagle, a sort of nature preserve and mucky boating pond, a place you went to get laid in your car, your tape deck on and your BAC way over the limit. And the third out at Fort Keogh, the military base–cum–ag research facility that was as old as Miles City itself, founded on the same site, in fact, as the original cantonment headed up by General Nelson A. Miles—the town's namesake.

None of these places was new to me, but I saw them all differently with a soundtrack playing as I passed them by: an 1800s white-washed bunkhouse with a caved-in roof set to gangsta rap. The Penney's and Anthony's window scenes— dark in the early-morning hours, mannequins in sweaters and winter jackets, scarves and mittens, fake leaves scattered on the ground—set to riot grrrl. Strictly speaking, we weren't allowed to listen to music while we practiced; but I was an initially unexpected bonus for the team, had placed in the top ten at all of our meets thus far, and I suspected that the whispers about Coach Lynn Rosset's preference for the ladies might have also played in my favor.

Maybe I should have thought harder about this prefer-ential treatment as a potential area for big trouble, as added weight to any rumors that might land on me about my own "preferences," but I was just happy to get to run to whatever Lindsey had mixed up for me: sometimes Prince and R.E.M., sometimes 4 Non Blondes and Bikini Kill, sometimes Salt-N-Pepa and A Tribe Called Quest.

I'd also taken to wearing my headphones in the hallways at Custer, between classes, even when I'd go to the bathroom or my locker during study hall. I'd keep my head down, my thoughts lost to whatever song was on, me somehow both in a high school in Miles City and also in some other world entirely. This was exactly what I was doing the day in October when I rounded the corner by the attendance office and crashed into some girl in corduroys and expensive-looking loafers, which is really all I saw of her until I looked up to mumble *sorry* and found myself staring at Irene Klauson.

"Oh, fuck," I said without really meaning to, my mouth open wide. I pulled the headphones from my ears and let them hang around my neck, the music still playing, a kind of muffled buzz emanating from me.

"Hey, Cameron," Irene said, seeming totally recomposed, or maybe she hadn't ever lost composure. She even folded her arms and did a kind of half smile, almost like a smirk, but maybe not quite.

Somehow it seemed like we'd already missed the right moment to have hugged, so we just stood there in front of each other. I hadn't seen her since Easter Break her first year away, and then it was with a whole group of us left-behinds, and we had all just kept asking questions about how great it must be to be Irene Klauson, and she'd delivered the shiny answers we were hoping for. I thought I'd see her during the summers, but she spent them on the East Coast as a junior counselor at some hoity-toity camp. We'd only written each other a couple of times, and that was right when she'd first left and was probably a little lonely, though she didn't ever say so in her letters.

She was taller, but so was I. She had on a blue polo shirt, a sweater honest-to-God tied around her neck, diamond studs that glinted even under the bad fluorescent hallway lights. She had her hair pulled back like I never remembered her wearing it. I was in a long-sleeved T-shirt from the previous year's state swim meet and my warm-up pants, a sloppy pony-tail, just an older, taller version of the me she'd dropped off in front of my house a couple of years before. But in her time away it was like Irene had become grown-up Irene.

"What are you doing back?" I asked.

"Maybrook does a fall break. A bunch of my friends went to London, and I could have gone, but Mr. Frank asked my parents if I wanted to come and talk to his science classes about what's going on with the dig."

"Why not just have your dad come and save a plane ticket?" I was feeling our old competitiveness despite myself.

She waved to someone in the hallway behind me. "He's really busy, and he's not the best public speaker. I'm more relatable." She paused, considering, I think, whether or not she should say what she ended up saying next. "We don't really need to save on plane tickets anyway."

"Must be nice," I said.

"It is," she said. "It's very nice."

I felt like she might just end things there, the way she kept looking past me into the hallway, the way it felt like her body was almost leaning away from me, like a magnet pulling her along, and I didn't want her to go. So I asked, "What is going on with the dig, anyway?"

Irene ignored that question or didn't hear it or decided it wasn't worth answering. "My mom tells me you're in the paper all the time for sports," she said.

"Yeah, I guess. Are you still riding?"

"Seven days a week. We have our stables and all of these trails through the woods, right on campus." She ran one hand through her hair in a way that mirrored my memory of her mom. "My boyfriend, Harrison, rides too. He's a polo player, actually. He's really good." She tried to pull the mention of *boyfriend* off as casual, but we had too much history for it to work.

"His name is really Harrison?" I asked, smiling.

"Yeah," she said, jerking into that stiff pose again. "Why's that so funny?"

"It's not. It just sounds like the kind of name you'd expect from a rich guy who plays polo."

"Well, he is and he does, like I said. I'd make fun of your boyfriend's name too, but, you know"—she leaned in a little closer—"there's not one to mention, is there?"

"Yes, actually," I said, smiling, trying to undo what it was that I'd done. "The weird thing is that his name's Harrison. And he plays polo." It didn't work.

"Whatever," she said, not even looking at me anymore but pretending to be interested in the kid in the attendance office asking for something or other. "I need to go—my mom's waiting outside in the car."

"Yeah, go ahead," I said. "You should call me sometime this week."

"Maybe," she said, just like I knew she would. "I'm really busy." And then Irene seemed to remember her new breeding and added, in the kind of voice characters in movies set in the Victorian era use when reading aloud the formal letters they've written to one another, "It was nice seeing you, Cameron. Give my best to your grandmother and your aunt."

"Um, okay," I said. "That was weird." But Irene was

already walking away.

I could still remember the exact way her boots used to *click-clock* as she walked; it was something about how she planted her foot, a distinct sound that I always paired with her. But those loafers she was wearing didn't make any noise at all on the shiny hallway floors. Nothing. Not one sound.

• • •

Somewhere around this time I became aware that Aunt Ruth was having sex with Ray the Schwan's man. I heard them one afternoon when Ruth thought I was off somewhere with Jamie, but I was actually in my bedroom, working on the dollhouse. I'd ganked a vial of metallic glitter and a tub of decoupage paste from Ben Franklin and was covering the floor of the attic with a thick carpet of glitter interspersed with pennies that I'd flattened into smears of metal by placing them on the train tracks by the feedlot. *The Witches of Eastwick* was in the VCR, the volume low.

When I was doing anything to that dollhouse, I was so much in my own world that Ruth could sometimes call for me three times before I'd hear her, so when I first noticed the moaning, I guessed it was from Cher or Susan Sarandon, but when I looked at the screen it was just Jack Nicholson alone in that big mansion, overacting and plotting revenge.

It wasn't that Ray and Ruth were being all wild, but it was sex, and there were certain sounds, and being in the room above them I heard those sounds. I didn't want to listen, but I didn't want to do anything to make them aware of me either, so I kept on with what I was doing, the best I could, anyway, and waited them out, and tried not to imagine what was going on, exactly, in my parents' old bedroom.

Ray seemed nice enough. He liked Monopoly and made

good popcorn and he did keep us stocked up with Schwan's stuff—even some of the high-end crab legs and whatever. He and Ruth loved to compare notes about traveling the cracked highways of eastern Montana to sell their wares, and I was glad they had each other to talk to about that shit. Sometimes they even caravanned to certain towns together.

When things had been quiet for a long time, I went downstairs, and the two of them were on the couch under an afghan, watching football.

"Hey, Cammie," Ruth said. "You just get in?"

I could have told her yes, but I didn't see the point. If anything, knowing that Ruth was having sex made her seem more like a real person to me. For two years she had been mostly just this force in my life, my parents' replacement, and someone whose standards I didn't think I could ever live up to. The Ruth who was into nonmarried sex was maybe someone I could get to know, so I said, "No, I've been in my room doing some homework."

Ray cleared his throat at this, loud, and breathed in a little. He didn't take his eyes off the screen but started fiddling with the tab on his beer can.

"We didn't even know you were up there," Ruth said, making a face I was having trouble reading. She wasn't blushing, she didn't seem embarrassed, necessarily, but she didn't look like typical Ruth, either.

"Yeah. I was," I said, leaving that hanging there as I went to the freezer for a Push-Em, feeling a little like I'd earned it. Then I wandered downstairs to Grandma's area. She was in her big recliner, crocheting an afghan for Ray in the colors he'd picked: Custer pride, of course—blue and gold and white.

"There's my spitfire," Grandma said, looking up at me

over the tops of her reading glasses. "Aren't you a sight for sore eyes."

I slumped onto her couch. "You saw me at dinner last night. You saw me in the kitchen this morning. You saw me—"

"That's enough of that, smarty-pants," she said. "You know what I mean."

"Yeah," I said, because I did. We hadn't really done anything together for a long time, just the two of us.

"So what do you have to say?" she asked. She always asked that.

"Nothing," I said, pushing up the last of the orange sherbet from its paper tube.

"You know you're only bored if you're boring."

"Maybe I am boring," I said.

"I never have thought so," she said. "Go on and hand me that navy, will you?" She pointed with her hooks to a tube of yarn in a basket near my feet. "And don't drip that thing all over my floor while you're doing it." I kept the Push-Em in my mouth while I tossed the roll to her.

Then we just sat like that for a while, listened to the ag report on her radio.

"Ray still up there?" she asked me eventually.

I nodded. "I think he's staying for dinner."

"So what do you make of him?"

"I don't know. I think I like him okay," I said. "He seems nice."

"I think you're exactly right about that," she said. "I think he's a nice guy, hard worker. Now the fellas she was dating back when your folks got married—all hat and no cattle, those guys, and Ruth was just something to wear on the arm. But I think this one might stick."

"You think that already?" I asked. I guess I hadn't really

thought that far ahead, about Ruth, about whatever she might plan for her own future. "They just got together."

"Not just, Spunky," she said. "Not when you're Ruth's age. You forget that she's had just about as much change to her life as you have. I think this is a real good thing for her."

"I'm glad then," I said. I meant it. And then I said, I hadn't planned to, I just did, "I saw Irene Klauson at school the other day. She told me to say hi to you."

"What's she doing back?"

"Visiting," I said. "She was on fall break. I think she's gone again now."

"You should have had her over," Grandma said. "I'd have liked to say hi. You two gals used to be thick as thieves."

"Not anymore," I said, feeling sorry for myself again, thinking we'd end it there.

But Grandma said, "No, not since they died, huh?"

"Not just that, Grandma," I said.

"No," she said. "Not just that."

• • •

Coley Taylor wasn't one of the ranch girls who were always wearing their blue FFA (Future Farmers of America) jackets and spending all their free time in the farm shop. The farm shop was this all-metal Quonset of a building sprung up in the faculty parking lot. They held some of the ag classes there; students worked on tractors and identified grain funguses, cussed a lot. Some of those farm-shop girls were actually as townie as I was, so they overcompensated with gleaming hubcap-size belt buckles and by blowing Seth and Eric Kerns—future National Finals Rodeo champions and high school demigods—in the boys' pickup during lunch.

Coley didn't need to cowgirl-up her persona. She was the

authentic version. She drove the forty-some miles into town from her family's ranch every morning, and then back again after classes. She'd been in kindergarten through eighth at the little country school in Snakeweed, and was first in her class of twelve, but then they stopped letting Snakeweed do high school credits, and those twelve joined the rest of us.

I had biology with her fall semester of freshman year, and Coley didn't huddle at the back table with the other FFAs, though they had saved her a seat. She picked the table dead in the front of the room and asked intelligent questions about dissection methods, while I spent the semester watching the summer highlights fade from her hair, which had a little natural curl and which I imagined smelled like peony and sweet grass. I spent a lot of time imagining the smell of Coley Taylor's hair.

With her at the head table were a couple of student council kids, including Brett Eaton, who had the jaunty good looks of an ad for astronaut recruitment. Plus he was a genuinely nice guy and a decent soccer player. They were an item by Halloween, which at that point didn't upset me as much as it did those cowboys at the back table who spit wads of Copenhagen into the lab sinks when Mr. Carson wasn't looking.

Sometime that December, in the days before Christmas, Coley and her mom joined Gates of Praise. It was the time of year when the strays return (Grandma Post included) for two or three Sundays so they feel like they've earned their holiday. I hadn't noticed the Taylors during the crowded service, but while I was arranging powdered doughnuts for what I referred to as the "coffee communion," partaken of only by the over-sixty crowd and obligated church newcomers, in they came. Coley and her mom *cut quite a figure*, is what Grandma said. And they did. Both of them somewhere around five ten, both of them slim but not skinny, and both of them in turtleneck sweaters—Coley's black, her mom's red. It was at a time when Cindy Crawford was still cover-modeling and making workout videos and hosting that lame style show on MTV, but that morning in the fellowship hall I would have given Coley the edge over the supermodel with the famous mole.

I had moved on to fanning out the paper napkins (which was a joke, because Ruth redid practically every little half-pinwheel that I made) by the time Coley noticed me. Or by the time I noticed her noticing me. She was standing just slightly behind her mom and strobed me a huge smile right before this old ranch-hand bachelor grizzled his way in on her for a kiss on her cheek. When he moved on to her mom and I could just see her face beyond his flanneled reach, she winked at me. A wink coming from anyone else, like that ranch hand or one of the community-college boys who hovered around and took the leftover doughnuts to their dorms, would have been predictable and annoying—something you did to the orphaned tomboy. But the way Coley did it made me feel like we already had some sort of secret between us.

If it hadn't been coffee communion, there would have been a whole lot more teenage classmates around, kids who knew Coley better, her crowd. Firepower was then some ninety members strong. But I was made instantly more appealing that morning when stacked up against the under-twenties currently snacking in the hall: a motley crew of shrieking and running elementary-school kids glad to be free of the pews they'd sat in for the last hour and a half; Pastor Crawford's ever-increasing brood, only one of whom was old enough for high school, and he had skipped out right after the service; and Clay Harbough, the computer genius who, despite being so gifted a programmer that he was allowed to spend his afternoons in the Custer computer lab setting up systems and wowing the librarians, spoke in a rapid monotone to his Nikes and smelled often of black licorice, which I never once saw him eating.

Considering my competition, I wasn't all that surprised when Coley launched herself toward me, even though the most we'd ever said before was *Are you done with that scalpel?* I was surprised, however, when she didn't stop at the other side of the long table to talk to me over the platters of foods built for coffee dunking but instead came right around to my side, the server's side, and stood next to me like she had always been there, every Sunday, helping fan the napkins.

"So what do you think the dissection final's gonna look like?" she asked, leaning in front of me to grab a packet of orange-spice tea. I flinched at the way her sweater sleeve brushed across my chest, felt my heart twitch around for a second. It was uncomfortable, like an itch buried deep inside my lungs.

"No clue. Probably me with a pair of forceps pulling at intestines while Kyle sings 'Enter Sandman' under his breath." I liked watching her stir her tea with the little red straw, three turns clockwise, then rotate, then repeat.

She laughed. I liked it.

"Yeah, that kid's a hoot," she said. Coley Taylor made sipping cheap tea from a chipped yellow JESUS IS LORD mug seem cultured and Julie Andrewsish. "You guys are a thing?"

I was both horrified and sort of flattered. Kyle Clark, lab partner, was as rocker-dude as Custer High could offer, and so asking me if I was dating him meant that Coley somehow thought that I was rocker-chick enough to do so, which wasn't a mistake that anyone made very often.

"No. Definitely not. We've just known each other forever. Like everyone else in our class," I added.

"Not me." She smiled again, her face just a few inches from mine, and I felt the itch.

I stepped back a little. "Be glad, or you'd already know that Kyle puked SpaghettiOs on me at third-grade field days." Talking to Coley as she drank tea in her chic outfit, all of her so put together, made me feel like I might as well have still been in third grade, my gangly pose with my stupid arms hanging weirdly at my sides. I busied myself, putting out more of the heavy cake doughnuts even though the plate was already stacked high. With each doughnut some of the glaze and frosting pasted itself in the spaces between my fingers.

"Sorry," she said. "I guess I shouldn't assume that everyone's dating their lab partners."

"Well, you set a good example, right?" I focused on the now-towering doughnuts, wondering how that sounded to her. Bitchy? Or worse, jealous?

But she laughed and grabbed my arm for just a second, which made me tense up all over. "Yeah. Exactly. I thought you guys must be together because you always seem to be having a better time with your fetal pig than me and Brett."

"You mean Hambone?"

She smiled into her mug. "You guys named your pig?"

"You guys didn't? There's your problem. You could do Porky, but it's pretty obvious. What do you think of Coulda-Been Bacon? But you have to say Coulda-Been really fast, so it sounds like a name." I was doing my little stand-up shtick, the one I did for pretty girls, so they'd like me quickly and wouldn't try too hard to actually get to know me beyond my role as wisecracking Cameron the orphan. Maybe it was a little like flirting, but also a kind of protection: *Don't get too close; I'm just jokes without substance.* And it seemed to be going over, so I would have kept on if Ruth hadn't suddenly been there with us too, a cloud of White Diamonds (her new fragrance, compliments of Ray) settling over the table. She took the doughnut box from me, and my weird arms just had to hang there again.

"This is way too many, hon," she said, plucking this custard filled and that raspberry glazed and reboxing them. "Coley, I just met your mother. We're so glad to have you here to worship with us." She finished with the doughnuts, set the box down, and wiped her hands on a napkin before offering her palm to Coley. "I'm Cameron's aunt Ruth. You're both freshmen?"

Coley answered right as Pastor Crawford pulled in for a maple bar, "Yeah. We were just talking about dissection."

"Well, that's a way to spend a Sunday morning. Good gravy, girls, you're no fun." Aunt Ruth grinned her Annette Funicello grin and put her hands on her hips and did some sort of hula-hoop motion, a move that played like the 1950s and a poodle-skirted malt shop.

Pastor Crawford kept hovering, chewing, laughing at Ruth, some of the tan icing flaking onto his collar. "You know," he said, "I'm having one of those great moments of epiphany." He paused and chewed more. Pastor Crawford was the king of the drawn-out revelation. Eventually he turned to me. "Cameron, Coley's going to start coming to Firepower, and I know that Ruth's been driving you. Why don't you two gals ride together instead?"

It was a move that I can only assume he meant as gregarious and pastorly, but really he had just forced me into the truck of one of the it girls in my class, since I was the sad sack without her own car whose aunt or grandmother had to pick her up and drop her off.

While I was grinning like a jack-o'-lantern and shrugging, rolling my eyes, trying to play off these meddling adults to

Coley, she answered, "Yeah, that'd be good," and she didn't hesitate or anything, but there was something so grown-up about her that I thought maybe she was just better at maneuvering these awkward chitchats than I was, and so I didn't take much comfort in her easy tone.

I also wished that we could have this conversation without the group of adult onlookers planning our playdates. "You know, like half of the school comes here on Wednesdays," I told her. "And I start track in March, anyway. Don't feel obligated to pull a *Driving Miss Daisy*."

"Don't be stupid," she said, "I don't." Her mom was beckoning her from a table of really old people, and as Coley turned to head over, her face too near mine, a smile flitting across it, she said, "We could just call him Fetal Piggly Wiggly, right, Miss Daisy?"

It probably doesn't seem like much that she would play off my lame movie reference, mention the grocery store from that scene where Miss Daisy finally accepts a ride from her own chauffeur, but I'd been making movie references just like that for so long that they came out without me even thinking about them, and certainly without me expecting anyone but Jamie to make one back. And definitely not one based on the grocery-store scene from *Driving Miss Daisy*. And most definitely not someone like Coley, who I thought I had already figured out just by sitting behind her in science for a semester.

In the Fetus Mobile on the way home, Ruth gave Grandma the Taylor family rundown. Mr. Taylor had died from lung cancer two years before, but Coley's older brother, Ty, and her mom were still running the cattle ranch, making it work. Ty was supposed to be some sort of debonair wild card, a real cowboy, and after her husband died Mrs. Taylor had fallen apart some—drinking and staying out and *making bad choices*—but she had recently found her way back to Christ.

"She's getting things back on track for her family," Ruth said. "That takes real courage."

It was Coley, as she understood it, who had been keeping things together in the interim. Coley, according to Ruth, was pretty and smart and just *a real go-getter*, loved by all.

"I'm glad that you two are friendly, Cammie," Ruth said, eyeing me in the rearview mirror the way she liked to. "She seems like a very put-together young lady, and maybe if you get to know her, you won't have to spend so much time with Jamie and the boys, you know—"

"Jamie's my best friend," I told the mirror, cutting her off. "I don't even really know Coley. We just have a class together."

"Well, now you can get to know her," Ruth said.

"Yeah, whatever," I said, because it was easier than again trying to explain high school politics to a former head cheerleader. But I just figured Coley would offer me the obligatory ride the following Wednesday, and it would be a little awkward, but she would be sweet about it, and then she'd mention, casually, that she had an errand to run before Firepower the next week and *could I get a ride with my aunt*, and then we'd forget about this arranged friendship altogether. Which would definitely be for the best, I decided that night in bed, when I closed my eyes and saw her drinking tea and opened them and still could see her, and I wanted so much to see more.

CHAPTER EIGHT

It took until March, the still-crispy days of early-season track practice already under way, for me to stop waiting for Coley to tell me about that errand she had to run. By that point she and Brett had adopted me as some kind of tag-along kid sister, despite our being the same age. The only problem was that the more time I spent with the two of them—in a corner booth at Pizza Hut creating contests that involved shooting straw wrappers at various targets, or in the top row of the Montana Theatre, watching whichever movie was showing that week, a tub of popcorn on Coley's lap for all of us to share, or boonie bashing at the Honda Trails in Brett's beat-up Jeep, AC/DC blaring from the stereo—the more I fell in love with Coley Taylor. But the weird thing was that I really liked Brett, too. I would have these moments of jealousy over the tiniest of things—Brett grabbing Coley's hand as we crossed a street or Coley ruffling the back of his head as he drove us somewhere—but for those first months I was mostly content just to be near her and to make her laugh, which was harder to do than with other girls; I had to try harder, which made it more worth it.

• • •

Prom season, with its torrents of confetti and satin gowns and sparkle stars to accompany the Van Gogh *Starry Night* theme, was met with the flannel-cloaked apathy of the late-blooming grunge crowd that made up a very small but riotous portion of the Custer High Senior Class of 1992. Some of the grunginess had trickled its way down to my class, too, a Hacky Sack cluster here, the smell of patchouli there, but it seemed to have mostly infected students nearest to graduation. Those almost-adults, many of them with college acceptance letters already tacked to bulletin boards in their bedrooms at home, were into raging against machines and not washing their hair, and certainly not punch fountains and dyed-to-match pumps and a spotlighted Grand March through their soon-to-be-former high school gymnasium. I could totally sympathize, and I had my share of flannel shirts; I just wasn't full-blown grunge. However, when the administration announced a mandatory formal dress code (in response to the hallway buzz that several of the senior grunge couples planned to attend Starry Starry Night barefooted and in unisex jumpers made entirely of hemp), most of the senior class sympathized too, and the FFA kids and the jocks and student council geeks united with the grungeheads to begin an outright boycott of the prom.

The promise of low ticket sales, coupled with the poor fundraising efforts of the junior class, whose car washes and bake sales had yielded far less than was needed to throw such an event, resulted in a first-time-in-history scenario for Custer High: freshmen and sophomores would be allowed to attend prom, *in formal attire*, and at the *very fair* price of only ten dollars extra per couple.

"You're coming, Cam," Coley told me, appearing next to my locker right after last period and just before I was due at track practice. It seemed like she just appeared, anyway. School was out for the day, it was just barely starting to feel like spring, and everybody streamed through the hallways drunk on 3:15-p.m. freedom, leaving the rush of students headed for the main doors only long enough to pause at their lockers before rejoining it, like all of it was choreographed, every movement rehearsed, every sound and sight a special effect—the slam and rattle of the metal locker doors, the *call me laters* and *fuckin' chemistry tests* loud and throaty, the thick smell of just-lit cigarettes as soon as you hit the outside steps, the sound of mix tapes blaring from cars as they tore away from the student parking lot, windows down on both sides. I usually liked to soak in all of that for a minute or two, just linger at my locker before heading off to change for practice. But that day there was Coley.

Vice Principal Hennitz had just explained the "new deal" prom scenario during the end-of-day announcements in that pasty voice of his, each word somehow sticky sounding: *Prom is a place for decorum, and in offering you underclassmen this opportunity, the administration and I feel confident that you will treat it as such.*

Because we'd been presented with this opportunity literally minutes before, I knew exactly what Coley was talking about with her *you're coming, Cam,* but I pretended not to so she'd have to work even harder to convince me. I liked the feeling I got when she needed something from me.

"What are you talking about?" I asked her, pretending to dig for something in my backpack.

"Only the primary event of the spring fashion season," Coley said in this highfalutin socialite voice she did really well. Then she switched it off to add, "If you're gonna double with me and Brett, you need to find a guy to actually make you a double." She did this thing that she always did with her hair where she put it up in back and held it there with a pencil all in one move and it always got me how incredibly, carelessly sexy she was when she was doing it.

"I guess I can see if Grandma is free. What night is it again?" I asked, trying to keep that locker door between us. Brett was almost always around when Coley was, and when he wasn't I sometimes still got all flustery like that first coffee communion at GOP.

"Don't do the thing where all you do is make a bunch of jokes and it becomes impossible to talk to you about anything," Coley said. "This will be classic—we'll never have the chance to crash prom as freshmen again."

"There's absolutely nothing in what you've just said that makes your argument any more convincing," I said.

She reached around the locker door and grabbed my arm all dramatic-like. "I'll call Ruth. I'll do it. I'll call her and tell her you're being a weirdo loner again and won't come to prom and you know she won't let off you. She'll have all sorts of ideas about eligible bachelors."

"You're a terrible person and I hate you."

"So who do you want me to ask? Travis Burrel would totally go with you." Coley pushed the locker door open wider and stepped around it, helping herself to the pack of Bubblicious I had on the top shelf and, as she was doing it, brushing up against me in a way that she didn't even notice and in a way that made me notice nothing else.

I backstepped into the hallway a little so that we weren't wedged into that space so tightly. "Travis Burrel would go to prom with anyone he thought he might be able to dry hump on the dance floor."

"So you want me to call him first?" The gum coated her words in all-sugar strawberry.

"Yeah. Get right on that. I'm gonna be late," I said, trying at the same time to push her out of the way with the back of my arm and also grab my backpack, my practice bag. She didn't move very far and I had to reach around her again, brush up against her again, feel a little shudder roll along my body and end in my stomach, again, just to latch the door, clip shut the padlock.

She stayed right next to me as we wove back into the hallway, walking against the stream toward the women's locker rooms. "C'mon, just ask Jamie; you know you're going to anyway."

Coley and I had to separate to get around a girl who was mostly eclipsed by the size of the poster she was carrying, some sort of project about World War Two—a picture of Hitler doing his mustachioed *Sieg heil*, a gaunt concentration-camp victim, a couple of American soldiers smoking cigarettes and scowling at the camera, the captions beneath each photo in glitter-bubble letters. If this had been the movie version of my life, I knew, somebody who did teenage stuff well, some director, would have lingered on that poster and maybe even have swelled some sort of poignant music, put us in slow motion as the hallway continued on at regular speed around us, backlit the three of us—Coley and the posterboard chick and me—and in doing so tried to make some statement about teenage frivolity and prom season as it stacked up against something authentic and horrible like war. But if renting all those movies had taught me anything more than how to lose myself in them, it was that you only actually have perfectly profound little moments like that in real life if you recognize them yourself, do all the fancy shot work and editing in your head, usually in the very seconds that whatever is happening is happening. And even if you do manage to do so, just about never does anyone else you're with at the time experience that exact same kind of moment, and it's impossible to explain it as it's happening, and then the moment is over.

"Ask Jamie today because I want to buy the tickets tomorrow," Coley kept on, back at my side again, the full-color atrocities of a war both of our grandfathers had fought in *clip-clopping* away from us, offscreen where they belonged, not staring us down during prom season.

"Jamie isn't gonna want to fucking go to prom. I don't want to fucking go to prom. The whole point of the boycott is that nobody in this school wants to fucking go to prom."

Some shaggy junior in a Pantera T-shirt turned and shouted as we passed him, "I'll fuck you at prom!" His two equally shaggy buddies high-fived him and giggled the way high school boys and certain cartoon characters giggle—Barney Rubble, for one.

"You're a troglodyte," Coley yelled back. We were at the blue metal door that signified the locker room entrance. She grabbed both of my arms at the biceps. "Jamie will go with you if you ask him, even if he doesn't really want to."

"Coley, *I* don't really want to."

"But I do, and we're friends, and this is the sort of thing friends do for each other," she said with a kind of earnestness that maybe would have been laughable if I wasn't so much in love with her.

"Oh, is this the sort of thing?" I asked, both of us knowing that I would ask Jamie to prom that very afternoon and that he would give me shit about it but would eventually say yes because that's the kind of guy Jamie Lowry was. "What are the other sorts of things friends do for each other? Do you have a list?"

"No, but I'll make one," she said, waving at a group of shiny juniors who were mostly Brett's friends. They were lolling around the pop machines and called her over. "It's gonna be so, so good," she said.

"You so, so owe me," I said back from partway inside the locker room.

"You know I love you forever." She was already walking toward the knot of fresh-faced couples on their way to soak up the sunny afternoon, no doubt, like some sort of J.Crew ad, and leaving me to think about that list of "things friends do for each other" the whole time I was changing, the whole time I was jogging over to the track at the community college, the whole time I was doing extra laps after practice because I was just barely late. If Coley ever were to actually write out a list like that, I knew that I'd do each and every single thing on it. I just knew that I would.

● ● ●

I'd mentioned my Coley crush to Lindsey in a few brief paragraphs in one of my letters, but I filled in all the angsty details during a three-hour phone conversation we had the weekend before prom, while Ruth and Ray the Schwan's man were at a couples' Bible weekend in Laramie and Grandma was napping in front of the TV, empty cellophane wrappers from those sugar wafers on the coffee table. She was favoring the strawberry variety that month, so she had weirdly pink wafer shards and sugar crumbles in the creases of her shirt, like the fiberglass bits that had sometimes coated my father's overalls when he was installing insulation.

It was Lindsey who had called me, so it was her mom who would get the phone bill, not Ruth. And when it took her twenty minutes just to tell me about an Ani DiFranco concert she'd been to the night before, I knew this would be a long session, so I grabbed a couple of Ray's Bud Lights from the fridge (I was pretty sure he knew that I was taking them sometimes, but he wasn't saying anything to me or to Ruth), and then I took the cordless phone into my room and spent the better part of those three hours decoupaging the floor and ceiling of the guest bedroom of the dollhouse with stamps saved from Lindsey's letters. Lindsey wrote me a lot, probably four letters to each one of mine, but I still didn't have nearly enough stamps to do the whole thing. It was just a hopeful start.

While I had been running track, and contemplating Leviticus and Romans, and being the tag-along sister to Custer High's favorite couple while in private imagining Coley every time I watched any movie with even a hint of lesbianism (Coley as Jodie Foster in *Silence of the Lambs*, Coley as Sharon Stone in *Basic Instinct*—that movie had just, finally, come to Miles City), Lindsey had been getting it on with, to hear her tell it, every lesbian in the Seattle area between the ages of fifteen and twenty-five. Many of them had names, or probably they were nicknames, that sounded frightening to me in a "too cool" sort of way: Mix, Kat, Betty C. (for Betty Crocker? I wondered, but never asked), Brights, Aubrey, Henna, and on and on.

Lindsey was good with details and she was always very specific about which conquest had smelly white-girl dreads, and which girl had totally shaved her head, and which girl wore a leather jacket and rode a Harley, snorted coke, was anorexic and too bony and whose body felt like scaffolding; but there were so many different girls that I couldn't keep track of any of them once the phone call or letter ended, and I didn't usually need to, because Lindsey herself would have seemingly forgotten those girls and moved on to a half dozen more by the next time we spoke or she wrote.

"Betty C. has a tongue ring, you know? Well, a stud, actually, but it's crazy because I heard those make a difference but I had no idea just how much of a difference, you know?" This was typical Lindsey style of conversing, phrasing everything in such a way that it forced me to ask her to explain things to me, keeping her forever in the role of my personal lesbian guru.

"It made such a difference how?" I asked, situating a flag stamp next to a stamp of the State Bird of Maine, the black-capped chickadee.

"Seriously, Cam, grow an imagination—while she was going down on me. It's like, it's this tiny piece of metal, you know, but if you know how to use it—and Betty C. does, she totally does—it's otherworldly."

"Yeah, I got that part," I said, because I *had* actually understood that she was talking about oral sex but was still so unsure of the mechanics of it all, the actual process, what it was like on either end, that I had a hard time understanding how the tiny piece of metal made any significant difference. When I daydreamed about Coley and me, it was always a lengthy fantasy lead-up to our first kiss, and then a whole lot more intense kissing, shirts off, maybe, some touching, but never anything else. Ever. It was such foreign territory that my brain couldn't even imagine the map for it.

"Right, okay," Lindsey said. "I forgot what a sexual aficionado I was talking to. You and your varied conquests out in cattle country."

"Whatever," I said. I took a drink of the beer, which was growing warmer by the minute. I wasn't such a big fan of drinking alone, but something about these phone calls with Lindsey made the alcohol seem necessary, partly because I liked the idea that while she was filling me in on everything I wasn't doing (and she was), I could be breaking the rules too, and partly because I needed to be just a little numb to listen to her exploits.

"The point is," she said, "I'm totally getting one the next time Alice goes out of town."

Lindsey had recently started referring to her mother only as Alice, and usually with disdain, which annoyed me, because as far as I could tell, Alice, the city-living, former-hippie type with liberal leanings, was a pretty awesome choice in the mom category.

"She lets you do whatever you want, anyway," I said, with more hostility than was probably warranted. "Why not just get one now if you're gonna do it?"

"She does not let me do whatever I want," Lindsey said. "She grounded me, or she tried to, over the goddess fiasco."

(Lindsey had recently tattooed a Triple Crescent symbol—which, according to Lindsey, represented some Wiccan things and also the three stages of the moon and of a woman's life—in purple on the upper part of her left shoulder.)

"And it's like really, Alice? How puritanical can you get? It's my body. She's the one out at Planned Parenthood with an A WOMAN'S BODY, A WOMAN'S RIGHT TO CHOOSE sign, and she goes postal because I *choose* to put something meaningful on my own shoulder."

"Did you seriously just say that getting an abortion is like getting a tattoo?" I asked, not because I thought she was necessarily wrong, but because I knew it would piss her off.

"Yeah, that's what I said if you have a first-grade understanding of logic," she said. She put on what I thought of as her professor voice. "The point is not the severity of the action done to the body, Cameron; it's a matter of the ownership of the body in question, and even if I'm fifteen, my body belongs to me."

I took another drink and put on my best sarcastic-student voice. "So again, I ask you, why wait on the tongue ring?"

"Because they heal like a bitch. Sometimes you have to go a solid four days on just milkshakes, and if you take it out you're screwed. I'm waiting until Alice'll be gone for at least that long. And then once it heals, I can take it out, if need be, while I'm around her."

"Gotcha," I said, opening the second of the two beers and checking at my door to listen down the stairs, make sure I could still hear *Columbo*, which I could. Not that Grandma was much for climbing the flight up to my room.

Then there was a pause in the conversation, with maybe twenty seconds of quiet between us, and because that almost never happened when we spoke, it felt especially uncomfortable; and when Lindsey didn't end it, I said, just to say something, because even though lately Lindsey had become a little bit sneering and self-important, she was still my one and only connection to authentic, real-life, not-in-the-movies lesbianism and I wanted to keep her on the phone: "I'm going to prom with Coley Taylor."

"What the fuck? Why were you sitting on that? Your Cindy Crawford cowgirl crush? You have to be shitting me—you're not even old enough to go to prom."

"Well, not *with* her, with her—not as dates. But we're going together as couples. Coley and Brett and me and Jamie." I was glad to have kept her from hanging up even if it was embarrassing to admit this. "They changed the rules for this year," I added, "because not enough upperclassmen bought tickets."

"Of course they didn't," she said. "Prom is an antiquated institution that reinforces outdated gender roles and bourgeois dating rituals. It's worse than cliché."

"Thanks for remembering to always make every moment a teaching moment," I said.

"Well, I'm fucking sorry that I have to, but this is not healthy progress for a dyke in training. Pining after straight girls—straight girls who are, by the way, in happy relationships with good-looking straight boys—when you live in a town filled with angry, Bible-pounding, probably gun-toting cowboys is a total no-win."

"Who am I supposed to pine after in Miles City?" I asked her. "It's not like I have a buffet of every lesbian imaginable just hanging around the local tattoo parlor, waiting in line to get their tongues pierced."

"Piercing parlors and tattoo parlors aren't always one and the same," she said, and then softened some. "Do you think Coley has any idea about you?"

"I don't know. Sometimes, maybe," I said—which was only partly true. The whole truth is that once, just once, when Brett had canceled our movie date last minute because of a math test he needed to study for, Coley and I went anyway, and even though I was my usual fidgety, alone-with-Coley, electrified self as we sat together in our top-row seats, she had seemed sort of electric too—not making eye contact and pulling her arm back when we'd both set it on the armrest between us at the same time. "But she's definitely not gay," I said, as much to myself as to Lindsey.

"So then what's the best that could possibly come of this?" she asked me, and then went on before I could answer. "That's what you have to ask yourself, because it seems like there's all sorts of things that could be really bad about this scenario, and not much that could be good."

"Yeah, I get it," I said, draining off the last of the beer and putting the can beneath my bed. I had been saving beer cans for a while then, cutting shapes out of them, tiny shapes— flying birds and diamonds and crosses—as small as I could make them, often cutting my fingers in the process. I was using the shapes on the pattern I was doing in the dollhouse nursery. "But I can't just stop having a crush on her because I get it," I said. "You know that's not how it works."

"Okay, but what's inspired this megacrush, anyway? I mean really—why the fuck Coley Taylor?"

Which, of course, was an impossible question to answer. "It's just how she is. I don't know—it's how she says things and what she's interested in, and the way she's somehow more grown-up than anyone I know, and she's funny." I paused, realizing how stupid and obvious I sounded.

Lindsey went on for me. "And how her ass fills out her jeans and—"

"You're seriously ten times worse than all the guys on the track team combined. You are," I said.

Lindsey laughed, then she put her professor voice back on. "Hear me out, my foolish and young apprentice: There's dykes out here who only go for straight girls, or straight-by-day, slut-by-night girls, to try to turn them or whatever; but they never get anywhere beyond one night, and they always end up pissed off and sad when the girl inevitably says something like how she was only experimenting or shit-faced or whatever, and that she's really into guys, not girls. And that's at least out here, where there's bars and concerts and a whole dyke scene to loosen their inhibitions. Prom in Montana is so not that scene."

"Duh," I said, sounding like someone who had just pounded two cans of Bud Light.

"Just continue to jill off to her or whatever, but end it there. Seriously."

Since, in a previous conversation, Lindsey had taught me that jill off was the female version of jack off, I was spared having to ask her to clarify. "Well, I'm going to prom, still," I said. "We have tickets and outfits and the whole setup."

Lindsey snorted. "I bet Ruth is beside herself with excitement."

"She's making us all a sit-down, *gourmet* dinner. She keeps saying how *gourmet* it's going to be. She's used that word maybe twenty times."

"Of course she has," Lindsey said. "I bet she makes a bunch of things she thinks are totally representative of haute cuisine but in fact would make a trained chef weep with disdain."

"I don't know. Whatever. I'm just telling people when to show up."

"Trust me," Lindsey said.

• • •

Ruth made Schwan's chicken cordon bleu and a salad (with Kraft French dressing) and green beans amandine (also from Schwan's), and these really tasty fried potatoes that she insisted we call *frites* when we asked her to bring us more. She played the role of the server and stayed, with Grandma, in the kitchen and breakfast nook during the bulk of the pre-prom meal, entering the dining room only to refill our wine glasses with sparkling grape juice and snap photos of us eating our *frites*. But she was sort of sweet about the whole thing and obviously genuinely happy to have the four of us there, me behaving like her vision of a typical teenage girl. She bought a big bouquet of roses for the centerpiece and put out silver candlesticks and set the table with what had been my great-grandma Wynton's lace tablecloth and wedding china—the stuff my mom used to use on the big holidays and sometimes my birthday.

The food tasted especially good to Jamie and me because we'd smoked quality pot in my room before Coley and Brett had arrived and dinner was served. This had been one of Jamie's conditions for attending prom: "We need to be fucked up for the whole thing," he'd told me after saying yes. "And I'm wearing a black tux with a black shirt and tie. All black, like a Bond villain or something, because that's dope as shit. And my Chuck Taylors."

That night he'd come over early wearing just that ensemble, his head freshly shaven. He came early ostensibly to bring me the wrist corsage—tiny pink roses and baby's breath—that he said his mom had picked out. Ruth was wary about me having him in my room, which was weird since he'd been up there so many times before, but she told him how dashing he looked and then called up the stairs to warn me that he was headed my way. I was still in sweat pants and a T-shirt, the too-short (I thought) black dress that Coley had picked out for me hanging safely in my closet, away, I hoped, from any pervasive smell of marijuana. Jamie took off his jacket and put it in there too.

We'd smoked together twice before with the same group of guys as always, me still the only chick allowed, and both times in the key room at Holy Rosary. Because of those occasions I'd decided that pot was a poor substitute for booze and didn't like the way it scorched my throat and down into my lungs, left them raw even the next day. I also didn't like how it made me paranoid; I wasn't sure if that was because it really did make me paranoid or because I'd heard that pot was supposed to make you paranoid; but both times I had been absolutely convinced that we were going to be caught in the hospital and kicked off the track team—so much so that I'd kept crouching behind file cabinets and hushing the group of giggling guys and making everyone listen to the weird, echoey sounds of the hospital for minutes on end.

"We can't be obviously fucked up, Jamie," I said as he packed a little blue glass pipe that I'd not seen him with before. "We have dinner and Grand March to get through."

"This is better stuff than you've smoked before," Jamie assured me. He pulled out a yellow Bic and lit the pot, took the first hit. I had to wait for him to go on, which he did in starts and stops as he held the smoke and released it.

"Travis Burrel's brother got me this shit."

I waited.

"He's in college at MSU-Bozeman with Nate."

I waited.

"This is the real deal—the stuff those East Coast granola ski-bum fuckers come to Montana to partake of. All part of a real Montanan collegiate experience." He craned his neck to exhale the sweet smoke out the open window, finally done, and passed the pipe to me.

"Because we grow it better here?"

"Fuck no, we grow ditch weed here, chica. This shit's from Canada, comes right over the border. Hydroponic all the way."

"What does that even mean?" I asked, the glass pipe warm in my hand.

"They grow it without soil, just minerals and shit. But all you need to know is that it fucks you up with more class." Jamie smiled his big-toothed Jamie smile, a fleck of ash on his stretched top lip, which he nabbed with the tip of his tongue.

I rolled my eyes but took my first hit and thought maybe it did seem less harsh than what we'd done before. "Let's do half of it now, see what the deal is, and maybe sneak the other half before we leave for the school," I said after exhaling. I was thinking mostly of Coley and not wanting to disappoint her. I'd seen her drink beer at a couple of keggers that ranch kids had out on their parents' land, but pot was something I felt like Coley Taylor would not approve of, would think was lame and strictly for the Dungeons & Dragons/Magic set and the granolas.

"What's happened to you, JJK?" Jamie asked, shaking his head and crossing his arms as if he was the guidance counselor asking me about slipping grades or truancy. "First you make me take you to prom, now you're fucking pussying out on the best pot you've ever smoked? I was afraid this might happen."

I took the bait. "What might happen?"

He toked and held it for an overly long time, making me wait yet again. And then he said, blowing the smoke right at me, "My little girl is becoming a woman."

"Fuck off," I said while he laughed and laughed. I took the pipe and took my turn, took another, and was going to prove my point with three when the pot hit me in that rolling rush that it always hits in, and I considered the weight of my tongue, the feeling of shifting sand behind my eyes, and the way the strained left hamstring that had been bothering me all season was already feeling loose and slippery; I decided that maybe I'd proved my point enough.

And then time passed the way it does when you're high, and Jamie took maybe one more hit, maybe three, and we talked about the dollhouse and Jamie suggested that there should be a tiny grow room in the back of the house, with replica heat lamps and marijuana plants made of actual marijuana buds, and I countered that it would cost like a hundred bucks to have enough tiny "plants" and what a waste just to glue them all to a table in a dollhouse, and Jamie said the whole point would be how cool the authenticity of such an endeavor was and if we ever got desperate for a high we could just set a fire in that room, and then I told him that was arson and the dollhouse police wouldn't stand for it, or something like all of that, or maybe nothing like any of that, and then Coley and Brett were there, and Ruth was calling up the stairs for us, and prom night had officially arrived with me high in my sweats and T-shirt.

"Just a sec," I yelled through the door as Jamie emptied nearly an entire can of Cinnamon Freshness room spray in a sticky-sweet aerosol mist that clogged the air and made it smell like cinnamon-flavored pot.

Coley did not wait just a sec and was up the stairs and knocking while Jamie giggled in the corner with the can held out in front of him in both hands, like a gun. "Show her in," he kept saying, then giggling more, then trying to stop it. "Do show her in."

I didn't have to because Coley knocked again and then just opened the door, singsonging, "I hope you're behaving yourselves in here."

And there she was, just as perfect as always but more so, in a pale-yellow dress with teeny-tiny straps and tiny daisies woven in her hair and not too much prom makeup but perfect and *glowing* and *fresh* and *dewy* and all the adjectives they used in the "How to Apply Prom Makeup Like a Pro" articles I knew that Coley had clipped and read and made happen, though she didn't need to, as lovely as she was without the beauty advice and the makeup.

We were standing very close, Coley still at the top of the stairs and me just inside the door. I felt myself staring and it felt like a long time and neither of us had said anything and I didn't want to turn around to see if Jamie was still pointing the can.

"Just how high are the two of you?" Coley asked me, shutting the door even though that meant Brett was left alone downstairs with Ruth and Grandma, which was hardly fair.

"We don't know what the devil you're referring to, madam," Jamie said, having done something with the can. (The something, I found out very early the next morning when I finally made it home, was stuffing it under my pillow like a gift from the Weed Fairy.) He walked to Coley in a straight-spined, Rex Harrison–in–*My Fair Lady* sort of way, took her hand, bowed deeply, and kissed her knuckles. "If you'll excuse me, lovely ladies, I must freshen up before dinner and have a chat with that Brett, the old scallywag." He took his jacket from my closet and did the stiff-spine down the stairs. I still hadn't moved.

"I'm actually glad that you're not dressed, because your hair will be easier to do this way," Coley said. She opened a bag I hadn't noticed her carrying and took out a curling iron and a hair dryer and various plastic tubes and tubs of makeup and laid them all on my bed.

"What first?" I asked, hoping that maybe we would just stick to the task at hand and skip over any more talk about how high I might or might not be. "Always hair," she said, putting a hand on each of my shoulders and pushing me back and down until I was seated on the edge of the bed.

"Figures," I said, lolling my head around because it felt good to do that but also trying to be a real sport about it. Coley and I had been halfheartedly arguing about the need for me to have "prom hair" since I'd agreed to go.

"Brett's going to be genuinely heartbroken if you two are too baked to share the bottle of Jim Beam he has. He's been saving it for a special occasion for months. Seriously. Months." She was busy undoing my ubiquitous ponytail.

"We're not that high even," I said, liking the feel of her fingers in my hair and also feeling a little bit throw-uppy and twitchy having her so close to me, leaning over me.

"I hope not," she said, spritzing hair spray and brushing and using the curling iron, and doing other things too, things that I didn't ever take the time to do. "Because the night, my dear, is young."

"I thought you'd be mad at me if you found out we smoked," I said, which was not the kind of thing I'd have ever admitted to Coley without the pot egging me on.

"I already knew that—of course. It's Jamie's thing, right?"

"But Jamie's not me," I said.

"Close enough sometimes," she said, yanking on something.

"No," I said. "Not close enough."

"Okay, whatever," she said. "I am sort of surprised you didn't wait for us."

"Since when do you smoke?" I was somehow offended by the idea of Coley having a habit of recreational drug use without my being aware of it.

"I don't," she said, leaning down to grin at me, her face huge and bright and so, so close to mine. "But I just told you, the night is young."

Here is how the young night grew older:

After dinner and pictures and pictures and pictures, Brett and Coley making most of the necessary conversation with Aunt Ruth so that Jamie and I could avoid doing so, the four of us loaded into Grandma Post's Chevy Bel Air, which seemed a markedly cooler car than it had not so many years before. Brett played chauffeur and Ruth took even more pictures of us loading up, rolling down the driveway, pulling into the street, until finally we were around the corner and free from the flash of her newish pink Sally-Q camera—at least until Grand March. We'd told her we were leaving a little early to drag a couple of Mains (drive the Main Street loop) and to stop for pictures at Brett's aunt's house. Instead, Brett pulled into a space by the community college track, the parking lot empty, the lone jog-walker in a teal running suit puffing through a lap, and the coast as clear as it was gonna get. We took turns with the Jim Beam until Jamie said he didn't want to drink as much of that shit as he was going to need to get through prom, produced his pipe, and after watching him pack it, Coley spoke for the group when she said she'd "give it a whirl," but only if we did it outside, because she was "not showing up to prom reeking of marijuana."

We borrowed scratchy stadium blankets from the trunk and Jamie and Brett took off their jackets. The puffing jog-walker did a perfect comic double take as the four of us—Coley and I wrapped in wool cocoons with bare legs and strappy shoes, Jamie and Brett mostly in their tuxes—crossed the parking lot to the thin cluster of juniper bushes and cottonwoods, found cover next to one of the picnic tables, and lit up. Coley coughed and coughed. Brett coughed and coughed. Jamie jogged to the Coke machine just outside the doors to the recreation center and bought a Sprite to cool their throats, jogged it back, and proceeded to pop open the too-jostled can and spray himself in sticky lemon-lime.

"Shit balls," he said, shaking drips of pop from his fingers and handing what was left in the can to Coley. "Are you guys feeling it, at least?"

"Can't tell," Brett said. "My lips feel like beehives. Does that mean I'm high?"

"As a spaceship," Jamie told him, reaching for the pipe. "But maybe one more for the road."

"No more for the road," Coley said, grabbing my arms and attempting to make me spin with her, which I didn't do. "I feel peaceful. And also like the world is made of pudding. This is nice. This is enough for now; we should go."

And after spritzing ourselves with almost the entire contents of the tiny bottle of Red Door perfume that Coley had in her clutch, and liberally sampling the PepOMints Grandma kept in the glove compartment, we did.

• • •

We had to line up for Grand March behind a partition arranged at one end of the gym. Vice Principal Hennitz was taking tickets and supposedly checking breath for booze, but Brett's winning grin and tremendous soccer season earned him only a vigorous nod and a smile, and then the four of us were in the door, at prom. It was too much hair spray and eyeliner back there, everybody a little bit sweaty and the whole thing already feeling deflated. When our names were announced we had to climb separate risers perched on either side of some platform, done up in glitter paint and apparently intended by the prom committee to look like a lunar surface. Once up the stairs we were to then meet in the middle, join hands, smile for one photo, and exit together. They had video cameras hooked up, so all this was playing on a screen hanging from the retracted basketball hoop. The bleachers at the opposite end of the gym were filled with all manner of doting relatives and with fellow high schoolers in various degrees of fuckup-ed-ness, some of them cheering for their favorite couples but most of them mocking the whole production—which isn't to say that some of us in line weren't doing the same.

I had to concentrate to walk in the heels Coley had picked for me, not that they were particularly tall, but certainly more so than my sneakers. Because of that concentration, and the pot, I didn't much hear the bleacher section until I was already in the middle with Jamie, hands together, the spotlight on us, and in the distance the rapid flashing of a couple of cameras—Ruth's, certainly, and probably Jamie's mom's. Jamie, unable to resist his moment on the big screen, put one arm around my back and dipped me low like a tango dancer. More cameras snapped. People clapped and whistled. Somebody booed.

During Coley and Brett's five seconds in the spotlight Brett gave Coley what was described by two junior girls in nearly identical purple dresses as "just an adorable" peck on the cheek, and Coley filled up the screen with her fucking amazingly sweet smile, and the bleacher contingent, even the bitter and scorned girls in the back row, *awwww*ed like people do when a precocious puppy takes a bubble bath in a Disney movie. But this wasn't the prom moment that got me.

Other moments that didn't get me include the first dance, which they let the parents and onlookers stay for, and which in this case was to Mr. Big's "To Be with You." Coley and Brett didn't have much time for intimacy with Coley's mom stopping them every two seconds to smile and pose, but when I did catch a look at the two of them, they seemed very happy in a completely stoned sort of way. Jamie and I were getting the same camera treatment from Ruth and his mom, but Jamie kept bobbing and weaving us around other dancers to keep us safe from their lenses, so much so that Jamie's mother eventually walked right through the couples into the middle of the floor and pulled at Jamie's jacket, asking why the two of us couldn't *just dance like normal people so we can get a picture, damn it.*

After that the parents left, and then it was a bunch of faster songs, and Jamie actually had some moves, most of them comic, all of them big but impressively rhythmic, somehow. And then it was two quick pipe hits each in the third stall of the girls' bathroom in the senior hallway, which the four of us escaped to fairly easily but had a hell of a time getting back from. The classrooms and hallways beyond the gymnasium were "officially closed," supposedly to prevent just the kinds of activities we were partaking of. But there were only so many chaperones, and the punch fountain needed constant surveillance.

While Jamie made the most of his all-black ensemble, slinking the length of the hallway and stairwell to ensure the coast was clear, Coley and Brett took some advantage of their high and did more kissing in that bathroom than they'd ever done in my presence before. And still that wasn't the moment that got me.

And it wasn't the next couple of slow songs. And it wasn't watching Coley dance sweetly with, and not at all to ridicule, this weedy FFA kid who had it bad for her and wore just how bad on his blushing face. And it wasn't even when Coley asked me to dance. Brett and Jamie were off posing for one of those photos small-town professional photographers always like to take and then hang in their store windows—a black-and-white with a bunch of the high school jocks, jackets slung over their shoulders, arms crossed, all of them refusing to smile and instead glowering at the camera.

Other girls had been dancing together all night, in groups and couples, but "November Rain" was a little bit slower and a little bit mushier a song than typical girl-girl dancing fare; and even still, with the cardboard stars overhead and way-too-high Coley holding me tight, our dance felt strangely meaningless and hardly romantic and not at all like anything I'd ever privately wished for when I thought about her. I was conscious of the couples around us who might be watching, and I was glad when it was over.

The moment that did get me was maybe five songs before the DJ thanked us for coming and they turned on the overhead lights and we all squinted and looked at each other in harsh fluorescent and noticed how squashed so-and-so's hair was and how the food table was all used up and dirty and rumpled and how some of us maybe looked a little like that too. Before that, Jamie and I were sitting one out in the bleachers and Coley and Brett were twisted up together on that gummy floor, all the couples around them members of Custer's Most Committed Relationship Club—not the couples who just got together for prom, the real deals. I was staring at Coley. I was. Her head on

Brett's shoulder and her eyes closed and several of the daisies now gone from her hair. She had taken off her shoes, we all had, and so she was tiptoeing it through this dance, the bottoms of her perfect feet black, but it didn't look like she could feel the floor anyway. Not from where I was sitting. I was still high enough to have a very bright kind of daydream where I was the one dancing with her that way, at our prom, with everyone knowing that we were together and girls in purple dresses whispering about how sweet and adorable it was when I kissed her. And I thought I was having a private moment, there from the dark of the bleachers, just watching Coley. But I felt the kind of prickle you get at the back of your neck when someone is watching you and you're about to get caught, and I turned my head and Jamie wasn't looking at the dance floor anymore; he was looking at me.

"Jesus, Cam," he said, not that quietly. "Try to keep it in your pants."

In my chest it felt like I'd just done the 200 IM. "You want my attentions all to yourself, huh?" I asked, trying lamely to smile and play him off like an idiot.

"Okay, sure," he said. "Whatever." He stood up. "I don't want to talk about fucked-up shit like this anyway. I'm gonna go see if I can find Trenton and score a cigarette." He was already two rows down, jacket slung over his shoulder and his face angry for real, not for the camera.

I stood up, followed him without knowing what I was supposed to say but unable to let whatever had just happened hang over me there in the bleacher section. My brain felt all linty like I'd been keeping it in the hatch in the dryer, and I couldn't get a handle on how best to make this go away fast.

When I'd caught his step and was just behind him, I leaned in over his shoulder and tried: "I don't have a thing for Brett, if that's what you meant. Jealous much?" I had intended to say this in my best sneer, but I didn't sneer all that well to begin with, and here I was high, and also it was hard for me to even make it sound plausible in my own head.

We were in the big lobby just outside the gym where the concession booths and trophy cases were. There were plenty of promgoers out there, milling around in their now-drooping finery, the heavy entrance doors propped open and the night air drifting in cool enough to be cold. Jamie answered me louder than I expected. "Yeah, I know that. You wouldn't have the problem you have if that were the case, huh?"

A knot of speech and drama kids who had dressed in Renaissance-style attire mostly borrowed from the school's prop room turned and looked at us. Despite the very non-period glasses and haircuts and braces that some of them sported, I felt in that moment like they were the chorus in my unfolding tragedy. I actually took Jamie's elbow and pulled him through the entrance doors, and he let me do it; but Hennitz was standing just outside, hands clasped behind his back, looking out at the school lawn and the ground-lit metal sculpture of Custer some alum had donated the year before.

"It's two of Custer's fastest," he said, turning to us and smiling in that vice-principalish way. "Did you make the most of your big night?"

"Sure," Jamie said, linking his arm to mine. "It's been a gay old time."

Hennitz chuckled. "You're not all really saying that again, are you?" he asked, seeming genuinely bemused. "I can't ever keep up with the lingo." He turned to go in, turned back. "Now remember, if you leave the steps you've left the premises and I can't let you back inside." He left us there on the wide cement stoop.

"Sure thing, dickhead," Jamie said to the space where Hennitz had been. In one graceful movement he perched himself on the top rung of the metal handrail.

A couple of kids I didn't know were on the far end of the stoop, lounging, the girls wearing their dates' jackets over their bare shoulders. It was chilly out there, worse yet when a breeze lifted the hem of my dress and left me with a series of shivers, one after the next. I bit back on my molars and clenched my shoulder blades together. I didn't have any of the right words to convince Jamie of anything. I looked at my still-bare feet, which were already stinging from the cold of the concrete. I willed myself not to fucking start crying.

"You want my jacket?" Jamie asked, his voice softer.

I shook my head no without looking at him.

He hopped down and put it over my twitching shoulders anyway.

"God, don't cry, Cameron," he said, his voice softer still, and he never, ever called me Cameron. "I really didn't mean to make you cry."

"I'm not," I said, which was just barely the truth. It was now or never. "When did you first know?" I asked him, still watching my feet. My toes had gone all white at the tips.

"What do I know?"

"About me."

"What about you?" His voice was only sort of teasing.

"Why do you have to be such an asshole about this?"

"Because what do I know, really? I know that you and that girl Lindsey are still pretty fuckin' chummy and she had the look about her. So that I know."

"What look?" I asked, finding his face.

"The dyke look. Fuck." He shook his head and snorted, banged the heel of his hand against the rail hard enough for it to hum a clangy, hollow sound the lounging couples noticed. "You want me to just call you a dyke? Is that like your party prize or something?"

"Yeah, that's what I want," I said, crying for sure now, and mad at myself for it and mad at Jamie, too. "Maybe you could spray paint it on my locker, just to be safe. So I won't forget."

I turned to go but Jamie pulled me back to him, and even though I'd seen that happen in like four hundred movies, nobody had ever done it to me and I didn't know that it could work just like that. One second I was full-force out of there and then I was crying hard against his chest, which was embarrassing and made me feel weak and was still something I let happen for a little while, anyway.

"Does everybody know?" I asked when I pulled myself away and used Jamie's jacket sleeve to wipe up the mess I'd made of the *dewy look* Coley had worked so hard on.

"A couple of the guys on the team have talked shit," he said. "But it's not an everyday thing."

I made a face that said *Oh really?* It involved raising my eyebrows and sort of pushing out my lips and cocking my head, and I could feel how stupid it looked even as I did it.

"It's not," Jamie said. "They like you, so it's like, *She's just a jock*, or whatever."

"But that's not what you said in the bleachers—"

"Because it's bad fucking practice." His voice was up again. "Jesus—you think people are saying shit now? Why don't you keep on with the Coley Taylor thing awhile longer and see what happens?"

I couldn't stop the way I was blushing, just like I never could. "We're friends," I said. "Seriously. I've never even . . ." I didn't know how to end that.

"You and me are friends too," he said. "For way longer.

It's like, how do you even know?"

"Who said I know anything? Or anything for sure."

Jamie shook his head. "Well, when you're around Coley, you sure act like you do. At least sometimes you do." He paused a second, seemed to work on his next words. "So if what you're telling me now is that you don't know for sure, then that's stupid. It is. You could give a guy a chance, find out."

And even though probably there were dozens of times I should have noticed before, it wasn't until right in that moment that I knew Jamie had a thing for me. Or that he thought he had a thing for me. And everything we had been talking about or around those last few minutes became suddenly more complicated and more uncomfortable, and it was now the exact kind of scene that I fast-forwarded through in movies—too much tension, too little air, nothing to undercut it all.

Some kids we both knew came outside just then, all of them laughing and loud, sweaty with sticky bangs and flushed faces. "One more song before last dance," one of them told us. Then they all seemed, at once, to notice that they'd interrupted some prom-night drama: Jamie's tense stance, my messy face.

They offered us shoulder shrugs and apologetic smiles, waved their packs of cigarettes at us, mumbled things about not wanting to smoke on top of us, and made their way down a couple of steps and over to the other handrail.

"If you don't know for sure, then what's the big thing about trying stuff out?" Jamie said, not looking at me but looking out at that statue, just like Hennitz.

I still didn't have any of the right words. "It's more like maybe I do know and I'm still confused too, at the same time. Does that make sense? I mean, it's like how you noticed this thing about me tonight, you saw it, or you already knew it—it's there. But that doesn't mean it's not confusing or whatever."

"Yeah, but I don't know anything about you for sure." He turned to look at me again. "That's what I'm saying. Sometimes when I hang out with you, you're like more guy than I am. But other times I want to . . ." He finished by doing this overdone thrusting movement with his hips, grinning like a perv. Which was stupid but felt much better than wherever we had been a second before.

"That's just because you're a disgusting teenage boy," I said, hitting him hard in the arm to get him to stop his gyrations. "That doesn't really have anything to do with me."

"Well, if I like girls and you like girls, that makes you a disgusting teenage boy, too," he said, hitting me back, and not that gently, either.

"Never," I said, and thought that maybe we had cleared something big, left it behind us, but then Jamie leaned over and kissed me. I could have turned my head away, I had time to duck or move or push his face, and I didn't. I let him do it. And I kissed him back, sort of. His lips were dry and his chin a little bit rough and he tasted like sour smoke and too-sugary sherbet punch, but there was something charged about kissing him, some sort of thrill because it was so unexpected.

Jamie's mouth was too busy, but he wasn't exactly a bad kisser. We kept at it long enough for the smoking section to give us a hoot and a whistle, and then I pulled back, not because it wasn't interesting kissing Jamie—it was, sort of like a fucked-up science experiment, and it was kind of nice, even, somehow—but because there we were on the school steps at prom and I liked to do my experimenting behind closed doors, and now Jamie's hands were behind me, one on my back, one on my head, and he was gaining momentum and I wasn't.

"Oh! Mission aborted! Advanced move denied!" It was

Steve Bishop, one of the smokers, yelling from his perch on the rail, the rest of them laughing along.

"Only for now, Bishop," Jamie yelled back. "And only because I'm a gentleman."

"That's not how it looked from over here, big guy!" Steve kept on, but Jamie smiled and gave him the two-handed flip-off and kept his attention on me.

"So that was the shit, right? You see what I'm saying?" He fixed his jacket because it had slid to the back of my shoulders.

"No. What are you saying?"

"That we should do more of that," he said. "Duh, JJK. The obvious choice."

"Maybe," I said, which is exactly what I meant without knowing at all what I meant. "Let's go do the last dance."

Which we did, Coley and Brett wrapped up tight right next to us. Jamie kissed me twice more during that dance (to "Wild Horses") and I let him, and after the second time I noticed that Coley had noticed our kiss and she winked at me over Brett's shoulder and wrinkled her nose and I blushed and blushed, and she noticed that too and winked again, which made me blush harder and hide myself in Jamie's shoulder, which I'm sure she noticed as well, and which Jamie noticed and was of course reconvinced by, pulling me tighter to him, and there I was sending the wrong signals to the right people in the wrong ways. Again, again, again.

CHAPTER NINE

S ince decades before I was born, summer in Miles City
was trotted down a banner- and flag-lined Main Street
and officially welcomed in by one event, always held the
third full weekend in May: the World Famous Miles City
Bucking Horse Sale. Ostensibly a series of showcases during which salty rodeo contractors came to bid on the finest
in debuted bronc stock, it was the four days of debauchery in the form of street dances, tractor pulls, and *authentic*
cowboy shenanigans that lured in city folk from both coasts
and boosted the town's economy until the next go-round.
Bucking Horse Sale (BHS) put Miles City in the Guinness
book of world records as the event that boasted "the most
alcohol consumed within a two-block radius, per capita, in
the United States." Pretty impressive if you consider Mardi
Gras in New Orleans or any major collegiate football game.
And we did consider them. Lots. And there was a strange
kind of local pride in our accomplishment, the town motto
for the weekend being: "If you can't get laid during Bucking
Horse, you can't get laid."

My parents and I had always gone to the parade Saturday
morning, lawn chairs and a thermos of sun tea, me troll-
ing the gutters of Main Street for pieces of saltwater taffy
or Jolly Ranchers that the already-tipsy-at-ten-a.m. float riders had flung off course. Next it was lunch at City Park, a

barbecue-beef sandwich greasing my fingers and making it hard to handle my sweaty cup of lemonade, and then my mom would have tours to give at the museum, and so maybe I'd meet up with Irene and we'd go to the rodeo together, liking best the shade under the grandstands where we collected the tossed-aside fifty-fifty tickets in big Styrofoam cups and tried to avoid the arcs of sunflower seeds and, worse, chew that plummeted around us like the heavy but staggered drops at the beginning of a thunderstorm.

Since my parents had died, Grandma had become a big fan of the DAR (in Miles City that stood for Daughters of the American Range, not Revolution) Cake Walk, a kind of tacked-on event. Bucking Horse Sale had lots of those. After the parade we'd head over to the library, come home with one German chocolate with coconut icing and a half dozen of Myrna Sykes's cinnamon rolls. But soon after prom night Grandma started feeling crappy, and the doctor told her she wasn't "quite managing" her diabetes with her diet alone. So when, a few weeks later, they put the Bucking Horse schedule of events in the paper and I asked her about our plans, Grandma, her Humulin vial in hand, told me she wasn't "fooling with the damn parade this year." Which was just fine by me, because with Ruth and Ray already signed up to staff about a zillion Gates of Praise–related BHS activities (a day care, an early-morning prayer meeting, a picnic lunch), as well as Ruth's Sally-Q booth at the fairgrounds, that left me with four days of authentic cowboy debauchery to spend as I saw fit; and it turns out that four days was more than enough.

Jamie, Coley, Brett, and I pregamed at Jamie's with beer and pot and then went to the opening street dance Thursday night. We got there early, before they roped off the area in front of the Range Riders Bar, and we should have been kicked out soon after, because the MCPD was out in much fuller force than typical and we were clearly underage, which was less of a big deal at later Bucking Horse Sale events, but the first night warranted extra vigilance. We *should* have been kicked out, but Coley's brother, Ty, was big shit that weekend, rodeoing for the exhibitions, but more important, he was one of the local, authentic, good-looking, and good-for-tourism twentysomething cowboys. And he had a word with someone or other working the little gate they'd set up, and all of a sudden the four of us couldn't be touched.

"But you're on your own for booze," Ty announced, swaggering over to us, working his way around a smattering of two-stepping couples, weirdly elegant in his dress Wranglers and vest. His hat would have looked cartoon-big if he hadn't worn it so well. "Don't let me catchya with a drink in your hand," he said to Coley, yanking on her ear. "I don't need to see none of that shit."

"*Any* of that shit," Coley said, thunking him on the chest. "Why would we even stay down here if we can't drink?"

"I didn't say you couldn't drink," he said, taking a theatrical swallow from his can of Miller. "I said I don't want to *see* you drinking. Out of sight, out of mind, your royal highness."

"I'm not royalty yet," Coley said. "You don't have to bow before me until tomorrow."

"So long as you name me court jester," Jamie said, doing this leprechaun sort of heel click he was fond of.

Coley had been nominated as queen of Bucking Horse Sale, which was a citywide competition, though usually an FFA girl from the Custer senior class ended up with the crown. Coley was the youngest girl to be nominated in something like thirty years, much to the annoyance of several of those seniors. She'd asked about retracting the nomination, but had offended the mustachioed guy at the head of the Montana Cattlemen's Association, which ran the election, so she'd decided to see it through, royal obligations and all.

"I won't win," Coley said. "They'll give it to Rainy Oschen. They should. She's been living for that crown." Then she took a couple of steps, and in a move that solidified yet again why I felt the way that I did about Coley Taylor, she did a perfect imitation of Jamie's heel click, and upon landing said, "But you'll always be court jester to me."

The band, some group out of Colorado, started up a foot stomper, and Ty nodded at a tiny but big-haired brunette across the street and motioned toward the dancing couples. He considered the four of us for a moment, actually shifting his gaze from one face to another, like he was looking at a police lineup. Then he put one hand on each of my shoulders, which was awkward, with that cold beer can crushing hard against my clavicle, pinned there by his giant, freckled thumb, which had a mostly dead fingernail, asphalt black and plum.

"Cameron, I'm putting you on Coley patrol for the next four days," he said, his beer breath hot and thick in my face. He wasn't wearing even a hint of a grin. "I can't trust the jester or the boyfriend, for obvious reasons. It has to be you—you have to keep her in line."

"'Help me, Obi-Wan Kenobi, you're my only hope,'" Coley said, clutching my arm, laughing.

I laughed too, but Ty still didn't let go.

"I'm serious," he said, his celery-green eyes hard on mine. "Don't let my sister ruin the good family name."

"No, that's your job," Coley said, shoving him toward the crowd. "Go dance with your cowgirl, hot stuff. I promise we'll behave."

162

"You need to use duct tape to stick to her, you do it," he said, walking backward, still hawking me. "Don't let me down, Cameron."

I laughed and said, "Sure thing, sir." But something about Ty made me nervous, something I couldn't quite pin down.

"Your brother's gonna be fighting them off all weekend," Jamie said as the four of us watched Ty claim his lady and twirl her into the center of the street.

"That's hardly a stud qualifier," Coley said. "I mean, if you can't get laid during Bucking Horse, Jamie . . ."

"Ouch," Brett said, taking her hand. "No need to crush a growing boy's dreams. Let's dance before Cameron has to defend her man's honor."

"Don't worry," I said as they headed out into the middle of the street. "He doesn't have any."

There had been lots of little jokes like this since prom night. Just teasing, mostly coming from Brett and Coley, since Jamie and I weren't really talking much about what was said on the school steps. What we were since prom was a good question, and not one I necessarily wanted an answer to. We'd twice taken the kissing to a shirts-off kind of place, both times in my bedroom, both times to a Lindsey mix tape; and one of the times Ruth had been fully aware of Jamie's arrival, the closing of my bedroom door, and Jamie's eventual departure. And she had said nothing.

It wasn't bad, the making out; it didn't make me feel wrong or even as weird as I thought that it might, but the whole thing did feel mechanical, or like a rehearsal, maybe, is the right way to put it: And I put in a tape, and I push Play, and the Cranberries serenade us, and I take off my shirt as Jamie takes off his, and we roll around on my comforter that smells like Downy, and Jamie has a weird indentation in his back, and his hands are so big and I can feel his calluses, and I can feel his heartbeat in my stomach, and he does this thing to the back of my neck that produces waves of goose bumps, and he hasn't yet pushed for the pants-off part the way the swell in his own pants worries me he might.

"I love how the so-called dorky prom, this thing you resisted, brought you two kids together," Coley had told me our first Monday back to school after our PDA in the glitter-star-filled gymnasium.

"We're not together," I said.

"Well, then what are you?"

"We're friends who are figuring shit out," I said, which at that point was the most honest and direct thing I'd said to Coley about me and my feelings, well, ever.

• • •

The Friday of Bucking Horse practically all the FFA kids, which was like forty percent of the school to begin with, were given excused absences, and then probably another twenty percent had parents who let them miss class, and the unfortunate rest of us who weren't goody-goodies or entirely uninterested, skipped. Jamie and I spent the morning at Holy Rosary with a couple of track teamers, rationing our pot allowances because Jamie couldn't get any more until later that evening and supplies were low. We used a couple of wobbly pushcarts for hallway races and eventually hallway crashes. We finally broke through the barricade at the top of the metal ladder on the ninth floor to climb through the hatch to the flat-topped, gooey-tarred roof, where we spray painted CLASS OF '95 on anything not moving and also a pigeon, which was moving, and so Jamie managed only a silver streak down one wing. We broke windows. We did handstands. We threw things into the empty, weedy parking lot. We did nothing that made any real kind of sense.

It was summer-hot on that roof, Jamie's shirt off soon after we got up there, the other guys' too, and me with my own T-shirt pulled up and tied around my middle, my belly button showing, my sleeves rolled and tucked in so that my arms were completely bare. At some point it became just me and Jamie, and then my pulled-up shirt came off altogether and we found a corner shaded by a huge duct with my back squished into that melty tar, sun-hot skin on skin. I remembered the feel of Lindsey, and I imagined what this might be like with Coley. For a few minutes I went with it, both in the moment and not at all, trying to match Jamie's intensity while pretending I wasn't with him. But I couldn't keep it up, and a police siren went by, and the clouds shifted, and Jamie's increased breathing pulled me back to that roof, and I had to get out of there.

I sat up, pushing Jamie off without giving him warning. "I'm starving," I said, reaching for my shirt. "Let's go to the fairgrounds and make Ruth buy us lunch."

"Give a guy a second, Post—fuck," Jamie said. "We're kind of already doing something."

I stood up, did some quick lunges like my legs needed stretching, which they didn't. "I know, I'm sorry, but I'm seriously hungry," I said, not looking at him. "I skipped my Wheaties this morning."

"Completely fucking lame," he said, leaning back on his elbows and squinting up at me. "We can't even go to the Sale until after school's out—Ruth thinks you're in chemistry right now."

I pulled on my shirt, reached down so as to help Jamie up, and babbled. "So we'll tell her it was a half day. Or we'll just tell her we left early; she'll get over it. Maybe we won't even see her; it's packed out there. We can find Coley, score a hamburger."

Jamie ignored my hand and pushed himself up, turned away from me. "Yeah, let's fucking go find Coley. Should've known." He jerked open the lift for the hatch.

"C'mon," I said, tugging on the T-shirt he hadn't put on but had tucked into the waistband of his shorts. "I'm just really hungry."

"Whatever," he said. "What I don't get—" He shook his head, said *Fuck it* under his breath.

"What?" I asked, without wanting him to answer.

He sneered. "For like two minutes I was like, *Holy shit, here we go—Cameron's actually into this for once.* And now we're off to find Coley." He started down the ladder into the darkness below.

"Then let's not find her," I said, following after. "Let's do Taco John's. Whatever." This was a desperate sort of suggestion and Jamie knew it. Probably his greatest temptation after pot were the Super Potato Olés at Taco John's, which went well with the pot. We ate there with such frequency that I usually put up a fight for someplace else.

"I have an idea," Jamie said from below me. "Why don't I drop you off with Pastor Crawford and you can ask him to pray for your perverse disease." I heard him jump from the last rung, his sneakers slap the cement floor.

"You're being such an asshole," I said, my foot searching for another rung and finding only air. I jumped too.

"You're being such a dyke," he said, not waiting for me, taking off down the hallway.

We didn't talk in Jamie's Geo. He blasted Guns N' Roses and I pretended to be really interested in the same out-of-the-passenger-side-window scenery I'd been staring at my whole entire life. He drove us to the fairgrounds and paid the three bucks to park. He put on his T-shirt. We walked the packed dirt path, clots of dust kicking up behind us like behind Yosemite Sam in the cartoons—that dirt as soft and dry as flour. We walked side by side but not really together. The grounds smelled like manure and spring, the prairie wind lifting the scent of new sand reed and the just-blooming lilacs that edged the paint-chipped Expo Hall. What was left of my high was mostly worn off, but there was enough there for me to appreciate being outdoors in spring in a way that I wouldn't have otherwise.

Inside the expo building we didn't see Ruth but found Coley right away, staffing a booth with the five other Queen of the Bucking Horse Sale nominees. They were raffling off a quilt and a dozen steaks to benefit the Cattlemen's Association, and the glass jar in front of Coley had the most tickets. She wasn't only the youngest; from where I stood she was by far the prettiest in her tight black tank top with one of her brother's stiff, white pearl-buttoned shirts tied over it and a sort of beat-up straw cowboy hat, her perfect hair pony-tailed for once, two of them, actually. She was sipping a Coke through a red-and-white straw and smiling her big smile at some cowboy stopped at the table. He had his thumb hooked in his belt buckle and was wearing a google-eyed look like a guy shot by Cupid on a crappy drugstore valentine. I knew that look. I'd worn that look.

Coley jumped up when she saw us, ran around the table, and hugged us both like we hadn't been together less than twelve hours before. She could pull off that kind of thing, but when someone like Ruth did the same, it didn't work at all.

"This is a little like torture," she said in my ear, smelling like Old Spice and cigarette smoke, which must have been left over on Ty's shirt. She handed me the Coke and I took a long swallow, met Jamie's stare, offered him the cup, but he turned away.

"How much longer do you have?" I asked.

"Half an hour, forty minutes, something like that," she said, squeezing my arm. "Wait for me?" Then she considered us both again, went back to my ear. "Are you two high already?"

"Not already," I said. "Already finished."

"A big morning, was it?" She smiled, the signature Coley wink.

"Hardly," Jamie said. "Cameron couldn't wait to get over here to see you. She's been thinking about you for hours."

I jumped in fast. "Jamie's playing the role of baby right now because I wouldn't go with him to Taco John's."

"Oh, you poor thing," Coley said, now grabbing Jamie's arm. "They have pacos at the concession booth. Is that an acceptable stand-in? I'll treat you. Well, I'll get my mom to treat you; she's working over there right now." Coley had the knack for smoothing things over, making people smile and go along, but I guess it didn't always work.

"I don't think so," Jamie said. "I'm gonna head out. See if I can find Travis." He still hadn't looked at me since Coley had offered me her drink.

"You're coming back, though?" I asked.

"Depends," he said. "I'm sure you can man up without me." He walked off into the clatter of the hall.

"What's the deal?" Coley asked, both of us watching his long stride and black shirt weave through the crowd around the tangles of cowboys, standing out as he went, mostly because of the shorts and his half-bare legs in all those stems of denim.

"Just a bad high," I said. "He's been cranky since we smoked."

"You fool kids and your drugs," Coley said. "When will you ever learn?"

• • •

Coley wasn't crowned Queen of Bucking Horse Sale 1992. It went to Rainy Oschen, just like Coley claimed it should, though some people seemed scandalized by the election process and there were murmurings that it was fixed, that if ballots had indeed been counted properly, Coley would have landslided it.

"Whatever," she said after the dusty crowning ceremony held out in the center of the arena, the bull riding just finished, the calf roping up next. (Even the runners-up got crowns, albeit of the smaller, silver variety.) "I'd honestly rather win as a senior, or as a junior. If I even get nominated again."

"Are you kidding?" Brett said, putting his arm around her. "It's in the bag."

We were grouped together at one of the entrances to the grandstands blocking traffic, but we didn't care. The night was just chilly enough to remind us that it was still technically spring, and the place was packed, everybody too loud and too drunk and high on Bucking Horse fever. I'd been scanning for Jamie for most of the evening and hadn't found him. And hadn't necessarily expected to.

"How many more days of this?" Coley asked us, pulling off her crown and sticking it on my head. "It already feels like forever."

"No way," Brett said, taking the just-placed crown off my head and putting it back on Coley's. "You don't get to tire out on my last night of Bucking Horse."

Brett had been selected as one of two Miles Citian players

to compete in a statewide soccer match to determine the all-stars who would represent Montana in some national high school soccer league taking place in the summer. The match was in Bozeman on Sunday, and so he was heading there with his parents promptly the next morning, right during the parade.

"Don't remind me," Coley said, now putting the crown on Brett's head. "I wish I could skip and go with you."

"Not a chance," he said, kissing her hand. "You're part of the royal brigade."

We moved outside the arena, where it was less crowded and the smell of grilling burgers was smoking the air. We parked ourselves as near to the beer booth as we thought permissible, hoping to spot someone to buy for us, or at the very least let us sip from their can. A round ended and the beer line swelled into a lake of thirsty patrons waving their tens at the beefy ladies working the booth. Two of those patrons were Ruth and Ray, hand in hand, Ruth wearing a denim skirt and a red scarf with brown boots and hats printed on it.

Ray saw me before Ruth did, and I nodded at him and wondered if that could maybe be that, but he pointed me out to her and she walked right over, gaining some appreciative glances, I noticed, as she went.

"There you are," she said. "I was starting to think we weren't going to see you before Monday."

"Blame my brother," Coley said, as if letting Ruth in on something, which was exactly the kind of thing Ruth loved. "He appointed Cam my official keeper for the weekend."

Ray joined us, handing a beer to Ruth, which I sensed wasn't her first of the evening, and after I cleared spending the next couple of nights at Coley's (contingent upon mandatory church attendance Sunday morning), and we heard about the

Sally-Q booth's success (*Seventeen new hostesses planning to open up their living rooms for hardware demonstrations!*), Ruth told me she wanted a word in private, so we moved a few feet away from the little knot, found a space wedged in so close to one of the big barbecue grills that my right side was all sizzling heat.

"Honey, this might upset you, but I want you to know that Ray and I saw Jamie tonight," she said, taking my hand and quieting her voice as much as the crowd would allow. "He's ahead of us a few rows in the bleachers and he and that Burrel boy are being pretty darned disgusting with a couple of girls they have with them." When I didn't say anything, she added, "I don't think they're Custer girls. Ray thinks maybe they're from Glendive." And when I still didn't say anything, she said, "I just wanted you to hear from someone who loved you."

"Okay," I said, trying to picture what these girls looked like and liking the slightly chunky, bleach blonde with black roots and too much makeup version the best. And even though I was surprised by the little bit of jealousy I felt, there was some relief in it too—as if the pressure was off me.

"Do you want to talk about it?" Ruth asked, even as some dustup disturbed the already-impatient beer line and the shouts of the crowd grew louder around us.

"Not really," I said. "Jamie can do whatever he wants." But then I added, "Thanks for telling me, though, Aunt Ruth." And she gave me a quick hug and a sad-Ruth half smile and went off with Ray.

"Did you get a talking-to?" Coley asked me, drifting over to the grill and leaving Brett with some of our classmates.

"Sort of," I said. "Jamie's in the bleachers with his tongue down some Glendive girl's throat."

"Ruth said that?"

"In a Ruthian kind of way."

"That slimy son of a bitch," Coley said, putting her arm around me. "Let's get Ty to kick his ass."

"Not worth it," I said, and that I meant, even though I knew that Coley didn't believe me. "Let's just go get really, really drunk."

"Don't you want to see what she looks like?" Coley asked, and I told her that I guessed I did just to humor her. From the closest arena entryway Coley spotted Ruth and Ray climbing the stairs, and when I couldn't find them in the stands, she actually took her hand and turned my head until it was facing the right direction, both of us tight together against the pull of the crowd, watching as they returned to their seats, and sure enough, there was Jamie just a few rows down. And I suppose we were sort of far away, but even so I could tell these girls were much prettier than the ones I'd put in my head. And Jamie was indeed all over one of them.

"They're beasty," Coley said. "Authentically vile. You can tell they're trampy from here."

"Can you?" I asked, smelling Coley's apple-scented shampoo, her soft hair brushing the side of my face. "Are they wearing the scarlet letter?"

"How are you being so cool about this?" She turned to look at me, our faces so, so close. "Is that what happened this morning before I saw you—you broke up? Is that it?"

"I've told you twenty times. There wasn't anything to break up."

"I know, but I thought that was just you being you."

"I don't even know what that means," I said. But I did know, and she was right; I had been totally arch about Jamie and me, just not in the way she was reading it. "Jamie and I are just better as friends," I said, trying again.

She started to say something and then didn't. We watched Jamie and his Glendive girl kiss, and then watched Ruth make faces at those kisses, shake her head for an audience of Ray, which made us both laugh.

"The good thing about it happening tonight is that it's Bucking Horse," Coley said, taking my arm and walking us out of there. "We can find you a cowboy in no time. Or two cowboys. Twelve cowboys."

And I wanted so much to say "Or how about a cowgirl?" Just say it, right then, in the moment, put it out there and let it stay and make Coley deal with it. But of course I didn't. No way.

• • •

After Coley's stint as runner-up on a crepe papered flatbed float in Saturday's parade, the two of us decided that we were officially tired of Bucking Horse. Brett was off to play in his big soccer match, Jamie was still dodging me in favor of a girl who might actually put out, and a bunch of thunderheads rolled in by noon, the way they always do at least once during the festivities, making everything gray and soggy and more than a little deflated.

Coley drove us out to her ranch and we spent the afternoon frocked in Ty's gigantic sweatshirts, drinking sugary mugs of Constant Comment (Coley's favorite) and watching MTV, hiding out from the social obligations of Bucking Horse. It was only the second or third time I'd been out at her house without Brett, and I was predictably anxious about that. Coley's mom made us grilled cheese with tomato soup before she headed into town to work her twelve-hour shift as an ER nurse. She'd told me to call her Terry probably half a dozen times, but I couldn't stop with the "Mrs. Taylor."

"Coley, honey, wouldya be sure and feed before it gets too late?" Mrs. Taylor said, standing by the front door in maroon scrubs, an umbrella in hand, an older, more worn version of Coley but still really pretty. "I have no idea when Ty will show his face." She kept checking her reflection in a mirror above their coat hooks, flicking the side of her hair a few times. "It's chicken-fried-steak night at the cafeteria. You girls want to come in and eat with me before you go out?"

"We're not going out," Coley said, and then she turned to me. "What is it you said about Bucking Horse, Cam?"

"That it's a bitter mistress," I said.

"Yeah," Coley said, laughing, though her mom was not. "We've decided that Bucking Horse is a bitter mistress and we'd rather eat ice cream and avoid it."

"That doesn't sound a bit like you," Mrs. Taylor said, looking from Coley to me, not necessarily unkindly but not kindly, either. "I thought you'd be downtown in the thick of things for sure."

"We're just gonna stay in and do nothing," Coley said, checking her own reflection in the coat-hook mirror and then pulling the hood of her sweatshirt over her head and backing up until she fell over the arm of the couch and sprawled with her head and trunk on the cushions and her legs in the air.

"Call me at work if you change your mind and head in," Mrs. Taylor said. And then from the stoop she added, "And tell Ty to call me too—if you see him."

We did see Ty not half an hour later, a dirty and busted-up version with a big cut under one eye and, as he put it, a "hitch in his giddy-up."

"I didn't think you were supposed to ride until tonight," Coley said, helping him off with his jean jacket.

"I'm not," he told us, putting on a big grin. "This is from one ornery son of a bitch named Thad. I shit you not. The fucker's named Thad. Now *he*'s the one looks like he got trampled by a bull."

"Nice, Ty," Coley said, inspecting the dried blood on the jacket's collar. "I thought we were trying to preserve the family name."

"That's exactly what I was doing, kiddo," he said, his head buried in the freezer. He emerged with a bag of frozen broccoli as his ice pack.

He drove off again after a shower, a serving of scrambled eggs and toast, and a clothing change: stiff jeans, a different hat, a fresh cigarette behind his ear. Coley was asleep next to me on the couch. The rain had mostly stopped and there were sunbeams spotlighting through the remaining clouds and lighting up sections of the hills outside their big living-room window. Next to that window was a framed family picture taken before Mr. Taylor had died. They were out somewhere on the prairie. Coley was maybe nine, in pigtails, all of them wearing soft denim shirts tucked into jeans. The picture had sort of faded somehow in the processing, almost a black-and-white but just tinged with color. Mr. Taylor, his mustache hiding part of his smile, had his arms around Mrs. Taylor and Ty, Coley was sort of perched in the middle, and Ty had his thumb hooked in his belt. They looked happy, which is the point in those kinds of photos, I know. But they did.

I tried to get up from the couch to look at it closer without waking Coley, moving only an inch or two and then waiting, trying not to shift the cushions, but I hadn't even put all my weight on my feet before she said, "Did it stop raining?"

"Yeah," I said, feeling like I'd been caught doing something when I hadn't, really.

"We should go feed, then," she said in a yawn, stretching wide her arms.

I grinned at her. "You think I'm gonna help you do your chores? You play the cowgirl, not me."

"Only because you could never hack it as a cowgirl, townie," Coley said, sitting up fast and gripping the hem of my sweatshirt, pulling me back onto the couch, which I didn't fight at all. She threw the fleece blanket she'd been wrapped in over my head and put a couch cushion on top of that, climbing atop the pile and staying there. I struggled halfheartedly, Coley resisted, I struggled more, the two of us eventually on the carpet between the couch and coffee table, the blanket still covering most of me and so it was between our bodies; but when a corner of it got pinned beneath my knee and pulled away and I could see how those too-big sweatshirts had twisted around us, leaving my stomach and Coley's back bare, I stopped pretending to struggle and actually pulled away from her, stood up, shook out my legs as if I was Rocky at the top of the stairs in Philadelphia.

"Retreat means defeat," Coley said, pulling her hair out of her face and lifting her arms for me to help her up, so I did but then backed off again.

"I didn't want to hurt you with my advanced physical prowess," I said, all jangly energy.

"Of course not. Wanna see if Ty has any booze in his room as payment for our labor?"

He did. Half a bottle of Southern Comfort, which we mixed with what was left of two liters of semiflat Coca-Cola stored in the door of the fridge. We drank some. We changed into jeans. I borrowed a pair of Ty's also-too-big boots, which reminded me of trips to the Klausons'. Outside it was muddy and smelled like grass and wild flowering crabapple trees and just-after-rain, the smell that laundry detergents and soap try to imitate with their "spring meadow" varieties but can never pull off. We loaded heavy bags of range cake into the slippery bed of the truck. Coley found a pocketknife and cut each bag open at the top. She ran back into the house and emerged with a cassette, which she put into the truck's player, hit Rewind. The tape was a Tom Petty mix, also once belonging to Ty. I'd sent a similar mix of Tom Petty & the Heartbreakers tunes to Lindsey as a kind of thank-you for all the artists she'd mixed up for me, but when I'd asked her what she thought of it during one of our phone conversations, she'd told me that Tom Petty was a male chauvinist and that his role as an Alice-eating Mad Hatter in the video for "Don't Come Around Here No More" was just additional fuel to a fire already started by what Lindsey claimed were lyrics showcasing his "limited abilities as a songwriter and his prurient interest in teenage girls."

I didn't share any of this with Coley, and it didn't change Petty's appeal for me, either. That afternoon in the truck Coley turned the volume up loud. We rolled down the windows, manual, not electric. We drank from our big plastic bottle. She'd rewound to the first song on side B, "The Waiting," which was our mutual favorite. She sang one line.

Oh baby don't it feel like heaven right now?

I sang the next.

Don't it feel like something from a dream?

Coley bounced us over the hills, down rutted roads of crumbly sandstone and shale, through trenches of fresh mud as thick and oily as modeling clay, and then cross-country, crunching wet sagebrush when it was in our path, which it often was.

In between verses we passed the bottle, noticed the purple crocuses that dotted some of the hillsides, their petals so thin they were nearly transparent, the sunlight cast through them, and those hillsides greener than they'd be for the rest of the summer. We listened to a few more tracks and then Coley rewound and it was "The Waiting" again, and then again, each time louder, each time better.

We found most of the herd through gate seven, down in a grove of juniper, one of those beams of sunlight warming their wet and tangled hides. The Taylors raised Red Angus. They were due to calve in a couple of weeks, and several of the way-pregnant heifers looked like hairy boxcars on legs. Their calves, I knew, would be velvety red-brown teddy bears with big, soft eyes: completely adorable. I moved to the bed of the truck and poured cake while Coley drove us in a zigzagging line, trying to spread out the cows for their meal.

We found the rest of the herd grazing in a patch of new grass maybe a half mile away. I finished pouring the feed. Both of us drank more. With some effort, Coley drove us up the rocky but slippery side of a partly pink sandstone hill they called the Strawberry, and after spinning the wheels in a marsh of mud near the crest, she parked. We lined the bed of the truck with the empty cake bags and spread the flannel blanket from the bench seat over them. Coley left the stereo on, turned up the volume even louder. We lay flat on our backs, our feet planted and our knees in the air, the just-setting sun coloring the remaining clouds in plum and navy with Pepto Bismol–pink underbellies and the sky behind them every candy-colored shade of orange, from circus peanut to sugared jelly slice. I could feel something happening between us, something even beyond my buzz from the liquor, something that had started with the wrestling on the couch, before that, too, if I was to be honest. I closed my eyes and willed it just to finally happen.

"Why don't you still talk to Irene Klauson?" Coley asked. It wasn't any more of a surprise than anything else she might have asked me right then.

"She's too cool for me now," I said. "I didn't even know that you knew her."

"Of course. The dinosaur heiress? Are you kidding?"

"But did you know her before that?"

"Yeah, especially when we were little," Coley said, twisting the bottle cap with just the smallest of fizzing noise escaping from what was left of the carbonation. "I didn't know you, but I'd see you two together at everything."

"At what?"

"At everything—the fair, at Forsyth's field days."

"We were together as much as we weren't," I said.

"I know," Coley said, handing me the bottle. "That's why I asked why you don't still talk to her."

"She went away. I stayed here."

"That doesn't quite add up." Coley let her right knee fall out to the side so that it collided with my left knee and stayed propped there.

"Her parents found dinosaurs and my parents died. Does that add up?" I didn't say it to sound mean, exactly; I was actually hoping that answer made sense.

"Maybe," she said, letting her other knee fall so now she was turned completely on her right side, facing me, both of her legs propped by mine, her elbow down and her right hand holding her head. "I guess some of my friends changed after my dad died."

I didn't have anything to say to that. We listened to Tom Petty telling us about *free falling*. Coley put her left hand on my stomach, just above where my belly button was. She pressed it there kind of hard.

"Did you sleep with Jamie?" she asked. Just like that.

"Nope," I said. "I'm not planning to, either."

Coley laughed. "Because you're a prude?"

"Absolutely," I said. "All prude, all the time." Then I waited a little and added, "You have with Brett, though, right?"

"That's what you think?"

"I guess so."

"Not yet," she said. "Brett's too nice a guy to pressure me."

"He is a nice guy," I said, trying to read what was happening and to be sure about it, but I couldn't.

"Sometimes I think I should wait, anyway. It used to be really important to me to wait, at least until college. Doesn't it seem like there's all this room to figure things out in college?"

"I guess," I said. She still hadn't moved her hand.

"What do you think Irene Klauson is doing at this very moment?" Coley's words were Southern Comforty and wet and warm at the side of my face, deep into my ear.

This was it, I decided, and so I said, "Making out with her boyfriend, the polo player." And then I added before I lost my nerve, "Pretending to like it." Those words just hung out there for a moment, out in the all-color sky, with the sound of raindrops flitting from pine boughs when the breeze hit them right.

She gave it a second, then asked, "Why pretending?"

I got scared. "What?"

"Why doesn't she like it?" Coley moved the fingers of the hand on my stomach, one at a time; she pressed in the

180

pinky, then released, the ring finger, release, the middle finger, release, again and again she cycled through them.

"Just a guess," I said. *I could just turn my head to hers, right now,* I thought, *and that would be that.* I didn't.

"I don't think that's what it is," she said. She took her hand away from my stomach, sat up, scooched to the end of the truck bed, the tailgate, let her legs dangle over the edge.

It was somehow easier with her down there, her back to me. Easier, but still not easy. I breathed in and out, in and out. Then I did it again. Then, before the moment was too far gone, I said to her sweatshirt hood, "She's pretending because she'd rather be kissing a girl."

Now Coley got scared. "What?"

"You heard me," I said, though it took effort to make the words steady.

"How do you know that?"

"How do you think?"

Coley didn't answer me. We listened to the pine boughs shake free more rain. It was growing darker with every word I wasted.

She turned to look at me, that colored sky all stretched out behind her, her face a shadow. "Come sit with me."

I did. I sat as close to her as possible. Our shoulders and legs touching. She was swinging her feet back and forth like a kid on a swing set. We sat like that for a while. The swing of her legs made the tailgate squeak, but only every so often.

Finally Coley said, each word spaced out, "There have been a whole bunch of times I thought you were gonna try to kiss me. Yesterday at the rodeo, even."

We waited some more. The tailgate squeaked twice.

She said, "But you never have."

"I can't," I said, just barely letting the words out. "I never

181

can do it." I watched Coley's boots swing out and back over the ground, the heel of one of them just grazing a clump of sagebrush, flicking water from it.

"I'm not like that, Cam. You should already know that I'm not."

"Okay," I said. "I didn't think that you were."

"I'm not," she said, and breathed in big. "But then what's weird is that sometimes I think if you kissed me, I wouldn't stop you."

"Oh," I said. I actually said "Oh." It was a clear, solid little word and it felt like a stupid thing to say because it was.

"I don't know what that means," she said.

"Does it have to mean something?"

"Yes," Coley said, looking at me. I could feel her looking at me, but I kept on staring at her swinging feet. "It does have to mean something."

I hopped down, right into the mud. I leaned up against the tailgate, trying to make out the slope of each hill as the twilight worked to make the range one stretch of shadows. "Sorry," I said, because I thought I should say something. I wondered if I could maybe walk all the way back to Miles City. I knew it would take me over an hour just to reach the highway, but in that moment it seemed like maybe the safer option.

But then Coley put her hand on my shoulder, just barely there, the feel and weight of her palm through Ty's thick cotton sweatshirt. That was all I needed. I turned around and found her face, and her mouth was already waiting like a question. I'm not gonna make it out to be something that it wasn't: It was perfect—Coley's soft lips against the bite of the liquor and sugary Coke still on our tongues. She did more than just not stop me. She kissed me back. She pulled me in with her arms, her ankles latching behind my thighs, and we stayed like that until I could feel my boots sinking so far into the rain-softened clay-thick mud beneath me that I wasn't sure I'd get them out. Coley noticed too, me now several inches lower than when we'd started.

"Holy fuck," she said when I pulled away.

"I know," I said. "Trust me, I know." I tried to lift up my boots and found that I couldn't, so I stayed planted there. "I'm stuck," I said. It was embarrassing.

"Oh my God, Cam. Oh my God." Coley had her hands over her face, which was right in front of me, I mean, right in front, inches away, but I couldn't move back any.

"Seriously, Coley—I'm stuck," I said. I put my hands on her thighs and was planning to grip her jeans while I attempted to jerk one foot free, but my touch freaked her out even more and she did a kind of Elizabeth Taylor gasp and jumped down from the tailgate and there was no room for us both in that small space, no way for me to move my feet, so I fell backward, literally in slow motion, Ty's boots still stuck in that thick mud-clay but the momentum pushing the rest of me back, back until there wasn't any farther to go.

I hit a clump of sagebrush but it couldn't hold my weight, and my back squashed down hard on its leathery leaves and stiff stems until my head was in the mud and my legs were in the mud and my fucking feet were still locked in those boots. I had cold mud squelched in my ears but I could hear Coley laughing, hard, big, for real, a whooping kind of laughing, and so I closed my eyes and shoved my sage-scraped hands into my jeans pockets and joined in, right there on the ground.

And when I opened my eyes again, Coley was standing over me, one foot on either side of my hips, but because of the diminished light and her angle, the way she was bent over me some, her hair falling toward me, I couldn't read her face.

"And we called her Grace," Coley said. Even without seeing her expression, I could tell she was smiling.

"You're very clever," I said.

"What just happened?"

"I fell on my ass. Big-time." I was stalling.

Coley knew it. "Before."

"I'm not sure," I said.

"Yes you are," she said, and then in a move I never could have guessed, she sat down on my hips, me pinned beneath her like when we were wrestling, but this was something much bigger. "You finally kissed me," she said.

"I thought you wanted me to."

Coley didn't say anything to that. I waited for her to, but she didn't.

"It doesn't have to be a big deal," I said. "It can just be one more stupid thing the two of us tried together."

Coley kept on sitting where my hip bones jutted out, all of her weight on me, and having her there was maddening; I wanted to pull her down on top of me. But she still didn't say anything. So I waited, and I panicked, and I listened to Tom Petty singing from the cab of the truck, and I thought about Lindsey and how she had warned me about this exact stupid thing, and how I just couldn't help myself.

I tried again. "C'mon, Coley. We don't even have to talk about it. It's no big deal."

"It is too," she said.

"Why?"

"For lots of reasons."

"Why?"

"Because I didn't really think I'd like it and I did." She said it like ammunition.

"So did I," I said.

"And that doesn't seem like a big deal to you?"

"It doesn't have to be," I lied. "It's not like I'm thinking you're gonna ask me to go steady."

"Okay, it's into the ether," she said, standing up. "But I want to stop now."

"Yeah," I said, hoping she couldn't see my face any better than I could see hers. "Me too."

I didn't spend the night. After we got back to her house and cleaned off, the two of us didn't even know how to sit on the couch and watch TV without what had happened sitting down between us, and eventually Coley said that she thought maybe she did want to go downtown after all, so we ended up at the hospital cafeteria having the too-much-gravied chicken-fried steak with a pleasantly surprised Mrs. Taylor, and then we found our way to another street dance and joined a group of FFA kids. When everybody decided to head out to the McGinns' ranch for a kegger, I told Coley that I was tired and was just gonna go home if that was cool, and she looked relieved about that. At least that's how I read it.

Aunt Ruth and Ray weren't home yet, and it was kind of embarrassing to come in before them, but Grandma was at the kitchen table eating sugar-free cherry Jell-O with mandarin oranges and cottage cheese. She was wearing the same purple housecoat she wore the night she told me about Mom and Dad. She'd worn it plenty of times since, but something about seeing her alone at the table in it was like putting bare feet in a snowbank.

"You want some, Spunky?" she asked me, offering her spoon and pushing the bowl across the table a few inches. "It's no German chocolate cake."

"No thanks," I said, but sat down with her anyway.

185

"Your Jamie called twice tonight," she said.

"He's not my Jamie, Grandma."

"Well, he's sure as hell not mine. Whose is he if he's not yours?" She worked an orange slice onto the spoon she'd already loaded with Jell-O.

"I don't know," I said. "He's his own."

"You're too young yet to be fooling with serious boy-friends, anyway."

I liked watching how she made sure that every bite had some of each of the dish's three components in it.

She swallowed and said, "I made your grandfather chase after me for purt-near forever, to hear him tell it. That was the fun of it."

"So how did you decide to let him catch you?"

"Because it was time to." She used her spoon to do a long swipe of the inside of the bowl, the metal against the ceramic making an uncomfortable noise. "That's something you fig-ure out when you do."

"Is that what it was like for Mom and Dad?"

"Most likely. In its way." She let the spoon rest against the rim of the bowl. "We're coming up on three years, kiddo."

I nodded, focused on that spoon and not her face.

"You wanna talk on that any?"

I shook my head no but then decided I owed her an actual answer for making the attempt. "Not tonight," I said.

"We're doing pretty good, huh?" She patted her soft, old hand on top of mine just a few times and then got up from the table, which was a labored process, and took her bowl, the spoon rattling against it, into the kitchen.

"I'm not doing so good, Grandma," I said, and I didn't whisper it, but she was already rinsing her dish in the sink, the water from the faucet whooshing against the metal basin, and there was no way she could hear me.

In my room I put on *The Hotel New Hampshire*, mostly just to again watch the half-second kiss between Jodie Foster and Nastassja Kinski. It was only a little before eleven and I thought about calling Lindsey, since it was even an hour earlier in Seattle, but I wasn't sure I wanted the lecture that I knew what I was gonna get, or her list of non-straight-girl conquests that would follow it.

Earlier in the week I'd finished decoupaging these pose-able wooden mom and dad dolls with words from the newspaper articles about my parents' accident and also from their obituaries. I'd nicked those dolls from Ben Franklin's craft aisle, had stuck them inside my track sweatshirt in the silk flower section, which was in the front corner of the store and completely overgrown with plastic vines and garish birds of paradise, a perfect place to hide loot. But for some reason, even though I could have easily stolen it, I decided to pay for the daughter doll I'd found. It was $4.95. That night I started on her, using words cut out of a "Dealing with Loss: Responses to Life Crises" pamphlet I'd had hanging around since Nancy Huntley's therapy sessions. *Numb* and *numbness* were in that twelve-page booklet seventeen times, so I set about making a numb shirt.

I'd been at it for a little while before I noticed the sheet of paper folded in the secret-note method (all the ends tucked together into a neat little square, perfect for palming in a class and passing across an aisle). Jamie had taught me how to fold it. The note was leaned up against the dollhouse-size picnic table I'd made by preserving some of Grandma's sugar wafers in clear enamel. The table had those too-pink strawberry wafer legs and a chocolate-and-white sugar wafer top, and it was drying on a couple of sheets of newspaper on the wide shelf above my desk. I wiped my sticky fingers on my jeans and peeled the note from the wafers; the top portion had stuck just a little.

I SNUCK IN WHILE YOUR G-MA WAS NAPPING.
SORRY. I THOUGHT YOU MIGHT BE HOME. YOU AREN'T.
I FUCKED THE GIRL ~~YOU~~ I KNOW YOU SAW ME WITH AT
BHS, (I DON'T THINK YOU KNOW HER AT ALL – HER NAME
IS MEGHAN.) WE'RE NOT GONNA GO OUT OR ANYTHING,
BUT THAT'S WHAT HAPPENED AND I WANTED TO TELL YOU
MYSELF. YOU <u>SHOULDN'T</u> HATE ME FOR IT. THAT WOULD SUCK.

I NEVER TOLD YOU (ON PURPOSE) THAT MY UNCLE TIM IS
GAY OR WHATEVER. MY MOM IS ALL PRAYING FOR HIM
BUT WHEN I SEE HIM AT FAMILY SHIT HE'S DOPE.
I MEAN HE'S NO PUSSY AND HE HAS A KICK-ASS HARLEY.

I WON'T TELL ANYBODY ABOUT YOU. TRUST ME ON THAT ONE.
YOU CAN.

– Jamie

"AND DON'T WORRY ABOUT NOTHING, NO CUZ WORRYING'S
A WASTE OF MY TIME."

–GNR– "MR. BROWNSTONE"

CHAPTER TEN

If you didn't just work on your parents' ranch or have an affinity for burger flipping, the two best summer jobs available to a high schooler in Miles City in 1992 were Scanlan Lake lifeguard and flagger (usually flag girl) for the Montana Highway Department. Getting either of those jobs meant that you had to know somebody in charge or have a special set of skills, like being a strong swimmer. But both of those jobs also meant good money, lots of hours, and that the whole thing happened outside. The downside of lifeguarding was teaching swimming lessons in the mornings: sobbing toddlers, anxious mothers in culottes, the difficulty of producing a lasting back float from a skin-and-bone, blue-lipped, and shivering six-year-old. The downside of being a flag girl was hour after hour spent standing on a stretch of black highway in the hazy heat of an eastern Montana summer. That and the constant danger of becoming the roadkill of some minivanned family speeding their way to Yellowstone. I got lifeguard; Coley got flag girl; Jamie was a brand-new black-and-purple-polo-shirted employee of Taco John's; and Brett, who had apparently impressed with his ball handling in that game he'd played during Bucking Horse, was selected as the Montana representative for this big-deal national soccer camp, which meant that he would spend part of June and all of July in California trying to maybe earn himself a college scholarship.

Jamie and I were pretty much back to our pre-prom friendship, but Coley and I had been expectedly weird together since Bucking Horse, so I worked hard to be extra amusing and also to offer up lots of private Brett-and-Coley opportunities to both of them, and the weirdness at least got back-burnered with the excitement of summer.

"So you kissed her, she rocked your world, leave it be," Lindsey told me when I phone-spilled most of the details, including my stuck-boot fall. "It's like one of many, many such kisses in your future, but for her it's the thing she'll obsess over after she gets the two point five kids and the mortgage. She'll ask herself as she's trying to sleep at night: *Why didn't I make it with that chick when I had the chance?*"

Lindsey was pressing me hard to come visit her for at least part of the summer. She had no interest in swim team and, with her dad actually in Alaska as anticipated, no reason for coming to Montana at all.

"I'm *supposed* to spend all three months with him, but my dad doesn't give a shit if I stay here. What am I gonna do in motherfucking Alaska, anyway?"

"Hot Inuit women," I said.

"Oh, lookit our little Kate Clinton."

"I don't know who that is," I said, even though Lindsey already knew this.

"Dyke comic. You'd like her. Alice is being such a fascist about this whole thing. As if three months in Alaska with my dad is going to make or break my development from fucked-up teenager to functioning adult."

"It might be cool."

"Yeah, totally cool," she said. "*Maybe* it could be. Maybe. But only if you come up and we find some sweet, north-of-the-border drugs and pick up where we left off."

She did a phone-sex operator voice. "I know all the right moves now, *Cammie*."

"Ruth won't go for that," I said.

"Yes she will. You could totally convince her that it'll be a learning experience. Just bill it as the summer of your lifetime. Get your grandma on board."

I knew that she was probably right, and that it might not have taken much at all to convince Aunt Ruth that a month or so in Alaska would be a good thing for me. But Lindsey was pressing for me to come in July, because she wasn't even going to get up there until mid-June and she needed a few weeks to situate shit with her dad. And July was gonna be Brett-free in Miles City. Despite myself, and the weirdness, and where things were currently with Coley and me, I'll admit that I was holding out hope: big-time hope.

So I told Lindsey that I'd try and make Alaska happen, and then I didn't try at all. Now I sometimes wonder how things might have turned out differently if I'd not made that decision, but you don't really get anywhere when you think too much about stuff like that.

• • •

Coach Ted had finally gotten his degree and was working as an athletic trainer for some college out East. They couldn't find anybody to replace him until almost the start of the swim season, and when they did, it was this total hack from Forsyth who usually taught water aerobics to pregnant women and knew about as much as Grandma about flip turns and stroke modification. Also, it was hard to take off weekends as a lifeguard at a lake most popular on the weekends, so with Lindsey gone and Coley around, I didn't join the swim team. I'd been on it for seven years. Other than school it was the most uniform part of my life. But not that summer.

While Coley donned an orange mesh vest outlined in strips of pearly reflective material for night jobs and got herself planted on an eight-mile stretch of roadwork hell between Miles City and Jordan, I spent a week with twenty or so fellow lifeguards learning the cross-chest carry, the submerged-victim approach, and, most difficult of all, the dreaded spinal rescue complete with deepwater backboarding.

The returning guards, many of them home from college for the summer, made the skills look easy and cool, and the few of us who were new tried to joke around with them, but we were too nervous to pull it off very well. The city had only just diverted water from the river to fill the Scanlan lakebed a week or so before our training, and in June that water was like swimming in snow-cone slush. Despite being in her sixties, Coach Ted's mom, Hazel, was still in charge, her steel-wool-colored hair in a close-cropped bob like a 1920s flapper, and had she smoked her menthol Capri cigarettes from a long-stemmed holder like a flapper, I'm not sure that it would have surprised any of us. But she didn't. And she certainly didn't smoke on the guard stands or even on the beach, but outside in the parking lot in the shade of the bathhouse and next to the bike racks, between our emergency enactments, still in her bathing suit, using her vintage-red flip-flops (she called them thongs) to elegantly twist each smoldering butt against the sandy pavement.

During our training she watched from the dock, her small face hidden behind celebrity-size mauve-tinted sunglasses, making notes on a grade sheet she kept dry against a clipboard plastered with a huge Red Cross sticker. While she judged our rescues, again and again and again, she chewed endless pieces of Wrigley's spearmint gum and snapped tight bubbles that were so loud they seemed like they should have hurt the inside of her mouth. She called us all "honey" or "dear heart" but was easily disappointed and let us know just how much in mandatory sprints of freestyle punctuated by the shrill pacesetter of her Acme Thunderer rescue whistle—which she told us she'd had since her very first time on the guard stand back in the 1950s. I, for one, believed her. And I wanted to impress her. I worked hard. Before and after our group sessions I practiced and repracticed my skills, both in water and out: those for CPR, for first aid. I asked the senior guards to watch my attempts and offer advice. One of them, Mona Harris—a college sophomore with a gymnast's build and a huge mouth, both physically and in terms of gossip—was the most eager to do this, shouting her corrections from the dock, telling me over and over to "try it again." And I would. Something about Mona intimidated me. She seemed to know just a little too much about everyone and everything; but she was a strong lifeguard and I was happy to have her help with my training, which apparently paid off, because Hazel soon presented me with three newly laminated official Red Cross certification cards, and also a red swimsuit with GUARD across the chest area in white letters, and my own Acme Thunderer rescue whistle. I had arrived.

• • •

By the time Brett left for soccer camp, Coley and I had, more by happenstance than anything else, developed what became an increasingly treacherous pattern. Scanlan's open swim hours were from two p.m. until eight p.m. every weekday. Coley would finish her shift, pick up her truck at the just-out-of-town highway department building, and caravan with many of her fellow crew members back into the city limits during my last rotation. This was the absolute best time to be on the guard stand: The sun had quieted its intensity and long shadows were beginning to stretch across the lake; the masses of mothers with tiny toddlers had stopped swarming the shallow end and had headed home for baths and dinners; we turned up the crappy stereo and let it blare, scratchy and tinny, out the bathhouse hatch where we usually returned clothes baskets and gave out sand buckets and kickboards.

The downtown exit took the highway crew directly past Scanlan. All of them were red faced and dusty and more than ready for a dip in the lake. That time of night, with only a few preteen all-dayers (lake rats) springing from the diving boards and maybe a family or two splashing around the shallow end, we were pretty lax about making anybody pay the entrance fee, especially a crew of dehydrated employees of the state of Montana. Hazel was just fine with this. Her standard policy was free admission to all former lifeguards, most anyone in a uniform, and everyone under the age of six. But she rarely was around to close up shop anyway, instead heading home sometime in the afternoon and leaving us to count the wrinkled bills kids had rolled or wadded and gripped tight and sweaty against their bike handlebars the whole ride to the lake.

Frequently we'd shoo out the rats, shut the bathhouse doors, and officially close, and then some of us remaining guards would swim around awhile with the highway department bunch, cannonballing off the high dive and competing in strictly-forbidden-during-open-hours chicken fights. Actually, we broke all the rules and regulations: We hung from the low dive, we dove from the deep-end guard stands, we skipped rocks out across the lake, and most horrific of all, we went underneath the docks.

There were three of them: the two long docks exactly fifty meters apart designating the officially guarded swim area, and one much smaller, square dock in the exact center of the deep end. Swimming down, finding the bottom of their wooden sides, and coming up into the air pocket beneath them was the biggest Scanlan no-no for an obvious reason—we couldn't see the kids once they were there, which meant we wouldn't know if they were drowning or doing any number of other forbidden actions. Which is exactly why below-center-dock make-out sessions were so popular with the preteens on up.

Sex and Scanlan went together seamlessly. Mona Harris was rumored to have lost her virginity late one night up against the metal ladder on the far side of the high dive; Bear and Granola Eric boasted of countless (and thereby questionable) after-hours locker-room blow jobs; and almost all of us were familiar with the appeal of the relative privacy of the below-dock world: the gentle slosh of the lake, the way the sun came between the soft boards in even slits, how closed in the sides were, making you fit tightly with whichever naked-except-for-a-swimsuit guy or girl you'd managed to bring in there with you. Sometimes somebody managed to pack some booze to these in-the-water soirees, and we'd swim a few cans of beer out below the lake's surface and crack them open beneath the cover of that sun-warmed wood.

For those first Brett-free weeks, Coley and I were careful never to be underneath the dock together without at least one other person along. Even though we'd started hanging out again, just the two of us, the weight of what had happened at Coley's ranch and the inescapably sexual world below those docks made both of us nervous.

After the lake we'd throw my bike in the back of Coley's truck and head over to Taco John's to score free Choco Tacos and nachos off of Jamie, or maybe we'd go to my house and take long, separate (of course) showers, eat whatever Ruth had cooked up, watch some TV, though even there we worked hard not to find ourselves alone in my bedroom for any reason, at least not without the door wide open. There was a steady crackle that buzzed between us during those early-summer days, like a radio set between station signals, the volume low, and neither of us said a thing about it. But it was there.

Coley was over one such night and we were half watching a *Magnum, P.I.* rerun with Grandma, the windows open and a big old black fan whirring in front of them but doing us no good, just blowing the curtains and the hot air around the three of us. We had a bowl of quickly thawing frozen grapes on the coffee table and a fat, black housefly was buzzing about them.

During a commercial Grandma said, "We have the cemetery on Saturday. I want you to go to Friendly Floral and get some nice arrangements." She produced two fresh-from-the-bank-crisp twenties from the pocket of her housecoat and handed them to me. She'd obviously been planning this moment, the announcement of this task, which made me that all-of-a-sudden kind of sad.

I'd cleared the day off with Hazel at the start of the summer, but it had seemed further away then than it actually was. "Ruth is at that big Sally-Q thing on Saturday," I said, loud and looking right at her, because Grandma's hearing was worse than ever and she had the TV turned up.

"I know she is," Grandma said in a stage whisper, because Tom Selleck was back on, jogging on white Hawaiian sand. "It's just going to be you and me, kid."

"I didn't know it was this weekend," Coley said, putting her hand on top of my hand, and even though it made us both flinch, she didn't move it right away. "I'm sorry."

"It's okay," I said.

"I've never been to the Miles City cemetery before."

"Your dad isn't . . ." I asked, without wanting to finish that sentence.

She shook her head. "He was cremated. He wanted to be left at the ranch."

This was territory that Coley and I hadn't ever covered in much detail, and now I think that avoidance seemed extra strange to the both of us, since dead parents was such a particular kind of commonality.

"I don't really know what my parents wanted," I said. "But the Miles City cemetery is what they got."

Coley squeezed my fingers. "You want me to come with you Saturday?"

"Yeah," I said. "That would be really cool of you."

So she did, and it was three instead of just the two of us, on a day a lot like the day we'd had the funeral, hot and dry, and Grandma even wore the same black dress she'd worn then, and the same rhinestone-studded brooch. Coley wore a little floral skirt and a linen top. I wore khaki shorts and a white button-down oxford shirt Ruth had bought me, a tiny polo player embroidered where the pocket would have been if it had a pocket, which it didn't. In honor of the occasion I did a sloppy job of ironing both the shorts and the shirt, and tucked the shirt in, too—but I rolled the sleeves just the same. It was too hot not to.

Grandma's forty bucks bought two big bouquets of everything except the white lilies I refused, and Ruth had arranged for a couple of really nice planters to be installed at my parents' plot, big copper things filled with red geraniums and ivy. Coley said how nice the gravestones were, and squeezed my shoulders while I squeezed Grandma. I cleared some papery brown leaves that had gathered up against the cold granite. Grandma took out one of her embroidered hankies and used

197

it. She told a little story about my dad once trying to cook *something or other fancy* for my mom, *early on in their courtship*, but he messed it up and started a kitchen fire. From that plot at the crest of the hill we could see across the main road and over the top of a backyard fence to watch a little girl as she went down a teal slide into an aboveground pool. Up the ladder, down the slide, and repeat, her long brown braid flopping behind her as she ran around the deck.

"I'm glad you came," I said to Coley, still watching the girl.

"Me too," she said. "This is a really nice place. It's not what I expected."

After a few more minutes Grandma needed to *get out of the sun* and so we all went to Dairy Queen and Coley and I had cherry Dilly Bars and Grandma first had just onion rings and complained about how much she wanted ice cream, and so then she had most of a Hawaiian Blizzard even though she shouldn't have, and we had to rush her home to shoot her insulin pretty soon afterward.

While Grandma napped, Coley sat on the edge of my bed and I sat in my desk chair. We had on *Adventures in Babysitting*, which Coley had never seen, but I don't think either of us was much watching Elisabeth Shue and her perfect blond curls hitch a ride from a hook-handed big rig driver, sing in a Chicago blues bar, and fight off the mob, all in one night.

I had taken a bunch of wrapped alcohol pads during CPR training, little squares of soft white paper with blue writing, like tiny pillows. I was planning to use them to make a padded cell in one of the dollhouse bedrooms, but right then they were just arranged in neat stacks in front of me—stacks I kept undoing and redoing. Coley got up, took the Quake Lake picture of my mom down from the TV, and studied it close, though she'd asked about it before and I'd told her the story.

"Your mom looked a lot like you," she said.

"When she was little," I said. "Not as much if you see her pictures from high school."

"What did she look like then?"

"She was really pretty. Miles of style."

"You're pretty," Coley said, like she hadn't just said that at all.

"No, you're pretty, Coley," I said. "That's not my area."

"Then what's your area?"

"Dollhouse interior design," I said, getting up and crossing in front of her to my swim bag, flung on the floor the previous night. I had a pack of gum in there, its waxy paper packaging damp from a week of wet towels.

Coley stood up and put back the picture, and when I tried to go to my desk chair she was still standing there, in that tiny walkway between the dresser and my bed, and I couldn't get past her.

"You want?" I asked her, holding out the orange Bubblicious.

"Nope," she said. And then we were kissing. That's exactly how it happened. I had a sugar-crystally lump of not yet really chewed gum lodged in my molars and Coley's mouth was all over mine and the door to my room was wide open and there was no going back and so we didn't go back. We went onto my bed, me on top of Coley, because she pulled me there, and we kept all our clothes on and made out to *Adventures in Babysitting* and Coley didn't seem nervous and she didn't seem unsure and we didn't stop until Grandma was calling up the stairs and asking about what we wanted to do for supper.

"We'll be right down," I yelled, turning my head toward the door but still very much on top of Coley.

"I'm still with Brett," Coley said to me then, as if that settled anything at all.

• • •

I think Coley got pretty good at convincing herself that what the two of us were doing with each other night after night after hot, still, big-sky Montana night was just some bound-to-happen-in-college-experimentation thing come early. And I tried hard not to let on that I knew otherwise, or at least desperately hoped for otherwise.

Our new thing was to go to the movies. Coley would come get me at Scanlan, take me home, and I'd shower fast while she chatted with Grandma. Then we'd head off to see whatever was showing. The only problem being that the Montana Theatre kept the same two movies, a seven o'clock and a nine o'clock, for a week at a go. And we never were in time to make the seven o'clock. So that summer we saw *A League of Their Own, Buffy the Vampire Slayer, Batman Returns,* and *Death Becomes Her* three to four times each. On the big screen, feet and feet of Michelle Pfeiffer as Cat Woman, Bruce Willis as a dorky plastic surgeon and not an action hero, Madonna in a vintage peach baseball uniform and a falser-with-every-screening Brooklyn accent. Though it was a theater built for hundreds, at the Tuesday- and Wednesday-night showings it was sometimes Coley, me, and fewer than ten other people in the entire place. Which is how we liked it.

"You girls are going to the show again?" Ruth asked us on more than one occasion when she happened to be home while I was changing. "The same movie? It must be pretty fantastic." But Ruth was with Ray, and always busy with Sally-Q and GOP, and by then we'd learned pretty well how to stay out of each other's way, especially because Ruth so loved Coley and thought she was *good for me.*

The old guy who had been taking tickets at the Montana for as long as I could remember always dressed in brown pants and a brown sweater vest over a collared white shirt and brown tie. He was flagpole thin, and the AC in there was arctic; we eventually took to bringing Grandma's stadium blanket with us. Ticket Guy had a messy nest of thin red hair and called us the *terrible twosome* and every once in a while would wave us through without making us pay, but whenever we guessed it would be one of those nights, we were wrong. When he did come through, though, we would spend big money on popcorn and a graveyard soda, sometimes Milk Duds.

We'd go to the very last row, up against the wall, the projection booth above our heads, center if we could get it, but if it was taken there were these cool, old-fashioned booth things on either wing of the aisles, though sometimes there'd be a creepy guy flying solo in one of them. My dad had told me that the theater hadn't changed much since he was a kid, and it sure hadn't changed any since my first memories of it: burgundy carpeting, big orange and pink light sconces that I knew were art deco because my mom liked to go on about them, and behind the snack bar and down just a couple of stairs, a lounge area with stained velvet couches and the entrances to these amazing pink-and-green-tiled bathrooms, one on either side. The doors to the bathrooms said GENTS and DAMES in thin gold letters.

After a few weeks the whole place, from the heavy smell of the popcorn to the cold darkness and hush of the theater, felt like some semiprivate cave we had discovered and laid claim to. We held hands. We wound our legs together. When we could, we made out. Even there in the dark and the last row it was completely risky, and while that was only part of the thrill for me, it might have been most of the thrill for Coley. I couldn't say for sure.

The movie itself was basically two hours of carefully maneuvered foreplay, so we'd leave the theater anxious and buzzing and wanting to be all over each other in the lobby, on the sidewalks as we walked to Coley's truck, even within the truck itself, parked downtown on one of the mostly empty side streets; but we couldn't do so much as hold hands without scandal and made ourselves walk a couple of feet apart, wouldn't even let our arms brush, which just made it worse. Maybe you can't really call what we were doing foreplay because it didn't lead to anything more.

After we left the theater, we might drag a few Mains, talk to the cluster of kids parked at the Conoco station, and then Coley would drive me home and that would be that. It wasn't as if the two of us could go anywhere that was a typical make-out destination, Spotted Eagle, or out behind the fairgrounds, or the long-abandoned drive-in, or Carbon Hill: We couldn't possibly pull up and park next to our partially naked classmates at any of those places. And after that first afternoon in my bedroom we seemed to have outlawed our respective houses without actually saying as much.

And what made it all the worse was that we didn't really discuss this thing we were doing, not in any detail. We just went to the movies and did what we could when we could, and then I tried my best to leave it all there, in the theater, gone with the roll of the credits, until we could do it again the next night. But while I was muddling through my days and waiting for those nights to come, a bunch of big things happened in rapid succession, or maybe they seemed small at first but turned out otherwise.

• • •

Big Thing No. 1: Ruth and Ray went to Minneapolis for a Bible weekend and an exclusive preview of the soon-to-be-open Mall of America—a preview that Ruth had somehow won via her Sally-Q sales—and they came back wearing matching blue I SURVIVED THE MALL TO END THEM ALL T-shirts and also engaged. Ray had asked me about his intended proposal beforehand, not really for my blessing, exactly, but something like that. I told him the truth: that I thought it was a great idea. I liked Ray. And more important, I liked Ruth with Ray. He gave her a monstrous gold ring with glinty diamonds all around, one that must have taken hundreds and hundreds of boxes of Schwan's flash-frozen crab legs to buy, and for days afterward Ruth played "Going to the Chapel" on the downstairs record player while she sorted her Sally-Q shit. They didn't see any point in waiting, and Ruth loved Montana in September, so they checked the church calendar and settled on Saturday, September 26, 1992.

People told them they were *movin' in an awful hurry*. At least one old rancher said exactly that during coffee communion after Pastor Crawford announced their engagement during the Sunday-morning announcements.

"How will you get everything done?" another woman asked Ruth. More women nodded, made big-eyed faces of disbelief.

"I've been mentally planning my wedding for years," Ruth said. "This'll be a piece of cake. Piece of cake."

Grandma said, just to me, later, "I tell you what, it's going to be one helluva ceremony. I can already see it."

• • •

Big Thing No. 2: Mona Harris caught me totally off guard. She and I got put on copper sulfate duty one Saturday night at closing. To distribute the copper sulfate, you had to unhook this really crappy metal rowboat from where it was chained to the fence and haul it down the beach and wedge it out into the cattails. Then one of you would get in and hold the boat against the side of the dock while the other loaded up awkward, thirty-pound sacks of the chemical, grabbed the oars, and got in as well. Then one person rowed and one flung the copper sulfate, which was in a bright-blue crystal form and looked both like tumbled beach glass and oversize fish tank rocks. It was only activated with water, but parts of you were always wet in that leaky boat, and at the bottom of the bags the sulfate was mostly crushed and powdery and our scooping and flinging cup inadequate, and some of it always landed on your legs or your arms, rewarding you with a bunch of little red chemical burns.

We just made it a verb, called it copper sulfating, and we had to do it on Saturday nights because the lake didn't open until noon on Sundays. That gave the chemical enough time to kill some lake weed, a bunch of those swimmers' itch snails, and a myriad of additional lake life, mud puppies and small fish, things we'd find floating on the surface the next day; but also by then it was supposed to have stopped its dangerous toxicity so that human swimmers could again enter the water.

I rowed, Mona flung, and we were mostly silent. The sulfate spattered across the water like hard rain and left a ferocious storm of bubbles at the surface before sinking slowly, dissolving all the way down.

We'd finished one bag and were on to the next when Mona asked, "Have you thought about college at all yet? Like where you maybe want to go?"

"Not really," I said, which was both true and not. I'd entertained daydreams of just following Coley to wherever.

"Bozeman's a pretty cool town," she said. "I've met all kinds of superchill people there."

"I'll keep that in mind," I said.

"The world's really big outside of Miles City."

I thought she sounded sort of like Irene and her ideas about the whole big wide world.

Mona went on, flinging a scoop, trying for nonchalance. "You probably already heard that I dated a girl for a while this year. Not that it's a big deal or anything. I don't mean to like make it an announcement or whatever."

I was glad I had my sunglasses on and hoped she couldn't read anything on my face. "I hadn't heard," I said. "Why would I have?"

"Don't freak," she said. "I figured Eric or somebody would have managed to share that with everyone by now. I was just trying to give you an example of the kind of things that can happen once you get out of Miles City."

I had bottomed us up against one of the banks of jungle-thick cattails and had to stick my oar into the muck to dislodge the boat. I pretended like this took all of my concentration so that I could avoid where we were in the conversation.

When we were moving smoothly on the water again, Mona said, "You don't have to get weird. I wasn't trying to stir shit up."

"You didn't," I said. "It's cool."

"I just have a few years' life experience on you."

"Well, my parents died," I said. "And tragedy makes you age in cat years. So I'm technically older than you."

"You're funny," she said without laughing or even smiling, really.

We were riding along the edge of something I wasn't ready to talk about in a rowboat with a girl whose motivations I didn't understand. So instead I asked Mona about her major and she humored me by telling me all about biofilm engineering, letting the other topic dissolve out there beneath the lakebed with the chemicals.

. . .

Big Thing No. 3: Gates of Praise welcomed Rick Roneous to lead a Sunday sermon and also as a guest speaker at a hastily planned Firepower. Firepower didn't meet regularly in the summer save a weekend camping thing that happened in August, a big kickoff to a school year of spirituality, so this reconvening was billed as truly a special something.

Reverend Rick was a big-deal Montana Christian made good: He had written a couple of books about practicing Christianity in a "changing world," and had recently returned to the state *he so loved* to launch a full-time school and wellness center for teenagers crippled by *sexual brokenness*. Also, he had Elvis-blue eyes and very hip shoulder-length brown hair (like so many pictures of Jesus and also rock star Eddie Vedder); and since Rick was youngish, only in his midthirties, and could play the guitar, he pulled off the Christian-as-cool thing pretty well.

At the sermon he wore a nice button-down shirt and a silvery-blue tie and read from one of his books, talked in generalities about the importance of Christian faith starting and staying in the family. But at the Firepower meeting we got jeans-and-T-shirt Rick, guitar in tow, and more than a few of the female members expressed their megacrushes in barely whispered whispers.

Coley and I sat next to each other, Indian style (though we were being told to now call it crisscross applesauce), on the gray carpet of the meeting room. We were careful not to let our knees touch, our shoulders brush, lest we call up our movie-night activities.

Rick lead us in the acoustic versions of a couple of songs by popular Christian rock acts, Jars of Clay for one, and everybody, including me, was impressed at the up-to-dateness of his repertoire. He tucked stray curls behind his ear and smiled at compliments in that shy kind of artsy-poet way that made husky Mary Tressler and birdlike Lydia Dixon giggle and wink at each other.

"We'll do this up casual, you cool with that?" Reverend Rick asked, removing the guitar strap and setting his shiny acoustic at his side, then turning back to us and tucking some more of that hair, despite its not needing to be tucked. "So ask me anything. What's on the minds of teenagers in Miles City, Montana?"

Nobody spoke. Lydia Dixon giggled again.

"You can't always be this quiet," Reverend Rick said, doing a semiconvincing job of appearing unaware of his celebrity status.

"You could tell us about what you're doing with your school in Montana or whatever," licorice-smelling Clay Harbough said to his lap, no doubt as anxious as I was to get this meeting over and done with, though in his case it was probably to get back to whatever he was doing with his computer that month, and in my case it was to avoid the topic that he'd just suggested.

"You bet," Rick said, smiling that shy smile. "It's a big summer for Promise—we're celebrating our third-year anniversary here in a couple of weeks."

"My parents just sent in a donation card," Mary Tressler said, all puffed up, seriously almost batting her eyes at the poor guy.

"Well, we certainly appreciate any and all of those," Rick

said, smiling back at her, not smarmy like a televangelist either, but with a genuine sort of smile.

"But it's for like curing gays or whatever, right?" Clay asked, talking more during this meeting than I could remember him talking ever.

Coley had to have known that this was what we were getting to—I knew it, this is what this guy did, what he was known for—but I could feel her, next to me, tense just a little at those words: *curing gays*. Maybe I tensed too. I tried to seem cool, though, cool like Rick. I made a point of keeping eye contact with him.

"We don't really use the word *cure* so much," Rick said, without seeming at all like he was necessarily correcting Clay, which was a real kind of conversational gift. "We help teens come to Christ, or in some cases come back to Christ, and develop the kind of relationship with him that you all are working on. And if we can do that, then it's *that* relationship that helps people escape these kinds of unwanted desires."

"But what if somebody wants to be that way or something?" Andrea Hurlitz asked, and then she told a story about some documentary she had seen at the church she used to go to back in Tennessee about how the only true cure for homosexuality was AIDS, which she said was God's way of curing it.

Reverend Rick listened to her story, and he nodded in places where you could tell Andrea thought she was making some big point; but when she was finished he said, breathing in some and tucking that hair again, "I've seen that film before too, Andrea, and I know people who hold that belief, but my own relationship with Christ has taught me compassion toward my neighbors no matter what the sins they're struggling with." Pause, hair tucking. "I know a bit about how this works from the inside. I was a teenager who struggled with homosexual desire, and I feel grateful, really, I feel blessed, that I had friends and spiritual leaders to help me, and I still have people help me. Mark, chapter nine, verse twenty-three: 'Everything is possible for him who believes.'"

Nobody knew where to look after that. I'd lock eyes with someone across the circle and we'd shift our stares, fast, to someplace else. I hadn't known that piece of the puzzle, that background about Rick, and judging from the faces of most of my fellow Firepower members, neither had they. Except for Clay Harbough, who looked like he was unsuccessfully attempting to eat a grin, his mission of revelation apparently accomplished.

"Do you all have more questions about this?" Rick asked. "This is not a shameful secret for me anymore. You can bet that it once was, but in Christ I have found redemption and a new purpose. So let's go ahead and talk about anything you want to talk about."

I had many, many questions, and I didn't dare look at Coley, but I knew that she did, too. There was no way that I was raising my hand, though, and nobody else did either until Lydia asked, "So do you have a girlfriend now?"

Everybody laughed, Rick included, and after he told us *not at the moment, but not for lack of trying*, and we all laughed more, somebody asked something about the different kinds of sexual brokenness and that led to a discussion of promiscuity in teenagers in general and then to the *appalling* teenage pregnancy rates around the country and then, predictably, to abortion, and we seemed to have fully moved on.

After the meeting Coley clumped with a couple of other members around the snacks table. Rick had put a pile of pamphlets about his God's Promise Christian Discipleship Program at one end next to a plate of peanut-butter brownies. She picked up one of the pamphlets and pretended to nonchalantly peruse it and then slipped it into her purse. I wanted to take one too, though I can't exactly say why. I guess just to see what it said, to see if there were like pictures of the kids who went there, more information about what actually went on, but there was no way that I could just grab it in front of everybody. Not like Coley could. She didn't need to sneak it, because nobody would ever suspect that she might be taking it because she needed to go there, or at least thought that maybe she did. Not *the* Coley Taylor of *Brett & Coley*. No way.

. . .

Big Thing No. 4—the Really Big Thing: Just a few days after Reverend Rick's visit, Coley got an apartment in Miles City. Her own apartment. Maybe that sounds big-city or glamorous or something, but it wasn't at all unheard of for kids whose families lived on ranches miles and miles away from Custer High. There were easily a couple dozen such students—four of them sharing a little bungalow not far from the school, or somebody renting out an old lady's top floor or, like Coley, a one-bedroom sixth-floor walk-up in the Thompson apartment building downtown, just a few blocks off Main Street.

Coley had mentioned the possibility to me before, but when Ty hit a deer driving back to the ranch one night, and then a couple of days later drove off the road and into an irrigation ditch (that having more to do with the alcohol he had been drinking than the rutted and curvy ranch roads), Mrs. Taylor decided that an apartment in town would be good for them all. Coley would stay there Sunday through Thursday nights during the school year; Ty could use it when he'd had too much to drink; and Mrs. Taylor would go there to sleep a few hours after she worked a twelve-hour shift and was too bleary to make the trip out to the ranch. But ultimately, it was to be Coley's place.

She told me that it was happening for sure when she came to pick me up at Scanlan. I was still on left chair, the lake wrapped in shadows from the cottonwoods and a family of out-of-towners playing a loud game of Marco Polo just beyond the rope line.

We'd been surprisingly steady since the Firepower meeting, since Coley had taken that pamphlet. In our typical style, we hadn't even talked about it, and we'd since been to the movies without any noticeable change in our routine. But Brett would be back in a week, and school would start fifteen days after that, and even if we weren't talking about it, our routine was most definitely gonna have to change.

Still, that evening, Coley in dirty work clothes, grit and dust in her hair, stood next to my guard stand and leaned one arm against its warm wood and flaky paint and told me in this excited voice of hers how great this apartment was going to be, despite the fact that she said it currently smelled like *bleach and feet*, and how she wanted me to help her decorate it, and how her mom had already taken her to Kmart and bought her a red metal teapot and a soft yellow bathmat and a bunch of vanilla and cinnamon candles, and how the bathroom had a claw-foot tub and black and white tiles, and how we could start moving her in the very next day.

CHAPTER ELEVEN

Lindsey once tried to explain to me this *primordial connection*, she said, that all lesbians have with vampire narratives; something to do with the gothic novella *Carmilla* and the *sexual and psychological impotence of men when facing the dark power of lesbian seduction.* As such, I'd heard all about "the scene" in *The Hunger* before ever seeing it for myself. I did eventually rent it, though, and while "the scene"— wherein Catherine Deneuve as Miriam, the ageless Egyptian vampire, and Susan Sarandon as Sarah, the doctor on aging, tumble around Miriam's big silk-sheeted bed and totally get it on, and also do their vampire-blood-sisters-exchange thing with white curtains billowing all around them, blocking the shots of their tangled bodies at the most inopportune of moments, forcing me to rewind again and again—*is* very steamy and erotic and all of the things Lindsey described it as, it's what comes before that scene that gets my vote as the much, much hotter moment.

That's the moment when Susan/Sarah, flushed by Catherine/Miriam's piano playing—and probably also by her low voice and hypnotic but sometimes hard to decipher accent—spills three drops of bloody sherry on her very white, semitight T-shirt, and then there's a jump-cut to her attempting to rub it out with a wet rag, creating a fraternity-movie-type wet T-shirt situation, and at that point all Catherine Deneuve has to do is walk behind her and gently trail her fingertips along Susan's shoulders and cause this intense moment of eye contact between the two of them, and it's go time: Susan Sarandon just peels off the T-shirt entirely maybe five seconds after that.

And even though it was just some artsy vampire movie with David Bowie and two, to my knowledge, non-lesbian-in-real-life actresses, that single moment, the shoulder touch, the way they met eyes, it seemed completely true to me, and way more powerful or erotic or whatever than the sex itself. Maybe that's because the first time I watched *The Hunger* I'd actually *had* a moment like that, but none of the "sex itself."

I had rented it sometime in my first months after knowing Lindsey, but at that point she'd given me so much lesbian-knowledge-building pop-cultural homework that I guess it was one assignment I'd forgotten to mention to her as checked off the list, because she sent it to me, a videotape in the original box with a pink PREVIOUSLY VIEWED MOVIE sticker placed inconsiderately over Catherine/Miriam's face, in a care package that came all the way from Anchorage, Alaska. A care package that I didn't really deserve given that I'd only written her once since the start of summer, and even more so considering how I'd blown off her plans for our Alaskan reunion in order to court Coley Taylor.

The package was waiting on the dining-room table for me when I got home from work in a hurry to shower and change. For the first time in a long time Coley wasn't with me. This was how we'd planned it. She was at her new apartment, the one that had been swarming with family and friends the last couple days, Ty and his cowboy cronies hauling furniture and hanging shelves; Mrs. Taylor's crowd, nurses and GOP-goers, bringing old dishes and pots and pans; people stopping by with cases of soda, with frozen meals, with potted plants. Now finally everything was settled, ready to go, and we had made a date for our first ever nontheater, private-screening-for-two movie night. I was supposed to swing by Video 'n' Go and rent something, anything, to serve as the outward reason for our get-together—one to be spent completely alone, with a door that locked, both deadbolt and chain, and a brand-new queen-size bed in the other room.

But then smack in the middle of these plans came this package from Lindsey. I opened it while taking the stairs to my room, two at a time, trying to both tear apart the box and also to pull off articles of clothing as I went, unwilling to let any amount of time that I could be spending with Coley go to waste. I got a paper cut from the corner of the cardboard, one that I aggravated by pulling at the packing tape. I littered shredded newspaper as I went. I didn't stop to pick it up. Inside, along with *The Hunger*, were two mix tapes, a bag of chocolate-covered nuts and raisins labeled Real Alaskan Moose Droppings, a snow globe with a fly-fishing grizzly bear inside, and a postcard with a couple of busty and tanned big-smiling women in neon bikinis standing in a very large, seemingly very cold snowbank, pines and cedars all around them, and the neon purple caption: *Alaska's Finest Wildlife*.

On the back of the postcard Lindsey had written:

POST CARD

PLACE
STAMP
HERE

Cam,

FOR CORRESPONDENCE

FOR ADDRESS ONLY

Your coded and brief letter
confirmed my suspicions that
you're spending your summer in
pursuit of that which is sure to
end in heartbreak :, but I love
you for trying... use the vid and
chocolate as weapons of seduction.

XXOO

Linds

Cameron "Baby-Dyke" Post
1349 Wibaux St.
Miles Shitty, MT 59301

P.S. Aren't you glad I put
this *inside* the package?

I *was* glad that she had put the postcard inside the package. And though, at first, I read her seduction suggestions as jokes, *The Hunger* was in fact a movie that I knew Coley hadn't seen, one that I had sitting on my bed and could just bring with me, saving myself a few otherwise wasted minutes at the video store. I mulled it over in the shower, where I used Ruth's extensive lineup of personal body scrubs and moisturizing washes and refreshing rinses—all of them in various shades of creams and greens, perfuming the whole bathroom with their *natural plant extracts* and *fortifying vitamins and minerals*. Somewhere between leg shaving and toweling off I decided just to go for it. I'd bring *The Hunger*, tout it as a wacky vampire story, put it in the VCR, and let things happen from there.

The dark wooden stairwells and long hallways of Coley's apartment building were thick with hot air and the smells of various tenants' dinners: definitely fish sticks for 3-B and maybe McDonald's or Hardees for 5-D. The whole place whirred with the sound of in-window air conditioners. On the sidewalk outside the building they'd dripped on me, fat drops of machine-induced rain, and inside those ripe hallways, their constant humming along with the muffled sounds of TVs and stereos made Thompson Apartments feel at once alive and also a good place to hide out, to be unseen.

Outside Coley's door, which was glossy reddish wood with 6-A painted on it in black, I stood for a moment before knocking. I was holding the video, the bag of Moose Droppings, and a Gal-on-the-Go Necessities Only pink toolbox, an apartment-warming gift courtesy of Ruth and Sally-Q. I could hear the radio on inside, the country station, Trisha Yearwood singing about being "in love with the boy." I was sweating, and not just because of the heat in that hallway. I took a bunch of deep breaths that didn't really do much to calm me down. I wondered, for maybe the first time ever in my life, if I should have dressed better, something other than my same-as-always tank top and shorts. I looked at my dark-brown toes, forever the tannest part of my tan body, so dark they looked dirty even right out of the shower. I looked again at the door and worried that Coley was watching all this through the peephole Mrs. Taylor had gotten the landlord's permission for Ty to install. I knocked.

She didn't answer right away, so she couldn't have been peepholing me, or maybe she just wanted me to think otherwise. I heard the metal click of the deadbolt and the slide of the useless (according to Ty) chain lock, and then we were face-to-face, both of us in tank tops and shorts (Coley's much shorter than mine, or maybe it was just that her legs were endless), both of us with shower-wet hair, and both of us grinning shy, weird grins.

"Okay, so it's magma hot in here," she said, stepping back so that I could come in.

"Any excuse to use the word *magma*," I said as she relocked the door.

The shades were all drawn and a single lamp did a bad job of lighting one corner of the living room. The space was filled with Trisha Yearwood still singing and also the loud chug of the apartment's sole air conditioner, one that Mrs. Taylor had found at a garage sale and that Ty had tinkered into functionality. It was in the bedroom, and Coley was right: It wasn't doing much to cool the place off.

"On the plus side it smells way better," I said, leaving my flip-flops by the door because I saw that Coley was barefoot and I had worked out this plan to try to follow her lead all evening, even with the minor things.

"You think?" She walked ahead of me into the tiny kitchen with its olive linoleum floor and olive-painted cabinets.

"Undeniably. Much, much better than my first visit."

Coley opened the door to the fridge, talked to me with her head stuck in it. "So I made that cabbage-and–ramen noodle salad of my mom's that you said you liked, and a fruit salad and a chicken salad."

"You've gone all Becky Home-Ec-y," I said, backing out of the way so that Coley could unload a stack of Tupperware bowls onto the countertop.

She peeled off the lids, stirred each salad with its own wooden serving spoon. "I'm too classy for that. Try gone Martha Stewarty."

I switched on my best announcer voice. "Well, certainly Martha would approve of this exquisite pink plastic toolbox complete with a Busy Lady hammer, a pair of pliers, a tape measure, and both a flathead *and* a Phillips screwdriver." I held the box the way I imagined Vanna White might, showcasing it for all its glory.

"God love Ruth," Coley said, opening the kit while I held it. She took out the hammer, practiced a couple of imaginary nail blows. "Wow! Useful *and* comfortable. I'll never go back to a man's hammer again!"

We both laughed at that, there in the shades-drawn semidark of the kitchen, close together in a small space and totally alone. The ease of our laughter somehow made us remember our nervousness, both of us at once. They were playing the ag report on the radio, that guy with the gummy voice. Coley put the hammer back and I put the case on the counter. She got us plates from a cupboard above the sink, from a shelf newly lined with contact paper sporting tiny, perfect yellow pears, each with a single, also perfect, green leaf. We'd done all the drawers and cupboards the day before.

She dished up our plates and I got us silverware. We were careful how we moved our bodies, careful not to brush against each other or even to stand too close, which took precise maneuvers in that small space.

Coley nodded her head toward the bag of chocolate and the movie. "So what'd you rent us?"

"I didn't," I said, opening the fridge so that she could reshelve the bowls.

"What'd you bring, then?"

"Lindsey sent it. It's a vampire thing with Susan Sarandon. It's okay. Kind of weird."

Coley emerged from behind the door with a plastic pitcher filled with an orangey-yellow concoction. "You've already seen it?"

"I've already seen everything."

"We can drink to that." She motioned for me to move out of her way, opened the cupboard under the sink, pushed aside the Pine-Sol, and removed a bottle of rum.

"Ty left this," she said. "And he specifically told me not to drink it."

"So obviously we'll be drinking rum and whatever's in the pitcher," I said.

"Orange/pineapple juice."

"Very tropical."

Coley gave me her wink. "Absolutely. We can start with rum and juice and work our way up to rum and rums."

We did this next part like a ballet, careful and precise, barely any talking between us, the presence of what we had planned for the evening, though as of yet officially unspoken, as thick and heavy as the heat. We carried our plates into the living room, set them on the coffee table, came back and mixed our drinks, made them strong, added ice from the purple plastic trays Coley's mom had just bought for her. We drank big swallows in the kitchen. We clinked our glasses. We drank again, then refilled those glasses to their tops with more rum. Coley carried our drinks and I brought the video and the chocolate, switched off the radio on the way. I put the tape in the VCR and took the remote from the top of the TV, brought it over to the couch with me, pressed Play. We sat, plates on our laps, as far away from each other as possible, each against the opposite brown armrest, with much greater distance between us than we ever had at the theater. I worried, right then, that we wouldn't move from those spots all night.

We ate and watched the movie's moody, hard-to-follow intro, with Bowie and Deneuve at a foreign-seeming dance club, neither of us speaking until Coley said:

"This is really weird, right?"

"The movie?"

"Yeah. What'd you think I meant?"

"I don't know," I said.

Coley put her plate on the coffee table and reached over and took the remote from where it was partially wedged beneath my thigh. She had to touch me to do this, and both of us were very aware of that. She pressed Pause. The frozen scene left the screen in a bright, sterile, white hallway, with David Bowie and the female half of a couple he and Catherine Deneuve had lured back to their apartment pressed together, all black leather and punk hair and piercings.

Coley turned to me with this intense look and asked, "Is it gonna be like this all night?"

"The movie?" I asked again, grinning.

Coley grinned, too. "You are such a smart-ass. Thankfully I've chosen to overlook your many immaturities."

"Yes, and I'm ever so grateful, ma'am," I said.

"I'm sure." She grabbed the video's case. She studied the back and then read in an overdone Dracula voice, "Nothing human loves forever." She did the Sesame Street Count cackle, tossed the case back onto the coffee table. "Why did she send this to you?"

"Didn't I tell you? Lindsey's a vampire."

"Well, that was my guess." Coley jiggled her drink at me, a notice to get to work on my own. "Seriously, why?"

"You'll find out once we watch it."

"Somehow I doubt that," she said. "You two and your secrets via the postal service. Why is it bothering you that I'm asking if we're about to watch it anyway?"

"It's not." I took a big bite of the fruit salad, a really big bite, two grapes and a bunch of slices of banana.

"It definitely is."

I hadn't told Coley all that much about Lindsey and me. She knew that she sent me shit all the time. She knew that she was into chicks. But what she knew was definitely lacking in detail. I put my own plate on the coffee table and said, "If you just push Play, then all the secrets will be revealed."

"No way. Too easy. How about you give me three guesses?" Coley pulled her bare legs up onto the couch and folded them beneath her, turned herself toward me completely.

I did the exact same thing with my own legs.

"Oh my God, you're so tan," she said, looking at my knees, which were a close second to my toes in darkness, mostly because of all those hours up on the guard stand.

"So are you," I said.

"Not my legs." She untucked one of them and extended it down the length of the couch until her red-toenailed foot was in my lap.

"Well, you work in jeans," I said. "What miracle of solar power were you hoping for?"

She could have pulled her leg back after that, but she didn't, and I pretended like having it there was just a slumber-party, girls-being-girls kind of thing. I didn't know what the hell to do with a foot in my lap, anyway. I'd seen a movie with toe sucking, but that seemed entirely out of my range of ability and also fairly unappealing, as nice as Coley's toes were, not to mention that such a move would be a gargantuan leap from whatever it was we were doing at the moment.

Talking seemed the best route. "So make your three guesses," I said.

"Okay." She closed her eyes for a second, folded her hands in her lap, and readied herself as if a contestant on a game show answering the big-money question. "Okay. Is it—because it's superscary and it's gonna freak me out and I'll want you to spend the night because I'm afraid to be alone?" She did the corny double eyebrow raise at me.

"Not even close," I said. "It's like artsy scary, and not even, really. There's barely any blood. You won't be afraid to be alone."

Coley nodded her head like a knowing TV psychologist. "Mmmm-hmmm, mmm-hmmm. Just as I thought." She studied the frozen image on the screen, looked back at me. She asked, with more seriousness than the last question, "Are they all gonna have vampire group sex?"

"A solid guess," I said, blushing despite myself. "But no. No group sex, vampire or otherwise."

"None anywhere in the movie?"

"No. None at all." I thought about it, then pointed to the TV. "Well, I mean, right now two couples are making out at the same time, in the same room, but only one on one, so that's not really a group. Does that make sense?"

"Yeah," Coley said. She just looked at me, not for too long, and then she picked up the remote and pressed Play, just like that, Bowie and the chick back in action.

"What about your third guess?" I asked.

"I already know what it is."

"Oh really?" I said.

"Oh really," she said.

She pulled back her leg and fitted it beneath her again, and for maybe fifteen seconds I felt like I'd fucked something up without knowing how or why. But then she scooched herself to the middle of the couch, close enough to offer me her hand, which I took, and I also moved myself toward her, and we wrapped ourselves up just like at the theater, but better, tighter, and Coley traced her supersoft fingertips over the top part of one of my bare legs, making me tickle and itch in the best way, and we finally got the first kiss of the evening out of the way and I was ready to do more but Coley said, "I just want to watch until it happens."

And I said, "Until what happens?"

And Coley said, "You're not half as tricky as you think you are."

And I said, "Okay."

After that I got up once to refill our drinks, and when I came back, we wound ourselves together again.

When, in the movie, white T-shirted Susan/Sarah rang the doorbell at Catherine/Miriam's creepy-fancy town house, Coley said, "I knew it," and even just her saying that made me shiver along the length of my spine.

We barely made it through *the scene*, left the tape playing as we bumbled our way, still twined together, toward the bedroom.

The chug-whirring air conditioner was even louder in there, but it was noticeably colder, too. Coley, her tongue in my mouth, lifted the bottom of my tank top and then stopped with it pulled halfway up. I finished the job for her and then removed hers as well. It wasn't as complicated as they sometimes make it seem, for laughs, in certain movies. Coley pulled back the summer quilt and we tumbled onto the cold sheets together, shivering, laughing, pulling the quilt up and over us, giggling at our goose-bumped skin, the softness of those chilly sheets, the hot closeness of our bodies. As we wound our limbs and warmed a pocket beneath the covers, things got more serious again.

I could have spent hours just tracing my lips over her perfect skin, feeling the way certain bones made ridges and valleys, smelling her tangerine lotion, the small noises she made when I found certain, unexpectedly pleasurable areas: just below her armpit, these tiny soft hairs at the back of her neck, her collar bone, which jutted out like the thin metal rod and spokes of an umbrella's undercarriage, her heartbeat steady and fast there.

"You're so soft," Coley said at one point, like a breath. "Your skin is so soft and you're so small."

"You too," I said, which was a lame response, if true, but I was at my least articulate.

I kept on with my exploration, tiny, tiny kisses, just grazing my lips over her breasts, her ribs, her stomach, and Coley pressed and moved against me in encouraging ways.

I stopped at the waistband and silver button on those tiny khaki shorts. I slipped just one finger beneath the band, not far, just against the place where her hipbone pushed out, and I felt her tremble, just barely, but still.

"You tell me when to stop," I said.

She breathed in big, blew it out, and said, "Not now."

And her saying that, just that, *not now*, made my want of her flutter up inside me again and again like tiny explosions from Black Cat firecrackers, one after another: just her saying that.

I undid the button, found the metal pull of the zipper, and worked it down, the noise it made impossibly loud and definite. When it reached the end of its track, I stopped and asked, "How about now?"

"Not now," she said.

Pulling off her shorts, small as they were, was more complicated than our tank tops had been, but I worked slowly, and stopped to kiss parts of her legs that I hadn't ever had the chance to visit before. When I got the shorts all the way down to her feet, Coley shifted to help me free them. I heard her take in a breath.

"Now?" I asked.

She laughed a small laugh. Then she said, "No way."

I didn't know exactly what I was doing, but I figured it out. I couldn't tell if Coley assumed my expertise or if it just wasn't that hard to gauge what she wanted, to make a move, judge her reaction, be it slight or large, and then continue from there or reassess. At first I used just my fingertips, then more of my hand, and when Coley started to move hard against me, I just kept on with what I'd started out doing originally, and explored with my mouth. I didn't get to do this very long before her whole body tensed and her breaths came in ragged jumps and her thighs pressed together against my head and I stopped at what I hoped was the right moment. It seemed like it was. But I didn't know what to do in the aftermath, where to put my body, what to say. I felt like maybe there were things to be said, the right things, but I didn't know how to put those words together. Instead, I stayed where I was, rested my head on her stomach: it felt and sounded like her heart had somehow slid down into it, each beat pulsing loud and superfast in my ear.

Eventually Coley said, "Come up here."

I kissed my way back up her body, just more tiny kisses.

When I got to the pillow, she said in her sweet, quiet voice, "Wow, Cameron Post."

I grinned a big grin, a grin that would have embarrassed me, I know, if someone had shown me a mirror right then.

But then Coley's face shifted some, her features forming an uneasy sort of look, and she said, "I don't know how to . . . I don't know."

"It's okay," I said.

"No, I want to try. I just don't have, like you had Irene and Lindsey, and I—"

"Irene and I were twelve. We barely kissed. And Lindsey and I never got this far."

"But still, it was something. Isn't she all wild?"

"Not then," I said. "It wasn't like this at all, anyway." I reached for her face and she let me kiss her, then pulled away.

"It has to have been something like this," she said.

"It wasn't."

"Why not?"

Now I breathed in deep, let it out. "C'mon, Coley," I said. "You already know why."

"No I don't."

I said this next part with my face turned into my shoulder, looking away from her. "Because I've been in love with you since forever."

"I didn't know that," she said.

"Yes you did."

"I did not," she said, turning away from me and onto her side. I couldn't tell if maybe she was crying or about to cry.

"Coley," I said, just barely touching her shoulder, feeling like I'd made a really big mistake. "It's okay, I don't even—"

"It goes against everything," she said, some of her voice buried in the pillow. "This is like—it's just supposed to be silly and whatever. I don't want to be like that."

"Like what?" I asked. Somehow, even after what I'd just done, what *we'd* done, I felt ashamed, the guilty party.

"Like a couple of dykes," she said.

"What does that even mean?"

"You know what it means."

"To who?"

"How about God, for one," she said, turning and looking at me dead on.

I didn't feel like I had a good answer for that. I knew that Lindsey would have, but I wasn't sure enough to make a case.

"Doesn't this feel really big to you?" she asked. "I mean like too big? It's like the more time we spend together, the harder it is to turn off."

"Maybe that means we're not supposed to turn it off," I said.

"Maybe it means we shouldn't have started in the first place," Coley answered. But then, and this wasn't what I expected, she kissed me, hard, and pretty soon after, she pushed me onto my back and covered me with her body. We kissed like this awhile, even more intensely than we had before, almost like Coley was trying to rid herself of this thing, like she could maybe just get it over and done with, forever, if she was aggressive enough, forceful enough.

Eventually she moved her hand down my body, slowly, and she pulled her mouth away and said, "I'll try," with a kind of serious determination that made me smile but also made me want her to "try" all the more.

She had made it to my stomach, her soft hair and mouth trailing my skin, making me shiver, when the room, which had felt like our own small world, cut off and entirely private, exploded with the sound of someone pounding hard on the apartment door, a sound as scary and out of place, right then, as gunshots.

We both went rigid. Coley jerked her head. More pounding. And then Ty's door-muffled and drunken voice, full of laughter. "Open up, girls! This is the police. We know you're consuming alcoholic beverages."

Coley was off me and standing next to the bed before

he had even quite finished what he was saying. "Shit, get dressed," she said in a low but panicked voice I'd never heard from her before.

We were fast. We didn't have much to put on. But even still, Ty had time to work his key in the lock and open the door the few inches the chain would allow him to. "C'mon, gals" came a different guy's voice, one that was a little louder with the door open that crack. "You passed out in there?"

Coley threw the quilt back in place and I tried to smooth it out some.

After the cave dark of the bedroom, even the one lamp in the living room seemed too bright, and Coley looked rumpled, her hair messy and flying with static, her face red, like she'd been up to something, and I could tell by the way she was looking at me that I appeared just as wrong.

"Take your drink," she said, already at the coffee table, grabbing hers, smoothing the back of her head with her other hand.

I didn't understand her intentions. I looked at her like the village idiot would.

And so she looked back at me the exact way that you would look at the village idiot when she was about to ruin something or already had. "Pick up your drink so they just think we're sloshed," she said in the same harsh whisper voice.

I did what she said. I also picked up the remote and again pushed Play on the tape. It had rewound itself.

Coley took big strides to the door. "We're gonna need to see some IDs, fellas," she said, her voice fake and bright like a talking plastic cowgirl doll. "For all we know you could be Pine Hills escapees."

"We are," Ty said. "We cleared the fence and now we fucking have to pee. Open up."

"Then move your nose out of the way so I can shut it and undo the chain," Coley said. And then she did just that.

There were three of them in boots and Wranglers, shirts tucked in, gleamy belt buckles: the works. I'm sure it helped us that they were drunk, stupid drunk, their perceptions already fucked up.

Ty motioned at Coley's drink on his way to the bathroom, undoing his belt as he went. "I knew it was the Malibu," he said. "I knew it." He slammed shut the door, but not in the way you would if you were really mad, more in a drunken, accidental, closed-the-door-too-hard kind of way, and from behind it he shouted, "I trusted you to keep her on the straight and narrow, Cameron. My wrath is upon you."

The shortest of the three, a guy with a thick neck and small-man, big-muscle syndrome, put his arm around Coley and said, "Hey, good-lookin'. You've weeded up in my absence." He squeezed her to him, and it made me clench my jaw.

Coley kept on with the plastic voice and said, "Hey yourself, Barry. Last time I saw you, you were passed out in the back of Ty's truck with some poor lady's bra on your head."

"Sounds about right," he said, squeezing her again and laughing a big drunken laugh. Coley laughed too, and even though it was her fake laugh, just watching her flirt—flirt in the exact same way that I had seen her do so many times before and had found charming maybe, or cute—so soon after the bedroom, after our nakedness, our quiet intensity, after the feel of her beneath me, on top of me, was pretty much unbearable.

The other guy came over to me, stooped and smelled my drink, made a face, winked at me, and said, "Something girly, huh?"

"Yeah," I said, looking at him, glad to have a reason not to look at Coley.

He jerked his chin toward the TV, where Bowie and Deneuve were back at the club, dancing. "What's this movie?"

"It's about vampires," Coley answered fast for me.

"Oh yeah?" the short guy, Barry, said. "You girls trying to scare yourselves? Good thing we showed up."

In the bathroom the toilet flushed, water whooshed in the sink.

"No, it sucks," Coley said. "We were gonna turn it off and go out."

Ty strode back in, the front of his hair wet and his forehead dewy, like he'd just dunked his head under the faucet. He ran his hands over his face a bunch of times, fast. "Where the hell's 'out'?"

"Just out," Coley said. "As in not here."

She worked her way from beneath Short Guy's arm and came to me, reached out her hand toward me, and I thought for one split second she was going to unbelievably, amazingly, prove something about us to these guys, and I sucked in my breath as her hand grazed my tank top, just at my waistband. But all she was after was the remote, which I had shoved into my pocket without even realizing that I'd done it. It wasn't hard to pull out, barely in there in the first place. She stopped the tape and I was still holding my breath.

"Hey," the guy next to me said, turning from the now-blank TV screen. "That looked interesting."

"It's really not," Coley said.

"You girls look like you've been up to something," Ty said, twisting on the tiny penlight he kept on his keychain and shining it in my eyes, making me squint.

"You're the one who looks like you've been up to

something." Coley pushed his hand and the light out of my face.

"We have," he said. Then he whipped the light toward the glass in Coley's hand, lit it up funny from the side so it glowed orange-yellow. "What have you two juvenile delinquents concocted, anyway?" He grabbed her glass and took a drink from what was left and then made a face even uglier than the one made by the taller guy who had smelled mine. "What a fucking waste of my rum."

Barry had thoughts on this. "All you have to do is mix it with some Coke, gals. That's the best drink you're gonna make with rum."

"A piña colada is pretty damn tasty," the taller guy said.

"Only if you're in the islands, mon," Ty said, doing a bad Jamaican accent and heading into the kitchen, flicking on the light in there.

"A piña colada is a pussy drink," Barry said. "It's just about what these gals have here anyway."

"Nah, you gotta have coconut milk," the taller guy said, and at the same time Ty shouted something from the kitchen about how *fucking much of the fucking bottle* we'd downed.

Taller Guy and Barry kept on debating the faggoty nature of fruity drinks as they meandered to the kitchen, and simultaneously Ty started in on a loudish and surprisingly well-sung chorus of "If you like piña coladas, getting caught in the rain . . ." and Coley, next to me, not looking at me but looking at the backs of the guys as they jammed up the kitchen, whispered, "You should feel my pulse right now. Thank God I did the chain, right?"

And I thought if I opened my mouth to say something back I might shout at her like a crazy person; just shout or cry or even kiss her, something big and dramatic and something

I wouldn't be able to keep hold of once I'd started doing it. So I said nothing.

My silence registered and she finally looked at me and said, "I think it's okay. They don't know anything."

I still didn't talk.

"It's okay now, Cam."

Before Coley could stop me, or I could stop me, I put my fingertips on the soft skin at the side of her neck, right at the edge of her jawline, just the lightest touch in a place that only minutes before, *minutes before*, I had been kissing, a place right over her carotid artery. I touched her there with those cowboys in the kitchen, as likely to turn around any second and see us as not.

Coley slapped my hand away like you would an ant, or something even worse, something that didn't belong on your skin at all, ever. "What are you doing?" She didn't even really whisper the words but mouthed them big and ugly so that I couldn't mistake them.

"I was feeling your pulse," I said, not that quietly.

Coley moved away from me in the direction of the kitchen but kept her head turned toward me, still just mostly mouthing her words. "What the hell's wrong with you?"

"You said that I should feel it," I said.

"Now here, ladies, is a drink," Barry said, turning around in the kitchen's doorway, a glass with a newly mixed brown beverage in hand.

"Rum and Coke?" Coley asked, taking it from him without waiting for a confirmation, downing a big swallow.

"What's left of my rum," Ty shouted. "You two are a gypsy band of thieves."

"A duo of thieves, not a band," Barry said. "Where the fuck did you learn to count?" He grabbed the glass back from

Coley, put his mouth over the same place she had, drank half of it in one gulp.

I thought I might pass out. My body felt jangly and sharp and uncontrollable, like chunks of glass were floating all around inside my limbs. I couldn't be in that apartment with them for one more second.

"You want some of this?" Barry was shaking the drink at me.

"Nah, I've got to go," I said, not looking at him or any of them. I walked to the door, slid my feet over my flip-flops, wedged the plastic divider between my big toe and its neighbor. I could hear Barry repeating to Ty and Taller Guy that I was leaving, and they all seemed very confused by this news.

I had the door open when Ty pushed through the jam-up in the kitchen and came toward me. "Not because of us, right? We didn't mean to drive you off."

I couldn't look at his face. I couldn't look behind him at Coley, even though she had followed him. "No," I said to the apartment's ugly carpeting. "I got too much sun today or something. I'm supertired all of a sudden."

"But you're okay other than being tired?" Ty asked, his hand on the top of the door, keeping it open, his arm sort of blocking my way out. "You seem upset."

"Just tired," I said.

"How are you getting home?"

I had driven the Bel Air. I didn't even know where I had left—

"Here's your keys," Coley said, handing them over like she'd just conjured them up, a magic trick.

"You sure you're good to drive?" Ty asked, still blocking me.

"She's better than you, Ty," Coley said. "Let her go home and go to bed."

"I'm fine," I said. "I'm perfect."

"You call us when you get there," Ty said, and then he slid his arm away and let me pass.

I could tell somebody was watching me from the doorway as I walked down the hallway, as I started down the first flight of stairs, but I didn't look up to see who, mostly because I needed to believe that it was Coley, but I knew better that it was probably just Ty.

CHAPTER TWELVE

The next day Coley didn't come to pick me up at Scanlan after work, and even though it made me even angrier, and sadder, I wasn't that surprised about it. I rode my bike out to Taco John's, and as I pulled up, I could see Jamie through the glass door, working a big mop in front of the beverage station.

"Power Trip Troy just stopped by to check time cards and he gave us a bunch of shit to do," Jamie said when I walked in. The place was empty. "And Brian's already baked, so he's annoying as fuck."

Brian, who had recently dyed his hair Teenage Mutant Ninja Turtle Green, was behind the counter, two stairs up on a step stool and doing a bad job of pouring a pillow-size plastic bag of tortilla chips into the warming machine. He had the bag lined up wrong, with the opening to the machine, and chips kept falling, two and three at a time, landing like crispy autumn leaves on the fake Spanish tile–style floor.

"I have my dinner break in twenty minutes," Jamie said, pony-riding the mop handle until he was back behind the counter. "You want I should fix you a supernacho?"

"No, I'm fine," I said. I waited for him on the wooden bench of an empty booth with my beach towel wrapped over my legs because it was way too cold in there to immediately follow the nine hours I'd just spent in the sun. There was ballpoint pen and marker graffiti all over the cream-and-brown-striped wallpaper next to the booth. Minuscule graffiti, most lines punctuated with at least one exclamation point:

I love Tori! yer mom luvs Tori! Go Cowboys!!!
Tori who? TORI SPELLING? 90210 SUCKS DICK!!!

I thought about asking the guys for a pen and adding my own, but I wasn't sure what to write: *I love Coley Taylor. I'm pissed at Coley Taylor. I fucked Coley Taylor. Coley Taylor fucked with my head.*

I didn't ask for a pen. A couple of truckers came in and took me in, my towel-wrap, my swimsuit top. I waited some more while Jamie made them enchilada platters and then nodded at me from behind the counter that it was break time, that he could meet me outside.

He had already lit up by the time I got to the concrete pad at the back of the building. The bright-orange Taco John's Dumpster had wasps swirling all around it, and there was a giant plastic bucket filled with brown grease slop just outside the workers' entrance, but the night was calm and the sky was starting to turn that summertime purple it turned every once in a while, and the painted cinder block wall of the restaurant felt warm and smooth against the bare skin of my arms and shoulders as I leaned against it and accepted the joint from Jamie's thin fingers.

"Where's Coley at?" he asked.

He had to wait until I had released the sweet smoke in my lungs before I answered. "Fuck if I know," I said, trying to sound cool and mean and not hurt.

"My poor lass." Jamie gripped my shoulder and made a big, fake, pained face. "Has the young suitor Brett returneth to claim his bride?"

"Tomorrow," I said, taking the joint from him even though he hadn't yet offered it back, hadn't even had the opportunity to hit again himself.

"So don't you want to try any last-chance moves on your woman on this, your final night of alone time?"

"It's all really messed up," I said.

"Yeah," he said, smacking a wasp to the ground with his work visor and then smearing it on the concrete with his sneaker. "I told you it was fucked up from the start."

"Well, it's even worse now, Captain Foresight," I said, afraid that I might cry and not even sure quite where it was coming from and mad about it, about always, always crying in front of Jamie.

"How come?" he asked, getting the last of the wasp off the sole of his shoe, one thin wing still twitching. He took the joint back from me.

"It just is. And there isn't any going back from it, either. There's no undoing or whatever."

"Did you ladies actually consummate your nonrelation-ship?" Jamie had tried for his usual smart-ass tone, but I could tell he meant his question.

I didn't answer him. The joint—it was small to begin with—was mostly caked, but there was enough left for one solid hit. "You wanna shotgun this?" I asked.

He knew how to read my nonanswer. "Niiiiice, JJK," he said, doing a man punch to my upper arm. "This *is* fucked up. You're now like officially the other woman. You're a lesbian home wrecker."

I took in as much smoke as I could and flicked the butt out into the alley, and after a few seconds Jamie leaned over and opened wide and I sealed my lips to his dry mouth as best I could and exhaled, waited, and then pulled away. And then I did start crying like a giant, beach towel–wrapped baby, and Jamie put one arm around me and then both arms around me and we stood in a hug out there on that hot cement stoop and didn't let go until a truck crammed with high schoolers, kids in the cab and bed, pulled into the drive-through lane and Brian opened the heavy door to the workers' entrance and hollered for backup.

"It's gonna be cool," Jamie said while I pulled off my towel wrap and draped it over my shoulders, used one end to wipe at my face. "It'll be better with Brett back, anyway. Now the pressure's off. We just gotta find you a slutty Glendive girl. Somebody out of the city limits."

"That's the answer," I said. "When in doubt, it's always a slutty Glendive girl."

"It's always a slutty girl," Jamie said situating his wasp-killing visor on his head at the jaunty angle he favored. "But there's no rule says she has to be from Glendive."

After he went in, I thought about riding my bike to the Montana Theatre, just to see if maybe Coley would be up in the last row, just to see if maybe. But even though I went a couple blocks past my house in that direction, I turned around well before I got there and rode home. Grandma was on the front porch, sitting in the half dark, eating a thick wedge of sugar-free banana pudding pie with graham cracker crust.

"No picture show tonight, huh?"

"Not tonight," I said. "Did anybody call for me?"

"Anybody who?"

"Just anybody, Grandma," I said.

"No anybodies I know, cranky," she said. "Sounds to me like you have a somebody in mind, though."

Ruth and Ray were on the couch watching something

on TV that I didn't even pause long enough at the doorway to distinguish.

"I put a couple of catalogs in your room for you, honey," Ruth called after me as I started up the stairs. "I circled the ones I like best. You only have two months to pick—two months!"

I showered with the cordless phone on the sink so I could hear it. It didn't ring. I played this game where I convinced myself that if I stayed in the shower Coley would call and if I got out she wouldn't and so I just let the hot water run and run and run until it was cold and that was fine too because it was so hot in the bathroom anyway, and I stayed in even with the water growing colder and colder and she still didn't call.

In my room I didn't put on a movie. I didn't work on the dollhouse, either. Ruth had left the bridal-wear catalogs on my desk. I flipped through them, Ruth's blue marker circles on page after page. The maid of honor dresses she'd picked all looked nice, and surprisingly plain, like she was really trying to think of me and what I'd want to wear, but I still couldn't imagine myself in any of them. Coley had said she'd help me find something in Billings for the wedding, that we'd make a weekend of it.

I tried to turn off my lamp and sleep, on top of the covers, my shirt and hair wet, the fan on, the phone lying on the bed next to me, but it was still early and I wasn't tired. I played one of the new mixes from Lindsey, a bunch of bands and singers I'd not yet heard of, but it felt like too much work to try to *really* listen to new songs sung by new voices, too much thinking, somehow, so I changed to Tom Petty and felt sorry for myself and then mad at myself for feeling like that and then sorry for myself again. And Coley didn't ever call.

. . .

Mona Harris and I had a rotation in the bathhouse together the next afternoon. I'd been a shitty lifeguard for the past several hours, looking at the lake but not actively scanning the water at all, instead imagining Coley and Brett's reunion night in the greatest possible detail, playing out one scenario after another just to torture myself. I came up with a lot of scenarios that did the trick.

"Will you slather me up?" Mona asked as I walked in from the beach, removing my sunglasses, letting my eyes adjust to the cool dark.

She already had her swimsuit straps peeled off and hanging at the sides of her arms, a white bottle of Coppertone SPF 30 in one of her hands.

I nodded. She handed it to me.

"It's the end of summer and yet watch me burn," she said as I squirted a little pool of the thick, white cream into the center of my palm. "If I forget to lotion even once, I'm a lobster."

I coated her warm back, the skin pinky white and freckled all over, but definitely not tan like the rest of us lifeguards.

I finished and Mona pulled her straps back and I set the lotion on this shelf that was like a community graveyard of half-used bottles of every sun lotion or oil or stick ever invented.

We sat at the check-in table without talking, the crappy, scratchy radio on behind us. Mona was flipping through a water-wrinkled *People* magazine that had been in the bathhouse since June, and I was using the metal handle of the fly swatter to work on a skull and crossbones that someone else had already started carving into the tabletop. Then a couple of lake rats ran in from the boys' locker room and told us that some of the other lake rats had tossed their clothing and towels up onto the roof of the bathhouse, which happened at least a dozen times a summer because the locker rooms were open air with just cement partitions for stalls and kids would stand on the wooden benches and hoist stuff up onto the bathhouse roof just to be assholes.

"You going up or me?" Mona asked, but I was already out of the metal folding chair and on my way to get the ladder so I could retrieve the T-shirts and the sneakers and the stretched-out, grimy tube socks with a couple of dollar bills shoved down into the toe.

The boys waited on the ground as I tossed things down to them and told them to put their shit in baskets next time, but once the roof was clear, a part of me wanted to stay up there, hide out. It was just a flat, square expanse of hot tar, sort of like the Holy Rosary roof only much, much smaller and much, much closer to the ground. Granola Eric waved at me from left chair, obviously not doing a particularly good job of keeping his eyes on the water either. I waved back. I caught the glint of the sun off the lake and everything in front of me, beneath me, glowed white and hot; and as my vision readjusted, the beach and the street and the Conoco across the way went from ghost outlines to fuzzy color to finally their normal, solid selves. Then I climbed down.

I slammed the side of the ladder against the doorway trying to bring it back into the bathhouse and I jammed my thumb behind it and it hurt and I swore a bunch before I actually got it put away, Mona watching me the whole time, laughing some.

"You having a rough go of it?" she asked as I sat down.

"Whatever," I said.

"I'll take that as a yes," Mona said, and then she reached

over and flicked my arm with her thumb and pointer finger, hard, just above my wrist.

"Fuck!" I said. "That hurt." It did.

"No it didn't," she said, smiling.

"Yes it did," I said, but it made me smile too, for some reason. "That's workplace abuse and I don't have to stand for it."

"Write me up," she said. "I'll find you the necessary form."

"Too much effort." I tried to flick her back but I only managed a weak one near her elbow because she kept moving her arms all around.

Then whatever it was we were doing ended, the moment all used up in the way that sometimes happens and the mood just shifts, and you're both aware of it, and that's all there is to it. I went back to working on the skull, Mona the magazine.

But not very many minutes later she said, "She's gorgeous, right?" She turned the magazine toward me so I could see this two-page spread of Michelle Pfeiffer photos: Michelle Pfeiffer on the beach and walking her dog and cutting veggies for what looked to be an enormous, all-color salad in her fancy, big-windowed kitchen.

"Yeah, she's pretty," I said.

"She's at her hottest in *Grease 2*," Mona said, sliding the magazine back.

"That movie sucks."

"I didn't say the movie was good. I said she's hot in it."

"I don't think I noticed her looks because the movie she was showcasing them in sucked so badly," I said.

Mona smiled a slow smile at me. "So you just didn't notice her at all? It was like she was invisible in every scene?"

"Yeah," I said. "Exactly like that."

"Wow," Mona said, taking her whistle from the table,

putting it back around her neck. "That's an incredible talent you have."

I waited. Then I said, "She's hotter in *Scarface*, anyway."

"Hmmmm," she said. "I'll have to think about that."

I looked at the clock. We had to rotate out in a couple of minutes. I stood up, got my bottle of Gatorade from the big community cooler that Hazel brought ice for every morning.

"Can I have a drink?" Mona asked, already standing behind me, assuming my yes.

I passed her the bottle. She drank a lot before handing it back.

"You're kind of shy, huh?" she said, getting her towel from the hook. "Like little-kid shy."

"No," I said. "Not at all."

"It's okay," she said. "It's not an insult."

"But it's not true."

"See, you sound like a little kid right now, even," she said, laughing, leaving the bathhouse to relieve the right rover.

It wasn't that I didn't still think about Coley, and Coley and Brett, and Coley and me, for my next several hours outside; it was just that I punctuated all those thoughts with new thoughts about Mona, and Mona's possible motivations, and a couple of times I even just plain stared at her while pretending to scan my area, a whole lake between us and my sunglasses covering the exact direction of my gaze.

Of course Coley didn't show up after work, not with Brett newly back in town. A few of the other highway department guys did though, and they had a case of beer with them.

I wasn't gonna stay, but as I was hanging my whistle on my designated hook, Mona came into the bathhouse and grabbed my towel where it was wrapped around my waist, her fingers sliding between towel fold and swimsuit at my hip. She held on while she said, "You're staying, right?" And then I was.

While she covered me from the curiosity of the last departing lake rats, I poured a can and a half of Coors into my empty Gatorade bottle. We hid as many additional cans as possible in towels and sand pails, locked the main doors, and joined the highway guys in the trek down the beach toward the docks and the deep end.

One of those guys, Randy, said to me, after snapping my left suit strap, "We figured you'd have played hooky today, too."

"What do you mean?" I asked.

"Coley called in sick this morning," he said. He did air quotes with his fingers around *sick*.

"Nah, Ty did it for her," one of the other guys said, coming up alongside us.

"Same dif," Randy said. "We all guessed that you two gals had made for Billings or somewheres. Maybe she's actually sick."

We stopped at right guard stand to unload our bundles. I could feel Mona looking at me.

"Her boyfriend just got back into town," I said. "That's the kind of sick she is."

"Ohhhhh," Randy said, doing a slapstick kind of elbow jab in my direction. "Lovesick, huh? That's the good kind."

"That's what they tell me," I said, taking a big drink from my bottle and then twisting on the cap and chucking it into the lake and following its trajectory with the arc of my own racing dive.

We chicken fought for a while, me and Mona on broad, slippery shoulders, wrenching and pulling at one another, laughing when we toppled into the water's dark surface, again and again. We later rated each other's jackknives and cannonballs, but only Mona and I managed flips off the high dive. When the two of us wound up together beneath center dock, it felt inevitable and not weighty at all. The highway crew was tooling around in the shallow end, chasing a mud puppy, and even though Mona said something like "I can't believe I'm one of those college girls who go after high schoolers" three or four times, that didn't stop us from making out down there in the slits of light that colored the water around us chartreuse. And that's all it was. Maybe ten minutes of making out. Mona and her thick lips, her nearly translucent eyelashes. But I rode my bike home with a buzz from both the beer and the kissing, an older woman, a college woman, and *Take that, Coley Taylor, take that*, and I felt good for twelve blocks before I felt bad. Really bad. All of it thunking on me at once, feeling like I'd cheated on her, or weirdly, on us.

On the last streets before my house I decided that I would write Coley a letter. I would write her a really long letter and tell her that even if this thing between us was big and scary, we could figure it out because we had to, because it was love and that's what you do when you're in love. Even in my head it sounded like the lyrics to a Whitesnake song, but that didn't matter. I would write it all down. All of it. All the stuff that made me feel weird and mushy and stupid and scared when I went to say it, and sometimes even when I thought about it.

Pastor Crawford's car was in the driveway and I didn't consider that fact for a second. He was over all the time, Ruth and her committees. I put my bike in the garage, grabbed the newspaper from the porch, didn't really wonder why nobody else had yet done so, opened the door, threw the paper on the entryway table, and was already three stairs up toward my room when Ruth said, "We need you to come in here please, Cameron."

It was her saying Cameron and not Cammie that made the first little knot twist right at the base of my throat. And then when I was at the doorway to the living room, Ruth and Crawford on the couch, Ray in the big club chair, and Grandma nowhere, the knot got bigger, twisted harder, and it was my parents all over again but this time with Grandma. I was sure of it.

"Why don't you go ahead and sit here?" Pastor Crawford said, standing, motioning to the spot on the couch he had vacated for me.

"What happened to Grandma?" I stayed in the doorway.

"She's downstairs, resting," Ruth said. She wasn't really looking at me. Or at least she wasn't holding her eyes on me for very long.

"Because she's sick?" I asked.

"This isn't about your grandma, Cameron," Pastor Crawford said. He took the couple of steps over to me and put his hand on my shoulder. "We'd like you to have a seat so we can chat with you about some things."

Chat was a counseling-center word, a word that, when somebody said it like Crawford just had, never really meant chat at all. It meant a big conversation about the kinds of things you would never just chat with someone about, never.

"What'd I do now?" I asked, shrugging out from under his heavy hand and crossing my arms over my chest, leaning against the doorframe in a way that I hoped suggested that I couldn't care less, whatever. But I was running over sins in my mind as fast as I could call them up. *Was it the missing beer from the fridge? Was it Holy Rosary? Was it an intercepted package from Lindsey? Was it pot with Jamie? Check here for all of the above.*

The four of us traded glances. I could see Crawford

making the face he made when he was searching for powerful words during a sermon, but before he could get them out, Ruth made a freaky, strangled sobbing noise from the couch and muffled it fast with her hand. Ray got up to go to her, and when he did, a pamphlet slid off his lap and onto the floor. It was just one thin trifold, nothing I'd have noticed from across the room, but I sure did once it lay against the rug, its logo unmistakable: *God's Promise*—those pamphlets that cool Reverend Rick had stacked at the end of the snacks table. The pamphlet that Coley had taken, put in her purse.

After feeling for so long like I could get away with anything, *anything*—like I could just keep sliding free in the nick of time like Indiana Jones rolling out from under the impossibly fast slam of a metal gate, narrowly escaping a series of steel spikes, a gigantic rolling ball of stone in a closed-in tunnel, near misses, just close enough to give you a jolt—I felt the choke of being caught, and knowing it, and the kind of shame that sidecars that choke.

"I know you can see how difficult this is for all of us," Pastor Crawford said. "And we know that this is going to be very difficult for you as well." He reached out like he was gonna do the hand on my shoulder again, but then reconsidered and instead motioned me toward the club chair.

I went, thinking in those few moments that this all must have something to do with Lindsey, her packages and letters, maybe even those locker-room photos we'd taken, all of it evidence against me. I can't quite explain why I focused on Lindsey and only Lindsey, but that's what happened: I was convinced, sitting in that club chair, pulling my knees up into my chest, looking at no one, that this *chat* absolutely had to do with all that mail between us.

And so I was already working on the ways that I'd blame all this on Lindsey, her influence, her wicked, big-city abominations, when Crawford said, "Coley Taylor and her mother came to my house last night," and his words crashed through me like someone smashing cymbals together over my head. Ruth leaned into Ray, letting his blue-work-shirted chest do a better job than her hand of muffling her even bigger sobs.

From there on I had a hard time following Crawford's narrative. I tuned in and out, in and out, like a fucked-up set of earphones with a wire loose. I heard all of his words, I mean, I was right there and he was talking to me, but it was like he was telling some complicated, embarrassing story about somebody else. He told me about how Ty and the drunken cowboys had wrangled a story, "the truth," out of Coley after I had left her apartment two nights before, and in that story, "the truth," I was the pursuer and Coley the innocent friend, and a very angry Ty had convinced her to go to Mrs. Taylor the following morning, and Coley had then told her mother about Lindsey's corruption of me and my attempted corruption of her, my sick infatuation, and how she felt sorry for me, and how I needed help: God's help. Then Pastor Crawford told me about how he had had to deal with this news, how he had visited Ruth that morning, before she got in the Fetus Mobile for her sales trip to Broadus, me at Scanlan teaching my Level Threes the elementary backstroke—*chicken, airplane, soldier, repeat, repeat*—he and Ruth on the couch staring down the details of my ugly, sinful behavior. Once Ruth could pull herself together enough to stand, and that took hours, the two of them had searched my room, and there it all was: the mail I had wrongly thought of as the cause, not the cause at all but instead the corroborating proof to Coley's accusations, the letters and the videos and the note from Jamie, the photos, the mix tapes, the fucking stack of movie tickets I'd rubber-banded together and had been saving for the dollhouse, the dollhouse itself. But who could make any sense of that?

Pastor Crawford kept on in his steady, practiced, too-calm voice, talking about how it wasn't at all too late for me, about Christ's ability to cure these impure thoughts and actions, to rid me of these sinful impulses, to heal me, to make me whole, while I thought, over and over: *Coley told, Coley told, Coley told.* And then: *They know, they know, they know.* Just those two thoughts on repeat, steady like a drum rhythm. And it actually wasn't so much anger that I felt right then. Nor was it betrayal, even. Instead I felt tired, and I felt caught, and weak; and I somehow felt ready for my punishment, whatever it might be, just bring it on.

Pastor Crawford paused several times during his living-room sermon, for me to add something, or to question, I guess, but I didn't.

At some point he said, "I think we can agree that Miles City isn't the best place for you right now, spiritually or otherwise."

And I just couldn't help myself. "What does Miles City have to do with anything?" I asked the floor.

"There are too many unhealthy influences here," he answered. "We all think that it will be healing for you to have a change of scenery for a while."

I finally looked up. "Who all?"

"*All* of us," Ruth said, meeting my eyes, her own puffed up and mottled with mascara, the return of Sad Clown Ruth.

"What about Grandma?"

Ruth's face wadded up and she had to cover her mouth again, and Crawford jumped in quick and said, "Your grand-mother wants what's best for you, just like the rest of us. This isn't about punishment, Cameron. I hope you understand how much bigger than that this is."

I said, fast and mumbled, "I want to talk to Grandma myself," and I stood up to leave, to go downstairs.

But Ruth stood up too and she said, loud and sharp like a thumbtack, close to my face, "She doesn't want to talk about this! She is just sick about this, she's *sick* about it! We all are."

She might as well have slapped me. Ray and Crawford were both doing these O's with their mouths as if she had. I sat back down and *we* continued on with *our chat* and *we* had everything decided within the hour. Ruth would drive me to the God's Promise Christian Discipleship Program the following Friday. I would be staying for at least the entire school year, two semesters—with breaks at Christmas and Easter. *We'd* see how things had progressed after that.

Before he left, Pastor Crawford said a long prayer in which he asked for God's help in my recovery; then he hugged us all, even me. I let him, and afterward he handed me a manila envelope of application forms and rules for admittance that he'd had Reverend Rick fax over. The fee, by the way, was $9,650 per year, to be paid for with money left from Mom and Dad's estate, an education fund they'd set up for me. Simple enough.

GOD'S PROMISE

CHRISTIAN SCHOOL
& CENTER FOR HEALING

Residential Discipleship Program

*The opposite of the
sin of homosexuality is not
heterosexuality:
It is **holiness**.*

Purpose Statement

God's Promise is a Christian school and outreach center for adolescents yearning to break free from the bonds of sexual sin and confusion by welcoming Jesus Christ into their lives.

Our purpose is to provide support and direction while nurturing students' spirituality and personal growth through one-on-one and group support sessions, appropriate gender-modeling activities, constant spiritual instruction, and rigorous academics.

"You were taught, with regard to your former way of life, to put off your old self, which is being corrupted by its deceitful desires; to be made new in the attitude of your minds; and to put on the new self, created to be like God in true righteousness and holiness."

(Ephesians 4:22–24)

Guidelines/ Restrictions

Many disciples who come to God's Promise struggle with a variety of current behaviors and past histories that they are not equipped to deal with on their own. These include sexual addictions, drug and alcohol addictions, abuse, isolation, relational detachment, etc. Therefore, during the first semester, disciples are not permitted visitors nor phone calls—not even from family. Disciples may receive, after three months' time, mail, which will be screened by staff before it is presented to them. The purpose of these guidelines is to maintain a protected environment for breaking sinful patterns.

At the end of the first three months, leadership will assess Program parameters on an individual basis. They may lift some or all phone and visitation restrictions at that time if the disciple being assessed has grown in his/her walk with Christ.

Roommates/ Friendships

A principal tenet of the residential discipleship program is the importance of establishing and nurturing healthy, Godly friendships between all disciples. In particular, it is important that disciples learn how to develop healthy, nonerotic friendships with members of the same sex. These friendships are important not only in affirming appropriate gender roles, but also as a part of the healing process.

Further, at God's Promise we strive to replicate a collegiate or boarding school–type atmosphere for our students to help them prepare for *real-world* situations. As such, each participant is paired with a same-sex roommate. We see this as an opportunity for trust building and the further development of healthy, Godly, gender-appropriate relationships. Students must learn to function within a society that values friendships and bonding among individuals of the same sex, and fearing these kinds of healthy relationships is not progress.

However, we realize the delicate and special situation in which students are placed. As such, dorm rooms must remain unlocked at all hours of the day and night, and, unless changing clothing, students must leave their doors propped open until the lights-out hours of 10 p.m.–6 a.m. Further, random room inspections and "pop-ins" are performed by staff, unannounced, with regularity.

If we see components of a relationship, either same sex or opposite sex, that are potentially damaging to either disciple's walk with Christ (including sexual attraction, negative bonding over sinful/unhealthy desires or histories, or signs of emotional dependencies), we will implement guidelines to return these friendships to a Godly course.

If any disciple should experience sexual or unhealthy emotional attraction toward another disciple, he/she must immediately arrange to speak with either Rick or Lydia. Disciples MUST NOT TELL EACH OTHER ABOUT ANY POTENTIAL ATTRACTIONS. Such an action could cause both disciples extreme temptation. No dating is permitted during the program.

Erasing the Harmful "Gay" Image

God's Promise strives to maintain an environment that promotes Godly ways of communicating. Leadership will swiftly put an end to patterns of behavior or speech that promote or celebrate so-called gay or lesbian culture interests or mannerisms. Also, conversations that glorify past sins are not allowed. This includes sharing descriptive details of sexual encounters or fantasies.

Dress and Dorm Manual

During all scheduled activities (other than free time) that occur during the Monday-through-Friday school week, and also during worship services on Sundays, the Promise uniform must be worn by all disciples. During weekday free-time hours, (some) off-campus outings, and weekend hours other than worship services, uniforms are not required. However, clothing must be deemed appropriate by leadership.

All other instructions/
requirements for daily
life at God's Promise
are detailed in the dorm
manual, which will be
provided to disciples upon
their acceptance into the
program.

All Disciples Must:

- Be born again and
filled with the Spirit
of the LORD JESUS
CHRIST
- Understand and be in
agreement with the
guidelines established
and explained in the
God's Promise dorm
manual
- Actively participate
in all residential
discipleship activities
and acknowledge and
follow all programmatic
requirements

- Have a TEACHABLE
HEART, thereby being
open to receive
instruction, correction,
and support from
the God's Promise
leadership
- <u>**Agree that sexual
behavior in marriage
between a man and
a woman is God's
creative intent for
humanity and all
other sexual behavior
is sin**</u>

Part Three

God's Promise
1992–1993

CHAPTER THIRTEEN

I t was Jane Fonda who gave Ruth and me our official
welcome tour of the God's Promise Christian School &
Center for Healing. We were in the Fetus Mobile for six
hours straight before getting there. Six hours straight except
for when Ruth pulled into the Git 'n' Split in Big Timber to
get gas and *treats* and to let me pee. Ruth didn't even go. She
could hold it like a camel.

Back then Big Timber still had the only water park in
Montana, and it sat right alongside the interstate. When we
passed, I craned to see the strange toothpaste-green looping
slides as they towered out of a field housing cement vats of
too-blue water. The place was packed.

It was the last good week of August, and even whizzing
by like that, I could feel the urgency in the actions of the kids
as they swarmed about the place. Everything was heightened
the way it always is when summer is slipping away to fall,
and you're younger than eighteen, and all you can do is suck
your cherry Icee and let the chlorine sting your nose, all the
way up into the pockets behind your eyes, and snap your
towel at the pretty girl with the sunburn, and hope to do it all
again come June. I turned around in my seat and kept staring
until I could just barely make out those green twisting slides.
They seemed like tunnels from a science fiction version of
the future, with the charcoal and purple Crazy Mountains

all stretched out behind them like they didn't fit at all, like painted scenery at the school play.

At the Git 'n' Split Ruth bought string cheese and little cartons of chocolate milk and a tube of Pringles. She offered them up in the Fetus Mobile as though she was bearing frankincense and myrrh.

"I hate sour cream and onion Pringles," I told the dashboard, where I had my feet planted until Ruth pushed them down.

"But you love Pringles." Ruth actually rattled the canister.

"I hate sour cream and onion anything. All lesbians do." I blew heaps of bubbles into my milk with the tiny straw that came cellophaned to the carton.

"I want you to stop using that word." Ruth jammed the lid back onto the can.

"Which word? *Sour* or *cream*?" I plastic laughed with my reflection in the passenger-side window.

• • •

I had spent the week postintervention moving from numbness to outright, unabashed hostility toward Ruth, while she, on the other hand, became increasingly talkative and positive about my *situation*. She busied herself with the many *arrangements* to be made on my behalf: buying me dorm supplies, talking to Hazel about my early retirement from Scanlan, filling out paperwork, scheduling my mandatory physical, helping Ray haul the phone and TV and VCR from my room. That arrangement came first, actually. But the biggest arrangement of all: She canceled the wedding. She postponed it, that is.

"Don't," I said. She hadn't even told me she was doing it, actually. I surprised her in the kitchen, overheard her on the phone with the florist.

"It's not the right time now," Ruth had said. "The priority

is getting you better."

"I mean it: Don't. Don't stop the show for me; I'll live with not being there."

"It's not about you, Cameron. It's about me, and I don't want to have it while you're away." She had left the room after that. But she was lying, of course. It was completely *about me*. Completely.

• • •

I had to be babysat at all times. Someone in my condition couldn't very well be left alone. I met with Pastor Crawford each day, an hour or two at a go, but I never said much of anything. They were just Nancy Huntley sessions with God thrown in. I ate breakfast with Ruth, lunch with Ruth, dinner with Ruth and Ray. I stared out my window a lot. One afternoon I thought I saw Ty circling our block in his truck, around and around. I'm sure I did. But he never pulled up to the curb, put it in park; never charged up the stairs to teach me the violent version of the very same lesson God's Promise would be attempting to teach me soon.

During my lockdown Ruth was Ruth: chipper—forced, but chipper. Ray was Ray: quiet and even more unsure of what to say to me. And Grandma was nowhere. That whole week she ghosted around the house, wouldn't find herself alone in a room with me, took off in the Bel Air to who knows where for hours at a time. We ended up in the kitchen together one afternoon. I think she was hoping that I was still out meeting with Crawford, but I surprised her as she was mixing up a can of tuna with mayonnaise.

I didn't try to be proud. I thought maybe I had just one chance. "I don't want to go, Grandma," I said.

"Don't look at me, girl," she said, still mixing the mayo in thick. "You brought this on yourself. This is all your doing, every last bit of it. I don't know as Ruth's way is right, but I know you need some straightening out."

I don't think she realized that her word choice was sort of funny, and it wasn't really, right then, anyway.

"You'll be fine," she said, putting the mayo back into the door of the fridge, taking out the jar of sweet relish she wasn't supposed to eat. "You do what they say. Read your Bible. You'll be just fine."

It seemed like she was saying it as much for her as for me, but that's where the conversation stopped. I only saw her once more before we left. She emerged from the basement as we were loading the FM, gave me a loose hug that grew a little tighter right before she let go.

"I'll write you some, once it's allowed. You write too," she said.

"Not for three months," I said.

"You'll be okay. It will fly by."

• • •

Lindsey called once, she just happened to, probably wanted to know what I thought of the care package, but Ruth answered the phone, told her that I'd be *going away to school this year* and *wouldn't be able to continue to communicate with her any longer.* Just like that. I'm pretty sure she tried calling back, but I wasn't allowed to answer the phone. Jamie stopped by and Ruth at least let him come into the entryway, but she hovered in the other room, made it obvious that she was listening.

"Everybody knows now, huh?" I asked him. It didn't seem like there was any point wasting words by talking around the only thing worth talking about right then.

"They know one version," Jamie said. "Brett's been telling people. I don't think Coley has."

"Well, it's the only version they'd believe, anyway," I said. "Probably."

He hugged me fast, told me he'd see me at Christmas if the warden allowed it. That made me laugh.

• • •

I could have snuck out. I could have made secret phone calls. I could have rallied forces on my behalf. I could have. I could have. I didn't. I didn't even try.

• • •

By an hour outside of Miles City, Ruth had already given up on lecturing me on appreciating *God's gift of a facility like this right in my own state.* I think she had given up on instilling in me a positive attitude before we even got on the road, but she quoted some scripture and walked through her lines as though she had written her little speech out beforehand. And knowing Ruth, she probably had—maybe in her daily prayer journal, maybe on the back of a grocery list. Ruth's words were so stale by that point that I didn't even hear most of them. I looked out my window with my nose tucked into my shoulder and smelled Coley. I was wearing one of her sweatshirts even though it was too hot for it. Ruth thought it was mine or she would have piled it into the cardboard box with the other things of Coley's, of ours, that she and Crawford had confiscated, many of those things items from our friendship and not necessarily from whatever it was that we'd become those last few weeks: snapshots, lots of them prom-night pictures; notes written on lined paper and folded to the size of fifty-cent pieces; the thick wad of rubber-banded movie tickets, of course those; and also a couple of pressed thistles, once huge and thorny and boldly purple, now dried and feathery and the ghost of their original color, dust in your hand if you squeezed too hard, and Ruth did. The thistles I'd picked at Coley's ranch, hauled back into town, and tacked upside down to the wall above my desk. But the sweatshirt, buried at the bottom of my laundry basket beneath clean but not-yet-folded beach towels and tank tops, had escaped. It still smelled like the kegger campfire at which she'd last worn it and something else I couldn't place, but something unmistakably Coley.

For miles and miles I just let Ruth drone. I let her words crumble away between us, drop like those thistles into dusty bits on the seats and the console. All the while I smelled Coley, and thought Coley, and wondered when I would start hating Coley Taylor, just how long it would take for that to happen, because I wasn't anywhere near that place yet, but I thought that maybe I should be. Or that maybe I would be one day. Eventually Ruth stopped talking to me and twisted the dial until she found Paul Harvey and laughed like she was drunk and had never heard mild radio humor before.

Those whole six hours, the only other snips of dialogue between us, other than the Pringles incident, were:

RUTH: Please roll up your window; I have the AC on.
ME: And this affects me how?

RUTH: I wish you would stop slumping like that. You're rounding your shoulders and you'll end up an old lady with a hump.
ME: Good. It will go nicely with the horns I'm working on.

RUTH: I know that you read your manual, Cammie; I saw you. It says you have to enter Promise with a teachable heart if you want this to work.

ME: Maybe I don't have a heart, teachable or otherwise.

RUTH: Don't you want this to work? I just can't understand why anyone would want to stay like this if they knew they could change.

ME: Stay like what?

RUTH: You know exactly what.

ME: No I don't. Say it.

RUTH: Stay in a life of sinful desire.

ME: Is that the same category for premarital sex?

RUTH: (Long pause.) What is that supposed to mean?

ME: I wonder.

Only a few miles before the turnoff to Promise we passed the sign for Quake Lake. It was battered and the metal was crunched in the middle, as though it had fallen down and been driven over by a semi and then put back up. I think Ruth and I noticed it at right the same time, and she turned to me, actually took her eyes from the road to look at me, for just a few seconds. But Ruth somehow managed not to say anything. And I didn't say anything. And then we turned a corner and it was just trees and road in the rearview and that sign wasn't some big signifier at all, but just one more place marker we'd driven by on our way. At least that's what we both pretended right then.

The girl who met us in the Promise parking lot had an orange clipboard, a Polaroid camera, and a prosthetic right leg (from the knee down). She seemed about my age, high school for sure, and she waved that clipboard while walking toward the FM with surprising speed. Maybe I shouldn't have been surprised: She was wearing running shorts.

Ruth didn't even have the chance to say something like

"Oh, lookit this poor thing" before the poor thing herself was at Ruth's door, throwing it open and flashing a picture, all in what seemed to me the same moment.

Ruth made a gaspy-squeaky sort of noise and shook her head back and forth and blinked her eyes the way one of the *Looney Tunes* did after smacking into a brick wall.

"Sorry about the shock. I like to get one right away," the girl told us, letting the big black camera hang around her neck, pulling her head down some. The photo slid forward like a tongue, but she didn't pull it free. "Just as soon as folks get here I snap one. It has to be the very first moment; it's the best."

"Why's it the best?" I asked her, walking around the Fetus Mobile to see that leg up close. Her real one was bony and pasty white, but the fake one had some girth, some plasticky definition, and was Beach Barbie tanned.

"You can't use words to describe it—that's why the photos. I think it's because it's the purest moment. The most undiluted."

Ruth did a weird kind of chuckle after she'd said that. I could tell she was uncomfortable with this girl as our greeter.

The girl finally plucked free the picture and held it up so only she and I could see it. The shot was mostly Ruth's head too close to the lens and her mouth a line of displeasure, with me seeming far behind her, almost smiling.

"I'm Cameron," I said. I knew that if I didn't speak, Ruth would, and for some reason I wanted this girl to like me right away. Maybe because whoever it was I had been expecting to meet us, this girl wasn't her.

"I know. We've all been talking about you coming. I'm Jane Fonda." She was smiling and rocking a little on that leg. It squeaked like a bath toy.

"Serious? Jane Fonda?" I smiled back.

"I'm always serious," she said. "Ask anybody. So the deal is that Rick's in Bozeman at Sam's Club buying food and stuff. I'll give you the grand tour and then he'll be back before too long." She leaned toward me. "Sam's Club and Walmart give us a big discount, and free food, sometimes. Mostly chicken breasts and bananas. He does a decent barbecue chicken, but he gets the cheap toilet paper—the scratchy kind you have to double up on."

"There are worse things," Ruth said. "Shall we bring the luggage now?"

"Indubitably," Jane said.

"I can't believe your name is actually Jane Fonda," I said. "That's crazy."

She tapped her clipboard against her leg two times and it sounded sorta like when I was little and would tap my plastic drumsticks against my Mr. Potato Head. "Talk about the tip of the iceberg," she said. "We swim in crazy here."

• • •

The grounds at Promise had a little of everything that western Montana is famous for, things that the state tourism board makes sure show up on postcards and in guidebooks: golden-green fields for archery or horseback riding, densely wooded trails dotted with Indian paintbrush and lupine, two streams that, according to Jane, were just *aching with trout*, and a so-blue-it-looked-fake mountain lake only a mile and a half's hike away from the main building. Both sides of the campus (the compound) were bordered by the grazing land of cattle ranchers sympathetic to the holy cause of saving our souls from a lifetime of sexual deviance. Even that hot August afternoon, the wind down from the mountains was crisp, and on it rode the sweet scent of hay, the good spice of pine and cedar.

Jane Fonda took us cross-country, that squeaky leg sur-prisingly springy, and Ruth determined not to lose step with a cripple, even if not losing step meant bouncing the battered, green, Winner's-Airlines-issued wheelie suitcase now packed with my stuff over prairie-dog holes and sagebrush. I lugged a pink Sally-Q case, one that Ruth had told me she would be taking back with her, but I could keep the Winner's one. Out with the old, in with the new.

Jane sort of motioned to the chicken coop (eggs were collected each morning by students on a rotating schedule); to an empty horse stable (they were planning to get some horses, though); to a cluster of metal-roofed cabins used only during the summer, for camp; to two small cabins where Reverend Rick and the school's assistant director, Lydia March, lived. But Jane wasn't so much a tour guide as someone we might have happened upon in a foreign town, someone who felt obligated to show us around a little. As we walked, I stared at the back of her T-shirt. On it was a black-and-white print of a female athlete, maybe a volleyball player, judging by her shorts and tank top, stretching after an exhausting match— her ponytail limp, her brow dewy. Next to the image were the purple words SEEK GOD IN ALL THAT YOU DO.

The main building was built, I think, to resemble an aspen lodge, with log siding and a grand entrance; but once we were inside, it felt just like Gates of Praise back in Miles City, but bigger, and with dorm rooms. The floors were all that industrial laminate poorly imitating hardwood. The windows were too few, fluorescent lighting everywhere. Someone had made an attempt with the main room—a fireplace, cheap Navajo-style woven rugs, a moose head over the mantel—but even that room smelled like disinfectant and floor cleaner.

"Where is everybody?" I asked, and was first answered by a cavernous echo of my own voice.

"Most everybody's in Bozeman with Pastor Rick. Lydia's

somewhere in England—that's where she's from. She visits a couple times a year. But I think some disciples are at the lake, maybe. Summer camp just ended last week, so this is like transition time before the regular school session starts. Freedom time." She flicked on a light switch and started down a hallway.

"So you kids just do whatever you want this week?" Aunt Ruth trot-trotted a little to catch her, the suitcase wheels spinning sprays of dirt and grass on those shiny floors.

"I mean not really. We just don't have as many group activities, but we still do our Bible study and one-on-one sessions." She stopped at a closed door, which had two things taped to it: a poster of the Christian rock band Audio Adrenaline and a Xerox copy of the Serenity Prayer, the purple ink so faded and the paper so yellowed and curled that it somehow had gained an air of history, almost of authenticity.

Jane tapped the door with her clipboard. "This is you. And Erin. She's in Bozeman with Rick."

Aunt Ruth *tsk-tsk*ed her head some. She still hadn't come to terms with the roommate thing. Who could blame her? I hadn't either. I'd been given her name earlier in the week and I'd been regularly picturing my new roommate, Erin, as a bespectacled, chubby girl with unruly curls and a smattering of acne across her perpetually flushed cheeks. Erin would be a pleaser. I just knew it. She would be working hard, asking God to help her so that the grungy but holy men in that poster on our door might actually do it for her—goose bumps on her neck, a prickle across her chest. Praying to Jesus to help her want them the way she had that girl from her study hall, from her science lab. *He's a tall drink of water* she would tell me about some male movie star, some action hero, and then she would giggle. Erin would most definitely be a giggler.

We were still waiting outside the door. Jane nodded at the

handle. "You can go in," she said. "We don't lock anything here. The doors aren't usually even shut, but since no one's in there, it's fine, I guess." She must've seen my face because she added, "You'll get used to it."

I couldn't quite believe her.

Erin's half of the room was done up in lots of yellows and purples: a yellow bedspread with purple pillows, a purple lamp with a yellow shade, a massive bulletin board with a yellow-and-purple-striped frame, the whole thing collaged with snapshots and Christian concert tickets and handwritten Bible quotes.

"Erin's from Minnesota. Big Vikings fan," Jane said. "Plus she's a second year, and she's earned some privileges you don't have, I mean with the posters and whatever." She looked at me, shrugged her shoulders. "Yet. You'll get them eventually. Probably, anyway."

My half of the room was sterile and blank, and I hadn't really brought much to change that. We put my bags on the new-looking twin mattress. I wasn't sure if I was supposed to unpack right then, so I just pulled out a few random items and set them on my desk hutch: a stack of brand-new notebooks and a box of pens, purchased by Ruth; Kleenex; a picture of Mom and Dad and me one Christmas; Mom's pre–Quake Lake picture; the picture of Margot and Mom, which Ruth had looked at sort of funny while inspecting my luggage but had let me keep. *Make an effort,* I thought. I added my *Extreme Teen Bible.*

Ruth was examining that big bulletin board. She seemed to be noticing my lack of color in the face of all that was the Viking Erin. Maybe it made her a little sad for me. She reminded me to grab the reading lamp and alarm clock from the Fetus Mobile before she left with them.

"I think you're going to do really well here, Cammie. I mean it." She reached out to put an arm around me and I stepped away from her, pretending that I had a sudden and compulsive interest in looking out the window I'd be looking out all year. The view was unbelievable, so there was that, anyway.

Thank God Jane got us out of there. "Would you like to stop by the dining hall? Rick thought you might be hungry. There's sandwich stuff."

"Sounds good," Ruth said, already out the door.

Jane squeaked fast behind her. I paused at the bulletin board. There was one girl repeated in every photo. Had to be Erin. I was right about everything but the acne. Her skin was as clear as those girls in Noxzema ads, maybe due to her prayers before lights out. *God grant me flawless pores. God grant me a healthy glow.*

• • •

We were only just finished with egg salad on white when a big blue van pulled up outside, and the sliding door with the silver God's Promise logo slid open, and my fellow diseased poured out like a rush of holy water to pass over me and cleanse me and envelop me into their stream.

It was *Hi, I'm Helen. We're just so glad that you're here.* And *I'm Steve. We just bought tons of Cap'n Crunch. Are you into Cap'n Crunch? So good.* And Mark and Dane said they'd show me the lake, and Adam said he'd heard that I was a runner, and that he ran in the mornings and had seen tons of elk and deer and even a moose once or twice. *And those things are freakin' huge.* And it was these tight little embraces, and touching my arm, and these shiny, shiny eyes, and everyone smiling at me like we were all plastic characters out of some board game like Candy Land or Hi Ho! Cherry-O. And the thing I kept thinking was: *Is it really okay to be doing all this touching?*

I looked at Jane, who seemed just as royally awkward, that

271

camera still hanging from her neck, and I checked to make sure, in all this goodness and light, that her fake leg hadn't suddenly healed itself, sprouted anew and perfect and pure. It hadn't. That was something.

The Viking Erin was the last off the van. She stepped from it like it was a carriage once sprung from a pumpkin, all these bright-eyed well-wishers her subjects, her court, and me the new lady-in-waiting. She was confident in her denim overalls and sandals, her curls shiny and healthy; everything about her—even her roundness, her softness—made her seem somehow healthy. Maybe I was totally wrong about this girl. Maybe she was their leader?

She shrieked when she saw me. And then the giggle, a trajectory of such giggles. As we hugged, she said everything that prayer on her door, that bulletin board, had told me she would. How she was so glad to again have a roommate, and so glad we would take this journey together, and so glad that I was athletic, because she had been really trying to become so herself. I was more pleased with me in that moment, in the actualization of my intuition, than I would be for weeks.

But while Erin was cheerful and pleasant, she lacked a certain something that some of her equally affectionate class- mates did not. I just couldn't place it, that something. I studied Jane's face, tried to read it. One final embrace from Adam shrouded me briefly in a sweet, sticky smell that I struggled for a moment to identify, but only because of my surround- ings. In the embrace's release I caught the scent again. Unmistakable. Marijuana. These homos were high as kites.

Ruth was over with Reverend Rick, who was in his rock- star weekend attire of jeans and a T-shirt, and when we caught glances, he gave me a big smile and a wave. He seemed just the same as he had when he'd visited Gates of Praise. And Ruth wouldn't know this smell if she was handed a joint. If she was handed a bong. Were they all high? Was Pastor Rick high too? I couldn't get a read on Jane. She was talking with the Cap'n Crunch guy about the group's purchases. A couple of them were already dispersing to their rooms, to the kitchen. *Freedom time*, Jane had said. I would have taken my high outdoors.

Despite how unnatural the movement, I leaned in close to Erin as she listed off various furniture arrangements we might try in our room, *for fun*. I pretended like I was having trouble hearing her. "So you're all about the Vikings, huh?" I asked, inhaling deeply. Nothing except dryer sheet–smelling overalls.

"You know it! Don't worry—you'll get decoration privileges soon. Maybe you'll become a Vikings fan in the meantime." Erin started up a lengthy question-and-answer session, and for the second time that day, it was Jane who played my rescuer.

She was just so authentic with that clipboard. "Sorry, you two," she said. "Rick needs to meet with your aunt. He said I should finish showing you around."

I thought that I was done with Jane as semidisinterested tour guide, but seeing the clipboard, the implied authority of the good preacher, and Erin was off to our room. She couldn't wait, though, she told me, until we could *just gab and gab*.

Jane said something to Reverend Rick. He nodded at me again, everything just so, well, cool, relaxed. Then Jane took me to the hayloft of the main barn. She struggled climbing the ladder, its wood old and gray, but she struggled like it was a common thing. I could tell she came here often. Me a townie kid and always discovering things of such importance in barns.

"So now you've met your fellow sinners," Jane said as she motioned for me to sit at the loft's edge, which I did, while she settled in next to me. She had to put her hand against a post to do it, but she was surprisingly nimble. Everything was surprising: Jane, the place itself. "Any thoughts, observations?"

I just went for it. Why not? "Were they *all* high?" I asked as our legs swung free over the edge, Jane's with that squeak every second and a half or so.

She laughed a small laugh. "Good for you," she said. "It's not everyone—there's actually only a few of us repeat offenders."

"So you too?"

"Yeah. Me included. You didn't think Erin was one, didja?" Jane did this little smile, but not at me. Out at the barn.

"No. I figured that out pretty quick." I flicked pieces of hay over the edge just to watch them flutter and sail. "Doesn't Reverend Rick catch on? A couple of them smelled like they came straight from Woodstock."

"He can't smell. Not at all. He hasn't ever been able to—since birth. You'll hear all about it. He loves to find meaning in his not being able to smell." Jane flashed a quick picture of some falling hay. She used that camera like a whip.

"What about everybody else?"

"You just met them. They don't need to get high. God is the best high, right?" Jane actually hooked my eyes to hers with that line. But she wouldn't let them stay that way.

"Why don't they tell on you?"

She smiled to herself again. "Sometimes they do."

"What does that mean?"

"You'll see. Whatever you think this place is, you'll be in for a surprise. I mean it. You just have to be here for a while and you'll understand."

"It's not like I have a choice," I said. "I'm stuck here. This is where I am."

"Then I'm guessing you'll want in."

"With what?"

"The pot," Jane said, so matter-of-factly.

I hadn't thought it would be this easy. Or maybe it wouldn't be easy at all, but she had offered. "Absolutely," I said.

"Do you have any money?"

"Some," I said. We weren't supposed to bring any money with us; that was in the manual. But I'd rolled about $500 worth of lifeguarding cash and leftover bills from Dad's dresser drawer, twenties and fifties, into tight little bundles barely thicker than chopsticks, and I'd hidden those in various locations throughout my luggage, so that even if some of them were found, others might escape.

Jane was messing with the straps and buckles on her leg, pulling at things. It was grossing me out. The stump was all covered with a brace and padding, but I was afraid that if she didn't stop messing with it soon, it wouldn't be.

She noticed me noticing this. "I keep some of the stash in my leg. I have a little compartment hollowed out. You'll get over it."

"I'm fine with it," I said, throwing lots of hay and not looking.

"No you're not. But you will be after a couple of hits." In her fingers was a baggie with a good amount of pot in it, and also a soapstone pipe.

I was impressed. "I'm impressed," I said.

Jane packed the pipe like someone who had done it plenty of times before, replaced the bag, and pulled forth a red Bic. "I'm resourceful. I'm actually a bit of an off-the-land type, you know? I was born in a barn."

It seemed like the setup for a punch line. "Oh yeah. You and Jesus."

"Exactly," she told me, exhaling, passing the pipe.

It was strong but harsh, potent is maybe the word, though

not necessarily enjoyable going in. My eyes watered immediately.

"You'll get used to it," Jane said as I hacked like a sick cat.
"I do the best I can for what's essentially ditch weed."

I nodded at her, squinting, and tried again, let the smoke fill
me up while closing my eyes, passing her the pipe before letting
myself fall back into the hay. "Where do you guys buy from?"

"From me. I grow it a couple of miles from here, just
enough to last us the winter. If we're careful," she added
before sucking in again.

I propped myself up on my elbow and studied her as she held
in the smoke. "No shit? You're the resident weed farmer?"

She passed the bowl again and settled herself down in the
hay with me. "I just told you; I'm an off-the-land type."

"So how'd you end up here?"

Jane raised her eyebrows in what I guessed was supposed
to be a mysterious way. "The tabloids," she said, offering
nothing else.

"Like because of your name?" I asked.

"Sort of. Not exactly."

Jane was relishing this moment, I could tell. She'd been
around long enough to see new students come to Promise and
leave Promise, and she knew exactly what I was looking for:
her story, her past, the sequence of events that had led her to
this place to be saved, just like me. Something about being
sent to Promise made me desperate to hear her tell it, to hear
all the stories of all the students, right up to the part where
their parents, their aunts, whoever, drove down that road and
into the parking lot to drop them off. I don't know why the
desperation, exactly. I still don't know. Maybe it was feeling
like we all had shared history, somehow. That understanding
somebody else's path to Promise would help me make sense of

my own. What I know is that all of us, *all of us*, collected each other's pasts and shared them, like trading Garbage Pail Kids cards—each one wackier and stranger and more unlikely than the next. But I don't think anybody's ever quite trumped Jane's.

Her whole story was suspended in the thick fog of strong pot and a hot August afternoon in a hayloft, so the way I remember things, and the way she told them, might not be one and the same. But that doesn't matter so much as the realization I had while she was telling it—namely that my own past maybe wasn't nearly so movie-of-the-week as a lifetime in Miles City had convinced me it was.

• • •

Jane was raised until the age of eleven on a commune just north of Chubbuck, Idaho. The way she told it, it was as if roadies for the Grateful Dead had crossed with some Amish, and this place was the result. It was good land, left to one of the founders by a grandfather. The commune citizens dug crystals of quartz and amethyst out of the ground, polished them up, sold them at touristy gem shops or art fairs. They grew corn and carrots, Idaho potatoes for sure, and hunted deer and elk. Jane's mother was a beauty, a dark-haired woman from New Mexico, and she was the commune's princess, loved by all. And given all that loving, Jane had two dads.

At a place like that, Jane told me, paternity tests meant nothing. Who can truly claim ownership of a soul? Of a life? Shit like that. One possible father was Rishel—the commune mechanic with watery eyes and a slouchy walk and always a roll of all-cherry Life Savers in his back pocket. The other possibility was Gabe. He was some sort of professor. He'd work at a community college for a semester teaching literature and poetry and then spend the next semester on the commune. He rode a Vespa and had a little beard, smoked a Sherlock Holmes pipe mainly as a prop.

Somehow those men, who in high school might have slunk away from one another in an empty hallway, found respect for each other out there on that commune. Or at least something like respect. The naming of the baby was only a minor roadblock.

Rishel wanted Jane, for his mother: a wedding-cake maker from Chubbuck who had put her head in her bakery's oven after finishing a five-tier. Gabe wanted Jane for, you guessed it, his own mother: a breast cancer–surviving meter maid from Saratoga. And there was no question of the last name, Jane would take her mother's, and it was Fonda, and they had all enjoyed *Barbarella* (for varying reasons—Gabe: ironically; Rishel: genuinely), so there you go. Jane Fonda it was.

Gabe called the name a triumph of postmodernism.

Rishel called the name simple and straightforward. Plain. A good choice.

Jane Fonda was born in the commune barn in December, with a retired ER nurse named Pat pulling her free. Pat was apparently the nurse straight outta *Romeo and Juliet*, loud and self-assured, with a mass of gray braids and pink hands like slices of ham. Pat and her lover, Candace, a retired cop, had recently moved to the commune to spend their pensions toward the good of the whole. Before Idaho they'd lived on one of the lesbian separatist Womyn's Lands in Southern California, owned and run by several of Berkeley's Gutter Dykes. Pat and Candace had enjoyed their time in a womyn-only utopia until they'd headed to Canada for a folk festival, stopped to see friends in Chubbuck, and just never quite made it back.

Pat and Jane Fonda were close. Then Pat died in a snow-mobile accident, the same accident during which Jane mangled her leg. So in one afternoon, there went her leg, from the knee down, and there went her nurse and role model. Gabe hadn't been back on the commune for maybe two years before that, and Rishel never knew quite what to say about tragedy without still sounding like *The Farmer's Almanac*.

Not on the night of Jane's birth, not at all, but later, Jane's mother would glean from the evening all kinds of Christian significance. The manger, the month, the bright starry night, even the trio of wise-ass commune musicians plucking out tunes to birth by and passing around a pie for all to share. No one could ever quite get straight why Jane was born in a barn in the first place. They had a couple of cabins, several warm tepees.

"Because it was God's hand," Jane's mom had later decided. Jane's mom was sticking with that.

After that snowmobile accident, soon after, Jane's mother found Christ in the supermarket checkout line. She was on commune "nongrowables" detail that week: toothpaste, TP, and Tampax. One of those shock papers caught her eye—a supposed picture of Jesus on the cross had formed in a dust cloud over Kansas. And why the hell not? If crystals could be powerful and chanting could make you whole, then why not? And the other featured article on the cover of that tabloid? A story about Hollywood Jane Fonda's difficulties filming her new workout video: *Jane Fonda's Pregnancy, Birth, and Recovery Workout*. Jesus and Jane Fonda on the cover of one magazine, right there, staring her down in the checkout lane: It was too much to be just coincidental.

Jane's mom, now with a cripple for a daughter, was ready to leave the commune, to do her believing from a suburban split-level with a Dairy Queen close at hand. She was never entirely okay with Pat and Candace, even before the accident. Some things were just more unnatural than others. She blamed the dead Pat, maybe rightly, for Jane being a cripple, and for maybe infecting her daughter with something more. Just a few days before the supermarket tabloid she had discovered Jane with the red-haired, toothy daughter of one of the commune's newest families. Both girls had their shirts off, playing "chiropractor," they said. (The new girl's father was one.) But they were too old for playing doctor. So Jane's mom did something about it. And they moved. And this time, her mother married a good man: a church-going, lawn-mowing, youth T-ball–coaching man. And it wasn't too many years later that Jane Fonda wound up at Promise.

"But what did you do, specifically?" I asked Jane that day in the hayloft. "To land you here, I mean. What was the final act?" She'd long since put the pipe back into her leg compartment. We'd been up in the thick heat and sweet stink of that loft for close to an hour, maybe longer. I hoped that Ruth was looking for me, that she had been looking for me for a while, that she was ready to drive off and leave me but couldn't because I was nowhere to be found and still technically, at least for another few minutes, on her watch.

"What didn't I do?" Jane said. "That's the typical stuff, anyway. I just told you all the good parts."

I shrugged my shoulders. That "stuff" she was leaving out didn't seem typical to me.

"What? You want to hear about how I was *still* playing doctor with girls at fourteen? Only nobody calls it playing doctor when you're fourteen. Besides, what I was doing with those girls was more gynecologist than general practitioner."

I laughed. "Your mom caught you again?"

Jane shook her head at me, like I was way slow on the uptake. Probably I was. "She didn't need to catch me with anyone. I was living my sin right out loud. I was calling myself a proud member of Dyke Nation, and I got a friend to use her brother's electric razor to shave off all my hair. I tried to hop a Greyhound to the coast, either coast, wherever, more than once. You can't *catch* somebody doing something they're not hiding."

I asked the inevitable question. The only one left to ask. "So are you *cured* now?"

"You mean you can't tell?" Jane asked, doing that weird grin she did so well, the one that didn't reveal anything.

I would have thought of something to say back to her, but Pastor Rick and Aunt Ruth came into the barn. They looked up at the two of us, parked there at the edge of the loft. Rick smiled his dimpled, rock-star smile. Ruth looked calm. Well, calmer than she had looked when we'd arrived.

"Isn't this nice out here?" Ruth asked. "All this fresh air."

"We're very blessed to have these grounds," Rick said. "We make good use of them, huh, Jane?"

"Indubitably," Jane said.

"It's a beautiful place, it really is," Ruth said. "But I suppose . . ." She looked up at me.

I looked right back down at her, trying to reveal nothing, just like Jane. Nobody said anything for lots of seconds.

Then Rick asked, "You've got a long drive ahead of you?" He didn't say what some adults might have—*Your aunt has a long drive ahead of her, Cameron*—to scold me, to make a point, to back up Ruth. He could have, but he didn't.

"I do," Ruth said. "Though I'm just going to Billings tonight. I have a Sally-Q party there tomorrow afternoon."

She explained Sally-Q to him while Jane and I stood up, brushed away the straw stuck to us. Rick pretended to be interested in what Ruth was saying about *tools for women*. Or maybe he wasn't pretending at all.

At the ladder, as she was maneuvering her leg onto the top rung, Jane said to me, quietly, "You're not going to feel any better if you're wretched to her as she's leaving."

"How do you know what I'll feel like?"

"I know whole bunches of things," Jane said. "And that I know."

• • •

This was our good-bye: out, alone, next to the FM, the breeze down from the mountains still cool and spicy, the sun still hot, glinting off the white paint of the hood, Ruth hugging me tight, already crying a little, and me with my hands shoved in my pockets, refusing to hug her back.

"Rick and I talked about this anger you have toward me," Ruth said into my neck. "You have so much anger in you."

I said nothing.

"The worst thing I could possibly do right now is give up on you because I let your anger get to me. I won't do that to you, Cammie. I know that you can't see it now, but *that* would be the terrible thing to do. Not bringing you here; giving up on you."

I still didn't say anything.

Ruth put one of her hands on each of my shoulders and pushed back from me, held me at arm's length in front of her. "I won't do that to you. Your anger with me won't change my mind. And I won't do that to your parents' memory, either."

I jerked out from under her grip and stepped back. "Don't talk about my parents," I said. "My parents would never send me to a fucked-up place like this."

"I have an obligation you can't understand, Cameron," Ruth said, keeping her voice level and calm. And then, more quietly, she said, "And to be clear, you don't know everything there is to know about your mom and dad and what they'd want for you. I knew them both for a much longer time than you did. Can't you even consider for a minute that this is exactly what they would do in this situation?"

What she said wasn't any profound thing, but it landed on me like a football tackle all the same. It was just the place to hit me to make me feel weak and stupid and guilty, and most of all, afraid, because she was right: I didn't know much at all about the people my parents had been. Not really. And Ruth had called me on it, finally, and I hated her for doing it.

Ruth kept going, "I don't want to leave you this way, with all this anger between us—"

But I didn't let her finish. I took a step toward her. I made myself look right at her. I was careful and slow with my words. "Did you ever think that maybe it was *you* coming that made me this way? Maybe I would have been fine, but then every single choice you've made since they died was the wrong one?"

The face she made confirmed just how terrible my words were, and they were lies, of course. But I couldn't stop. I didn't stop. I got louder. The words just came and came. "Who do I have but you, Ruth? And you let me down. And now you have to send me here to try and fix me, quick, before it's too late. Before I'm fucked up for good. Quick! Fix me, fix me fast, Jesus. Heal me up! Quick, before it sets in for life!"

She didn't slap me. I so wanted to head back into that fake lodge with a bright, hot, red slash across my face. But Ruth didn't slap me. She stood sobbing tears more genuine than any I'd ever seen her cry over me. I believed that, the authenticity of those tears. Those sobs kept on coming, even as she got into the FM and pulled away. I could see her heaving great sobs through the window, unable to look at me, or unwilling, and I felt that, finally, finally, I had actually done something awful enough to deserve that reaction.

• • •

That first night at Promise, after Erin and I had circled around and back again our lives and dreams and newfound purposes—hers authentic, mine made up for my present company (accept Jesus's help, heal, find a fella)—I listened to the sound of her breathing, the rustle of the covers on her bed, all the other sounds that you hear in the night when you're staying in a new place with a bunch of other people. I thought not of Coley but of Irene Klauson, away at boarding school on her first night, hearing these same kinds of sounds, thinking, maybe, of me. Eventually all that thinking and quiet noise put me to sleep.

I dreamed that the real Jane Fonda came to visit me at Promise. I hadn't rented that many movies with her in them, but *On Golden Pond* had been on TV one afternoon. Katharine Hepburn's in it, but she's already all-shaky Katharine Hepburn and she keeps telling her husband, an even older Henry Fonda, to look at "The loons, Norman! The loons!" Jane Fonda's supposed to be like the fuck-up daughter or something, but her dad is crotchety and old and probably has dementia, and so it's hard for them to resolve anything. Maybe they do eventually. I don't know, because Ruth came home and I had to help her with something and I missed the rest of it. I'm not even sure about the significance of the loons.

But in my dream Jane Fonda is all tanned angles and blond hair blowing out behind her without any real wind, and I'm giving her this tour of the place. We go through all the buildings, and then when we open the door to leave the cafeteria, all of a sudden we're at Irene Klauson's ranch at the height of the dinosaur dig, but it's like it is Irene's ranch and it isn't, the same way it always is and isn't in a dream. And when we step out onto the ranch, into the sunlight, and I smell the churned-up dirt, I think maybe Promise is where I'm supposed to be. Something about that smell, and the way the light is settling, seems somehow right.

I try to ask Jane Fonda about this, but she's not standing next to me anymore. She's over by the barn with some tall man in a gray suit. It takes me a long time to walk to them, like I'm walking on one of those blow-up bounce houses at a carnival, and the ground shifts up and down, the surface all puffed with air. Not until I'm almost right in front of them do I see that it's Katharine Hepburn Jane's talking to, but the young Katharine Hepburn, in a man's suit and tie with all that billowy auburn hair. And then Katharine Hepburn sort of bounds her way to me, over the ground, which is still more balloon than earth, and she says, "You don't know anything about God. You don't even know anything about the movies." Then she leans in with red lips too full and big to be real and she kisses me with them, and when we pull apart I have those lips between my teeth, but they're wax. They're the oversize wax lips like from Halloween and my teeth sink into them all the way up to my gums, and they're stuck there. And I want to say something, but I can't, because those lips are all stuck on my teeth and my mouth can't get around them to form the words. And then Jane Fonda is laughing from somewhere far off—though I'm not sure if that part is still my dream.

CHAPTER FOURTEEN

During my first one-on-one session we did my iceberg. I guess it was really a two-on-one, because both Reverend Rick and a woman I'd never met before that day, Promise Psychologist/Assistant Director Lydia March, were there "supporting" me. The language at Promise was all about support, not counseling: *Support sessions. Support workshops. Support one-on-ones.* I learned later that I wasn't special and that everybody at Promise got an iceberg of their very own. The icebergs were black-and-white photocopies of a drawing Rick had done. When he first handed mine across the table, it looked like this:

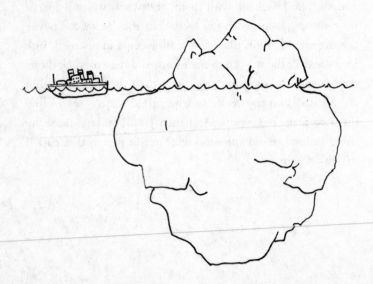

"So you know the deal with icebergs, right?" He asked.

I studied the picture for a little while, trying to work out where he was going with this. We had spent half an hour talking about how I was adjusting, about the classes I'd be taking, about any concerns I might be having in regard to the rules. We had not gotten to just how this place was going to cure me, and I didn't understand how this drawing might be a step in that direction. And not understanding bothered me; I didn't want to be tricked into revealing anything important. I stayed quiet.

Rick smiled. "Let me try that another way. What do you know about icebergs? Anything?"

I made my answer as unhelpful as I could, given my uncertainty. "I know that one spelled big trouble for the *Titanic*," I said.

"Yep," he said, smiling his smile, tucking his hair. "It did. Anything else?"

I looked again at the drawing. I kept looking. This was weird.

"Surely you know something more about them," Lydia said. "Enormous islands of ice adrift in the oceans." She had an English accent, and not that I knew anything about the variations of such accents, but hers was clearly more of the refined, posttransformation Eliza Doolittle variety than the pretransformation flower peddler Eliza Doolittle variety. "Think about the expression *tip of the iceberg*," she said.

I looked at her. She didn't smile. She didn't look mean, necessarily, but serious, all business. She had one of those faces with too many sharp points, her nose, her cheekbones, severely arched eyebrows; and she wore her hair pulled back supertight to her head, like the backup faux-guitar-playing women in that Robert Palmer video, so it seemed like her forehead went on forever. She did have great hair, though. It was really white, like a perfect shade of white, *Unicorn Tail* or *Santa's Beard*, and with it all pulled back tight like that, into a ponytail, it looked somehow futuristic, like she might have come off the *Enterprise*.

"Tip of the iceberg," she said again.

I had just heard that expression recently but couldn't remember where, and I didn't have time to think about it with them both looking at me with such expectation. "You mean because so much of it is below the surface?" I asked.

"Exactly," Rick said, smiling even bigger. "You nailed it. We only see about an eighth of an iceberg's total mass when we view it from above the surface of the water. This is why ships sometimes got in trouble, because the crew thought that what they were seeing on the water seemed pretty insignificant, manageable, but they weren't prepared to handle all the ice below the surface."

He reached over and slid the drawing back across the table and wrote a couple of things on it, then slid it back over to me. Next to the pointed mass located above the water's surface it read: *Cameron's Same Sex Attraction Disorder*. He had also written: *Family, Friends, Society* above the ship.

Now I could see where this was going.

"Would you say that the tip of the iceberg, in this drawing, anyway, looks pretty scary to the people on the boat?" He asked.

"I guess," I said, still looking at the paper in front of me.

"What does that mean, *you guess*?" Lydia asked. "You need to answer these questions with a bit of reflection. We can't support you if you aren't going to put forth any effort."

"Then yes," I said, looking at her and speaking deliberately. "The iceberg's tip, as it is drawn in this picture, features many sharp angles and pointy protrusions, and it is looming ahead of the ship in a precarious manner."

"Yes," she said. "It is. That wasn't so hard. And because it's so big and so scary, it's all the people on the ship want to focus on. But we know it's not the real problem, is it?"

"Are we still talking about the drawing?" I asked.

"It doesn't matter," she said. "The real problem for the people on the ship . . ." She paused to tap-tap her finger on the drawing, right on top of the words *Family, Friends, Society*; then she took that same finger and pointed it at me, getting me to look at her face, before continuing. "The *real problem* is the massive, hidden block of ice holding up that scary tip. They might manage to steer their ship around the ice above the surface but then crash directly into even bigger problems with what's beneath. The same is true for your loved ones when it comes to you: The sin of homosexual desire and behavior is so scary and imposing that they become fixed on it, consumed and horrified by it, when in actuality, the big problems, the problems we need to deal with, they're hidden away below the surface."

"So are you gonna try to melt away my tip?"

Reverend Rick laughed. Lydia did not. "Something like that, actually," Rick said. "But *we're* not doing anything; you're going to do it. You need to focus on all the things in your past that have caused you to struggle with unnatural same-sex attractions. The attractions themselves shouldn't be so much the focus, at least not right now. What's important is all the stuff that came before you were even aware of those feelings."

I thought about how young I was when I first considered kissing Irene. Nine. Maybe eight? And there was my crush—you could call it a crush, I think—on our kindergarten teacher, Mrs. Fielding. What could have possibly happened to me to make me "struggle with same-sex attraction" by the age of six?

"What are you thinking?" Rick asked.

"I don't know," I said.

Lydia sighed big. "Use your words," she said. "Your big-person words."

I decided I hated her. I tried again. "I mean, it's interesting to think of it this way. I haven't ever really, before."

"To think of what?" Lydia asked.

"Homosexuality," I said.

"There's no such thing as homosexuality," she said. "Homosexuality is a myth perpetuated by the so-called gay rights movement." She spaced out each word of her next sentence. "There is no gay identity; it does not exist. Instead, there is only the same struggle with sinful desires and behaviors that we, as God's children, each must contend with."

I was looking at her, and she at me, but I didn't have anything to say, so I dropped my eyes to my iceberg.

She kept going, getting increasingly louder. "Do we say that someone who commits the sin of murder is part of some group of people who have that identity feature in common? Do we let murderers throw themselves parades and meet up in murderers' clubs to get high and dance the night away and then go out and commit murder together? Call it just another aspect of their identity?"

Reverend Rick cleared his throat. I kept looking at my iceberg.

"Sin is sin." She seemed pleased with that, so she said it again. "Sin is sin. It just so happens that your struggle is with the sin of same-sex attraction."

I could hear Lindsey in my head telling me to say *Really? Well, if homosexuality is just like the sin of murder, then who dies, exactly, when homosexuals get together to sin?* But Lindsey wasn't sitting there with the two of them. And Lindsey wasn't exiled to Promise for at least a year. So I kept the Lindsey part of me quiet.

"How are you feeling about all this?" Rick asked. "We're throwing a lot at you, I know."

"I'm good," I said, too quickly, without thinking about his question at all. I added, "Well, maybe I'm fine." I had a headache. The room we were in, this little meeting space off Rick's office, was just big enough for the table and three chairs we now occupied, and the small space smelled too thickly, too sweetly, of the potted gardenia sitting on a shelf beneath the window, all shiny leaves and maybe half a dozen blooms, some of them already brown and decaying on the stem. Being there made me almost wish for Nancy the counselor's office: the couch, the celebriteen posters, the bites of food from the office staff, the lack of sin indicated by my presence.

"So what do I do with this?" I asked, holding up my iceberg.

Rick pressed both his palms to the table in front of him. "We're going to spend your one-on-ones, as many as it takes, attempting to fill in the stuff below the surface."

I nodded, even though I wasn't sure what he meant by that.

"It will be hard work," Lydia said. "You'll have to confront things I'm sure that you'd rather not face. One of the most important first steps is for you to stop thinking of yourself as a homosexual. There's no such thing. Don't make your sin special."

Lindsey in my head said, *Funny—my sin seems pretty fucking special considering that you've built an entire treatment facility to deal with it.* What I said out loud, though, was "I don't think of myself as a homosexual. I don't think of myself as anything other than me."

"That's a start," Lydia said. "It's uncovering just who the 'me' is, and why she has these tendencies, that will be the challenge."

"You'll do just fine," Rick added, smiling at me his

genuine Rick smile. "We'll be here to support you and guide you through all of it." I must have still looked doubtful, because he tacked on "Just remember that I've been right where you are too."

I was still holding my iceberg. I shook the paper back and forth a few times, fast, and it made that cool, sail-flapping noise paper makes when you shake it like that. "So I should take this with me?"

"We'd like you to hang it in your room," he said. "You'll write on it after each one-on-one."

That iceberg was my first, and only, decoration privilege for the following three months. I hung it directly in the center of the bare wall on my side of the room. I started looking for everyone else's icebergs, now that I knew what to look for. Sometimes disciples (we were supposed to call ourselves disciples and to think of ourselves as disciples of the Lord and not just fucked-up students) who were further along in their programs would have partially buried their icebergs beneath the typical kinds of ephemera that show up on teenagers' walls—though the posters and flyers and pictures belonging to Promise teens had more to do with Christian activities and bands and less to do with, say, naked cowboys or Baywatch girls. But adolescent collages are all sort of the same, regardless, and the iceberg photocopies were distinctive enough that I could eventually spot them.

Written in the ice below the surface on each disciple's picture were phrases and terms that didn't make much sense to me until my own one-on-ones progressed and I started writing similar kinds of things.

I studied everyone else's *below-the-surface* troubles with such regularity that I can remember some of them pretty much word for word:

Viking Erin (my roommate):

> Too much masculine bonding with dad
> over Minnesota Vikings football. Jennifer's
> extreme beauty = feelings of feminine
> inadequacy (inability to measure up),
> resulting in increased devotion to Girl
> Scouts, attempting to prove my worth (as a
> woman) in inappropriate ways. Unresolved
> (sexual) trauma from seventh-grade dance
> when Oren Burstock grabbed my breast by
> the water fountain.

Jennifer was Erin's sister, and there were some pictures of her on the bulletin board. I didn't blame Erin for feeling inadequate: Jennifer was a stunner. I asked Erin about why they let her decorate with Minnesota Vikings colors and memorabilia if it was such a problem area for her.

She had her answer all worked out. She'd obviously spent some time on it, because she said it just like I'm sure Lydia had said it to her oh so many times. "I have to learn to appreciate football in a healthy way. There's nothing wrong with being a woman who is a fan of football. I just don't want to look to my football bond with my father to confirm my sense of self, because the confirmation confuses my gender identity, since the activity we're bonding over is so masculine."

Jane Fonda:

> Extreme, unhealthy living situation at
> commune—Godlessness, pagan belief
> systems. Lack of (stable and singular)
> masculine role model in upbringing until
> adolescence. Inappropriate gender modeling

and "accepted" sinful relationship: Pat and
Candace. Early exposure to illegal drugs
and alcohol.

Adam Red Eagle:
Dad's extreme modesty and lack of physical
affection caused me to look for physical
affection from other men in sinful ways. Too
close with mom—wrong gender modeling.
Yanktonais' beliefs (winkte) conflict with
Bible. Broken home.

Adam was the most physically beautiful guy I'd ever met.
He had skin the color of coppered jute and eyelashes that
looked like a glossy magazine ad for mascara, though you
couldn't often see them because of his black, shiny hair, which
he let hang over his face until Lydia March would inevitably
come at him with a rubber band stretched out between her
thumb and pointer finger, saying, "Let's get it pulled back,
Adam. There's no hiding from God."

Adam was tall and he had long muscles and he held himself like a principal dancer with the Joffrey, all grace, all
refined power and strength. Sometimes we ran the trails
together on the weekends, before the snow came, and I
found myself checking him out in ways that surprised me.
His father, who had only recently converted to Christianity
"for political reasons," Adam said, was the one who'd sent
him to Promise. His mother opposed the whole thing, but
they were divorced, and she lived in North Dakota, and his
dad had custody and that was that. His father was from the
Canoe Peddler band of the Assiniboine, a voting member
in the consolidated Fort Peck Tribal Council, and also a

much-respected Wolf Point real estate developer with may-
oral ambitions, ambitions that he felt were threatened by
having *a fairy for a son.*

> *Helen Showalter:*
> Emphasis on me as athlete: maleness
> reinforced with softball obsession (bad).
> Uncle Tommy. Body image (bad).
> Absent father.

> *Mark Turner:*
> Too close with mother—inappropriate
> bonding (with her) over my role in church
> choir. Infatuation with the senior (male)
> counselors at Son Light's Summer Camp.
> Lack of **appropriate** physical contact
> (hugging, touch) from father. Weakness
> of character.

It wasn't difficult to tell Reverend Rick the things I knew
he was looking for me to say. He would shut the door to his
office and ask about my week and my courses, and then we
would start up wherever we had left off and I would tell him
some story about me competing with Irene, or about how
I hung out more with Jamie and the guys than with girls
my age, or something about Lindsey's influence over me. We
talked about Lindsey a lot—her big-city powers of suggestion, the enticement of that which is exotic.

It wasn't that I was lying to Rick, because I wasn't. It
was just that he so believed in what he was doing, what we
were doing, whatever it was. And I didn't. Ruth was right: I
hadn't come to Promise with a "teachable heart," and I had

no idea how to go about making the heart I did have into the other version.

I liked Rick. He was kind and calm, and I could tell that when I told him yet another story about my being rewarded and encouraged for masculine behaviors or endeavors, he thought we were really getting somewhere, that this "work" was benefiting me, and that I would eventually come to embrace *my worth as a feminine woman* and, in doing so, open myself up for *Godly, heterosexual relationships*.

Lydia, on the other hand, was sort of scary, and I was glad that, at least for now, I had one-on-ones with Rick. I'd heard people describe someone as "prim and proper" before, but Lydia was the first person I think I would have used those two words to pin down. When she led Bible study, or even if I saw her in the dining hall (which was not that big a room at all, certainly not a hall), or wherever, she instantly made me feel like I was sinning right then, pretty much just by being alive, by breathing, like my presence was the embodiment of sin and it was her job to rid me of it.

By Thanksgiving my own iceberg looked like this:

There were nineteen of us disciples that fall, which was an impressive six more than the year before. (Ten of the disciples were returners.) Twelve guys, seven girls, plus Reverend Rick, Lydia March, four or five rotating dorm monitors and workshop leaders, and Bethany Kimbles-Erickson—a twentysomething, semirecently widowed teacher who drove her grunting maroon Chevy pickup from West Yellowstone Monday through Friday to oversee our studies. (She and Rick were also now dating. Very chastely.) Out of the nineteen of us there were, at any given time, at least ten disciples really committed to the program, to conquering the sins of homosexual desire and behavior, to melting their iceberg tips in the hopes of eternal salvation. The rest of the disciples got along pretty much the way that I did: faking progress in one-on-ones, amicable interactions with staff, and burning off steam through a series of sinful, thereby forbidden, thereby secret interactions with each other.

At first, the constant scheduling, the routine of the place, was the hardest thing for me. After years of running wild with Jamie, with whomever, being unable to lock my door, to take off on my bicycle, to put in a video and watch it three times in a row, felt like the worst kind of punishment: way worse than meeting once a week to talk with Reverend Rick.

If we weren't in chapel, we were in the classrooms. There were two, and they each had a bunch of small tables and plastic chairs, a big whiteboard up front, the requisite ticking clock and pull-down maps, standard classroom fare; but when you looked out the windows, it was still all blue-purple mountain range and picture postcard, and the land and sky went on forever and ever, and every single time I looked out the windows too long, I felt like I was disappearing. And I looked out those windows for too long all the time.

Bethany Kimbles-Erickson didn't teach so much as she corrected homework and occasionally might clarify something if one of us raised our hands while reading or working silently. The quiet in the classrooms was how I imagined a monastery. At times it was so thick and solid, I would scrape my chair back as hard as I could and go to sharpen my pencil, or to get a book I didn't even need, just to break it. They ran things this way mostly because we weren't all in the same grade and had come from different schools in different states, we had vastly different transcripts to consider, and it was next to impossible for someone to stand in front of the room and teach us ten different subjects at the same time. Our curriculum was mandated by the State of Montana and our sponsor school, Lifegate Christian, in Bozeman, where we would go in both November and May to take final exams. Study plans and learning goals were worked out one disciple at a time, and the whole thing was run as sort of an independent study in every subject. This was just fine with me. It meant a lot of "work at your own pace" time, which I liked, but some students definitely struggled, and Bethany would spend hours sitting next to those students, or crouched over them, or at a separate table where I guess she did her teaching one-on-one.

First thing every Monday she provided each of us with photocopied packets of homework and reading assignments tailored to the state requirements for students at our grade level. To complete this homework, we used textbooks from the Promise library, a series of four six-shelf bookcases that held a bunch of older-edition textbooks and a set of encyclopedias, some other reference books, a shelf of "classic literature," and two or three shelves of books on Christianity, as well as current and back issues of *Christianity Today* and *Guideposts*. I'm not sure what I'd been expecting, but the textbooks themselves weren't really any different from those I'd had at Custer. Actually, I'm pretty sure that the government/economics book was the exact same text used for that class at Custer. And although there were a couple of science books that specifically denied the fossil record as proof of the earth's nonbiblically correlating age, and also predictably discounted evolution as hogwash, there was also a book of essays by scientists who were evangelical Christians, such as Robert Schneider, essays that actually made the case that one can believe in evolution without denying the theological notion that God created the world and all that is in it. Finding that book on the shelf surprised the hell out of me. It made me wonder who had made sure that it was there, who had advocated for its inclusion.

If we weren't in the classrooms, we were on cooking, cleaning, or evangelical detail. The first two are obvious, and I got pretty good at casserole making for twenty plus. We did several versions with cans of soup and Tater Tots, onions, and hamburger, and also a few with cans of soup, rice, chicken, and peas. These mixtures came out of the oven bubbly and brown and so heavy that it took two of us in pot mitts to lift the jumbo-size baking dishes to the counter. We also did a lot of instant pudding for dessert, and that made me think about Grandma.

Evangelical detail is maybe less obvious. Two or three of us would be assigned to work in the main office copying and then addressing the Promise newsletter to donors, and also addressing donation request cards from these master lists of Christians from all over the country. Exodus International supplied us with those master lists, and also videos and worksheets and workbooks. They were the "largest information and referral ministry in the world addressing homosexual issues." Occasionally, during evangelical detail, one or two of us even got to talk on the phone to major donors about the kinds of progress we were making, but for those first months I wasn't asked to do that.

If we weren't working a detail, we were in a workshop, a one-on-one, or a gender-appropriate activity. This meant lots of group sports for the guys, and fishing and hiking expeditions, or they'd take them to one of the neighboring ranches and let them help out for a few hours, really cowboy it up. For us girls it meant trips into Bozeman to various beauty parlors run by typically big-haired ladies sympathetic to our unique beauty needs, and also baking sessions and occasional visits from Mary Kay or Avon ladies. Once, a woman from the labor and delivery unit at Bozeman Deaconess Hospital did a presentation about pregnancy and infant care that featured dolls sort of similar to the Rescue Annie infant mannequins I had used in lifeguard training, and that made me think about Hazel. And Mona. And Scanlan. But not really all that much about the joys of motherhood, which seemed to be the point of the presentation.

If we weren't in a one-on-one or work detail or doing a gender-appropriate activity, then there were of course study hours and journal/reflection hours and prayer/devotional hours, and every other Sunday we would load into one of the two Promise vans and head into Bozeman for worship services at the Assembly of God megachurch: Word of Life. We had our own pews and were semicelebrities among the congregants. On alternate Sundays, though, Reverend Rick just did the sermon in our own chapel, and some of the local ranchers and their families might join us. As much as I liked excursions away from the compound, I preferred the Sundays we stayed at Promise, the entire congregation mostly just us disciples. At Word of Life I felt like a big, shiny, obvious goldfish, a goldfish well known to have homosexual tendencies, so basically a big, gay goldfish in a tank with eighteen other such goldfish, wheeled in and parked in a pew for two hours, much to the delight of the crowd. At those services it seemed like everyone who looked at me, whether they smiled, or glanced away, or clasped my hand during the meet and greet, was thinking: *Is this the service that's going to do it for her? Is she already becoming just that much less gay, and is this the service that will tip the scales to the side of the Lord? Might it happen before our very eyes?*

Despite all the routine, those of us who wanted to break the rules still managed to do so. We did have scheduled free-time hours on the weekends, and sometimes study hours could be manipulated, and depending on who you got stuck with for that week's work detail, so could those hours.

Jane Fonda, Adam Red Eagle, and I were the potheads. Steve Cromps could be convinced; he just wasn't a regular. Mark Turner, who happened to be Adam's roommate, had recently caught Jane smoking up on the path to the lake, and though he'd not tattled, at least not yet ("because," Jane said, "it just isn't his way"), he certainly hadn't accepted her offer to partake, either. Mark was the son of some big-deal preacher from Nebraska—a guy with two thousand–plus members in his congregation, and his billboards, complete with his picture, lined the interstate. I found out about all of this early, not because Mark bragged, or even spoke about it, really, but because he was basically an expert on the Bible, a child prodigy on the subject, and so he was often asked to recite passages during our Sunday services. What I'd noticed about him was his seriousness. But Jane thought there was more to him than that. He was, she said, "someone to be wary of." I didn't know quite what she meant by that, but this was typical of my understanding of Jane's observations.

Adam and I helped her harvest the last of her marijuana plants in latish September. She had been complaining that the early frosts had already killed off a bunch of them and that she wouldn't get what was left picked in time to save it. I offered to go with her and she gave me one of those unreadable looks of hers, but then she said, "Why not."

When I met her outside the barn at the time she'd said to, carrying the beach towel she'd told me to bring, Adam was there with her, chewing on a tiny pink straw from the Capri Sun juice pack he'd purchased the last time we'd all gone to Walmart. Adam was almost always chewing on something, and so Lydia was almost always telling him to try harder to "curb his oral fixation."

"He's coming with us," Jane said, Polaroiding Adam and me in that whip-fast way of hers.

"You might want to work on the part where you say *cheese*," I said. Jane barely ever showed anyone her pictures, though she had to have hundreds and hundreds of them. She'd already taken dozens of just me, but I'd only seen maybe three of them.

"What would be the point if you were posed?" she asked, removing the Polaroid and putting it in the back pocket of her khaki pants before taking off toward the forest. Adam and I followed behind.

"Apparently you can't interfere with art," he said to me when we were a few yards down the trail. I didn't know Adam well enough to tell how much of what he said was a joke, or if there was any joke to it at all.

"You think Jane's an artist?" I asked.

"It doesn't matter what *I* think," he said, sort of smiling at me around that straw. "Jane thinks she's an artist."

Jane stopped and turned around to face us. "Hey, wacka-doos—I am an artist. And amazingly I can hear you from all the way up here, these six feet in front of you."

"Artists are sensitive," Adam said, doing the hushed voice of some nature-documentary host who's spotted something wild. "They must be treated with care and sometimes caution."

"Indeed," I said, trying on the voice for myself. "Observe how the artist appears skittish and out of control when confronted by insensitive nonartists."

"Those who lack talent are understandably frightened and jealous when in its presence," Jane said, and then she took another picture of us: snap, flash, spit.

"The artist reacts with hostility," Adam said, "using her advanced image-capturing device to stun and immortalize her victims."

"My aesthetic approach requires spontaneity," Jane said, pocketing that picture and resuming her march forward. "You two feel free to look up *aesthetic* when we get back to the lodge."

"Does it have something to do with homosexual attraction?" I asked, not as loudly as Jane but loud enough. "Because it sure sounds like it does, and if that's the case then no thank you, sinner. I know your tricks."

"We'd better look up *spontaneity* while we're at it," Adam said, definitely smiling now.

"For sure," I said. "And *approach*. And *requires*. It's weird that we've been able to understand anything the artist has said to us, what with her massive vocabulary."

"I haven't, actually," Adam said. "I'm not even sure where we're going right now. She tried to explain it to me, but too many big words, you know? I just nodded my head in the places where it seemed like I should."

Right then I decided that Adam was my favorite person at Promise.

Farmer Jane's pot patch wasn't far from one of the main

hiking trails, the one to the lake, but Jane knew what she was doing, which plants to grow near, how to disguise her path. Even after following her out there and spending better than two hours tooling around among the smelly crop, I probably couldn't have found it on my own without taking forever to do so. I guess that Jane knew this or she wouldn't have brought us along.

The beach towels we each had draped over our shoulders served two purposes. The first was to make it appear, should we happen upon fellow disciples, that we were headed to one final, autumnal dip in the lake before the full brunt of fall and winter stopped our swimming. The second was for transport: to conceal the harvest. Jane also had a backpack with her for that purpose.

Lots of the leaves on the trees had already turned to shades of yellow, from canary to yield sign to lemon sherbet, and the fall sunlight was distilled through those leaves, the rays bouncing into the shadows around us in that chunk of forest. As we walked, Jane whistled songs I didn't recognize. She was a good whistler and a fast walker, the squeak of her leg comforting, like the chug of a train or the whir of a fan, a piece of machinery doing its job. I liked following just behind her; she had such purpose to all of her moves.

Her patch was in a kind of clearing, at least enough of one for the plants to get their required daily amounts of sunlight. I don't know what I had been expecting, but all these tallish, übergreen shrubs lined up in neat rows and bearing the actual, real-life leaves I'd seen immortalized on so many patches sewn to backpacks and black-light posters and CD cases were surprisingly impressive. And fragrant. Adam seemed impressed too, kind of smiling at the whole spread, the two of us shaking our heads at Jane's industry.

"All this by yourself?" I asked.

"It's best all by yourself," Jane said. She moved in between the plants, carefully, delicately, trailing her fingers just against their leaves. Then she looked off into the thick cover of the woods, all purposefully, her head high, like a stage actress, and said, "'And when that crop grew, and was harvested, no man had crumbled a hot clod in his fingers and let the earth sift past his fingertips. No man had touched the seed, or lusted for the growth. The land bore under iron, and under iron gradually died; for it was not loved or hated, it had no prayers or curses.'"

"What is *The Grapes of Wrath*, Alex?" Adam said.

"No idea," I said.

"We read it last year," Adam said. "It's good."

"It's more than that. It's necessary," Jane said. "Everybody should read it every year." Then she let herself slip back into Jane from wherever she had just been. She stuck her hands on her hips and said, "And here are the two of you, thinking that it just showed up, somehow, in little plastic Baggies, all shredded and ready for your rolling papers."

Adam began to sing, "There was a farmer grew some pot and Artist was her name-o."

Jane and I both laughed.

"And Homo was her name-o," I said. "It just sounds better."

"Not to Lydia," Jane said.

"What's her deal?" I asked.

"She's impersonating the mother from *Carrie* as a career choice," Adam said.

"Hardly," I said. "She's not nearly dramatic enough, and I've never once heard her say 'dirty pillows,' either."

"That's only because you don't flash your dirty pillows like you should," he said. I laughed. We were standing at the edge of the pot patch, right where the forest floor of trampled leaves and undergrowth met the dark, churned-up soil that Jane had obviously worked and worked. I think neither of us was quite sure if we were officially welcome to enter the patch or not.

Jane had knelt next to a massive bush of a plant and was doing something to the stalk, but I couldn't quite see what. "Lydia's a complicated woman," she said from behind that plant. "I think she's actually sort of brilliant."

Adam made a face. "But completely deluded."

"Sure she's deluded, but you can be both," Jane said. "I'll tell you what: She's not one to be trifled with."

"God, I love you, Jane," Adam said. "Who uses the word *trifled* but you?"

"I bet Lydia would," I said.

"Of course she would," Jane said. "It's a good word; it's very specific in its meaning and it sounds nice on the tongue."

"I can think of something else that sounds nice on the tongue," Adam said, doing a goofy double elbow jab at me, and then adding, "bu-dum-chhh."

"So we can just take this as our confirmation that you're every bit the man half today," Jane said, and Adam laughed, but I wasn't really sure what she meant by that.

"Lydia's hard work must finally be paying off," he said in this Paul Bunyan kind of man voice.

"Where did Lydia even come from?" I asked.

Adam switched to a really bad English accent and said, "From a magical land called England. It's far, far across the sea—a place where nannies travel by flying umbrella and chocolate factories employ tiny, green-haired men."

"Right," I said. "But why's she here at Promise?"

"She's the bankroll," he said. "She's majority stakeholder in Saving Our Fucked-up Souls Enterprises."

"Plus she's Rick's aunt," Jane said, standing and walking

toward us, a couple of acorn-size buds in her hand.

"No way," I said, exactly at the same time Adam said, "No shit?"

"She is," Jane said. "Rick talked about it once during my one-on-one, or it came up somehow, I don't remember; it's one of those things that's not specifically a secret but they're specifically secretive about it."

"God," Adam said, "Aunt Lydia the ice queen. I bet she gives things like wool socks as Christmas gifts."

"Wool socks are completely useful," Jane said. "I'd be happy with a big box of wool socks beneath the tree."

Adam laughed. "That's possibly the dykiest thing you've ever said."

"Which is saying something," we both said in unison.

Jane shook her head. "Practicality has nothing to do with sexuality."

"That would be nice on a T-shirt," I said. "What with the rhyming and all."

"Yeah, you mention that to Lydia when we get back," Adam said. "I'm sure she'll have a batch printed in no time."

"Where'd she get her money?" I asked.

"I haven't the foggiest," Adam said. "But my personal theory is that she was a big porn star back in England and came here to escape her past and use her hard-earned devil money to do God's work."

I nodded. "Sounds reasonable."

"I'm ever so slightly enamored of her," Jane said, digging for something else in her backpack, eventually producing a small stack of lunch-size paper bags.

"Of course you are," Adam said, overdoing his laugh. "Why wouldn't you be?"

Jane stopped rummaging, looked at him. "She went to

school at Cambridge, you know? Hello: the University of Cambridge. Have you heard of it?"

"Yeah I have," he said. "That's in Cambridge, Florida, right?"

I laughed at both of them.

"Who cares where she went to school?" Adam said. "All kinds of crazies go to good schools."

"I think she's mysterious," Jane said, resuming her digging. "That's all."

"Come on," Adam said, bending all the way over at the waist as if entirely exhausted by Jane's reasoning. "The solar system is mysterious. The CIA is mysterious. The way they record music onto records and tapes is fucking mysterious as all get-out. Lydia's a psycho."

"Recording sound isn't really that mysterious," Jane said, walking back over toward us, so, so careful of her plants. "It's a fairly straightforward process."

"Of course it is," Adam said. "And of course you know all about it."

"I do," Jane said, taking us each by the elbow and leading us into the patch. "But I won't tell you now because now is not the time. We came here to harvest."

For the next hour or so she showed us how to pluck the heavy green buds, carefully, and how she wanted them wrapped in pieces of the brown paper bags she'd taken from the kitchen. She scrutinized things like the textures and colors on those buds, the little fibers, which Jamie had told me were called simply "red hairs" but which Jane referred to more accurately as the pistils.

She spoke like a botanist about using them to determine peak THC-to-CBD potency and thereby recognizing maximal harvest time, but then she added, "It doesn't matter a whole heap because we're picking anything and everything that might even give us half a buzz while we're all snowed in during a blizzard come February."

"Hear, hear," I said to that.

"Hear, hear," Adam said.

"Hear, hear is right," Jane said back. "It's a boon for you all that my nature is to be a provider."

"It's the Christian thing to do," I said.

"Indubitably," Jane said. She stretched her neck and squinted at the sun, using the back of her forearm to wipe her brow, her face determined and proud, just like a sepia-tinged portrait of an Old West pioneer missionary woman come to convert the natives and settle the land, only this time the crop wasn't corn or wheat, and this time it was Jane who was in for conversion.

Adam waved a hairy, nearly golf-ball-size cluster of buds in front of Jane's face. "Are we allowed to sample the harvest, O wise Earth Mother?"

She grabbed the cluster from him. "Not what we're picking," she said. "We have to dry it first. But I came prepared, as usual, because my nature is to be a provider."

"And an artist," I said.

"Yeah, don't forget artist," Adam said.

"It's true that I am many things," Jane said, leaving the plot and heading just into the trees, leaning her back against the tall, thick trunk of a Douglas fir and sliding to the ground, where she rolled up her pants to the knee and unfastened her leg, which (she was right) by then I was used to seeing her do.

Adam and I settled in beside her while she packed the pipe. It was perfect there on the floor of the forest on an early-fall afternoon, getting high. It was almost possible for me to forget why the three of us were together, the sin we had in common, the reason for our friendship. Jane had a couple of those little green cans of apple juice with her, like from snack time in preschool, and she had a pack of beef jerky too, and we sat and ate our little pioneer-type meal and passed the pipe.

We were good with smoking and not talking. All of us did so much talking at Promise, even those of us who didn't really say anything in all that talking. Every so often a breeze would kick up and a few handfuls of those yellow leaves would flutter to the earth, the light passing through them.

At some point Jane asked, in a lazy sort of way, "So have you started to forget yourself yet? Or is it still too early?"

I had settled onto my back to consider the almost overwhelming height of the firs and hemlocks as they poked like half-closed green umbrellas into the sky. And when Adam didn't answer, I sat up partway, leaned back against my elbows, and said, "You're asking me?"

"Yeah, you," Jane said. "Adam did summer camp, so by now he's all but invisible."

"I'm not sure what you mean," I said.

"Promise has a way of making you forget yourself," she said. "Even if you're resisting the rhetoric of Lydia. You still sort of disappear here."

"Yeah," I said. I hadn't thought about putting it that way, but I knew what she was getting at. "I guess I've forgotten some of me."

"Don't take it personally," Adam said. "I'm the ghost of my former gay self. Think the Dickensian Christmas Past version but with my face."

"I thought you were never a 'gay self,'" Jane said.

"You and word choice," he said. "I wasn't, technically. I'm still not. I was just using the most handy term available to make a point."

I did my best Lydia. "You were *promoting the gay image*

310

through the use of sarcastic comments and humor," I said. "I'm probably going to have to report you."

"Not the gay image," Adam said, with more seriousness. "No gay image here. I'm winkte."

I'd seen that on his iceberg and had wanted to ask him about it. "What is that?"

"Two-souls person," he said, not looking at me, concentrating, instead, on the long pine needles he was braiding. "It's a Lakota word—well, the shorter version of one. *Winyanktehca.* But it doesn't mean gay. It's something different."

"It's a big deal," Jane said. "Adam's too modest. He doesn't want to tell you that he's sacred and mysterious."

"Don't fucking do that," Adam said, throwing some of the nonbraided needles from his pile at her. "I don't want to be your sacred and mysterious Injun."

"Well, you already are," Jane said. "Put it in your peace pipe and smoke it."

"That's outrageously offensive," he said, but then he smiled. "It's the Sacred Calf Pipe, anyway."

"So you were like named this or something?" I asked. "How do you say it again?"

"Wink-tee," Adam said. "It was seen in a vision on the day of my birth." He paused. "If you believe my mother, that is. If you believe my father, then my mother concocted this *nonsense* as an excuse for my faggy nature, and I need to just *man up* already."

"Yeah, I'll just go with your dad's version," I said. "Much simpler."

"I told you we'd like her," Jane said.

Adam hadn't laughed, though. "Yeah, you're right," he said. "My dad's version is easier to explain to every single person in the world who doesn't know Lakota beliefs. I'm not gay. I'm not even a tranny. I'm like pre-gender, or almost like a third gender that's male and female combined."

"That sounds really complicated," I said.

Adam snorted. "You think? Winktes are supposed to somehow bridge the divide between genders and be healers and spirit people. We're not supposed to try to pick the sex our private parts most align with according to some Bible story about Adam and Eve."

I didn't know what to say, so I made a joke, my usual response. "Listen, so long as you remember that it's Adam and Eve, not Adam and Steve, you should be just fine."

Nobody said anything. I thought I'd blown it. But then Jane started giggling in that way you do when you're high.

And then Adam said, "But I don't know any girls named Eve."

Which made me giggle along with Jane.

And then he added, "Plus I already let Steve jerk me off in the lake last weekend."

"Then clearly you're the mother of all gay lost causes," which wasn't even that funny, really, but the three of us got on one of those hysterical-laughter trains that lasts for so long you can't even remember why you started laughing in the first place.

Eventually Jane reattached her leg and went to finish something or other in the patch, and Adam wandered off to somewhere, and I just stayed put. I listened to the small, high-pitched sounds of the tree swallows and the nuthatches, and smelled the smoke and the wet ground, the good, musty scent of mushrooms and always-damp wood, and I felt all the ways in which this world seemed so, so enormous—the height of the trees, the hush and tick of the forest, the shift of the sunlight and shadows—but also so, so removed. I'd felt like this since my arrival, like at Promise I was destined to live in suspended time, somewhere that the me I had been, or the me I thought I was, didn't even exist. You'd think that dredging up your past during weekly one-on-ones would do just the opposite and make you feel connected to those experiences, to the background that made you *you*, but it didn't. Jane had just called it *forgetting yourself*, and that was a good way of putting it too. All the "support sessions" were designed to make you realize that *your* past was not the *right* past, that if you'd had a different one, a better one, the *correct version*, you wouldn't have even needed to come to Promise in the first place. I told myself that I didn't believe any of that shit, but there it was, repeated to me day after day after day. And when you're surrounded by a bunch of mostly strangers experiencing the same thing, unable to call home, tethered to routine on ranchland miles away from anybody who might have known you before, might have been able to recognize the *real you* if you told them you couldn't remember who she was, it's not really like being real at all. It's plastic living. It's living in a diorama. It's living the life of one of those prehistoric insects encased in amber: suspended, frozen, dead but not, you don't know for sure. Those things could have a pulse inside that hard world of honey and orange, the ticking of some life force, and I'm not talking about *Jurassic Park* and dinosaur blood and cloning a T. rex, but just the insect itself, trapped, waiting. But even if the amber could somehow be melted, and it could be freed, physically unharmed, how could it be expected to live in this new world without its past, without everything it knew from the world before, from its place in it, tripping it up again and again?

CHAPTER FIFTEEN

In October, disciple Mark Turner and I were on evangelical detail together in the business office. I spent our first session on the newsletter, written by Lydia and Rick and photocopied onto sky-blue paper, the God's Promise logo in the corner, four pages of articles about our various outings and community-service projects, a full-page profile on one disciple. That month it was Steve Cromps. What I did for two hours was this: staple, fold, stuff, stamp, repeat, repeat. Mark, however, was sitting in a spinny desk chair calling big donors and doing the spiel. He did it well, probably the best of any of us, and I could tell that not even five minutes into his first call. He did it well because he believed what he was saying. I still didn't really know him at this point, but because he was Adam's roommate, what I did know for sure was that he was completely committed to being at Promise, to being cured. (And also that he wasn't a tattletale—as far as we knew, and we'd have known by then, he never told anyone about Jane and the joint he caught her with, so despite her *wariness*, he seemed an okay guy to me.)

That chair he was in that day seemed too big for his elfin features. He was probably just shy of five one and had dainty everything—hands and arms and legs—and a little face with mahogany eyes and perpetually pink cheeks and pouty little Hummel-figurine lips. He had a black binder full of things to say, answers to give to various questions: Q. *Do you really think that you're getting any better there?* A. *In my time at Promise I've already grown in my relationship with Jesus Christ. I continue to grow every day. And as I learn to walk with him, so too do I learn to walk away from the sin of my sexual broken-ness.* But he didn't need the scripted, staff-approved answers to questions, because all of Mark's answers were naturally staff-approved. I watched him close a call with a donor from Texas, a guy who liked to be called every month, I'd heard, and now Mark was talking Cornhusker football with him, telling a story about the last game he'd been at with his dad and brothers at Memorial Stadium in Lincoln on a perfect October afternoon not all that different from the day we were having, just a twinge of frost in the air, warm cider in their thermoses, the Huskers propelled to victory, of course, by the sea of red in the stands. I really did watch him tell it. I stopped midfold and looked up at him, though he didn't notice me. He was animated, his eyes bright, the arm not holding the phone gesturing; and as he talked about some fourth-quarter turnover that was "just exactly a rabbit from a hat but on cleats and Astroturf," I wanted to have been there with him, just like I know the Texas guy on the phone did. But I didn't even care about college football. That wasn't it. Mark was selling the dream of an all-American autumn afternoon with the family. And there was nothing fake or gross about it—it wasn't like a Ford pickup commercial with stars and stripes in the background. It was simpler than that, more genuine. I guess because he believed in it for real. Whatever *it* was.

The Texas guy must have thought so too, because he made another donation, right over the phone. I know this because Mark said, "That's very generous of you, Paul. I can't wait to tell Reverend Rick. We couldn't do this without your support. Not just people like you, but you yourself. I want you to know that. What you give means something very real to my salvation. And there are no words of thanks I can offer that are enough for that."

I don't know how you can say stuff like that and not sound at least a little bit like an asshole; I know that I would have, and I'd never say those words anyway. But Mark didn't ever sound like an asshole. Not to me.

When he'd finished that call, was scanning for the next number, I asked, "How much is that guy sending now?"

He didn't look up from his list. "I don't know exactly," he said. "He's gonna work out the details with Reverend Rick."

I could tell that wasn't all of it, but it wasn't worth bothering him over. "You're crazy good at those calls," I said.

"Thanks," he said, now looking up and smiling a little smile. "That's nice of you."

"It's the truth," I said. "If you have to be that good, they won't ever ask me to do it."

He smiled again. "I like doing them. It gives me a sense of purpose the other tasks don't offer."

"Well, if you keep pulling in donations, they'll always have you do it."

"That's not why I like making them," he said.

"I know," I said. "I get it." But I'm not sure I did.

"Okay," he said, and went back to his list, checked the number, and lifted the receiver.

"Did you mean it?" I asked, leaning forward a little, across the table, wanting him to stop.

He did. He kept the phone in his hand but pressed the dial-tone button with the other. "Mean what?"

"That being here is necessary for your salvation?"

He nodded, then said, "Not just me. It is for yours too."

I rolled my eyes.

He shrugged. "I'm not trying to convince you. That's not my place. But I hope you do become convinced."

"And just how does that happen?" I asked, my voice still a little smug, but I meant the question.

"You have to start with belief," he said, letting up the button, punching the numbers. "That's where everybody has to start."

I thought about that while he made his next calls, while I kept on with the newsletters. I thought about it during Sunday service at Word of Life, and during study hours in my room, with the Viking Erin and her squeaky pink highlighter. What it meant to really believe in something—for real. Belief. The big dictionary in the Promise library said it meant *something one accepts as true or real; a firmly held conviction or opinion*. But even that definition, as short and simple as it was, confused me. *True* or *real*: Those were definite words; *opinion* and *conviction* just weren't—opinions wavered and changed and fluctuated with the person, the situation. And most troubling of all was the word *accepts*. *Something one accepts*. I was much better at *excepting* everything than accepting anything, at least anything for certain, for definite. That much I knew. That much I believed.

But I kept on watching Mark, his calm ways, the sort of peace he seemed to have, even though he was at Promise, just like me, just like the rest of us. I bugged Adam about him all the time, to give me details—what he did when they were in their room together; what he talked about.

"I think the system is already working," Adam told me one evening when I'd been asking a heap of Mark-related questions that he couldn't really answer. We were on dinner shift together. We'd put two tuna-noodle casseroles in the oven, cleaned up the dishes, and snuck out to the hayloft for a quick smoke because we knew Lydia and Rick were both in one-on-ones.

"What system is that?" I asked, taking the joint from him but dropping it onto my lap as I did. I plucked it up, inhaled.

"The conversion of your sexuality," he said, taking the joint back. "I think you're nearing the proverbial breakthrough." He had a piece of hay between his lips already, his *oral fixation*, and he left it there even while he was toking.

"Why do you say that?" I asked.

"You haven't stopped with the Mark Turner questions for days," he said, smiling. "It's a tad tiresome from my end, but bravo—I'd say a full-on hetero schoolgirl crush. Any moment now I'm expecting to see you drawing hearts with his initials in your pink Trapper Keeper."

I laughed. "My Trapper Keeper's purple, not pink, loser."

"Details, details," he said, waving his hand. "It's the passion I'm concerned with. *L'amour.*"

I shoved him. "I don't have it bad for Mark Turner," I said. "I just want to figure him out."

Adam nodded like a counselor, like Lydia, and brought his hands together in a pyramid to his lips while he said, "Mmm-hmm. And to be clear: by *figure him out* you mean climb onto his erect penis, correct?"

I laughed. "Yes, that's it exactly," I said, but then I couldn't help myself; I *was* sort of obsessed with Mark Turner. "You don't think he's interesting? His seriousness or whatever? I can't even imagine him doing anything gay enough to get sent here."

Now Adam laughed. "What—because there's an official gay barometer now? His parents weren't going to send him, but then they caught him listening to Liza-with-a-Z for the third time that month, and that was it: finally he'd *done something gay enough!*"

"Well, that's how it works, doesn't it?" I said. "I mean pretty much like that."

He shrugged his shoulders. "I guess," he said quietly. "If your crime isn't bigger."

"Yeah," I said. We smoked in silence after that. I was thinking about Coley, of course, of course I was. I don't know what Adam was thinking about.

After a while he asked, "Who would it be for you, though, here, if not Mark? I mean to mack on?"

"God, I don't know," I said. "No one. I don't think anyone."

"Come on," he said. "If you were picking, though. If you were forced to."

I waited. I thought. "Bethany Kimbles-Erickson," I said, laughing, but meaning it.

He laughed too, his shiny black bangs across his face. "I can see that. It's the schoolteacher thing. It's a classic scenario. But of the student body now—who?"

"You say," I said. "This is your thing, so you say first."

"I've already hit it with Steve. A few times."

"Right," I said. "So Steve's your answer?"

"Not really," he said, looking right at me, wearing something akin to Irene Klauson's old dare face. "Maybe it's you."

My stupid blush, again, again. "Sure," I said. "Then the system's working on you, too. Glad to know it's not just me."

He did a face of exasperation. "I'm not gay, Cam. I told you. It doesn't work like that for me."

"It works like that for everyone," I said.

"That's a really small way of looking at desire," Adam said.

I shrugged. I didn't know what to say to that. I studied the gray barn wood, toffee and mint green–colored lichen grow-ing on it in places. I flicked some of it off with my finger.

"You wanna power-tunnel this?" he asked, holding up what was left of the joint, which wasn't much.

"I don't know what that is," I said.

"Yeah you do," he said. He gestured with the roach. "I flip this, put the lit end in my mouth and blow while you cup your hands around my face and inhale. People call it a shotgun, too."

"That's not a shotgun," I said.

"I beg to differ," he said.

"You touch lips when you shotgun," I said, taking the joint from him. "It's more like kissing. I'm pretty sure you already know that."

"That's baked frenching," Adam said. "That's some-thing else."

"Well that's what I want to do," I said.

"Are you sure?"

I nodded. Then I inhaled, for as long as I could, and that was for quite a while, thanks always to my swimmer lungs. Then I held it, and then I motioned to Adam and he brought his mouth to mine and we sealed lips and I exhaled. And then we kept on kissing for a while from there, for long enough that we burned the tops of the casseroles.

Kissing Adam wasn't like kissing Jamie, not exactly: it didn't feel like rehearsal for the real deal, for something bet-ter. But it wasn't like kissing Coley, either. It was somewhere in between, like kissing Lindsey, I guess, most like that. I liked it. I liked doing it, and I didn't have to pretend that it wasn't Adam I was with in order to like it. But I didn't, I don't know, I didn't long for it, either. *Longing* is sort of a gross word. So is *ache*. Or *yearn*. They're all kind of gross. But that's how I had felt about touching, kissing, Coley. It's not how I felt about Adam. And I know it's not how he felt about me.

• • •

Promise had rules, lots of rules, many of which I broke with regularity, and it wasn't too long before I was caught. It was a fairly minor infraction really, considering that I might have been apprehended smoking pot or making out with Adam (which we'd taken to doing on occasion after our first go at it, up in the hayloft, out in the woods, clothes mostly on), or openly mocking the practices and *support* of Promise in exactly the sarcastic, textbook *gay-image* kind of way that I was supposed to be ridding from my life. But it was none of those things. The Viking Erin caught me shoving a pack of really nice, twelve-color, fine-tipped, professional-grade markers into the back waistband of my pants, up under my shirt and sweatshirt, at the Montana State University bookstore while we disciples were there, waiting to watch a Campus Crusade Christian rock concert out on the main quad.

The thing is, I had plenty of money to pay for the markers, but I couldn't do that because (1) I wasn't supposed to have brought that money with me to Promise, and my work-detail money was low because it took forever to earn and I bought a lot of candy with it; and (2) Even if I'd used work-detail money and maybe borrowed against future earnings (which was occasionally allowed), all purchases had to be shown to a staff person, with receipt, before we boarded the vans back to Promise, and I would then almost certainly have to explain what I planned to do with the markers, which was a secret worth stealing for. Only I didn't know that Erin had wandered into the art supply section to find me so that we could "grab a good spot to watch the show."

"What did you just do?" she asked me, and before I could answer, she said, so loudly she was almost shouting at me, "You're stealing! You just stole something. You have to tell. You have to go and tell Rick right now."

"I haven't even left the store," I said, keeping my voice low in the hopes that she might follow suit. "It's not stealing until you leave the premises. Just let me put them back. Here, I'll do it right now."

I pulled free the markers and made a big show of placing them back on the shelf, with the other marker packs of the same variety, but it wasn't enough.

"No," she said. "No way. You were gonna steal them if I hadn't seen you. You had the sin in your heart, and that's what counts. You need to talk to Rick about it, or Lydia, because I don't want to tattle on you, but you need help with this." She was teary by the end of her little lecture, and I could tell that it had taken something out of her to confront me the way she just had.

I tried to talk like I thought Reverend Rick might, kindly but with authority. "Erin, do you really think I need to talk to someone about a pack of markers that I'm not even gonna take? They're back on the shelf."

Erin shook her head, her curls bouncing softly, her cheeks red. "I wouldn't be much of a friend to you if I turned a blind eye to your sin. It says in Ephesians, 'Let him that stole steal no more: but rather let him labor, working with his hands the thing which is good, that he may have to give to those in need.'"

"Seems like they're talking about a dude," I said, trying a smile.

Erin did not smile. She stood there blocking me from moving forward, her arms crossed in front of her chest, right over the picture of a bearded, muscle-bound Jesus bearing a cross that read: THE SIN OF THE WORLD. (She wore this shirt a lot. I had memorized the back of it too: in big, red letters, in the exact font used to market Gold's Gyms, was GOD'S GYM—OPEN 24/7.) It was hard for me to look at her shiny face as she stood there making what I knew she thought of as an absolutely necessary stand against evil for my salvation, so I looked at her folded arms instead.

A couple of college students in baggy flannel shirts with chunky, matted white-kid dreadlocks came down the aisle, brushing past us on their way to the oil paints, both of them noticing Erin's shirt, too.

"It's the Christian campus invasion," the shaggier of the two said to his buddy.

"Like the Crusades without the good times of murder and pillage," the buddy said back.

"And shit-fuck music."

At this last comment, clearly said with the express purpose of our overhearing it, Erin looked like she might begin to really cry, like breakdown cry.

I sighed and shook my head. "I'll go tell Rick," I said. "Not Lydia. But I'll tell Rick."

She nodded at me, then leaned in for a big Viking hug, and I could feel her damp cheek against my neck, smell her perfumey deodorant doing its job.

"It's the right choice," she said while still locked in the hug.

I didn't just do it because she was crying. I did it because I knew that if I didn't, she would have been compelled by her guilt, her need to get me *support*, whatever, to tell on me anyway, but that decision for her would have been unnecessarily cruel. Also, Erin and I had settled into a mostly comfortable routine as roommates. She talked on and on about anything, about everything, about all the time; but I got used to that and sometimes really liked having her there, a steady stream of one-sided conversation that I got very good at tuning in and out of. Erin wasn't a Mark Turner, at least she didn't seem so to me. Her faith was showy, a performance for herself as much as the rest of us. I didn't understand it, and I definitely didn't want to emulate it, but I appreciated all the ways she thought she was working the program, that pink highlighter squeaking across one passage after another, hoping the very next one might do the trick, convince her once and for all that she wasn't this wrong thing anymore. I wasn't yet ready to have her write me off as a lost cause. I liked her thinking we were somehow in this together.

Telling Rick was as painless as I had expected it would be: He thanked me for coming forth, hugged me, we prayed together. But he told Lydia, too, said that they had to put a star next to shoplifting in my file as a "problem area for sin manifestation." And Lydia didn't just pray it away, but instead informed me that this sin of stealing was symptomatic of some of those below-surface issues I still wasn't really dealing with, and now, in addition to my one-on-ones with Rick, I had to meet with her once a week, too. On top of that, my three-month probation period was due to be up in a matter of days, but this infraction cost me an "indeterminate additional amount of time" without mail or decoration privileges, and without calling home. Apparently I had a care package from Grandma and a letter from Ruth and a letter from Coley, of all people (opened, read, and approved by staff), waiting for me in the locked mail closet in the main office, but they would have to sit there awhile longer. Also, Aunt Ruth was notified of these developments, though that news actually pleased me a little.

While both Rick and Lydia did ask me why I felt the

need to steal markers when Promise had a couple of bins of art supplies in the study rooms, they accepted my answer of "wanting them for my very own and coveting their expense and quality." The truth was, while I missed watching movies and I missed listening to music and I missed the hospital and Scanlan and Grandma and Jamie, and Coley, of course her, I really pined for my dollhouse. Or not the dollhouse itself, maybe, but whatever it was I'd been doing to it for so long. Even as she'd boxed and bagged all the remnants of my perversion, Ruth hadn't touched the dollhouse, and I hoped (needed) for that to still be true in my absence: for that fucked-up dollhouse to be there waiting for me. I had been planning to use the markers I never got to steal as part of a substitute kind of dollhouse project, this one inside a couple of half-gallon plastic cottage-cheese tubs cleaned and now hidden beneath my bed. The cottage cheese was sold to Promise at cost by a family who went to the Word of Life church and who very much supported the mission of our conversion. This family ran a local dairy that sold everything from those tubs to pounds and pounds of butter and ice cream and other cheeses of the noncottage variety, all under the product line Holy Cow Creamery. Their packaging had a picture of a cow with a halo over its head and fat, somehow cowish wings growing from its sides. We were supposed to collect the empty tubs in stacks in the kitchen for the dairy to restock with more product, but I'd nicked two of them the last time I was on cooking duty, and I'd planned to take more. They were no dollhouse, but they were something. I'd already stolen some decoupage adhesive and Krazy Glue from Walmart during a visit, and sometimes I'd take scissors or paints from the study rooms and return them before anybody noticed; but I had been attempting to build a stockpile of my own supplies, and the markers were key, and then Erin had come along.

Filling those tubs with stolen bits and secrets and then hiding them beneath my bed, mere feet from nosy Erin, our door always open, *come on in*, was risky and stupid and I just couldn't help myself. I guess I didn't want to. I couldn't really make sense of what they meant as objects, though I did feel like there was plenty of meaning in the act of working on them; but I knew that someone like Lydia would think that she could decipher *me* through those tubs, that they were maybe physical representations of the below-water iceberg bullshit. And that was trouble. That was reason enough not to work on them, not to have them at all. But I did.

• • •

We did a big Thanksgiving meal, hosted the neighboring ranches, some people from Bozeman. Adam and I volunteered to do the potatoes the morning of, bags and bags of them to scrub and peel and cube and boil before mashing them with Holy Cow butter and cream. We smoked half a joint with Jane beforehand, and then sectioned off a little corner of the kitchen to ourselves. For an hour or so it was nutty in there, loud and hot and smelling (for everyone but Reverend Rick) like all the good holiday-food spices, like cinnamon and nutmeg, sage and thyme. It was fun too, actually, everybody with their tasks: a couple of people working on the turkeys and stuffing, Viking Erin making the requisite green bean and French-fried onion casserole, but quadruple the size most people would make. Rick had on this mix tape he liked with all these contemporary Christian bands, but some really cool old gospel songs too: Mahalia Jackson, the Edwin Hawkins Singers. I'd heard that tape enough times by then to sing along, despite myself. (We'd all heard it enough times.)

At one point Rick noticed me doing the chorus to "Oh Happy Day," which is just a hard song not to join in on. He was singing it too. He backed over to me, doing a kind of butt-wiggle jazz shuffle, his hands all gooped-up with sticky, precooked stuffing. He held them out in front of him like mitts or casts, like he was letting them dry there, and he leaned his head in toward mine so that we could harmonize, I guess, or maybe just imagine a microphone in front of us, we two some famous singing duo: Sonny and Cher or Ike and Tina, maybe Captain & Tennille.

Adam reached over, his potato peeler in hand. He stuck it in front of our mouths so we didn't have to pretend the microphone. Everybody else in the kitchen was clapping along with the choir on the tape and watching us. I took the potato peeler from Adam, gripped it in my best Mahalia impersonation, and closed my eyes, fuck it, belted like a pro. We finished out the song like that, increasingly louder, reckless, goofy as all get-out. My excuse was the marijuana, but Rick didn't have one other than being Rick.

Helen Showalter whistled hard when it ended. Told us to "Go on, you guys—sing another one." She sounded like an old trail boss as she said it (Helen was always sort of gruff when she was having a good time, a little hard and scratchy), and we weren't supposed to use *guys* when referring to any group with women in it, but Rick didn't correct her.

The song playing now, though, was some sappy Michael W. Smith track with too much synthesizer, and there was Lydia, walking into the kitchen with a big box full of dinner rolls and two pies from the bakery in town, and the moment was over.

"I don't do encores," I said.

"Encores of what?" Lydia asked.

"Nothing," I said.

"You missed it," Viking Erin said. "Reverend Rick and Cameron were performing."

"I am sorry I missed that," Lydia said, unpacking the box. Then she added, fairly quietly, mostly to the big sack of rolls in her hand, "Though I'd say Miss Cameron is almost always performing."

Rick kind of gave her a look, just a small one, like *lay off* or whatever, but I don't think she noticed. "No excuses, next time we do karaoke," he said, smearing a swipe of stuffing along my cheek like an older brother or a youngish uncle might. Rick was big on karaoke nights. Promise had its own machine. Maybe it was Rick's personal machine. I'd never sung when we'd had them before.

The kitchen cleared out pretty soon after that, but Adam and I weren't done. You never have too many mashed potatoes come Thanksgiving. We were mostly silent, sort of entranced by the monotony of peeling and chopping.

At some point Adam asked sleepily, "So how come you never talk about the girl?"

"Who?" I asked.

"Oh, don't do the thing where you pretend to be confused. The girl. Your downfall."

"Who says there was just one?" I said, doing a corn dog wink at him.

"It's always just one," he said. "The one—the big one. The one who changes everything."

"You first," I said, but I was stalling and he knew it.

"This tedious modesty of yours," Adam said. "You've already heard all about Mr. Andrew Texier and his fondness for my outstanding oral abilities. A fondness diminished only by his fear of his father. And my father. And the entire Fort Peck football team."

"He didn't deserve you," I said.

"Few do," he said. "Very, very few. C'mon, spill it." He whacked me on the ass with his peeler. "It's not polite to keep a lady waiting."

"What do you want me to talk about? She's there and I'm here."

"Yes, but she sent you here. That's a story."

He'd been reading my iceberg. "You've been reading my iceberg," I said.

"Of course," he said. "But you said something once too." He rolled a couple of just-peeled potatoes across the counter to me.

"I don't remember that."

"Too much ganja," he said.

He had me there. "She didn't send me here so much as it was a fucked-up situation and she panicked and I got sent here," I said.

He raised his eyebrows. "So where'd they send her?"

I swallowed, then said, "Nowhere."

"That is a fucked-up situation."

I didn't say anything to that. We were done with the peeling, finally. Adam rinsed off his peeler, moved the trash can over to just beneath the counter, and used his hands to wipe the slippery skin pieces into it, where they fell in delicate swishes and heavy, wet clumps, rattling the plastic trash bag as they went.

"Was this mystery girl the fairest in all the land?" he asked.

"Sort of," I said, chucking potato chunks into the big pot, letting some water splash up over the top. "She's definitely pretty."

"Our nameless Snow White," he said, gesturing out to the empty room. "Lover of ladies."

"Snow White," I said back. "Mistress of movie night."

"And breaker of hearts," he said, rubbing me on the shoulder, for effect, not for comfort.

"She didn't break my heart," I said.

Adam made the twisted-up face of visible doubt.

I tried to mimic the face back while I shook my head no. "I just told you, it was a fucked-up situation right from the beginning."

"That doesn't mean anything where hearts and breaking are concerned."

Right then Rick came back into the kitchen, hands washed, shirt changed into a holiday button-down. He hung his REAL MEN PRAY apron (a gift from Bethany Kimbles-Erickson) back on its hook, just behind where Adam and I stood.

"Come with me a second, Cam, will you?" he asked, touching my elbow. To Adam he said, "She'll be right back. I won't leave you alone on spud service for long."

"We're almost done anyway," Adam said. "It's just boiling and mashing from here on out."

Rick and I walked in silence down the hallway to the main office. There he pulled a set of keys from his pocket and opened the mysterious mail closet. He gave me the box from Grandma, a little crushed and dented on one side, but there it was. He also gave me a stack of rubber-banded letters. The one from Coley I'd known about; the two from Grandma I could have guessed at; the other four, from Ruth, I hadn't either known about or guessed at.

Rick again locked the closet. "We told them to go ahead and write you, if they wanted to, just that we didn't know for sure when you'd be ready to get them."

"Why am I ready now?" I asked. The letter from Coley was on top, her handwriting right there beneath my fingers. I pulled and snapped the rubber band against the envelopes a few times.

"I like what I saw in the kitchen this morning," he said. "Breakthroughs don't always happen during a session. Sometimes it means more if they don't."

"Why is singing along with a tape a breakthrough?" I asked. *Snap, snap, snap.*

Rick covered my snapping hand with his. "It was more than that and you know it. For three minutes you didn't have that steel wall up around you you've had since you got here. The one that's back up now. You were letting yourself be vulnerable, and it takes vulnerability to change."

"So now I can just have these?" I asked, lifting up the stack of letters a little. They felt weirdly dangerous in my hands.

"Yes, absolutely. They're yours. You can have decoration privileges, too. Some. You can have some. Lydia has a sheet with the specifics, and she'll go over that with you."

"I don't feel any more cured," I said. It was my most honest moment with Rick up to that point.

Rick shook his head, closed his eyes, and overdid a sigh of exasperation. "We don't cure people here, Cameron. We help them come to God."

"I don't think I feel any closer to God, either," I said.

"Maybe God feels closer to you," he said.

"Is there a difference?"

"Read your mail," he said, opening the door. "Just don't leave Adam for too long. I promised him."

I checked out the care package first. Grandma had sent two bags of mini Halloween candy bars and a pack of nice white cotton running socks, and she'd baked brownies and blondies. They were now weeks old, but I tried a couple anyway. They tasted old. One of her letters talked all about how hard it was to bake with sugar and not eat anything she was making, but that she was willing to do it for me. Then she admitted that she actually had eaten some of the brownies. *But not too many.* The other letter was mostly about a new family of squirrels that had taken up residence in the backyard, and her alternating fascination and annoyance with them. She didn't mention where I was or what I might be doing. Ruth's letters, on the other hand, were all about how much I was missed, how much she was praying for me, how hard she knew this must be for me. Then I got to the one she must have sent first, and it was about how terrible she'd felt when driving away from Promise back in August, how she'd had to pull over to get herself together, and she chose the spot just before the sign to Quake Lake and it was like God was telling her to go there. Just to go there. So she did.

I hadn't been to Q.L. since I went back with some flight attendant friends once in the eighties. This time I pulled into a scenic overlook and just cried and cried while I thought about what you had just said to me about how I probably am partly to blame for your condition. I had to really wrestle with that, Cameron, and I still am wrestling, but I'm willing to admit that maybe I am. I can take some of that blame. I can shoulder it. I saw you turning from God and acting out, unsure of yourself, and I let you go your own way instead of actively helping you to become the woman I know you can be. I so want a life of happiness for you. I hope one day you'll see that this is the path to that happiness and, more importantly, to a lifetime beyond this one.

I re-enveloped that letter and put it aside. I took in a
breath. I reached for Coley's, considered all the elements:
the stamp, a Virgin Mary Christmas version—it was sort of
early for that; her neat penmanship; the soft, pearl-pink color
of the envelope. I pulled free the letter, one single sheet of
matching pink stationery.

Dear Cameron,

    *I am writing this letter because Pastor Crawford and
my mother think it is a good thing for me to do. I am
currently working through what happened between us, as
I know you are too, but I am very angry at you for taking
advantage of our friendship in the ways you did, so angry
that it makes it hard even to write to you. I thought that it
was too soon for you to hear all of this, but Pastor Crawford
asked the people at Promise and they said that it's good
for disciples to see how much their sin can damage others
and the destruction it can cause. I feel so sick and ashamed
when I think of the summer. I've never known shame like
this. I don't know how I let you control me like you did.
It's like I wasn't even me anymore. My mother started
saying that even during Bucking Horse Sale, and she was
right. I'm not saying that I didn't sin, too. What I'm
saying is that you already had this thing in you. I didn't.
However, I was weak, and you saw that and used it to
your benefit. I sometimes just sit and stare into space and
wonder why I did that, but I don't have any answers yet.
I'm working on them. Brett is being very supportive and
he even says that he's not mad at you, because he's a bigger
person and a better Christian than that. I know that you
will be home for Christmas and maybe by then I'll be
ready to see you, not alone, but at church, I mean. I don't*

know, though. I pray that you are finding GOD and in HIM are ridding yourself of this. I pray for you every night and I hope that you pray that I will heal from all of this as well. I have a long way to go. I feel like damaged goods right now.

Coley Taylor

I read it a few times to be sure that I got it all. The worst part was, somehow, that she had signed her last name. I put it back in its matching envelope. I put all the envelopes in the box from Grandma. I got up, took the box, shut the door to the office, walked down the hallway, counting my steps, making them even and precise. It took me thirty-eight to get to the kitchen. Jane was now standing by the counter, she and Adam laughing about something.

"Hey, hey, Patty Privileges!" Jane said, using a long-handled wooden spoon to point to the box in my hands. "You get anything good?"

I shook my head.

"Mail call, soldier," she said. "Who sent you what?"

"I got a letter from Snow White," I said.

Jane laughed and said, "Just Snow White, none of the other Disney princesses?"

But Adam said, "No way? They let her write you? Lemme see."

I handed it to him. He held it out so Jane could read it too. They did. Adam sort of gasped when he was somewhere in the middle; I don't know which line made him do it. Then they were finished reading, they must have been, her letter wasn't that long, but neither of them talked for a while.

Jane eventually said, "Well, she sure sounds like an enormous sack of good times."

Since she'd tried for a joke I tried for a smile. Neither quite worked.

Adam waited a little longer, and then he came over and put one arm around my shoulders, the letter in the hand at his side. He said, "I don't care what you say, if she hadn't before she has now."

"Has what?" Jane asked.

"Broken Cam's heart," he said.

"This girl?" Jane said, snatching the letter from him. "This Christian android–sounding thing?"

"She did," I said.

"Well then, you glue it the frick back together," Jane said. "You can't let her." She rattled the paper in the air, fast and angry. "Not this girl. No way, kids. Not pink-stationery girl."

She turned, letter in hand. She flicked on the garbage disposal, pushed up the faucet handle so the water ran full blast, and fed the letter, one big gulp, to the drain. It was gone in a single fast and crackly gurgle. Then she turned off the disposal, pushed down the faucet, wiped her hands on her pants like that process had been muddy or something. "There. Now there was no letter," she said. "That girl exists only as you want to remember her. I'd recommend not remembering her at all. That's it. There was no letter from a clone who spits out dumbed-down Lydia talk like a stupid parrot. Okay?"

I was maybe a little stunned.

Jane took the few steps to me. I was still there under Adam's arm. She took me by the chin and said, her face right up to mine, "Okay?"

"Okay," I said.

"Okay. Let's smoke again before we stuff ourselves," she said. "That's always a nice Thanksgiving tradition."

CHAPTER SIXTEEN

Christmas came just like that. I rode in a Promise van to Billings with a bunch of disciples. Everybody in there was catching a flight that they couldn't catch from Bozeman. A flight to some part of the country that wasn't Montana. Everybody but Adam and me. Aunt Ruth was meeting me at the airport to drive me to Miles City for two weeks of holiday visitation. Adam's dad was meeting him at the airport to do the same thing, just not in Miles City.

While we'd had a few feet of snow at Promise, once we cleared the Bozeman pass, a lot of the state was wanting for it. For most of the drive the land alongside the highway was barren, dead, browns and grays, the big sky that wintertime dirty white it gets, plum and blueberry and gray mountains sometimes off in the distance, but otherwise a world of cold dirt: a world on mute. We had the same Christmas album on repeat for at least a hundred and fifty miles before Lydia, riding shotgun, finally just turned the stereo off and we were left to listen to the wind alongside the van, the sound of the engine, whatever was playing in our heads.

Even though I knew, both at the time and after, that Jane's garbage-disposal show had been mostly a kind of magic trick, a big, shocking maneuver to keep me from drowning in the wake of Coley's letter, it had sort of worked. I guess sometimes you can recognize that you're being manipulated and still appreciate it, even respond to it. And there was the part about Jane being right too, that the Coley Taylor I'd known, or thought I'd known, the Coley Taylor from the last row of the Montana Theatre, from the bed of a pickup truck, was certainly not the same Coley Taylor now walking the halls of Custer High as a girl tainted by my perversion, a victim of my sin. Or maybe they were exactly the same girl, but even if that was true, she couldn't be the girl for me.

So I wasn't hoping, the way that I might have, say, in September, that she had written the letter just to pacify those in charge of her healing, and that once I was home she'd seek me out for a secret rendezvous, explain herself, her sorrow over having written it, over having told in the first place. I wasn't even hoping for a tearful reunion filled with apologies: even just apologies on my end and *I forgive you*s on hers. But I *was* hoping, just a little, for a single shared moment, maybe in the GOP vestibule, or maybe the coffee hall, a moment when we would be close to each other, just a few feet between us, a moment when we would be looking at each other, face-to-face. I wanted the moment, but if I got it, I hadn't yet decided what to say. Something brief. Something memorable. It was hard to whittle away all the buildup between us to get to one solid something worth saying. But there was something to be said, I was sure, and I thought about what that something might be for most of the ride.

Ruth and Grandma were waiting just inside the airport entrance by a silver Christmas tree decorated with dozens of aviation ornaments: a helicopter piloted by Santa, built-to-scale models of passenger jets, a parachuting elf.

Grandma looked like she should have been grinning at me from a box of cake mix or a jar of old-fashioned preserves—her cheeks rosy, her powdered plumpness oddly healthy looking. Her stomach looked a little smaller than when I'd left, actually, and her formerly tenaciously black hair was now at least half old-lady gray, maybe even sixty percent old-lady gray. It was sort of startling how fast it had turned, or seemed to have turned, in my absence, like a lawn overtaken by clover in just one summer.

She was sort of rocking back and forth in her tan SAS comfort shoes, all of her twittering with anticipation, and when I hugged her, she said, over and over, "Well now, you'll be home for a while. Now you'll be home a good stretch."

Ruth, on the other hand, didn't look so good. She was in a new (to me) nearly floor-length red wool coat, a shiny green-and-gold Christmas wreath brooch at the lapel; she was put together, of course, she was still pretty; but her hair seemed flat and thin, not the shiny, healthy curls I thought of her with, and her face was sort of slack and puffy at the same time, like a layer of skin-colored modeling clay stuck on wrong over her real skin, with makeup tastefully applied but not quite doing the trick.

We barely got in our hugs, the scent of Ruth's White Diamonds reassuring, when Lydia approached with some forms, instructions for my care. While they talked, a few feet away, I introduced Grandma to everyone.

"Good to meet you. Pleased to know ya. Good to meet you." Grandma double-clasped everyone's hands in both of hers as she said her hellos. Then she dug a tin with frolicking snowmen on it from the oversize quilted bag on her arm and opened it to reveal a layer of waxed paper. "Go on and pull it off, kiddo; you look thin enough to need 'em."

I did. It was filled with those cornflake holly wreaths you make with lots of butter and marshmallows and green food coloring, three Red Hots atop each. They were all stuck together, despite Grandma's best efforts. By the time Lydia and

Ruth joined us, we all had Grinch green–tinted front teeth.

"Have a Merry Christmas, Cameron," Lydia said, patting me on the back a few times. "Your aunt Ruth has a two-week plan for you. Try to stick to it."

I didn't have to answer her because Viking Erin pulled in for a big hug and said, "Write me, write me, write me! And call me, too. Or I'll call you!"

Adam said, "Now don't you come back pregnant," in my ear as he hugged me.

"You either," I said.

It was strange to see all the disciples walk off into the airport without me. It made me feel lonely in a way I can't quite explain, especially since I was going home for the first time in months. But I guess that says something, maybe more than something, about what home now meant to me.

• • •

Somehow Ruth didn't tell me her news during our late lunch at the Cattle Company (we all liked their beer cheese soup). Nor did she mention it during the entire trip to Miles City, snow flurries kicking up the closer we got to our exit, flurries that spit out their final flakes during our drive down Main Street, a drive through the early darkness that winter had flung over the town, strings of fat, colored lights crisscrossing above us, the oversize red bells and wreaths hanging from stoplights seeming just a little more garish than I had thought them the Christmas prior. But they were garish in a way that I sort of loved—they were usual, they were just as they always were. Ruth didn't even spill it when we pulled into the driveway, the house decked out like I'd never seen it, way more than my dad had ever done: every straight line, every angle had a string of white lights along it, every one, our house like a gingerbread cottage outlined in dots of white frosting. There were evergreen wreaths circled with red lights in the center of each window. There was a big wreath, a huge wreath, of silver bells on the front door.

"Holy cow," I said. "You've been busy, Aunt Ruth." I made myself say *Aunt* and was proud that I had.

"Not me," she said. "This is all Ray. He worked on this for two weekends. We wanted to have it looking nice for . . ." She stopped there.

"For Christmas?" I said, finishing for her even though I assumed that she must have meant for me, for my homecoming but just didn't want to announce it like that.

"Mmmmm," she said, using the remote to open the garage door, acting like it was taking all her concentration to get the FM in there without scraping it up.

And her news, her big news, waited for other things to happen too. It waited for me to say hello to Ray and to comment on how nice the tree looked (artificial, yes, but nice). It waited while the four of us sat awkwardly in the living room together, pink Sally-Q mugs of quickly cooling cocoa in hand, none of us talking about Promise, about where I'd been for months, but instead talking about the high school sports teams, about some babies born to families in the GOP congregation, about new Schwan's products. Ruth's news even waited for me to rediscover my room, my dollhouse still there, still hulking in the corner. I was touching some of my works, just running my fingers over the smooth coldness of the flattened coins, the weave of the gum-wrapper rug, sort of mystified by what I'd created, when she said, "Cammie?" from halfway up the stairs, and by the time I'd turned and said, "Yeah," she was in my doorway.

She had two long garment bags in her right hand and she was holding the hangers sticking out of their tops high above her head, her arm straight up in the air, so that the bags were hanging their full lengths.

"What are those?" I asked.

"So these are just choices," she said, maybe trying for the bubbly, enthusiastic tone that normally came naturally to her, but it was a shade or two off. She came into my room, laid the bags across my bed like she had those funeral clothes years before.

"Choices for what?"

"I want you to know that I was going to write you, but I didn't know if you'd even get to read the letter before coming home, because of the—the mail restriction or whatever it was."

"Because I got in trouble for not stealing some markers," I said. "For leaving them neatly on the shelf from whence they came." I just couldn't help myself. It was so comfortable to be flip with Ruth, so expected.

"But you were going to had you not been caught," she said.

"But I didn't."

She chose a corner of the bed to perch on, careful not to squash the bags. "Okay. Let's not start this way. I didn't write because I thought you'd just have to wait to read my letter anyway, and then what would have been the point, because you'd have already come here before getting it and it would be old news by the time you got back to Promise."

"What news?" I asked. This was like playing some fucked-up version of The $25,000 Pyramid, and Ruth was bad at giving the right clues.

"The wedding news. Ray and I are getting married on Christmas Eve."

"Two days from now Christmas Eve?"

"Yes," she said, sort of quietly. Then she smiled at me. "Well, it's not a sad announcement, is it? I should say it with a little conviction: Yes!"

"Wow," I said. "Okay."

"Is that okay?"

"It's your life—you should get married when you want to." That's what I said, but she hadn't gotten married when she wanted to, not really. She'd wanted to get married in September. I hadn't asked her to postpone on my account, but she'd done it anyway. "Why'd you pick Christmas Eve?"

Ruth stood, worked the zipper on the top bag. "We just didn't want to wait any longer, and you're home, so that worked. The sanctuary is always so beautiful at Christmas with the poinsettias and the candles—we don't really even have to add anything." She slid kind of a champagne-colored dress from its sheath. It had a matching coat thing. It was fine. It was just fine to wear to a wedding. "This is choice number one," she said. "The next bag has two dresses in it, so there's three choices in all."

"Are these bridesmaids' dresses?" I asked, though I meant something more but didn't know how to work it into the right words.

Ruth kept her hands busy, her eyes on the bags, unhooking the hangers from one another, a twist tie keeping them bound. "No, I'm just having Karen and Hannah; I've talked about them before, you remember; they're good friends from Florida, from my Winner's flight crew; they're both flying into Billings tomorrow and I'm having them. You're still the maid of honor."

That was it. That's what I was wondering. "I can't be," I said.

Ruth stopped her busy hands, looked at me. "What do you mean?" she asked, but she had to know what I meant.

She really did look so tired, so un-Ruth, but I said it anyway: "I'll go to the wedding, I want to, but I won't be your maid of honor." I kept talking fast before she could interrupt.

"And I don't think it's fair to get upset about me saying that. You can't have it both ways."

She shook her head. "What does that mean, *both ways*?"

"You can't ship me away to get fixed and then show me off as your dressed-up niece starring in the role of Maid of Honor."

"That's not what I—that isn't even . . ." she said. And then she sighed. And then she said, in a quiet voice, "But that's fine, Cammie. I accept your decision." She pulled at the big, droopy collar of the turtleneck sweater she was wearing, blew her sigh toward her bangs like beauty-pageant contestants do to show how much they're trying to keep from crying, but she worked it out, no tears came. She said, "I really thought this would be a good thing. I thought you might do this because it could be a kind of healing moment for the two of us."

I stopped looking at her. I fiddled with the dollhouse instead. "I've already done a lot of healing this year. This break is supposed to be my vacation from healing."

Ruth huffed and threw the bag she had been working the zipper on onto the bed, where it slapped against the others. Her voice had a jagged edge to it. "Now see, I don't know how to talk to you when you're like this." She took a step toward me. "Is what you just said supposed to be funny? Was that a joke or wasn't it? I'm asking in a genuine way: I really don't know."

"Did you think it was funny?" I asked.

"No," she said.

"Then I guess if it was a joke it blew." I snapped off a clump of dried sagebrush from where I'd glued it as one of two tiny bushes flanking the dollhouse's front path. I'd taken that sagebrush from Coley's ranch. Now it crunched in a satisfying way in my palm as I tightened and tightened my fist around it.

"Fine," Ruth said. "This is obviously still how things are."

"Yep," I said.

She went back to the garment bags, shifted one on top of the next. "These are nice dresses," she said. "You can still wear one of them, maid of honor or not."

"I'll wear my Promise uniform," I said.

"If that's what you want," she said. "I'll just take them with me, then." She gathered up the bags, not so careful this time, just folding them over her arm, their hard plastic making a *vwoosh* noise against her body each step she descended away from me.

After she left, I let myself feel a little bit terrible for what I'd said, no matter how true, and then vindicated in my decision, and then terrible, and while I was doing this, I kept on exploring the dollhouse, all those bits and pieces of stuff, just this stuff, glued on all the surfaces. I also waited to feel like myself, as if it would land on me all at once, this feeling like I was me again because I was home. And it didn't come.

· · ·

People said it was a nice wedding. I don't know—maybe that's just what people say. I thought it was nice, but I didn't think it was nearly as lavish as the ceremony and reception I know Ruth had planned for all those years. It was nothing like that. I hadn't been to very many weddings, though, only three or four, with my parents, when I was little; so I didn't have a lot to go by.

This wedding immediately followed the GOP Christmas Eve service. Coley and her mom and Ty were at that service, and Brett and his family. They were in the same row, in the middle, not near where we sat at all. The Christmas Eve service was always by candlelight, the place packed, everybody a little dressed up, chatty, excited, but even still: People noticed me. They could have been noticing my blue flannel skirt, its pleats, my collared white shirt sticking out over my navy sweater, my hair shiny and tucked behind my ears, my altogether neat and presentable Promise-approved appearance, but I'm pretty sure it was more than that. I got a couple looks of flat-out disgust, sneers, people doing those big-movement side-to-side head shakes in my direction to perform their disapproval. I guess one semester wasn't enough to wash off the stain of my perversion. Brett caught my eye as people were leaving, a slow-moving river of bodies working their arms into their winter coats, chins down, inching zippers over their puffy sweaters, shoving hats on the tops of their children's heads. Ray and Ruth had gone off to the Sunday-school classrooms to change into their wedding clothes. Grandma and I were just waiting out the mass emptying of the sanctuary. Brett took me in fully, didn't hide his stare, though I couldn't read his face. And Mrs. Taylor pursed her lips, wore her disgust openly, twisted up her face to do it, but she looked away eventually. Coley was between the two of them, each of them holding one of her hands, but she didn't look my way, or at least she made it seem like she didn't. She still looked as perfectly Coley as she ever had, but seeing her didn't knock me over, it didn't sock the wind out of me, like I'd thought it might. I guess I'd felt that way, just a little, when first I'd glimpsed her, from behind, during the service. It was seeing the back of her head, her hair, just like all those weeks in the science room. It jarred me. But it wasn't something I couldn't withstand.

Now, as she left, I wanted to let my eyes follow her all the way out and into the vestibule, as far as I could watch, because it was like seeing her new, somehow, but Grandma was looking at me, and probably other people were too, waiting for my reaction, and so I looked away. I didn't see Ty leave the sanctuary. He wasn't with them any longer.

Then Jamie's mom came toward our pew, and I must have made some face, some hopeful look, scanning the people around her for Jamie, because she frowned at me, and then, in a move I considered prompted by a burst of Christmas spirit, she cut her way between a couple of people and leaned over to me and said, "Jamie's not here. He's at his dad's for Christmas, in Hysham."

I said, "Tell him I said hi. I miss him." I wanted to say other things but I couldn't.

"I'll tell him," she said. And then she cut back into the stream, but turned to me again, a few steps away, and said, "You look nice."

Once people went home to their trees, their eggnog, fifty or so of us gathered in the front few pews. Ray and Ruth looked exactly like the real-life versions of those plastic bride and groom wedding toppers: standard black tux, white dress, a bouquet of roses. Ruth had had, according to Grandma, quite a bit of trouble finding a dress she liked. Her NF tumor, the one she'd had since birth on her back, too close to her spine, had grown some, was more golf ball than walnut now, and she was (understandably) embarrassed by it. She'd found a doctor in Minneapolis who thought he could probably remove at least part of it, but not until April, not in time for a backless gown at her winter wedding. I thought the one she'd settled on suited her, and it had a kind of satin drape thing, like a superlong scarf, a wrap, that went over her shoulders and hid the tumor entirely.

Ray had three sisters, a brother, a bunch of cousins. They all came. Some of them had families, and they came too. The church organist, Mrs. Cranwall, played a couple of songs;

Tandy Baker sang "How Firm a Foundation." Ruth cried during the vows. Ray maybe teared up as well. Then we went to the fellowship hall, where Ruth's stewardess friends, who were sassy and loud—*a good time*, Grandma said—had strung those old-fashioned crepe-paper bells and played 45s on some record player they'd hauled in. I can't believe it was quite the reception Ruth was planning on for all those years, but it's what she got. We ate really moist red velvet cake and those cream cheese pastel pink, green, and yellow wedding mints with the sugar crystal outside—Grandma made those. I ate probably a dozen of them, liked the crunch of the sugar between my teeth followed by all that soft inside, so sweet it made my molars ache. I ate enough that I felt a little sick. People danced, drank ginger-ale punch, snapped photos on those disposable cameras. It was nice. Then it was over. Ray and Ruth went to a cabin out in the Pine Hills that belonged to somebody or other who had apparently set it all up for them, hauled roses and champagne out there. But they were going to return in late morning, and the Florida ladies would be coming over. We were all going to eat brunch, open presents.

Grandma and I got to spend the rest of Christmas Eve together, just the two of us, though it was nearly midnight when we got home. We had to rush into the house, the night air that sharp, slicing kind of cold, and the wind different from the mountain wind at Promise. It was prairie wind, relentless, building up speed over miles and miles of flat expanse, then hurtling down the small streets of Miles City like hundreds of whistling pinballs loosed and thrashing around corners and curves.

Once inside, we heard not just the whistling but something clashing against the roof, something hard and fast, and then twenty seconds might go by, and then another quick clash. My heart skipped around. I imagined Ty in his bulky Carhartt jacket outside our house. Ty waiting for us. It made no sense for him to be on the roof, I knew, but why should it make sense?

"You must have been good enough this year to get you a visit from Santa," Grandma said, while I tried, unsuccessfully, to press my face against the back-door window in such a way as to see what was out there.

"No way," I said, trying to grin. "He's probably here for you."

"You okay, kiddo?" she asked me, studying my face.

"Yeah," I said. "I'm fine."

"Lots of things going on," she said, touching my cheek.

"Yeah," I said. "Let's find out what this is." She kept studying me while I put my coat back on, pulled up the hood.

"How's that poem go?" she asked. "'Up on the roof we heard such a clatter, went to see what was the matter'?"

"Something like that," I said, opening the door, the wind already taking my breath. "Somebody's wearing a kerchief, I remember that." I stepped onto the back porch and the wind slammed the door behind me. I walked down the steps and all the way out into the center of the backyard, the dead lawn coated with just enough snow and ice for my footsteps to crunch, like over a thick layer of cornflakes. I looked up. That prairie wind had torn loose a whole string of Christmas lights from along the roofline and then had caught the string in its gust, was holding it aloft for moments at a time and then letting it dip, sometimes far enough to crash against the roof, before shooting it skyward again. It calmed me down to see that this was what was making the noise, it relieved me, all at once, made me a kind of giddy. And it was beautiful too, this lighted string thrashing against the dark night.

"What is it, Spunky?" Grandma called from the doorway.

"It's lights," I yelled.

"What is it?" she yelled back.

"Come see," I yelled.

She did. She hurried out with an afghan draped around her, her big slippers on. She stood next to me, looked up, smiled. "Look at that," she said, her words coming out in steamy puffs. "They're still all lit up."

"I know," I said. "It's neat."

"It is neat," she said. "That's one way to put it."

I put my arm around her. She put her arm around me. From out there in the backyard, in the ice wind, for as long as we could stand to, we watched that string of lights dip and soar and crash and rise again.

Later, after we'd said good night, gone to our beds, I could hear them, right above me, smacking into the roof, scraping along it, and a couple of times I even glimpsed the string, a whip of tiny lights, as the wind carried a part of it past my window. The next afternoon, after the honeymooners returned from their cabin, tired and punch-drunk, Ray hauled out the ladder, put on a thick pair of leather work gloves, climbed up to the roof, and restapled that renegade strand. And then they stayed put until he took them down, with all of the other lights, on New Year's Day, prompt as he could possibly be, because he said that it *really irked* him when people left their Christmas lights up *practically till Easter*.

· · ·

I never got my face-to-face with Coley. I never did manage to see Jamie, though he called from his dad's, once, and we talked for ten minutes or so, Ruth in the other room, not making faces or saying anything but for sure letting me know that she was there, that she was listening, so all the real content had to come from his end. He was dating Andrea Dixon, and unbelievably, according to Jamie, she *put out like a champ*. It made me sad when he told me he had to go, said that he missed my *gay face*. Other than that, I met with Pastor Crawford twice; Grandma and I baked a couple of low-sugar pies; Ray and I played Monopoly a bunch of times and I think he won them all. One afternoon Ruth gave me some worksheets from Lydia to fill out. I sat down and did them at the kitchen table. They were just like all the other stupid worksheets we had to do at Promise all the time. In this packet I had to read an essay by the Reverend John Smid titled "Exploring the Homosexual Myth," and then answer some questions about it, basic reading-comprehension kinds of questions. It didn't take long. Ruth asked me to bring the worksheets to her in the living room when I was done. I did. Ray was sitting in there with her. The TV was off and I could tell that they were waiting for me, and I could also tell that this meant we were going to have a *chat* about me, only hopefully this time there wouldn't be as many tears as there had been at the chat we'd had in August, or at least not as many revelations.

Turns out there weren't any tears at all: not from Ruth and not from me. Ruth told me, very calmly, that she had discussed my progress with Lydia and Rick *several times*, and that even if I had a good spring semester, which she *certainly hoped I would*, everyone thought it would be best for me to stay at Promise during the summer—during Camp Promise.

"The summer was a particularly bad time for you last year," Ruth said. She still looked tired, even now, with the wedding behind her. Her hair was kind of squashed and lumpy and her face looked old. Ray, however, looked like the guy who'd just won the very biggest stuffed animal at the carnival. He'd looked like that since I'd gotten home.

"I think last summer was a particularly good time," I said.

Ruth frowned at me. "What I mean is that you had too much freedom; there were too many opportunities for you to find yourself in trouble. Part of that is my fault, I know, but I can't stay home with you all summer and neither can Ray."

"Grandma's here," I said. "I can stay with her and she can babysit me, since apparently that's what I need."

Ruth made a tight line with her mouth. "No," she said, smoothing her lap with her hands. I hadn't seen her do that in a while. "That's not an option. If you don't want to stay at Promise, then there are other Christian summer camps I'm willing to discuss. Reverend Rick recommended several."

"I'll stay at Promise," I said.

"Well, some of them sound very nice. There's one in— where is that one with all the swimming activities?" she asked Ray.

"South Dakota, I think," he said. "You still have the brochure, don't you?" He smiled at me. "It seems pretty fancy."

"It is South Dakota," Ruth said. "They have both an in-ground pool and a lake and they—"

"No way," I said. "I'll stay at Promise."

"Okay, that's your decision," Ruth said.

I snorted. "Hardly."

"It's what you just now said that you wanted," she said.

"From the limited choices you've offered me," I said, but I could see her ready to rattle off more Christian summer camps, so I added, "But you know what: It's fine. Whatever." And then, even though it scared me to ask, I said, "What about next year, for school?"

"Well, we'll have to see how the summer goes," she said. "We'll just have to see."

. . .

On New Year's Eve the newlyweds went downtown and Grandma and I ordered pizza and made a huge bowl of popcorn and watched the CBS New Year's special and *not* *New Year's Rockin' Eve* because Grandma had a grudge against Dick Clark stemming from something or other he'd done on *American Bandstand* years and years before, way before I was born, even. But the less popular special was fine with me. It was the first TV I'd seen in months, and not only that, both Pearl Jam and U2 were going to be on.

"I have something else for you," Grandma told me while we were getting everything settled in front of the TV. She had a stack of paper plates and napkins in her hand, and I thought that was all, but when she set them on the coffee table, she put one of those padded mailing envelopes down too. "It's not from me, but I'm the one who snuck it away for you."

I picked it up. It had one of those professionally printed return-address labels with a silver, blocky monogram of MMK in its corner and California as the location.

"I guess Margot's not in Germany anymore," I said, remembering our dinner, the stolen picture. It seemed like a long time ago.

"I don't know what it is," Grandma said, "but I thought Ruth might not give it to you, no matter what, and she was such a good friend of your mom's. It came a week or so ago and I got to it first and hid it. You go on and open it up and I'll make sure it's legal." She winked a big wink at me.

"You're sneaky, Grandma," I said.

"You're sneaky," she said.

It was the Campfire Girls manual Margot had mentioned to me during that dinner, and also a nice letter about how sorry she was not to have been in touch more, and how she was wishing me well, and how she hoped to make it back to Montana again soon. There were also three hundred dollars in one-hundred-dollar bills, but they were pressed flat in the very center pages and I didn't even find them until I was flipping through it during commercials, and by then Grandma had already pronounced the manual "Just fine for you to have, I don't see why not," so I didn't say anything about them to her. The bills were stuck between a page that listed some of the requirements for becoming a Campfire Girls Torch Bearer Craftsman and a page with a poem, I guess it was a poem, or mantra, "The Torch Bearer's Desire," which just floated in a lake of white space given how short it was:

That Light
Which Has Been
Given To Me
I Desire
To Pass Undimmed
To Others

Margot had printed something, very small, beneath those words, tiny letters in pencil: *Here's hoping that cash is as good as light. Use it well. MMK.*

Sometimes I thought about Margot, randomly, like maybe when I couldn't sleep. I would wonder what she was doing, which exotic locale she might be in. And I would wonder what she'd think of my exile to Promise, always deciding, ultimately, that she wouldn't think much of it at all.

"Why do you think she sent you that?" Grandma asked, nodding at the book and loading my plate with too many pieces of pizza.

"Because she and Mom were Campfire Girls together," I said. "She said she thought I'd get a kick out of it."

"It was a nice thought," Grandma said. "You write her a nice thank-you and I'll send it." Then she added, "You don't need to go on and on about your treatment in it."

"I won't, Grandma," I said. It would be completely embarrassing, even though I knew she wouldn't approve of such a place, to tell Margot Keenan all about Promise in a thank-you card. "That doesn't even sound like me."

"You're right," she said. "It doesn't. You not being around has me forgetting your ways."

We watched the TV special pretty much in silence after that, except for one of us commenting on the size of the crowd a few times, how cold it looked. But then the host—this comedian, I guess, or actor, Jay Thomas—was doing some crappy shtick where he pretended to read from *TV Guide* the other options for television audiences should they want to change the channel, and none of his fake options were funny, something about Shannon Doherty and something about Suzanne Somers, but then he started talking about this "lost episode of *The Andy Griffith Show*," one where Gomer tries on a bunch of women's clothing and heads downtown to walk around until they "send him to the Marines to straighten him out." And it was stupid, and nobody laughed, but Grandma, on the couch next to me, she tightened up a little at those words: *straighten him out.* I could feel her do it. And maybe that would have been that, but maybe ten minutes later, this Jay Thomas guy, he cuts to his cohost, Nia Peeples, who's actually freezing it out down in Times Square in her leather coat and her hat and gloves while he stays warm in the Hard Rock Cafe with all the bands, and he tells her, "Remember, Nia, Times Square: Men are men. Some of the women are men. Some of the men are women, so be careful who you pet when you're out there."

And this Nia lady basically says that she can take care of herself, and the joke is over, or they move on, whatever, but right after that Grandma turned to me and said, "I don't know why they think those queer jokes are so damned funny."

"He sucks, that's why," I said.

Grandma waited a moment and then said, quietly, "It's not so bad there, is it, Spunky?"

"In Times Square?" I asked. "How would I know?"

"At your school," Grandma said, making sure not to look at me, but plucking stray kernels of popcorn from the coffee table, the couch, and putting them back into the bowl. "Is it very hard for you there?"

And I said, "It's not so bad, Grandma. It's pretty much fine, actually."

Then she waited a few more moments, the band on the TV superloud, their electric guitar noise almost painful to hear because they were maybe drunk and also because she had the volume up so high. She said, "But are you feeling any different because of what they've got you doing out there?"

I knew what she meant by different, she meant better, fixed, *straightened out*; but I answered her based on the word she'd actually used and not her intended meaning, and I said, "I do feel different. I don't really know how to explain it."

She patted my hand, looked relieved. "Well, that's good then, huh? That's what matters most."

We watched until the ball dropped, welcomed in 1993.

It was the first year, after a ban that had been in effect for decades, that they reinstated confetti, all colors and sizes, the long curlicue pieces and the tiny metallic cutouts, all of it flung from the upper-level windows and rooftops of those buildings surrounding Times Square. On the screen it rained and rained confetti, for minutes, and that glitter-rain, plus the cameras flashing and the lights from the billboards and the awesome mass of the crowds in their shiny hats and toothy smiles, made that world pop and shine and blur in a way that makes you sad to be watching it all on your TV screen, in a way that makes you feel like, instead of bringing the action into your living room, the TV cameras are just reminding you of how much you're missing, confronting you with it, you in your pajamas, on your couch, a couple of pizza crusts resting in some orange grease on a paper plate in front of you, your glass of soda mostly flat and watery, the ice all melted, and the good stuff happening miles and miles away from where you're at. At least that's how it made me feel that year.

CHAPTER SEVENTEEN

Adam Red Eagle came back from Christmas break with his gorgeous hair all shorn off, to right up against his scalp, just stubble there really, though it started growing in fast. His father had insisted, and Adam said there was no way around his father's insistence. He made his voice puffed up when he imitated him: *We're not savages anymore. And for Chriss sake we're not women, either.* The weird thing was that Adam's now nearly bald head did nothing to make him any less womanly, or less feminine; in fact, it accentuated his high cheekbones and amazing skin, the Dietrich arch of his eyebrows, his full lips, all of his beauty somehow now spotlighted without that curtain of hair.

A few other things had changed since our return. I now had decoration privileges (though items had to first be approved by Lydia, and since there was nothing approved that I felt like Scotch-taping up there, I just left my lonely iceberg adrift on a sea of drywall). I was also now far enough along in the program to be a part of weekly group support sessions, which replaced my one-on-ones with Rick but not, unfortunately, with Lydia. While home in Idaho, Jane had purchased quite a lot of killer pot off of someone she mysteriously described as an *old flame, a tragedy of a woman*, and she used that to supplement our dwindling stock. And finally, the Viking Erin had begun a New Year's regime of Christian aerobics, one that had already lasted past the first-week burnout of so many similar kinds of resolutions.

She'd brought back to Promise a couple of videotapes, three brand-new workout outfits, and a blue plastic aerobic step with black traction pads across its top. She was all business. The videos were from the *Faithfully Fit* line and both of them featured Tandy Campbell, a perky brunette "cheerleader for Christ" who was compact and trim and totally rocked her shiny spandex tank tops and black Lycra stretch pants.

Erin was so excited. I hadn't even unpacked my suitcase before she was thrusting those tapes in my face, Tandy beaming at me above the title: *Joyful Steps—Cardio for Christ.*

"Will you do it with me?" she asked, performing a mock arm curl with the tape. "Lydia says we can use the rec room if we get up early."

"I didn't even know that Jesus was into aerobics," I said. "I've always imagined him as a speed walker, maybe across water."

"How can you not know Tandy Campbell?" she asked, now holding both tapes straight out in front of her, one in each hand, and doing a series of arm extensions and retractions that I guess were supposed to be somehow aerobic, though they looked kind of like the moves a traffic cop might use. "She's a huge big deal. H-U-G-E—huge! My mom went to one of her power weekends in San Diego with two of my aunts. They got to meet her. They said she's totally tiny in person, but still a presence, a real dynamic presence."

"I bet my aunt Ruth knows about her," I said. "I bet she's a fan."

"I'm sure," Erin said, now doing some leg bends with the arm movements, which had grown noticeably less grand and precise, even in just the thirty seconds or so she'd been at it. "She's totally amazing; everybody's a fan. You have to do them with me—please? Please, please, please? I need a work-out buddy and you can't run right now anyway. You won't be able to until April, probably."

She was right about that. We'd had snow at Promise since mid-October, but there had been feet and feet added during our couple of weeks away, and now everything except for the main road, which one of the neighboring ranchers plowed for us, and the path to the barn, which we all took turns shovel-ing, was mounded in white drifts, some so high and strangely shaped from the wind that there was no way at all to tell what was under them, or where solid ground might begin.

I thought that I'd do the tapes with her a couple of times, see them enough to make fun of them effectively when I reported back to Jane and Adam. (Lydia had given Erin per-mission to invite all the female disciples to these morning workout sessions; however, Christian aerobics were not, apparently, an appropriately gendered activity for men.) I don't know if it was maybe the lure of the almighty VHS tape reminding me of my days of freedom, but it didn't take very many mornings before I was in the habit of waking up to Tandy and her shiny smile, her bouncy energy, her strangely endearing habit of renaming standard aerobics moves in Jesusy ways, even if her substitutions didn't really make sense and she overused the word *praise*: Grapevine = Praise-Vine; March It Out = March Your Praise; all manner of kicks or punches = Joy Blasts.

Other than those substitutions, and the syncopated *thump-thump-boom* of remixed gospel songs, the only thing discernibly Christian about Tandy's workouts were the warm-up and cool-down meditations, wherein she would use the Word to motivate us toward our fitness goals. Her favorite passage was Hebrews 12:11—*No discipline is pleasant while it's happening—it's painful! But afterward there will be a peaceful harvest of right living for those who are trained in this way.* And at first, Tandy's workouts were kind of painful and intense, Erin out of breath by six minutes in, and afterward both of us with bangs stuck to our sticky foreheads in the breakfast line, where Erin was also practicing discipline, even choosing cottage cheese and canned peaches on the days when Reverend Rick made his Rice Krispies–coated cinnamon French toast. Sometimes Helen Showalter would join us in the rec room, her movements clunky and her steps hard, shaking the leaves of the potted plants. Jane came once, to take Polaroids, mostly, and a few times Lydia came, to observe our behavior I guess. She sure didn't launch into a *step, joy-clap, squat, step.* But it was usually just the two of us. Erin's clothes were looser by a couple weeks in, and by Valentine's Day they'd replaced parts of her Promise Uniform with a whole size smaller and she'd had her mom send us a care package via the mail service offered by Greyhound Bus Lines (which took twelve days to arrive in Bozeman but was cheap for sending heavy stuff). Her package contained two sets of eight-pound dumbbells coated in purple rubber and a new tape to keep us motivated: *SPIRITUAL LIFT—Toning More Than Your Muscles.*

• • •

When I was seven or eight, I was sort of obsessed with those sticky-hand things you could buy for twenty-five cents from the toy dispensers lined up just inside the automatic doors at grocery stores. The hands were usually some neon color, five fingered but puffy and cartoonish, and attached to a longish cord of the same material. I collected all the versions: the glitter sticky hand and the glow-in-the-dark sticky hand and the jumbo-size sticky hand. I used to drape them over my doorknob and choose just one or two for any given day, like some girls might have chosen their jewelry. There wasn't much you could do with them, really, besides whip them at people and watch them cringe or squeal or laugh when the stickiness smacked their skin, though there was something satisfying in the way the weight of the hand would stretch thin the cord, so thin sometimes you were just sure it would snap, and then the whole thing would spring back to its original shape and size. The worst thing about the sticky hands was their propensity for collecting tiny fibers and hairs, dust, muck, and the difficulty of properly cleaning them after that happened. You couldn't, really, ever quite get them clean again.

The longer I stayed at Promise, the more all the stuff they were throwing at me, at us, started to stick, just like to those sticky hands, in little bits, at first, random pieces, no big deal. For instance, maybe I'd be in bed during lights out and I'd start to think about Coley and kissing Coley, and doing more with Coley, or Lindsey, or whomever, Michelle Pfeiffer. But then I might hear Lydia's voice saying, *You have to fight these sinful impulses: fight, it's not supposed to be easy to fight sin*, and I might totally ignore it, or even laugh to myself about what an idiot she was, but there it would be, her voice, in my head, where it hadn't been before. And it was other stuff too, these bits and pieces of doctrine, of scripture, of life lessons here and there, until more and more of them were coated on, along for the ride, and I didn't consistently question where they had come from, or why they were there, but I did start to feel kind of weighed down by them.

Part of what contributed to this weighing down was undoubtedly my new group support sessions. Our group consisted of Steve Cromps, Helen Showalter, Mark Turner, and superskinny, Southern-drawled Dane Bunsky, a disciple

I got to know better very quickly (support group had a way of making that happen). Dane was a recovering meth addict who was at Promise as the scholarship child of some megachurch in Louisiana.

We met in the classroom on Tuesdays and Wednesdays at three p.m., pushing the chairs into a circle, a chorus of metal scraping linoleum that was nails on chalkboard to me. Lydia would bring a box of tissues to each session, and she'd also wheel in a cart with a big urn of hot water on it and mugs, a container of instant hot chocolate mix, and also this completely addictive mixture of Tang and loose tea and instant lemonade powder that Reverend Rick made in big batches and called Russian tea, apparently as some sort of dated cosmonaut joke. We weren't allowed anywhere near the drink cart, though, until the fifteen-minute midsession break.

We started each session with a prayer chain. All of us, Lydia included, would join hands, and whoever's turn it was that day would start by saying: *I will not pray for God to change me because God does not make mistakes and I am the one who is tempted by sin: Change will come through God, but within me. I must be the change.* You had to say this exactly, word for word, and if you didn't, Lydia would interrupt the prayer chain and make the starter repeat it until it was perfect. My first go-round I kept forgetting the word *because* and I had to say the whole thing like four times.

After the starting prayer was said correctly, the starter would squeeze either of their hands, and the recipient of the squeeze would add something of their own, usually something about asking God for strength, or thanking Jesus for this time together, something, and then we'd continue around the circle. Sometimes the prayers were more personal or pointed, but since this chain was just the opening proceeding to an extended share session, usually not. We were supposed to keep our eyes closed during this time, to focus on Christ alone, but I got to know my brethren by the feel of their hands: Helen's thick grip and fast-pitch softball calluses, still not completely healed despite months of not playing; Dane's skin, cracked and rough; Lydia's thin fingers as icy as you'd imagine them, exactly so. When the prayers again reached the starting person, their job was then to say: *The opposite of the sin of homosexuality is not heterosexuality: It is Holiness. It is Holiness. It is Holiness.* I loved it when it was Dane's turn, because his accent and the lazy slow-speak way that he said absolutely everything, no matter what, made that mantra sound strangely seductive.

We were allowed to move beyond our childhoods in these sessions and to actually talk about more recent experiences we'd had concerning the sin of homosexual behavior and temptation, though Lydia would frequently cut short particular monologues with "That's enough of that—we're not here to glorify our past sins; we're here to acknowledge and repent for them." Or, once, "Too much detail, Steve! Too much! Let's remember who's in the details, shall we?" I think that was the only time I ever heard her even attempt something like a joke, which maybe isn't so much a criticism, because there was usually very little about support group that was funny.

Dane and Helen had both been molested, which Lydia said was *a common reason that people found themselves unnaturally attracted to members of the same sex*: in Helen's case because abuse from her uncle Tommy had convinced her that *being feminine meant being weak and vulnerable to such abuse,* and because it made her fear any sexual intimacy with men; and in Dane's case because he had been abandoned by his father at an early age and therefore had *an unhealthy curiosity about men*, one that *manifested into an obsession* when a much older boy placed in the same foster home forcefully suggested the two of them fool around. Dane had also spent time as a runaway hustling for meth, and those stories, full of older men and their dingy apartments and trailers, Dane's all-consuming addiction, were completely gruesome, even without the specific sexual details.

I had determined, after the first few sessions, that even with my dead parents, Steve's textbook lisp and unyielding fey ways, and Mark's preacher dad, we three couldn't really compete with Dane and Helen in the arena of justification for our sinful homosexual attractions. Their pasts almost sanctioned their fucked-up notions, but we three did the fucking up on our own. This was especially fascinating to me when it came to Mark Turner. Here he was, poster boy for a Christian upbringing, but yet here he was, at Promise, just like the rest of us. Only he wasn't like the rest of us. He was so perfect and good. Adam and Jane and I joked, sometimes, that he was a plant, that he didn't *struggle with same-sex attraction* at all but was at Promise as part of a holy mission, one intended to benefit the rest of us, to show us the way a model disciple would work the system. But then came the Thursday in early March when it was Mark's turn to share.

Like always, Lydia flipped through this old-school composition book she had, scanning whatever she'd jotted down from the last group share done by whoever was going. Usually she'd then ask some sort of question intended to elicit a lengthy response, but that day, with Mark waiting patiently, his giant Bible on his lap with literally hundreds of page markers and slips of paper protruding from it like feathers, she said, "Is there something specific you'd like to focus on this week, Mark?"

And I, for one, was dumbfounded, not only because she'd asked the question almost sweetly, certainly more good cop than bad, but mostly because in asking it she was relinquishing some control, handing it over to a disciple, and that I'd definitely never seen from her. For his part, Mark also seemed sort of taken aback; he shrugged his shoulders and wedged his eyebrows down and in toward his nose, and said, quietly, "I don't know. I can talk about whatever you think is best."

The last time he'd shared, I remembered, he'd talked a lot about one or two *impure* daydreams he'd had about an assistant pastor from his father's church. Fairly chaste daydreams, it had seemed to me. In one of them the two of them held hands outside while hiking. Maybe they were shirtless, too—but really, not much happened. I guess he could have stripped them free of any of the more damning details, just to make sure they were cleared for retelling, but I doubt it. I think Mark Turner's struggles were likely almost entirely those of thought and emotion, battling the way he felt about men—the way some part of him wanted to feel about them—but not anything he'd actually ever done with them.

"Okay," Lydia said, still flipping through her notes, but pretty obviously doing so to gather her words and not because she was actually gleaning anything new from them. "I know that you've had an especially hard couple of weeks, and I thought that maybe there was something more pressing than not for you right now."

"Every week is especially hard," Mark said, not looking at her but flicking the cover of his Bible so that it lifted open some and then fell back against his finger where he flicked it again. "Everything is pressing."

"Okay," Lydia tried again. "But is there something—"

"How about everything," Mark said. "How about

every single thing." He had raised his voice some, which was weird coming from him, unexpected, and he almost seemed like he was pulsating energy or rage or something, like it was sort of racquetballing around inside his small body, smacking here and there, and it was taking work to keep it contained. I was across the circle from him but I could see the way his neck muscles were taut, all of him rigid and uncomfortable. He gritted out this next part: "If you want me to say something about my father, then you should just say so."

Lydia, pen poised above her notebook, said, "It sounds to me like it's you who wants to talk about your father's decision."

"What's there to say?" he asked. "You read the letter, Lydia, same as me." He paused then, looked around the circle, a strange sort of grin on his face. "But I can share it with the group, the important part." He puffed himself up some, there on his chair, and changed his voice, made is a shade deeper. "'Your visit home at Christmas confirmed my fears that you are still very feminine and weak. I cannot have this weakness in my home. It sends the message to my congregation that I approve of it when I do not. You will stay the summer and we will readdress your progress come August. You are not ready to come home.'" He settled back in his chair, not much, but enough to tell us that he was done. He tried to look pleased, to smirk, but he wore it wrong. His face just looked, in that moment, feral. "'You are not ready to come home,'" he said again.

Through all of this, Lydia was calm as ever. She didn't even react to his comment about her role as mail screener. She finished writing something and asked, "What specific thing happened at Christmas, Mark? What led to your father's decision?"

He snorted. "I happened. Just me. Like always. It's enough for me to just walk in the room the way I am."

"What way are you, Mark?" she asked.

"I want to read something," he said, his voice louder than before, just edging on frantic but not quite there. "Can I read a passage? It's one of my father's favorites. He reminds me of it every chance he gets."

"Please do," Lydia said.

So then Mark stood and read aloud a passage that I don't think I'd ever heard before that day, but one that I've revisited again and again since: Second Corinthians 12:7–10. Maybe I shouldn't say that he read the passage, because even though he had his Bible open and held out in front of him, he didn't need to look at it very often.

"And lest I should be exalted above measure through the abundance of the revelations, there was given to me a thorn in the flesh, the messenger of Satan to buffet me, lest I should be exalted above measure. For this thing I besought the Lord thrice, that it might depart from me."

He paused here, looked up to the ugly paneled ceiling of the classroom, or beyond that, probably. He was such a small guy, and everything about him usually so composed. I'd heard him read Scripture lots of times before, his voice always clear and assured, just like the Sunday-morning Bible Hour broadcast. Mark's voice as he spoke this passage on this day, though, kept that nearly frantic tremble in it.

"And he said unto me, My grace is sufficient for thee: for my strength is made perfect in weakness. Most gladly therefore will I rather glory in my infirmities, that the power of Christ may rest upon me." He paused again here, squinted his eyes, and bunched up his face to keep from crying. He shook his head back and forth, fast, and then somehow forced out the rest of

the passage through the clench of his jaw, each word its own victory over a complete breakdown. *"Therefore I take pleasure in infirmities, in reproaches, in necessities, in persecutions, in distresses for Christ's sake: for when I am weak, then am I strong."*

Mark breathed out hard when he finished, like some guys do when they're repping weights, and he closed his Bible and in the very next instant let it drop from his hands. Its descent was impossibly slow, like it took movie editing to make it happen, but its sharp smack against the floor was entirely of the moment, and as loud and uncomfortable as it could possibly be.

Lydia tried to subdue that moment with her typical ice, and said, "There's no need for cheap theatrics. If you sit down, we can talk about the passage you've selected."

But Mark wasn't done with the theatrics, and he sure as hell wasn't sitting down. "I didn't do the selecting. Weren't you listening?" he said. "My dad selected it for me. He'd have it tattooed on my back if tattoos weren't condemned in Leviticus 19:28. *Ye shall not make any cuttings in your flesh for the dead, nor print any marks upon you: I am the LORD.*"

Lydia half stood and motioned her hand for him to take his chair. "Sit down, Mark. We can talk about all of this."

But instead of sitting, he moved into the center of our small circle, the farmer in the dell, and said, "You know the best thing about my dad's passage?" He didn't wait for anyone to answer him. "It has *for Christ's sake* built right in. It's built right in."

He started doing jumping jacks. He did. Perfect-form, hand-clap-above-the-head jumping jacks as he shouted, "'For when I am weak then am I strong!' In my dad's passage, weakness actually equals strength. That means I have the strength of ten Marks. Twenty! Eighty-five! All my weakness makes me the strongest man alive."

He stopped short the jumping jacks and crouched down then, so fast, and with military precision he put his two palms flat on the floor and shot his small legs out behind him, leveled off his back, and knocked out push-ups, one after another, chanting, "For Christ's sake," as he pushed back into start position from each. "For Christ's sake! For Christ's sake!"

He'd done at least five, Lydia saying, "Stop it, Mark. Stop all of this right now!" before she managed, as he was in the down position, to get her right foot, a foot clad in a black loafer, planted squarely on the small of his back. She seemed to apply enough weight to keep him from rising back up. She remained in that position while she said, "I'll remove my foot when you're ready to stand up and get control of your behavior."

But then Mark, with the strength of eighty-five Marks, like he'd said, grunting and sort of squealing through the grit of his teeth, the clench of his jaw, started extending those elbows and raising himself back off the ground, and Lydia, shifting her hip to allow for this new position, lost her balance, and though, once she was steady again, she tried to apply more weight to the foot, you could tell it was too late. Mark was powering through, and then, sure enough, he was all the way up, Lydia standing stupidly with one foot still on his back, but now looking like an explorer in a snapshot with her foot up on some rock or outcropping.

But just as soon as he'd made it, he was done, and he collapsed back to the floor, sobbing now, his face mashed into the laminate. He was making all kinds of noises, and saying things, I'm not sure what, exactly, I know I heard *sorry* a couple of times, and *I can't, I can't do it.* Lydia crouched down next to him, put her hand on his back, she didn't rub it or anything, she just placed it there and said, not to him, but to all of us, "Go to your rooms until dinner. Go directly to your rooms and nowhere else."

And when none of us moved, she said, "You will go right now and not a moment later." And we did. We gathered our notebooks and pretended, poorly, not to linger, watching Mark, who was still crying on the floor. As the rest of us walked to the door, I noticed Dane hover next to his chair, trying to stay, I guess. But Lydia shook her head no at him, and then he joined the rest of us in the hallway, where we looked at one another with big eyes and open mouths. And even though we walked back to our rooms as a group, we were a silent group, nobody really sure what to say, or what to make of what had just happened.

Finally Steve said, lowly, "That was intense—that was more intense than anything."

"If it was intense for you, think about how it was for him," Dane said, sharp and mean. "It wasn't nothin' for all of us, faggot."

"Jesus," Steve said, "I didn't even mean it like that." But Dane pushed past him, and after that none of us said anything; we just went to our rooms like we were told.

• • •

Mark wasn't at dinner. By then most all of the other disciples knew what had happened and I could tell everyone was waiting for him to show up. When Adam walked into the dining hall alone, there were obvious glances and whispers from the cliques in the food line and those already pulled up to a table, starting in on their mac 'n' cheese with cut-up hot dogs and a side of green beans and canned pears.

"What's the full report?" Jane asked Adam as he joined

our table, his plate holding three ice-cream scoops of the synthetic orange, glumpy noodles and pink hot dog bites.

"I don't know," he said. "I didn't even know anything had
happened, and then I come back from evangelical detail and
find Rick and Lydia in our room and Mark is like out of it,
completely, a total zombie; he's sitting on the edge of his bed
and the two of them are practically on top of him saying all
sorts of shit, but he's in la-la land. And I'm going, Is anybody
gonna clue me in, here?"

"What were they saying to him?" I asked.

"Just like the usual junk: *It's gonna be all right; you're facing
your sin and that takes courage; you just need to rest and pray*;
whatever. None of it was penetrating, at least as far as I could
tell." Adam had been loading up his fork with noodles since
he'd sat down. I usually loved to watch him eat mac 'n' cheese,
or anything else made with elbow noodles. It took him forever. He'd maneuver one noodle onto each fork tine, four in
all, little tubes stacked one next to another, and then spear a
piece of hot dog on the end, and then take a bite. But that
night his dedication to his food routine was annoying me.

His fork was loaded now, so he took his bite and said, "I
didn't hear much anyway, because two minutes after I walked
in, Lydia sent me to Steve and Ryan's room. But then at least
Steve told me all about Mark's show of strength, if Steve can
be believed. Did he really knock out a push-up with Lydia
standing on his back?"

"She wasn't completely standing on it," I said. "But she
had one foot on it, some of her weight."

"Our group never has this kind of entertainment," he said,
scowling at Jane as if it was her fault for not bringing the
drama. "Couldn't you do cartwheels or something?" He was
loading his fork again.

"I used to be able to do a spectacular crab walk," she said. "All the way across the floor and up a wall."

"That could work," Adam said.

I knew they were just doing what we always did, making a joke out of everything because it sucked to be here and we didn't want any part of it and why not just laugh everything off because we obviously knew better than any of the assholes running the place, but this time—I don't know, maybe because I'd actually been there and had seen Mark, had seen him lose his shit, had seen him sobbing with his face in the floor—the way we were treating what had happened made me even more annoyed, and I guess sort of angry, too.

"I can also juggle a little," Jane said, picking up the bowl her pears had been in and tilting it to her mouth, drinking the Vaseline-colored juice, then wiping her face before saying, "How do you think I could work that into a share session?"

"Maybe you could—" Adam started, but I cut him off.

"It was scary," I said, not looking at either of them but talking more loudly than I normally might. "He was completely out of control. It was hard to watch. I mean, it seemed funny at first, and great that Lydia couldn't get him to sit down, but when he just kept going, it really wasn't funny at all."

"It must have been a little bit funny," Jane said.

"Not really," I said, looking at her. "Not if you were in the room as it was happening right in front of you."

Jane made her patented unreadable Jane face, but I'd come to associate it with her disapproval or doubt or both.

"I get what you're saying," Adam said. "I guess it's just because we didn't see it that it seems too crazy to be taken seriously."

"It was crazy," I said. "And it was completely serious, too."

Jane kept her blank face on for the rest of the meal, but she didn't talk anymore about crab walking or juggling, either.

Later, in our room, the Viking Erin said she needed a hug and so I gave her one and it was not the worst thing ever. It was actually seminice. Then she said she was going to pray for Mark and asked me if I wanted to join her and I said I did. And I did. And it was sort of nice, too. Maybe not the praying itself so much as treating what had happened with a certain amount of respect. It felt like something better than just making a joke out of it, anyway.

CHAPTER EIGHTEEN

The next day neither Mark nor Adam was at morning prayers, nor breakfast, nor in the classrooms for study hours, and nobody seemed to have any info as to where they might be, not even Jane. I glimpsed Adam during lunch, but Rick had his arm around him and they were walking quickly down the hallway toward his office, and it was obvious that none of us were invited to join them.

At group Steve, Helen, Dane, and I sat and waited for Lydia, which had never happened before. The drink cart wasn't there, pushed up against its usual wall. The lights weren't even on, and none of us turned them on but instead just sat in the watery parallelograms of midafternoon, late-winter/early-spring sunshine that streamed through the big windows on the western wall. We waited for ten, maybe fifteen minutes, not saying much, and then both Lydia and Rick walked through the door and slid chairs into our small circle to join us. And then Rick walked back over to the entrance and flicked the light switch and the fluorescent lights buzzed on and made the room just a shade or two brighter.

Rick flipped his chair around and straddled it like a cowboy and patted his hands against the top of the plastic chair back, which was now in front of him, and said, "This is a hard day."

At that, Helen started crying, not loud or big, though

her tears were fat and slow to trail her cheeks, but she was a sniffler and her face got splotchy fast, and Lydia had to pass the requisite box of tissues for the second day in a row, probably, though I hadn't actually seen Mark take a tissue the day before.

"I'm sorry," Helen said, blowing hard into a tissue. "I don't even know why I'm crying."

"That's okay," Rick said. "That's absolutely okay." Though Lydia looked like she thought it was maybe less okay than he did. "I know yesterday's session must have been really difficult for all of you, and I'm sorry that you had to process that on your own last night. We needed to be with Mark."

"Where is he?" Dane asked with a little venom layered into his typically lazy accent, though he wasn't as hostile as he'd been with Steve in the hallway the day before.

"He's in the hospital in Bozeman," Lydia said, and Rick gave her a look, I guess because she was so abrupt, and so she added, "I don't see the sense in drawing this out."

"There's no need for cheap theatrics, right?" Dane said, sort of under his breath, but definitely loud enough for Lydia to hear him.

"No there's not," she said. "I agree."

Helen started sniffling harder, and since she already had the box of tissues on her lap, she just plucked them, one after another, like pulling petals off a daisy, until her hand was crammed with them, enough to cover the whole of her face when she put them in front of it.

"He tried to kill himself, didn't he?" Dane asked, which was probably what most of us were assuming, at least I was. Dane shook his head and pointed at Lydia. "I knew it was gonna go bad before we even got out of the room." It was a strange merging, this bite beneath Dane's accent. In group I'd heard him talk about things like letting a fortysomething father of three fuck him in the backseat of a Jetta so that he could score a hit (sans explicit details, of course); but even then his accent, the way he phrased things, usually made what he was talking about sound sort of like a campfire story, or something that happened once to someone else. All that detachment was gone from his voice now.

Lydia didn't jump to answer this one. She waited for Rick, who seemed to be having trouble deciding which words to use.

Eventually he decided on "No, it wasn't a suicide attempt, I don't think. But he did hurt himself pretty badly."

I thought that Reverend Rick would go on to explain; I think everyone else thought so too. But when he didn't, and Lydia didn't jump in to clarify, Steve said, "Well, did he have an accident or something?"

And Lydia said "No" just as Rick said, "Kind of—in a manner of speaking."

"How can it be both no and kind of?" Dane asked. "What the hell kind of sense does that make?"

"I'm sorry," Rick said. "That was confusing. I meant that Mark's injury was accidental in the sense that he wasn't really himself when it happened." But as soon as he finished speaking, Rick looked sort of mad at himself for having said it that way, for being so cagey with us, which wasn't his usual style, and he added, "Look, Mark was very confused yesterday; I don't need to tell you, you all saw that. He was in a lot of emotional and spiritual pain, and he caused himself physical harm to try to make all of that go away."

"Which is not an escape route," Lydia said, her voice sharp and clear. "It didn't work for Mark and it won't work for you."

Reverend Rick started again before Lydia could go on.

"What's important," he said, "is that we got him to the hospital, and his dad has already flown in from Nebraska to be with him, and he's stable; he's going to be okay."

"Fuck this," Dane said. He put his hands in fists and hit the sides of his thighs, twice. "Y'all are talking like a hamster wheel. What did he do? If he didn't try to kill himself, then what?"

"Yelling and swearing won't make you feel any better about Mark," Lydia said.

Dane snorted a mean kind of grunt. "See, there you're wrong again, 'cause it does, actually. It really does make me feel a fuck of a lot better to say *fuck, fuck, fuck* right now."

I guess because it was already tense in there, or because she was already worked up, this is the moment that Helen started giggling behind her wad of tissues in a way that she obviously couldn't control. She had a surprisingly girly giggle, like a cheerleader in a teen movie. "I'm sorry," she said, and kept giggling. "I'm sorry, I can't stop." More giggles.

Right then Reverend Rick slid his chair forward as he stood up behind it and clapped his hands and announced that this *wasn't quite working out* and that we'd be having brief one-on-ones instead of group and that we should each go to our rooms and wait until either he or Lydia came by to talk with us, except for Dane and Helen, who they would start with right then. Lydia was looking at him like she didn't like the spontaneity of this plan much at all, but I, for one, was glad to get out of there.

The Viking Erin was on dinner duty, so our room was empty when I got back to it. It smelled like houses sometimes do toward the end of winter, when they've been sealed off for too long, like old air, like dirty heating ducts, so I opened the window just a crack and stood in front of the stream of crisp air until I was shivering a little. There were angry clouds building up behind the mountains, black-gray clouds, great clumps of them colored just like cotton balls after Aunt Ruth cleaned off her eye makeup from a big night out, all gunky with mascara and eye shadow.

I sat in my desk chair, tipping it so that it was only resting on the back two legs, one of my feet propped against the corner of the desk, balancing me. I tried to do exercises in my Spanish workbook, but I mostly thought about all the terrible things Mark might have done to himself.

I wasn't sure if it would be Rick or Lydia or both of them who would come, and so I was glad, half an hour or so later, when just Rick knocked on the open door of our room and said, "Hey, Cameron. Have you got a few minutes for me?"

It was classic Rick, acting like he was just stopping in for a routine chat and not like he'd sent us to our rooms with the express purpose of meeting with him, but he was so unfailingly nice that it was hard not to appreciate the way he phrased stuff like that.

I wasn't sure where he'd sit, but he came to the back of the room, where I was, and pushed my shoulder forward, one firm nudge, so that my chair tipped back into position and he had room to pull Erin's chair from its slot beneath her desk. It was a friendly sort of thing to do, casual.

"You know sitting like that breaks the legs, right?" he said. "At least that's what my mom always told me."

"My mom too, but I've yet to see it happen," I said.

"Good point," he said. And then, with no more filler, "So is there anything you wanna talk about?"

"About Mark?" I asked.

"About Mark, about yesterday's group, about anything at all."

"He's gonna be all right?"

Rick nodded, tucked his hair behind his ear. "I think so. He really hurt himself; it's a serious injury. He'll be healing for a long time—all kinds of healing."

It felt impossible, talking this way, around this terrible thing that I both did and didn't want to know all the details of. I kept seeing these flashes of Mark with all of these Biblical kinds of tortures applied to him, his eyes gouged out or his hands impaled, and not knowing wasn't making it easier.

"Did he do it in front of you?" I asked, which seemed all the more horrible to consider, that maybe he'd wanted them to watch, or that he was just so out of it that he didn't know they were watching,

"No, he was in his room," Rick said.

"Why'd you leave him alone if you were so worried about him?" I didn't intend for that question to sound mean, exactly, but it did, and I didn't regret asking it.

"I don't have a very good answer for you," he said, and then he looked at his hands. He was just sort of running the fingers of one hand over the palm of the other, tracing his guitar-playing calluses. "It could have been your voice in my head all day asking me that. Instead it was my own."

I waited. He waited. Then he said, "He had calmed down considerably. It was very late when we walked him back from my office; Adam was in the room sleeping already. Lydia and I felt sure that Mark would do the same."

We both waited some more. The unsaid everything waited there with us, hovering over us both. I stared at this picture of Erin and her parents at the Living Bible Museum in Ohio, all of them in khaki shorts and tucked-in T-shirts, grinning big grins, posed in front of a display of Moses on the mount. I'd stared at it all year, mostly thinking about how they looked really happy; happy to be there, to be together. But now their smiles, so stretched and thick, looked sort of terrible, like plastic smiles or mask smiles, I don't know. They were giving me a headache, those stretched grins. I looked back at Rick and I said, "I don't know what else to ask you. I guess either you want us to know what happened and to talk about it or you don't. This all just seems really fake if you're not gonna tell us everything."

"I will tell you," he said. He said it just like that. "I'll tell you if that's what you want. It's, ah . . ." He paused, did something with his lips between a grin and a grimace. "Well, Lydia and I have a difference of opinion about this, but I think it's important to be honest with all of you, so that you know what happened exactly as it happened with no rumors or gossip wrapped around it. But it's very ugly, Cameron."

"I can handle ugly," I said.

He nodded and said, "But just because you can handle something doesn't mean that it's good for you."

I had this flash-memory of me and Hazel on the beach when she'd tried to warn me off lifeguarding with the same logic, but I was older now and felt it too, the weight of the months that had passed between then and now. "You just told me that it was important to be honest and now you're backing off," I said. "Dane's right—you do talk like a hamster wheel."

He tucked hair behind his other ear, though it didn't need to be done. "Dane's got a great way of putting things, doesn't he?"

"There you go," I said. "Spin, spin, spin."

"I'm not," he said. "At least I'm not trying to. I'm sorry; it's a hard thing to tell." He breathed in quick and blew it out and said, "Last night Mark used a razor to cut his genitals several times; then he poured bleach over the wounds."

"Jesus," I said. Rick didn't blink at the word.

"He passed out after that, and Adam heard the bottle of bleach hit the floor. Or I guess he could have heard Mark hit the floor too. Adam's the one who came and got me, and he helped me and Kevin carry Mark to the van after that. He was mostly out of it, completely incoherent; Mark, I mean."

"Why didn't Adam go get Kevin?" Kevin was a college student and one of the night monitors. He came two or three nights a week, but he arrived during study hours and was usually gone by breakfast, so unless you had to go to the bathroom, or were a light sleeper and noticed him when he did room checks, you didn't really see him. He'd caught me trying to meet up with Jane and Adam once after lights out, but he had just walked me back to my room. Told me to *go to bed.* I don't think he ever even mentioned my rule breaking to Rick or Lydia.

"He couldn't find him," Rick said. "I guess Kevin was making a sandwich in the kitchen and they just missed each other. Kevin's taking it hard too."

"Shouldn't you have called an ambulance?" I asked. I already knew why they hadn't: It was much faster just to drive him than to wait for one to get all the way out to Promise, but I was just trying to think of things to say because I didn't know what else to do and I didn't want to sit there in silence with Rick looking one of his ponderous looks at me.

"It would have taken too long," Rick said. "It was faster to drive him myself."

I nodded and said, "Yeah. Duh. I wasn't thinking."

"It's okay," he said. "What do you really want to ask me?"

I was picturing Adam waking up to what he woke up to, the plastic smack of the bottle on the laminate, the chemical smell of bleach, Mark on the floor with his pants down, bloody and gruesome and a fucking mess, and Adam just barely awake, all bleary and confused. What I said to Rick, though, was "I don't know." Then I waited a little while, and he waited, and then I asked, "Is Adam doing okay?"

Rick smiled this weird, sad sort of smile at me and said, "I think so, all things considered. I'm sure he'll want to talk to you about this. It's gonna take him some time to process."

That set me off. I hadn't felt like I was ticking down to something, at least I didn't think that's what I was feeling. I had just felt sort of numb and baffled, but right after he said that thing about it taking Adam "some time to process," I was like instantly enraged, just so fucking pissed at him, and at this stupid place, God's Fucking Promise.

"How the fuck do you work out something like this?" I asked, my voice the kind of shrill it gets when I'm too mad to cry but have that burning in my throat anyway. I hate my voice like that but I just kept on. "I mean, seriously, you wake up to find your roommate with a bloody mess on his penis? What's the worksheet Lydia's gonna assign for that? Maybe Adam can fucking put it on his iceberg now." I was so, so angry, as mad as I'd ever been, ever, in my life. I just started saying stuff, just whatever, anything, stuff like "You guys don't even know what you're doing here, do you? You're just like making it up as you go along and then something like this happens and you're gonna pretend like you have answers that you don't even have and it's completely fucking fake. You don't know how to fix this. You should just say that: We fucked it up." I said some other stuff, too. I don't even know what all I said, but it was loud and angry and I just kept saying it.

Rick didn't tell me to stop swearing or being such a ass-hole, not that he would have used that word but that's sort of what I was being even if what I was saying was true, but he didn't try to cut me off or jump in and stop me the way that Lydia would have. And that didn't really surprise me, because Rick was good at being calm. What he did do, and it did surprise me, is start crying himself. He did it quietly, but he didn't hide his face from me, he just sat in that chair, facing me, and cried. That stopped my tirade. It stopped it pretty fast. And then it was all the more terrible, the whole thing, when he said, still crying, "I don't know how to answer you right now, Cam. I'm sorry."

Rick didn't call me Cam, nobody was supposed to at Promise, because it was, according to Lydia, *an even more masculine adaptation of my already androgynous name.* Sometimes Jane and Adam and Steve might, because it would just come out that way, but they tried not to do it around Rick or Lydia, and Rick had definitely never slipped up before.

He really was a handsome guy, and his face was sort of horribly beautiful right then, maybe because it was so vulnerable, I don't know, but it was one of those moments that's just unbearable to be in the middle of, everything raw and open and thick with emotion, and it's not something I can really explain, even now, but I got up and I gave him a hug, a hug that was even more awkward because he was still sitting and I was leaning over, but I did it, and then, after a few seconds, he stood up and we hugged like that, which was a little bit less awkward.

Eventually he sort of backed a step or two away but still held me by my shoulders and said, "We got this backwards. I came in here to make you feel better."

"It's okay," I said. "I do sort of feel better."

"You're right to be upset about this, and to wonder how it might change what we're doing here. But for now the best thing I can tell you is that we'll let Christ lead us to our answers. When in doubt He's the best guy to follow, right?"

"Sure," I said, but I didn't mean it, because it was precisely because he hadn't tried to give me any answers, because he'd told me that he didn't have any, and had started crying and had seemed doubtful, unsure, that I was feeling any better at all. All that seemed more honest than anything else he (and Lydia) might eventually invent to deal with this because Christ had *led them to it*. That would just make it worse.

"This means something to me," he said, and he pulled me back in for another quick squeeze before he let go. "Thank you for letting me have this with you. I know it doesn't come easy."

"This isn't easy for anybody," I said. "It's not like it's worse on me. I didn't find him on the floor."

"I'm thanking you for being honest with me. It was brave."

"Yeah," I said. "Whatever." I didn't want to talk anymore about what had just happened; I hated that about Promise. Why couldn't a moment just happen, and both of us be aware of it, without having to comment on it forever and ever?

"Anything else you want to ask me?" Rick said.

And out of nowhere, I mean, completely unplanned, I said, "Is Lydia really your aunt?"

He made a face like *What the hell?* and then laughed and said, "I wasn't expecting that one." But then he added, "As a matter of fact, she is. Jane must have told you, huh?"

"Yeah," I said. "Right after I got here. I just wasn't sure if I should believe her."

"About that you should," he said. "Lydia was my mom's sister."

"Was," I said. "Not anymore?"

"My mom died a few years ago."

I nodded. "Sorry," I said. I had lots more questions I might have asked him about Lydia, about the two of them, about his dead mom, but it didn't quite seem like the time to be doing it, and anyway, Erin walked in, before she recognized that Rick was in the room, she just walked in and then said, "Oh, I'm sorry. I'll come back when you're done."

Rick said, "I think we are done, right?"

I nodded.

He walked to the door and said to Erin, "You stay; I'm just on my way to find Steve." Then he put an arm around her waist and squeezed, quick, and said, "It's a hard day, isn't it?"

Erin nodded but kept it together.

"We're all gonna meet in the chapel in twenty minutes or so," he said, one hand hanging on the doorframe and one hand looking at his simple watch, the one I liked, with the white face and the tan-and-navy canvas strap.

"We are?" I asked.

"Yeah, Lydia came and told those of us in the kitchen," Erin said.

I looked at Rick, who nodded, smiled, then patted the doorframe twice and left.

Erin wanted to talk about Mark and I didn't. I wanted to climb into bed, all my clothes on, and sleep. Better yet: I wanted a VCR and a stack of videos and I wanted to play them one after another after another. Erin hadn't heard all the details about what had happened—she'd just heard it was a *self-inflicted injury* and that he was stable. I didn't fill in the gaps for her, because I knew some other disciple would, eventually. I just didn't want to talk about it anymore.

But that's what was mostly on the agenda for the rest of the night. We had the impromptu chapel session where we prayed for Mark and we prayed for his family and for Adam, who I didn't even get to say anything to in private before the whole thing started. Then we prayed for us. Then everybody who wanted to say something got to say something, and that was almost everybody except for me and Jane. When it was Dane's turn, he was a lot more calm than he'd been during group, so calm that I wondered if they'd drugged him or something, though the idea of Lydia with some secret stash of sedatives was sort of ridiculous, and also sort of not. Then we had free time, and there were some snacks in the cafeteria but no dinner, because the disciples on dinner duty had been called away before the meal was finished. Reverend Rick went into Ennis to get pizza for us, a real treat courtesy of Mark's personal tragedy. Somebody, Lydia probably, started *The Sound of Music* in the activity room. It was one of like three secular films in the Promise video library, but I couldn't lose myself to it with so many red- and puffy-eyed disciples in there watching together and breathing and shifting around on the couches, the floor. Jane and Adam and I eventually just got up and left, and we knew we were going to smoke. We didn't even have to talk about it. We got our coats and went to the barn. It was snowing but not very hard, *a nice, quiet snow* is what Grandma would have called it. Fat flakes coming slowly. There was still quite a bit of snow on the ground too, from our winter's worth, but it had been melting all day, the early-spring sun on it, and the path was really slippery, water over packed-down ice. A few feet out, I fell, hard, my right hip crashing onto the ground, that section of my khakis instantly soaked. Adam gripped my elbow and pulled me up and said, "You okay, twinkle-toes?"

That made me smile, and I said, "I'm okay. What about you?"

And he said, "I've been better," and he linked his arm with mine and we finished the walk like that. It was nice.

It was cold in the barn and damp, the hayloft stinking and wet. We huddled together in a clump, our legs beneath these blankets we'd hauled out there in the fall. It was dark too, the few electric lights on the main floor doing little to light the mow. I had a headache, and my hip hurt where I'd landed, and my hands were red and cold: I was kind of a mess. We were all kind of a mess.

For a while we just passed around the joint that Jane had brought, without talking, until it was maybe two hits away from being caked, and then Jane said, "I didn't even know that Mark shaved."

"He doesn't," Adam said, taking the joint from Jane and holding it, elegantly, between his thin fingers. "That boy's all peach fuzz; he doesn't need to shave. It was my razor from my shower kit. It's a nice one, it's not disposable, it's heavy. My dad gave it to me for my birthday last year. I used to use it sometimes to shave my legs, but not now with Lydia on girly-man patrol." He toked, then exhaled before he could have gotten much effect and said quickly, "Not that I'm saying I'm ever gonna use it again. I don't even know where it is. Lydia took it with her last night after she helped me clean up the room."

"I'm sorry," I said.

"Me too," Jane said.

Adam nodded. Then he said, "The bleach went every-where. It must have been a brand-spankin'-new bottle, because it fucking made a lake on the floor. There's probably still some in there, under the beds or whatever. I heard this noise, and I knew something was weird, and then I could smell the bleach, but it was—you know how it is when you've just woken up, nothing was registering right—and then when I put my feet on the floor it was wet, but like soaked-through-my-socks wet."

Jane and I just kept nodding. What was there to say?

Adam passed me the joint for the final hit, which I took, happy to have something to do.

"Did the bleach soak all of his clothes, too?" Jane asked. "Because he was lying in it?"

"He was naked," Adam said. "He was completely bare-ass naked. I pretty much tripped over him getting to the light, and then when I turned it on, I mean, I didn't know, I just knew it was bad. He was slumped over so I couldn't see his, you know . . ." He paused, shook his head. "His dick. I should be able to say the word *dick*. Fuck. I couldn't see it, so I didn't know that he'd done what he did. I just knew that he was naked on the floor, there was a fucking lake of bleach, and it took like four more seconds until I saw blood leaking into the bleach and I went for Rick. I thought maybe he'd tried to drink it, or slit his wrists, or something. I thought he was dead, though. I really thought he was dead. That's what I told Rick. I said, 'Mark's dead. He's dead on the floor.'" He stopped, looked back and forth between the two of us. "That's really fucked up, right?"

"It's not," I said. "What else would you think?"

"Not that," Adam said. "I don't know." He pulled at a piece of yarn that had come loose on one section of the blanket, pulled it tighter and tighter around his finger, cutting off the circulation, making the tip swollen and red with bright white indentations. "I talked to his dad today," he said. "Did they tell you that?"

We shook our heads no.

Adam let the string binding around his finger loosen. He took what was now most definitely a caked joint from my hand. I had just been sitting with it. He put it out on the end of his tongue. He always did that. Then he said, "I wanted to go to the hospital, but his dad didn't want any of us there. He sent Rick back like the minute he got in from the airport. But he called here later to talk to me, and he said, 'Thank you for what you did for Mark. We'll remember you in our prayers. You please pray for Mark, too.' That's it. That's what he said, word for word."

"But think about the condition his son is in," Jane said.

"A condition he helped cause," Adam said, sneering. He stood up, kicked some clumps of hay. "He sends him here, tells him that he'll go to hell as a sodomite if he doesn't fix himself. So the kid tries and he tries and you know what, he can't, because it can't fucking be done, so he figures, I'll just cut off the problem area. Great plan, Pops."

"You're right," Jane said. "It's completely fucked. But his dad doesn't see it that way. He absolutely believes with everything in him that what he's doing is the only way to save his son from eternal damnation. The fiery pits of hell. He believes that completely."

Adam kept sneering, near a shout now. "Yeah, well what about saving him from right now? What about the hell of thinking it's best just to fucking chop your balls off than to have your body somehow betray your stupid fucking belief system?"

"That's never what it's about to those people," Jane said, still calm. "All that's the price we're supposed to pay for salvation. We're supposed to be glad to pay it."

"Thanks, Mother Wisdom," Adam said. "Your calm insight is so powerful in times like these."

This wounded look crumpled Jane's face, and then she got rid of it quick. But I know Adam saw it too, because he said, "Sorry."

"It's okay," she said. "I didn't mean to lecture."

"Don't just give me an automatic dick pass." He bent and kissed her cheek and said, "I don't get to be a douche just because my roommate lost his shit."

"Yes you do," Jane said. "You get to be whatever you want right now."

"Can I be an astronaut?" he asked, sitting down next to me again and pulling some of my blanket around him.

"Indubitably," she said. "You can even be the famed Neil Armstrong."

"You just picked him because the name Armstrong sounds sort of native, didn't you?" he said, barely showing a grin.

"I'm not staying at Promise," I said, just like that. I only decided, for sure, pretty much as I was saying it. "I'm not. I'm gonna leave."

"You wanna be an astronaut with me?" Adam asked, palming the top of my head and tilting it until my ear rested on his shoulder. "We can open up the first lunar 7-Eleven." He mimed the outline of a billboard with his hands, popped his fingers in and out like blinking lights, and said, "Now serving marijuana Slurpees. For a limited time only. Some restrictions apply."

"I'm serious," I said, and the thing was, the more I said it, the more serious I got. "I'm gonna figure out a way to leave. If I don't, I know Ruth will keep me here next year. I know she will."

"Of course she will," Jane said. "Nobody ever leaves because they're all better. You only leave if you can't pay anymore or you graduate."

"Or you're Mark," I said.

"Yes," Jane said. "Or you're Mark."

"Really?" Adam said. "Nobody's ever passed the program

or whatever? Gotten ex-gay enough to go back to normal high school?"

"Well, it's only been open three years," Jane said. "But nobody's done it that I know of."

"Because it can't be done," I said.

"And because there's no real test that could prove your transition anyway," Jane said, putting things back into her leg compartment. It was weird how sometimes I forgot she even had that thing—the leg itself, not the compartment, I could never forget that. "You can change your behavior, but if you don't have Lydia breathing down your neck, that will only last so long. Besides, it doesn't mean anything else about you has changed, inside, I mean."

"That's why I'm going," I said. "That and a million other reasons. I don't want to be here anymore."

"I'm in," Adam said, whipping the blanket off both of us, my skin goose-bumping immediately. "Let's do it right now, no more talking. I'll be Bonnie and you'll be my Clyde."

"I'll go with you," Jane said, with total seriousness. She almost had her leg reattached. "But we need to have a comprehensive plan. We need to work out the details."

"Just like a couple of lesbos," Adam said. "Comprehensive plan? Are we building a deck or escaping? Let's just go. I'll steal the van keys—seriously. Right now we do it. We could be in Canada by morning, all-you-can eat Canadian bacon. Now there's a euphemism for you."

"They'd stop our stolen vehicle at the border check," Jane said. "And even if they didn't, we don't have our IDs, we don't have much money, we don't know anyone in Canada. Or I don't."

I wanted to jump up with Adam and just do it, like he said, take action. But what Jane said was true. They kept our driver's licenses (those of us that had them) and other identification papers, or copies of those papers, in one of the locked file cabinets in the main office.

"So we get our IDs right now," Adam said. "And then we go."

"This is why we need a plan," Jane said. "This is exactly why. So that we don't get tripped up by all the details we forgot."

While she was speaking, there was a kind of low rumbling from far off, and if it hadn't been snowing when we walked out to the barn, I would have been sure that it was thunder.

"We won't ever do it," Adam said, "if we sit around and think about it forever. We won't. So let's just go."

"To where?" I asked.

"Who cares?" he said. "We'll figure it out on the road."

"I want to go too," Jane said. "But let's do it right. If we steal a van, they'll find us and we'll get sent back here within a couple of days. And then what was the point?"

Right as she finished, there was a drum roll of what now sounded unmistakably like thunder.

"Zeus is angry," Adam said, standing again.

"Was it thunder?" I asked, and then more thunder rumbled, this closer than the last, the storm moving quickly like they so often do in the mountains.

"It's thundersnow," Jane said as Adam went to the heavy wooden hatch that closed off the hay pitch. It was a bitch to move. We'd done it before, but the hinges were more rust than not, and the gray wood splintered into your skin like a sticker plant every time you got your hands on it. Adam worked at it anyway, though.

"Is it even still snowing?" I asked as I got up to join him.

"If it is, it's thundersnow," Jane said.

"I've never heard of that," I said as Adam and I managed to push the hatch out some, those bolts squeaking and screeching at our efforts, tiny splinters of that old wood already barbing my fingers.

"It's uncommon," Jane said, standing up. "It happened once when we lived on the commune. I can't believe I don't have my camera."

Adam and I kept inching the hatch and it went a bit farther, and then a bit more, until we could see mostly just a black sky and black ground, some sections blacker than others, with white snowflakes coming down much faster than before, blizzard fast, the snow a superwhite blur against all that blackness.

"It is," Jane said from behind us. "It's thundersnow."

"Oh my God, we get it," Adam said. "Stop saying *thundersnow.*"

But she was sort of vindicated, because then a blast of thunder crashed loud, the storm closing in around us, the kind of thunder that you feel in the walls, deep inside your body, and then a bolt of lightning made its jagged silver path across the sky, like the trajectory of a failing heart patient's EKG monitor. And then another, its flash lighting the snow on the ground, reflecting off the millions of crystals, impossibly bright and white, and then the whole area was completely black again, and then another flash, another great cracking noise and spotlight. One of the pines lit up momentarily, its snow-heavy bows, its massive height against the black nothingness, and then it was gone, and then something else got the spotlight, some other section of land that had been blackness just before, and all the while the thunder rumbled behind the spectacle and the snowflakes whirled and flew, heavier and heavier, so thick they seemed almost to clog the air. We three watched and watched together. I think it was probably the most beautiful thing I've ever seen.

"I can't believe I don't have my camera," Jane said again, her voice almost reverent.

"You couldn't ever get this into a picture," I said. "And you'd miss it while you were trying to."

"Rick's back," Adam said, and I looked in the direction he was staring and found the headlights he had seen, two faint orange dots coming closer and closer toward Promise, toward us.

"I want to go with you," Jane said. She took my hand. "I mean it. I'll do whatever."

"Okay," I said.

"You two aren't running off together and leaving me here," Adam said, wrapping both of his hands around ours. "Even though I can't quite believe that we're ever gonna go."

"We're going," Jane said.

"I don't have a plan," I said. "I know some people who might help us, maybe, if we can even find them. But that's all I got." I was thinking of Margot, the money she'd sent me in that Campfire Girls manual; I was thinking of Lindsey and her bad-assness; and Mona Harris, close by in Bozeman, at college. And for some reason I thought of Irene Klauson, too. Though I don't really know why.

"Then we'll find them," Jane said. I liked how sure she was.

"I have my staggering good looks to offer," Adam said. "And my unique and complicated understanding of sex roles. You can call it a mystical understanding, if you must."

"I've got the weed," Jane said, and we all laughed the way you laugh when you're trying to be brave in the face of something that scares you.

The headlights were bigger, and closer, just beyond the

metal-roofed cabins now, the bulky rectangle of the van barely visible through the snow, Reverend Rick and his stack of pizza pies, braving the thundersnow for all of us weary disciples.

"We'd better go in," I said. "Before they come looking for us."

CHAPTER NINETEEN

Mark Turner didn't come back to Promise. Not two weeks later. Not a month later. Never. At least not while I was there. Reverend Rick and Adam had to pack up his stuff and send it to him in Kearney, Nebraska. Adam never did get his fancy razor returned to him, not that he wanted it back, he said, but it disappeared from Promise, just like Mark. Just like the three of us were going to.

Pretty soon after Mark's *incident*, which is what somehow everyone started calling it except for me and Jane and Adam, a guy from the state came out to inspect Promise, the classrooms, the dorms, everything. He worked for one of the licensing departments. Then a couple of other guys came, and a lady. The lady wore a plum-colored pantsuit with a gold-and-plum scarf, and I remember thinking that Aunt Ruth would call the combined effect *a smart little look*. All the men wore ties and jackets, and everyone who came worked for one state agency or another. Most of these people spent their time in Rick's office, but one of the guys talked to each disciple for twenty minutes or so. I went in after Erin, but there was no chance to ask her what it was like; we just passed each other in the hallway outside the classroom where he'd set up shop for the day.

At first I liked this guy because he was so routine, and seemed, I don't know, professional, or at least he didn't talk down to me, or act like a counselor, probably because he wasn't one. He introduced himself but I can't remember his name, Mr. Blah-Blah from the Child and Family Services Department, I think. He started with a series of mundane questions: *How often do you eat meals? How much time do you spend on schoolwork, both in the classroom and otherwise, each day? How much time do you spend completing other activities? What is the level of supervision for these activities?* And then he asked a few less mundane questions: *Do you feel safe in your dorm rooms at night? Do you feel threatened by any staff members or fellow students?* (This guy used the word *student*, not *disciple*). *Do you trust those in charge here?* My answer to that question was the first I'd given that really seemed to interest him.

"Not really" is what I said.

He had been taking brief notes on a yellow legal pad, rarely even looking up at me, just reading from his stapled list of questions and then scribbling this or that and moving on. But now he paused and looked right at me, his pen hovered there. "You don't trust the staff here?"

I guess, in answering that way, I had been expecting a reaction from him, but then I was sort of unsure of what to do with it once I got it. "Well, I mean, trust them how?" I asked. "What do you mean by trust?"

"Trust," he said, doing one of those *this-should-be-obvious-to-you* kind of open-mouthed, head-bobbing faces. "Trust: belief in them and their abilities. Do you trust them with your safety and security while you're living here? Do you believe that they have your best interests in mind?"

I shrugged. "You're saying those things like they're completely simple," I said. "Or black and white or whatever."

"I think they are black and white," he said. "I'm not trying to trick you with these questions." I could tell he was losing patience with me, or maybe he just didn't like me very much. He had very hairy ears, I noticed. It was hard not to look at them once I did, actually, so much hair coming from the inside, and hair on the outside, too.

"Maybe if you lived here you would feel differently," I said. Staring at his ears was making me feel like I could start in on uncontrollable giggles, just like Helen at our group session. I concentrated on his tie instead, which was a deeper shade of yellow than his notepad, but not far off. It had cerulean fleurs-de-lis all over it. Cerulean. I still loved that word. It was a nice tie. It was very nice.

"I like your tie," I said.

He bent his neck to look at it, as if he'd forgotten which tie he'd chosen for the day. Maybe he had. "Thanks," he said. "It's new. My wife picked it out for me."

"That's nice," I said. It was nice, sort of. It seemed so normal to have a wife who picked out your yellow ties for you. Whatever that meant: normal. It had to mean not living a life at Promise. It had to at least mean that.

"Yeah, she's kind of a clothes horse," he said. Then he seemed to remember what he was doing there with me. He consulted his notes and asked, "Do you think you can tell me more specifically what you mean when you say that you can't trust the staff here?"

That time he did sound like every other counselor who'd ever asked me to elaborate on my feelings. I was surprised at myself for having picked him to open up to. I was surprised even as I was doing it. Maybe I picked him because I thought he would have to take me seriously, whatever I said, he seemed so fastidious and by the book, and he also seemed, precisely because of his position and that fastidiousness, a little nonjudgmental, I guess.

"I would say that Rick and Lydia and everybody else associated with Promise think that they're doing what's best for us, like spiritually or whatever," I said. "But just because you think something doesn't make it true."

"Okaaaaay," he said. "Can you go on?"

"Not really," I said, but then tried to anyway. "I'm just saying that sometimes you can end up really messing somebody up because the way you're trying to supposedly help them is really messed up."

"So are you saying that their method of treatment is abusive?" he asked me in a tone I didn't like very much.

"Look, nobody's beating us. They're not even yelling at us. It's not like that." I sighed and shook my head. "You asked me if I trusted them, and like, I trust them to drive the vans safely on the highway, and I trust that they'll buy food for us every week, but I don't trust that they actually know what's best for my soul, or how to make me the best person with a guaranteed slot in heaven or whatever." I could tell I was losing him. Or maybe I'd never had him to begin with, and I was mad at myself for being so inarticulate, for messing up what I felt like I owed to Mark, even if he wouldn't see it that way, which he probably wouldn't.

"Whatever," I said. "It's hard to explain. I just don't trust that a place like Promise is even necessary, or that I need to be here, or that any of us need to be here, and the whole point of being here is that we're supposed to trust that what they're doing is going to save us, so how could I answer yes to your question?"

"I guess you couldn't," he said.

I thought maybe I had an in, so I said, "It's just that I know you're here because of what happened to Mark."

But before I could continue he said, "What Mr. Turner did to himself."

"What?" I asked.

"You said what *happened to him*," he said. "Something didn't *just happen* to him. He injured himself. Severely."

"Yeah, while under the care of this facility," I said.

"Correct," he said in another unreadable tone. "And that's why I'm here: to investigate the care that is given by those who run this facility, but not to investigate the mission of the facility, unless that mission includes abuse or neglect."

"But isn't there like emotional abuse?" I asked.

"There is," he said, completely noncommittal. "Do you feel that you've been emotionally abused by the staff here?"

"Oh my God," I said, throwing my hands in the air, feeling every bit as dramatic as I was acting. "I just told you all about it—the whole fucking purpose of this place is to make us hate ourselves so that we change. We're supposed to *hate* who we are, despise it."

"I see," he said, but I could tell that he didn't at all. "Is there anything else?"

"No, I think the *hate yourself* part about covers it."

He looked at me, unsure, searching for what to say, and then he took a breath and said, "Okay. I want you to know that I've written down what you've said and it will go in the official file. I'll also share it with my committee." He had jotted some things down as I was talking, but I definitely didn't trust that he'd really written down what I had said, not really, at least not the way that I'd said it.

"Right," I said. "Well, I'm sure that will be an effective method for change." Now I hated this guy, and myself a little too—for hoping that I could make something happen just by answering a few questions honestly. For once.

"I'm not sure I understand," he said.

And I believe that he really didn't understand what I was trying to say; I do. But I also believe that he didn't really want to, because he probably wasn't so nonjudgmental after all, and maybe he even believed that people like me, like Mark, absolutely did belong at Promise. Or somewhere worse. And though I knew that I couldn't explain all of that to him, make what I was feeling fit neatly into words, I tried, more for me and for Mark than for this guy's understanding.

"My whole point," I said, "is that what they teach here, what they believe, if you don't trust it, if you doubt it at all, then you're told that you're going to hell, that not only everyone you know is ashamed of you, but that Jesus himself has given up on your soul. And if you're like Mark, and you do believe all of this, you really do—you have faith in Jesus and this stupid Promise system, and even still, even with those things, you still can't make yourself good enough, because what you're trying to change *isn't changeable*, it's like your height or the shape of your ears, whatever, then it's like this place *does* make things happen to you, or at least it's supposed to convince you that you're always gonna be a dirty sinner and that it's completely your fault because you're not trying hard enough to change yourself. It convinced Mark."

"Are you saying that you think the staff should have anticipated that Mark would do something like this?" he asked, jotting again. "Were there warning signs?"

At that I just gave up completely.

"Yeah, I'd say his verbatim memorization of the most fucked-up passages in the Bible might have been one," I said, looking right at him and trying to make my face as blank as his. "But here at Promise that's seen as a sign of progress. It's actually surprising that all of us disciples haven't hacked off our privates with the handiest sharp object. I'll probably do it when I get back to my room, first chance."

That changed his flat face but he controlled it again pretty fast. "I'm sorry that you're so upset," he said. He didn't say *I'm sorry that I've upset you*. He didn't take the blame; but he was probably right not to. It wasn't really his fault.

"I am upset," I said. "That's as good a word as any."

He had other questions for me then, and he tried a couple more times to get me to give him specifics about *this emotional abuse* I felt I had suffered, but even the way he said it made it sound so stupid, and me like a whiny kid who didn't like the appropriate punishment I was receiving on account of my bad, bad behavior. I gave him one- or two-word answers and it didn't take more than maybe three minutes before he'd recapped his pen and thanked me for coming and asked me to "please send Steve Cromps in next." So I did.

I don't know what any reports that were filed to state agencies about *the incident* concluded, but I do know that nothing much changed at Promise. Kevin the night monitor was fired, that was one thing. He was replaced by Harvey, a sixtysomething who used to do security for Walmart. Harvey wore squeaky, black, old-man sneakers and did this rapid, three-quick-blows nostril-clearing thing into his hanky every fifteen minutes or so. I felt confident that if he caught me outside of my room at night, Rick and Lydia would most definitely know about it. Also, our parents or *guardians* were told about *the incident*; probably that was required by law. Ruth wrote me a long letter about how sorry she was *that it had happened*. She didn't write anything about possibly doubting the treatment I was receiving, or blaming it, or worrying that a similar fate might befall me. Other people's parents reacted similarly. Nobody pulled their kids out of Promise or anything like that. (Well, except for Mark's parents, of course.) For a few weeks right after, we were an even more exotic band of sinners when we attended off-campus church services at Word of Life. But the luster of us somehow being gruesome by association wore off pretty quickly, and soon we were just run-of-the-mill sexual deviants again.

• • •

I remember that my dad used to say that Montana only has two seasons: winter and road construction. I've heard lots of people say it since then, but I still think of it as something my dad said, something I remember him saying from when I was really, really little. I know all the reasons why people say stuff like that, the good-natured kidding about a state you're actually completely in love with; the folksy way of articulating the suffocating qualities of a seemingly endless Montana winter and the dry heat and annoyances of the summer that so soon follows; the way a saying like that encapsulates just how present the natural world is in Montana, and how aware of it you are—the sky, the land, the weather, all of it. (Variations on the saying include: Montana has only two seasons: winter and forest fires; winter and whatever's not; hunting season and waiting-for-hunting season.)

I can tell you for a fact, though, that there was most definitely a springtime in western Montana in 1993. And thank God for that, because our escape plan depended on it. Spring started to trickle in by the middle of March, a little bit here and there, and it had flooded the entire valley where Promise sat before the end of May. At first all our snowpack grew slushy, thawing during the day, refreezing at night, and repeat, and repeat, and then it melted into the ground entirely, leaving every path muddy, some places swampy, which sure didn't stop Adam and me from resuming our trail runs, even when we had to wear sweatshirts and gloves, even when the second half of the run, back to the dorms, took almost twice as long as the first half, our sneakers so clumped up with thick mud that they might as well have been weights attached to our feet. It didn't matter whose bedroom you walked past, now everybody had their windows open, letting all the good spring smells float in, the wet earth and new growth and the indescribable scent of icy mountain wind as it rushed from those peaks still covered in snowcaps that wouldn't ever melt completely and weren't really all that far outside our windows.

By the time the first crocuses appeared—there was a huge patch of them behind one of the summer camp cabins, and also these tiny yellow flowers that spread like shag carpet across the most unlikely ground, creeping out of crevices in rocks and alongside the edge of the barn—Jane and Adam and I had settled on a time to escape. We were gonna go at the beginning of June, just after we took our exams at the Lifegate Christian School in Bozeman but before the start of Camp Promise. I'd been working ahead on my classes, and if I passed the exams I'd be in the twelfth grade in terms of course credits, which is where Adam would be. But Jane would be graduating; she'd be finished. It was most important to her to have her transcripts in order.

We were still working out all of the details of our plan then, the whole thing looming vague and uncertain ahead of us, but from the very start Jane was pushing for us not to go until finals were over. She'd been arguing with Adam about it. He wanted us to leave sooner rather than later, and he definitely saw June as later.

Jane and I were talking it over quietly one morning while on cleaning duty together, the two of us scrubbing the always mildewy shower stalls, our voices echoey despite our attempts to speak lowly. Those stalls were heavy with the smell of Comet, something I still couldn't be around without thinking of the terrible night Grandma told me the news. I was glad we had our escape plan for me to focus on instead.

Jane was in the middle of making yet another point about the benefits of waiting until June when I said, "I'm fine with going after finals, it's cool. I get it. But then why even bother leaving with us?"

"What do you mean, 'why bother'?" She squeezed her yellow scrub sponge into our shared bucket. "For all the same reasons you're bothering."

"I just mean that you'll be done," I said. "You can go to college. You don't have to escape."

"Hardly," she said. "I don't turn eighteen until August, which will make me a minor with a diploma until then, still technically under my mother's guardianship, and she'll want me to stay through summer camp, I can guarantee you that; the less time I'm under her roof, the better." She dunked her sponge again, it made a squelchy-splashy noise as she twisted it. "Besides, you think I'm actually going to pursue my higher education at Bob Jones University? Or maybe Wayland Baptist in ever-progressive Plainview, Texas?"

"Just because they made you apply to shit schools doesn't mean you have to go to those schools," I said. Bethany kept a file thick with brochures and catalogs for evangelical colleges, and Jane and a couple of the other disciples who would be graduating had spent some time that fall apply-ing to them, which was, according to Jane, a formality, because, she said, those kinds of colleges let in everyone who can pay and is either authentically evangelical or willing to play the part. And indeed, many, many acceptance letters from those colleges had been arriving at Promise all spring, nobody turned away.

"Of course I don't *have to*," she said. "But they didn't let me apply anywhere that I might actually want to go, and it's too late now to try for this fall. Unless maybe I find a community college somewhere." She had been squatting to dunk her sponge, and as she stood, I could tell her bad leg was bothering her. She kept shifting her hip so that her weight rested on the other leg as she passed her sponge up and down the shower wall. "It's such a farce. Did I ever tell you that Lydia did her studying at Cambridge? And she looks the other way while they have us apply to the University of Christ on a Cross."

"I've heard their field hockey team is outstanding," I said.

Jane threw her sponge at me. It missed and flew out of the stall into the sink area, where it landed with a gross squelch against the wall. I grinned and moved to get it, but Jane put her hand up, started that way herself.

"I don't even know if I want to go to college," she said. "I think I'd rather be a student of the world for a while."

"I guess," I said. "But if that's the case, it just seems like you don't have to go to all the trouble of the running-away part. If you're not planning to live with your mom while you're *a student of the world*, anyway."

"Heavens no," Jane said, returning to the stall. "There's nothing for me in her perfect slice of suburban America, sprinkles on top."

"Exactly," I said. "So if you're not gonna live with her or go to the college she wants you to go to, why not just tell her, and if she freaks and tells you to never come back, it's like the same thing as running away, anyway. I mean, no doubt Adam and I will be sent back here for another year if we don't leave. But not you."

"Do you not want me to come with you or something?" Jane asked, and she sounded hurt, especially for Jane, who barely ever sounded hurt. "You're thinking maybe Hopalong might slow you two down?"

"No—shit, not at all," I said, and I meant it. "It just seems like you're taking the hard way when you don't really have to."

She stopped scrubbing then and stood there with her dirty sponge dripping fat drops onto the tiled shower floor. "It's odd that you see it as the hard way," she said, "because I see it exactly opposite. I've known for what feels like the longest, longest time that I'd have to escape my mother one day, and it seems much easier to do that with this big action, something she can't ignore—that I've completely run away with all these people—than with anything I might say to her. I've said and said all the words there are to say about how her way isn't my way, and as far as I can tell, it's never made a dent."

"You think this will make a dent?" I asked.

"The great thing is that I won't be around to find out one way or another," she said, smiling a Jane smile. "Besides, this way I get to do it with you and Adam and not just me all on my own. At least when we start out."

This was where our plan got muddled, even after we agreed on a go time: where, exactly, it was that we were going, and just how long we would stay together after we got there. At first I think Adam assumed that we'd just move somewhere, all three of us, and I don't know, set up house or something, and that didn't sound completely unappealing to me until Jane reminded us that there would be people looking for us, that we were minors, and even worse, that once she turned eighteen and became an official adult, she could maybe be charged with aiding us in our flight or something. We weren't really sure about any of the actual laws involved, but certainly I'd seen enough movies to know that all the bad guys split up when they were on the run, so that if one was caught, not everybody else got trapped too. And we sort of liked thinking of ourselves as the bad guys, but the kind who you root for, the ones who you want to make it.

For a while the favored version of the plan was to escape while on a mass outing in Bozeman, maybe even immediately following our exams, like immediately, just leave from the Lifegate Christian School itself. But if we did that, it would be nearly impossible to bring any supplies with us, even a change of clothes, not to mention that Lydia was supervigilant about watching us when we left the compound, especially since my thwarted marker heist.

Adam still pushed for stealing a van, but both Jane and I eventually convinced him, for certain this time, that that getaway would get us tracked down faster than any other. Finally we decided that even with Jane's leg, cross-country trekking was our best option, especially considering that the three of us had an established outdoorsiness that would allow us, in those weeks of late spring, to realistically "disappear" on a hike for a portion of the day. We guessed that we could be gone from campus for probably six to seven hours before they'd go looking for us, or send anyone looking for us. Maybe more if we started out early in the day, said we were taking a picnic lunch. Plus, Jane really was, as she liked to remind us, *a bit of an off-the-land type*, and she could definitely read a map, work a compass, and build a fire.

There were dozens of campgrounds and trailheads and tourist traps, even a few tiny towns, within a fifteen- to twenty-mile radius of Promise, less depending on how you traveled it; and at any of those places we determined that we might be able to hitch a ride into Bozeman if we could just convincingly pass ourselves off as granola college kids, which we thought we could do: especially if we happened upon any actual granola college kids out hiking or camping.

"We'll have no trouble making friends," Adam said more than once. "I mean, we'll come bearing pot. It's *the* must-have get-to-know-you and thanks-for-letting-us-escape-our-degaying-camp gift of the year."

Once in Bozeman, the plan was, we'd track down former Scanlan lifeguard and under-the-dock-make-out partner Mona Harris, who I believed would be willing to, at the very least, let us crash on the floor of her dorm room for a night or two until we could figure out what came next. Even once we had this much of the plan tacked down, things got very murky again with the *what might come next* part: murky for each of us. I thought I'd try to somehow contact Margot Keenan. I wasn't sure yet how much I'd ask of her, or really even what I'd ask of her; but she was an adult I thought I could trust, someone I believed would help me and stay quiet about it. Jane planned to call her old flame, the *tragedy of a woman* she'd purchased the really strong pot off of at Christmas. She said this lady was a total wild card and that she might drive all the way to Bozeman to pick her up, or might tell her to go fuck herself, but Jane assured us that she wouldn't be interested in ratting us out to the authorities because it would "entirely go against her sensibilities to play the narc." Adam didn't know what he planned to do once we got to Mona's, but he seemed unconcerned about that. Whatever he decided, though, the idea was to go our separate ways from Bozeman, at least for a while: a while being until we were all eighteen. This part of the plan, the splitting-up part, however murky and unformed and kind of impossible to believe we'd ever even arrive at in reality, made me unbelievably sad to think of, all the same.

• • •

In early April, Jane got caught smoking up in the hayloft. (Somehow Adam and I weren't with her when it happened. We were on garbage detail; it just worked out that way.) Jane had just finished her one-on-one and had a few minutes before dinner duty, so she went to the barn just to take a hit or two, because that afternoon was so nice, completely flushed with spring. Apparently, Dane Bunsky, also on dinner duty, had followed her from afar. He'd been strange since Mark's *incident*, like he'd turned his anger into vigilance, not against Promise and its teachings, but for it, toward its goals. It was weird to see happen. Dane knew a thing or two about drugs; my guess is that he'd probably known about us smoking pot for a while, but this was the day he chose to go get Lydia and lead her to Jane, who had, as she put it, "a beautiful little joint between my lips when I saw first the white top of her head and then her face pop up over the edge of the loft. She actually climbed up the ladder to catch me; it was rather remarkable."

Remarkable or not, Jane was given a more severe punishment than any I'd seen distributed in my time at Promise: all free-time hours replaced with supervised or in-room study hours; all decoration and correspondence privileges revoked until the infamous *yet to be determined later date*;

parents informed; and, worst of all, mandatory one-on-one daily counseling with either Rick or Lydia, probably Lydia, because Rick had been traveling a ton, promoting both Promise and a Free from the Weight video series he was featured in as a success story.

Now Adam and I saw Jane only at meals or during other supervised activities like classroom hours and church services. And even then, Lydia would often come and eat at the same table with us, or sit in the same pew, continually grazing her icy eyes over us in a way you could feel even without looking at her. Through notes folded into tiny squares and passed in secret, and clipped sentences offered here and there, we found out that Jane had given up some of the pot she had hidden in the barn to appease Lydia and to hopefully convince her that was all of it, the whole stash. Lydia hadn't discovered Jane's prosthetic hiding spot. Jane didn't think she would. And best, Jane hadn't mentioned Adam and me as fellow smokers, nor had Dane, if he knew about us, which I'm pretty sure he must have.

"Your punishment couldn't really have come at a more inconvenient time, could it?" Adam said at breakfast one morning while Lydia was still in line, carefully spooning the least watery sections from the scrambled eggs bin onto her plate.

"Actually, I think it's providence," Jane said fast. "It's the best time of all." She looked around for spies, but a lot of the disciples weren't even in the room yet, or they were half asleep over their food. She lowered her voice even more anyway and said, "We still don't know how we're going to get our IDs out of the office. To make that happen, at least one of us needs to get special evangelical detail duties that none of us are candidates for right now. I'm going to use this punishment to pull a Dane Bunsky."

"What?" Adam said before I could.

"I'll spend the next month pretending to buy everything Lydia's selling," she said, her eyes bright and sort of wild. "Completely. I think you two should as well. But you can't make it obvious that you're doing it; you need a reason for your reform."

"I don't know what you mean," Adam said, and he was still speaking for both of us. "Dane's not pretending anything."

"He might not be trying to plan an escape, but he hasn't actually found Christ," Jane said. "Mark was his catalyst for change, for extreme devotion, and Lydia's loving that. I got caught with pot, and so during my one-on-ones I'm being really honest about my passion for smoking up—by honest I mean I'm telling Lydia that I smoke pot to deal with my guilt over my sinful sexual perversion."

"And that's actually working?" I asked.

Jane nodded. "As far as I can tell. I mean, I've never really opened up to her before, and she knows it, so she can't help but think we're making progress. And I just started. Wait until I cry."

"I've cried in my one-on-ones before," Adam said.

"Of course you have," Jane said. "Indubitably."

"Oh, excuse me my delicacies, you woman of stone, you," Adam said, pretending to pout.

Now Lydia was saying something to Erin, but her plate was full, her cup of tea in hand. She'd be joining us any second.

"I don't know how convincing I can be," I said. "I feel like she'll get what I'm doing right off."

"Even if she does," Jane said, "she won't really know why you're doing it. I just think that the less time we three spend with each other right now, and the more we seem to commit ourselves to Promise, the better. We have to sacrifice today to benefit tomorrow."

"Ugh, gross," Adam said. "You already sound like her."

"Good," Jane said. "That's the idea."

Lydia sat down at our table just after that and we all talked about things she brought up for us to talk about, none of which I remember.

● ● ●

Not so many days later I received, in the mail, the perfect catalyst for explaining a change in my behavior during my one-on-ones, though it didn't present itself as that right from the start. I mean, I didn't like get it and think, *Super, now I'll manipulate Lydia with this sob story*; it just sort of opened itself up to me as I went along.

What I got in the mail was a typed three-page letter from Grandma (with an additional handwritten one-page inclusion from Ruth) detailing the difficulties Ruth was having with her NF tumor, and the thwarted surgery that was supposed to remove it. The tumor had apparently been growing at what everyone called an *alarming rate* ever since Christmas, especially since Christmas, and it was now obvious that Ruth had this mass on her back. She wasn't able to easily hide it beneath her clothes any longer. Plus it was now also painful, and it was making her tired, this thing basically feeding off her like a tick or a tapeworm, and so her Minnesota surgery was pushed up by a couple of weeks, and both Ray and Grandma went to Minneapolis with her *to get the damned thing cut off*. But all had not gone well.

Lydia gave me the envelope at the start of a one-on-one, and since all disciple mail was still opened and screened before we received it, she already knew the contents. We usually got mail at the end of one-on-ones, or in a mass delivery to our bedrooms on Saturdays, so I knew something was strange even as she handed it to me. Then she said, "Why don't you read it now so that we can discuss it if you need to." And I actually got kind of worried about what I might find inside.

In her letter, Grandma talked a lot about the trip to Minneapolis and the hospital itself, and also *the very fancy visitors' wing, where they had these old typewriters set up for kids to play around on,* she guessed, but she had decided to sit down and type out this letter to me, just to see if she could still do it. *I feel just like Jessica Fletcher. You remember her, from "Murder, She Wrote"?*

```
This whole business has been a real mess.
The surgeons here only took off the top of
the tumor (nearly a pound and a half!) before
they decided that they dare not go any closer
to your aunt Ruth's spinal cord (though they
had told her originally that they were going
to do just that). Also, she lost quite a lot
of blood while they were operating and that
was worrisome, as you might expect it would
be. There was a whole g-damn football team
of these doctors in green clothes (I asked,
and they call them scrubs) and not one of
them felt right going any closer to her
spine. So now the biggest section of the
tumor is gone, but everyone, this whole team
of doctors, is convinced that it was just a
quick fix and the tumor will keep growing
again because that root (or whatever you call
it) is still there. They did go ahead and do
a biopsy on what they got and it was benign
```

(that's good--it means cancer free). But they
pulled a small one off her thigh (she's had
them there before, you remember) and that
one was malignant (the bad kind), so they
have to give her some radiation to kill
the cancer cells there. Also, Ruth has the
makings of another tumor on her stomach.
This one isn't hard like the one on her
back, but it is quite large, they said, for
a brand-new growth. So we came over here to
Minnesota to get just the one removed and
now we have a whole other kettle of fish to
deal with. How do you like that? I call it
a mess. Ruth has to stay here in Minnesota
for another two weeks for the radiation and
all, and then she has to be on bed rest at
home for some time as well, although I do not
expect that she will follow those orders to
the letter. (Though she should!) Ray is going
home to Miles City because he needs to get
back to work, but I plan to stay with Ruth
and keep her company. ~~I~~ We sure wish that you
were here with us, Spunky.

Ruth had this to say (to me, anyway):

I think your grandmother just about covered it. Who knew
she was such a typist?! I just wanted to write you and say
that I am doing well. I am tired, but I feel strong, and I
think this surgery was progress, even if it wasn't exactly what
I was expecting. I know what the doctors are saying about
regrowth, but doctors don't know everything, and I, for one,

am willing to hold out some hope that it will stay the size
they've left it now for another ten or twenty years or even
longer, who knows, maybe forever. . . . I've had it back there
for so many years with not one change to it that I do not
consider it foolish to think this might happen. As for the one
on my leg, I think the radiation will zap all of its cancerous
remnants away.

> *It is a blessing to have your grandmother here with me,*
> *and we talk about you every day. You are missed. I hope*
> *that you will add my recovery to your prayers for your own,*
> *and I want you to know that I am still praying for you too,*
> *Cameron. I love you very, very much.*

When I'd finished them both and was tucking them back into the envelope, Lydia said, "I was sorry to learn of your aunt's illness. This is something she's had for some time?"

I thought it was sort of funny that Lydia said *to learn of your aunt's illness* when what she really should have said was *I opened your letters and read all about your aunt's illness.* What I said, though, was "Yeah, but it's not usually like this. It's, normally, she just gets these little growths removed every few years and she's okay. I don't think it's ever been this bad."

"It's a form of cancer, then?" Lydia asked, her voice with that kind of hushed quality that some people always use to talk about cancer.

"NF isn't," I said. "It's a genetic thing where you get these tumors on your nerves—I don't really understand it that well, but it isn't actually cancer. But if you have it, you have like a much better chance of developing cancer, which I guess happened in the tumor on her leg."

"You must be worried about her," Lydia said.

"Yeah," I said, quick, because it was the response that I was supposed to give, the response that, whatever had happened between Ruth and me, I still should have felt like giving, but it wasn't honest. I wasn't *not* worried about Ruth; I mean, I didn't wish her sickness or more cancerous growths or whatever, but I was mainly thinking about Grandma in that big hospital in Minneapolis, wandering those long, antiseptic hospital hallways that always sort of glow green, getting herself and Ruth little snacks in the cafeteria, the kinds of food Grandma loved, slices of cream pies and a big salad bar to pick and choose from, watching her detective shows on the TV in Ruth's room, the volume too low for her to really hear it because Ruth was resting, then *click-clack*ing away on the typewriter in a sticky, crowded waiting room where everyone looked tired, was tired, just so she could send me a letter. Picturing Grandma carrying a tray topped with a couple of bowls of soup, riding an elevator up to Ruth's floor, made me sadder than picturing Ruth in her hospital bed, even though she was the one who was actually sick.

Lydia must have been saying something that I didn't hear, because when she said, "Is that something you'd like to do right now?" I had to ask, "Do what?"

And she pursed her lips and then said, "Call your aunt in the hospital. We can do so; as I said, I have the number."

"Okay," I said, hoping, as Lydia and I walked down to the main office, that I'd get to talk to Grandma, that she wouldn't be tooling around the gift shop or outside getting some air.

She wasn't. After Judy at the nurse's station connected me to the room, it was Grandma who said, "Yes, hello."

I couldn't remember the last time I'd spoken on the phone

with Grandma. Not since before my mom and dad died, I'm pretty sure. We used to call her in Billings sometimes on the weekends, though not that often, because usually she just came down to see us or we went to her. I've heard people say "tears sprang to my eyes" before, or I've read it, I guess, but I don't think that I ever really felt like that had happened to me, like I didn't have some sense that I might cry before I started doing so, at least not until Grandma answered the phone. I was just standing in the office with its officey smell of paper and permanent marker and the glue on the backs of postage stamps, and I was aware of Lydia standing just behind me—she'd dialed the number and was now planted behind me to monitor the call, my end, anyway, and then there was Grandma's voice from some hospital room in Minneapolis, but it was like her voice out of the past too, out of my past, her voice speaking to the me who I wasn't anymore and never would be again. And you know what, fucking tears sprang to my eyes. They did. They weren't there and then they were, and I had to kind of take in a breath before I said, "It's me, Grandma. It's Cameron."

After that kind of a beginning, the actual meat of the phone call wasn't all that interesting. Grandma was superexcited to have me call, I could tell, and she told me all about the good cafeteria food, just like I knew she would, and all about these beautiful pink flowering trees in the hospital courtyard that she didn't know the name of but that *sure made her sneeze*, and when the phone was passed to Ruth, she sounded tired, but also like she was trying to make her voice bright and not tired, which made her sound more sick than if she hadn't done that. She and I didn't talk for very long, but I told her that I hoped she felt better soon and that

I was thinking about her, which was true.

After I'd hung up Lydia, motioned for me to sit in the spinny desk chair, and she took the nonspinny desk chair just across the room, but it was a small room and we were sitting very close, looking at each other. She just let me think for a moment or whatever, and then she said, "So how did that go?"

And I said, "It was weird."

And Lydia said, "You know how I feel about you using that word during a session. It's a catchall: the way you use it, it's meaningless. Be specific."

And for once I was specific. I was completely and totally specific and honest about what I was thinking right then in that moment. "I don't know why," I said, "but when I was talking to them, I kept picturing the two of them in a room in a hospital, which isn't strange, I know, but it wasn't the hospital they're actually at, because I've never even been there, so how would I know what it looks like? Where I keep thinking of them as being is actually the abandoned hospital in Miles City. It's called Holy Rosary, and like, even right now, if I try to picture my grandma in Ruth's room, I just see it as abandoned Holy Rosary, all dirty and dark. I mean, I could change that picture, I think, and make it more accurate and put working machines and everything in the room, but that's where my mind goes if I just let it. I see them in Holy Rosary."

"Why do you think that is?" Lydia asked.

"I don't know," I said.

"You must have some idea," she said.

"Maybe because I've spent so much time there, more than I've ever spent in an actual, functioning hospital or whatever. Plus it's a pretty hard place to forget."

"But you weren't supposed to be there, were you?" Lydia said, flipping to a clean page in her notebook, which she hardly ever did during my sessions because we covered so little ground.

"No," I said. "We used to break in."

It wasn't like this was the first time that I'd ever mentioned Holy Rosary during a session. Of course we'd gotten to the topic of my *unhealthy friendship* with Jamie and the guys, what Lydia called my need to *inappropriately emulate the reckless behavior of certain teenage males*, which was part of my *incorrect gender identity*. We'd also covered, loosely, my underage drinking (which fell into that reckless behavior category), and we'd even gotten to what had eventually occurred between Lindsey and me, for the first time, in that abandoned hospital. But what fascinated Lydia, she told me, both that afternoon and for several one-on-ones to follow, was that I was connecting this place where I had experienced all kinds of sin with the guilt and sadness I was feeling over Aunt Ruth's illness. And, according to Lydia, there was much work to be done, and progress to be made in "understanding that connection, digging it out and pushing it into the light and really facing it."

I didn't know that much about psychology. I've learned a few things about it recently, I guess, since leaving Promise; but when it was happening to me, when I was in the middle of my one-on-ones or group sessions, I couldn't have told you where the religion part ended and the psychology part picked up. At least not when Lydia was running the show. With Reverend Rick, he might use a psychological term now and then, like *gender identity* or *root cause*, but most of the time he stuck to Scripture, to words like *sin, repentance, obedience*, and that's only when he was talking in that authoritative kind of way, which he didn't do very often, really. He mainly listened. But with Lydia everything mixed together, a passage from the Bible followed by an activity she'd gotten from NARTH—the National Association for the Research and Treatment of Homosexuality. Or maybe Lydia reminding us that *sin was sin*, and then talking about the *pseudo-self-affirming behaviors* associated with our sins. If the goal was to keep us from questioning the treatment we were getting in our support sessions because we didn't know what, exactly, to question, to disagree with—the Bible or the psychology she was using—it kind of worked. But I don't think it was necessarily so organized, so planned out as a means to manipulate us. I just think it really was the Wild West out there and they were making shit up as they went along. I mean, who was there to stop them? I know the word for all this now: it's *pseudoscientific*. It's kind of a great word: I like the *s* sound that comes twice in a row when you say it. But that day in the office with Lydia I didn't know the word *pseudoscientific*, and even if I had, I wouldn't have used it. I was glad she thought we were on the verge of uncovering something significant about my fucked-up *development cycle*, about just how I had become the vessel for sin that had earned me my place at Promise. I let her believe it, and not only because of Jane's insistence that the three of us should get in good with the management to hasten our escape, but also because I thought, *If I'm really gonna leave Promise forever, for good, and never look back, maybe I should spend the next month or so actually giving myself over to the place, its ways.* Not giving in to it, not that. And not somehow acquiring faith and devotion by snapping my fingers. I knew that I would never be a Mark Turner: I didn't have the capacity for it, or the upbringing, or the combination of the two, whatever. But I thought that if I could be honest with Lydia, really honest, and answer all of her questions fully, then maybe I could somehow figure out some things about myself. *What the hell?* is basically what I was thinking. What the hell?

CHAPTER TWENTY

A week or so after Lydia let me make the phone call to the hospital, Bethany Kimbles-Erickson brought me a pretty amazing book. You wouldn't necessarily think so the first time you saw it. Or at least I didn't. It was about the thickness of an issue of *National Geographic* and it had a soft paper cover that smelled like mildew and basement, and it was sporting a coffee ring over the title, which was: *The Night the Mountain Fell: The Story of the Montana-Yellowstone Earthquake.* It was written by some guy named Ed Christopherson and it apparently cost one dollar when he self-published it in 1960. I knew this because in black, bold lettering at the bottom of the cover it read: ONE DOLLAR. But now, thirty-three years later, Bethany Kimbles-Erickson had paid only twenty-five cents for it at the annual Word of Life rummage sale, held in the church's parking lot. That detail actually made me sort of sad for Ed Christopherson, wherever he was.

"I found it lying on the very top of a box of books I was moving to another table," Bethany had told me probably ten times since she'd given it to me. "The very top. It's one of those everyday kinds of miracles, it really is, because do you know how many boxes of books were at that sale? I would say hundreds. Really, honestly. And I didn't even glance at half of them."

Bethany tended to overuse the word *miracle* when describing coincidences, and even when she tacked on *everyday* to clarify just what kind of miracle we were talking about, it was still kind of annoying. So that's what I thought her discovery of this book was: another coincidence polished up to shine like a miracle. At least that's what I thought at first. I mean, without calling it a ~~miracle~~ I could still appreciate the perfect timing of her find.

Recently, those of us disciples who were in good shape for our final exams at Lifegate Christian, which included me, were allowed to work on independent projects in various subjects, Montana history being one of them. Just picking that as my subject made me feel sort of close to my mom and her work at the museum, but then I decided to research Quake Lake as my specific topic, to really find out all the history of its formation and how the facts might differ from family lore, and so Bethany's find was very, very timely.

Those of us working on projects had already been taken to the Bozeman Public Library once, and would get to go again before the month was up, but before Bethany brought it to me, I'd not yet come across Ed Christopherson's book. Actually, I'd spent most of my four hours at the library looking through microfilm archives of the *Bozeman Daily Chronicle*, reading eyewitness accounts of the earthquake and spending lots of time squinting at the grainy photographs that accompanied those articles, trying to imagine my mom in her pageboy, her Campfire Girls T-shirt, sitting in the backseat of the family car, Ruth next to her, the morning after, my grandpa Wynton driving, my grandma Wynton looking back over the seat to check on her girls every few minutes, the car filled up with the heavy burden and joy of all of them knowing that they had escaped the exact site of the earthquake's worst damage. But others hadn't—no official word as to how many yet, but certainly other campers had not been so fortunate.

I tried hard to imagine what my mom might have felt in the backseat on the long, hot, many-times-detoured-because-of-quake-damage drive home to Billings. Her father's neck would have been tense and strained, the radio, when it tuned in, all endless earthquake coverage, the bottle of ginger ale bought at a gas station sweating and warming from where she had wedged it between her thighs, Mom unable to drink any more after the first swallow, when she'd thought of the Keenans, almost certainly dead, and how could she sit in the backseat and drink ginger ale if that was true? At some point while I was imagining all this, I would switch over to remembering the terrible, seemingly endless car ride into Miles City with Mr. Klauson the night he'd cut short my sleepover with Irene, the night Grandma had told me the news about my parents' accident. This switch from imagination to memory happened automatically, young Mom in a car to me in a truck, a sort of reflex, I guess, but one triggered by what? Thinking of the sound of tires rolling over cracked, summer-hot Montana asphalt? Things left unsaid in moving vehicles? Guilt? I don't know. And then Bethany brought me the book: *The Night the Mountain Fell.*

It had everything. It had graphs and charts, a fold-out cardboard map of the entire Madison Canyon Earthquake area with these funny little hand-drawn symbols all over it, like two parachutes to indicate the smoke jumpers who were called in to fight a forest fire that was started as a signal fire by some campers who had survived the quake but needed to be rescued, their cars gone, even the road they traveled to their campsites on gone.

It also had tons of photographs, clear photographs that I didn't have to squint at: an upside-down Cadillac and the highway it had been on now cracked and broken away like snapping one of Grandma's sugar-free wafers; another highway, one that had circled Hebgen Lake, literally dropped off into nothingness, into the lake itself—now you see it, now you don't; harried men in untucked shirts hoisting stretchers with bandaged people on them; crowds of onlookers come to view the damage, their big-finned cars lining the sides of the nonruined highways; what one photo's caption called a "refugee family," all of them in pajamas as they walked down a street in Virginia City, the grandmother, in a white bathrobe, holding the hand of the youngest child, a little girl with square bangs, the mousy mother carrying a kitten, the eldest daughter with her arms folded across her chest, refusing to look at the camera but smiling a shy smile off to the side, and the son, with his blond crew cut and bare feet, grinning right at the lens. That photo had no father in it. Maybe he was the one taking the picture, but maybe not. I don't know—the caption didn't say.

But the photograph that made me rethink Bethany's use of the word *miracle*, and that also helped to finalize our escape plan. It was like the book itself: one that didn't seem so special at first glance. Most of the image was focused on two enormous boulders that had, the caption explained, crashed down during the quake, crushing a pup tent and *killing David Keenan, age fourteen, of Billings*. But *miraculously*, not disturbing the food on his family's campsite picnic table, nor the larger family tent. The picnic table was in the foreground, the boulders looming just behind it, having stopped their momentum, somehow, just in time to avoid the spread.

David was survived by his parents and sister, the caption read. I'd scanned the photo while reading during classroom hours, and then had flipped on though, brought the book back to my room even, and had gone on with my day, or part of my day, before that name, David Keenan, fluttered back across my brain and made me shiver.

I was folding ratty bath towels in the laundry room when I made the connection, and I went to get the book right away, leaving the dryer door open, a bunch of wadded towels still waiting to be pulled out, more in the washer waiting to go in. David Keenan was Margot's brother. David Keenan had kissed my mom in the pantry of the First Presbyterian Church in Billings. The book was on my desk, and once I picked it up, I flipped past the page the photo was on twice, my hands shaking. Then I flipped to it: Looking at that picture was like looking right into Margot's memory, something that should have been completely private. Those were her family's cups and plates on that table, their cardboard box, probably with a package of hot dog buns, a container of homemade chocolate chip cookies, maybe the stuff for s'mores, if s'mores were even around in 1959, I didn't know for sure. Margot would have been in the *not pictured* larger tent, safe, when her brother died. The photo credit was given to the U.S. Forest Service. Some stranger who had snapped up her family's tragedy. I thought that she probably wouldn't need this photo to remember that table, those boulders, just about exactly, but I wondered if she knew about its existence, knew that it was in this ONE DOLLAR book. And wondering about that, of course, made me wonder about my own parents and all the photos of their Quake Lake death that might very well be around: their car being pulled from the lake; their bodies being pulled from the car; their

IDs being pulled from my dad's wallet, my mom's purse. Probably there were lots of photos like that, in police files and newspaper articles, photos that I might never see, and thinking about that made me—for the first time since they'd died—want to go to Quake Lake and see things for myself. I'd told Margot Keenan that night at the Cattleman's—my double-cherry Shirley Temple so pink there on the table in front of us—that I didn't think I'd ever want to go to Quake Lake, ever. And she'd told me that was fine. She hadn't even said that maybe I'd change my mind one day, the way adults always talk about stuff like that. She'd just let it be. But now, mostly because of the book, that photo, I had changed my mind. And it was practically right next door, certainly within hiking distance if you knew somebody who could read a map, work a compass, build a fire. And I did know that somebody.

The next thing I did after studying the photo was go to the Promise library and take the fat dictionary off of the bottom shelf of the second bookcase and look up the word *miracle*. Sure, one of the definitions talked about the work of a *divine agency* operating outside of *natural or scientific laws*, and for that definition the usage example was: *the miracle of rising from the grave*. And yes, that definition seemed like way too much pressure for this particular situation I'd found myself in. However, the next definition—*a highly improbable or extraordinary event, development, or accomplishment that brings about welcome consequences*—worked much better. I didn't know yet if our escape plan would work, if I'd make it to Quake Lake as my *welcome consequences*. But Bethany finding the book, then me finding that photo, and then the use of the word *miraculously* in the caption to describe the undisturbed food on the picnic table: I was willing to call all that a *highly improbable or extraordinary development.* What sucked was that I couldn't tell Bethany Kimbles-Erickson about how she'd maybe been sort of right about everyday miracles, just this one time.

• • •

"Today shall we talk about the cottage-cheese containers under your bed?" Lydia asked me at the start of a one-on-one in early May.

"Okay," I said, not necessarily surprised that she knew about the containers (of course she did), just surprised that I hadn't heard about this knowledge beforehand in the form of some punishment for having them there in the first place. We were holding this one-on-one at a picnic table not far from the barn. An outdoor support session was a rare occurrence, especially when Lydia was conducting it; but it was the best day of spring thus far, high sixties and everything covered in crazy-bright sunshine, and even she couldn't resist being out in it. Probably too my recent willingness to actually partici-pate during our sessions had factored in.

"You must be wondering why I've never mentioned them," she said, running her hand just over the top of her swim cap–tight, French-twisted white hair.

"I guess I wasn't sure that you knew about them," I said.

"Of course you were." She flicked some tiny black bug off her notebook. "You certainly didn't go to any lengths to hide them. You must have known that they'd be found during room inspections, which indicates that you wanted them found."

"I thought that they could be like the Promise version of my dollhouse," I said. Which was completely true, just like everything else I'd said during our sessions since I'd made that phone call to the hospital. It was actually a lot less work, this complete and total truth business, than whatever it was I'd been doing before.

"Did you find them as satisfying?" she asked. We'd already spent an entire one-on-one and part of a group session, actually, talking about the dollhouse.

"Nope," I said. "Not really. I couldn't ever lose myself to them like I could with the dollhouse. I haven't even pulled them out since . . ." I thought about it, when that might have been. I shook my head. "I don't even know when it was."

Lydia opened a book that she carried around with her most of the time, but that wasn't her composition book. This one was small and had a black cover that looked sort of like leather. Maybe it was leather. She flipped a couple of pages, and I could see that it was a daily planner or journal, something with the date written on each page. "When you had just returned from break," she said, trailing her pen down the page as she scanned. "We did room inspections that next weekend and you had added—"

"Three Christmas lights," I finished for her. "Yeah, I forgot. They were from this string of lights that Ray had tacked up to the roof, but they came loose on Christmas Eve and the wind blew them all around."

There was a woodpecker jackhammering somewhere close by, or at least it sounded close by. I turned to look for it. The nonneedled trees hadn't leafed out yet, but their branches were covered in bright green buds, like they had wads of already chewed spearmint gum stuck all over them. I couldn't find the bird. When I turned back around, Lydia was looking at me the way she did when I hadn't yet said enough for her to ask another question.

"My grandma and I went outside because we couldn't figure out the noise. It was cool because they stayed lit while they got tossed around." I felt like explaining it this way was ruining my memory of that moment, but Lydia kept on with that look of hers. "Ray tacked them down again, though."

Lydia tapped her pen on the picnic table. "So how did you obtain three of these lights to put in the container that you had needlessly hidden beneath your bed, given that you already had decoration privileges?"

"When he took down all the lights, one strand was dead, and I pulled off three of the bulbs before we threw it away," I said, and felt stupid enough just saying it aloud without looking at the kind of smirk face Lydia was making.

"So it mightn't have even been the strand you saw with your grandmother," she said.

"Yeah, I guess not. I don't know for sure."

"And yet you felt compelled to take these three lightbulbs and hide them in your luggage and bring them all the way back to your room here at Promise and then glue them to the inside of a cottage-cheese container?"

"Yeah," I said. "That's exactly what I did."

"I know that's what you did, Cameron, but that's simply the chronology. We're trying to understand *why* you would do something like that. Why you continually do things just like this."

"I know," I said. I had my tan sweater on that day. It was a weekday so I was in uniform, and I was suddenly too hot.

Or maybe I wasn't suddenly too hot but I had just noticed that I was too hot, with both my sweater and my long-sleeved shirt, so I started to pull off the sweater and had it halfway up my torso, my chin tucked and arms in that weird midpull position with my hands gripping the sweater's hem and my elbows pointed up by my ears, when

Lydia said, "Stop that right now."

"Huh?" I said, stopping but maintaining the weird position.

"We do not undress ourselves in front of others as if all public spaces are changing rooms," Lydia said.

"I just got too hot," I said, pulling the sweater back down. "I have a shirt on under this." I lifted the sweater again, with just one hand this time, and pointed at my shirt with the other.

"An undershirt, or lack thereof, is not my concern. If you would like to remove an article of clothing, then you ask to be excused so that you may do so in private."

"Okay," I said, keeping the sarcasm completely in check because we'd already had several conversations about that, too. "I'd like to remove my sweater because I'm too hot. May I please be excused to do so?"

She checked her watch and said, "I think you can manage your discomfort for the remainder of our session, at which time you'll be free to return to your room and remove your sweater in private."

"Okay," I said.

Lydia was like this all the time. I mean, the more I opened up to her, was a model patient or whatever, the icier she got, correcting pretty much everything out of my mouth and at least half of my silent actions as well. But the thing was that her near-constant admonitions actually made me like her more. I think because witnessing her administration of ten zillion rules and codes of conduct, all of which she applied to her own life, made her seem fragile and weak, in need of the constant protection of all those rules, instead of the opposite, the way I know that she wanted to be seen, the way I'd seen her when I first arrived: powerful and all knowing.

"You're ready to continue, then?" she asked.

"Yeah."

"Good," she said. "Because I don't want you to avoid this subject by creating a disturbance."

"I wasn't doing that at all," I said.

She ignored me and continued with the pronouncement that it seemed like she'd worked out long before our session had even begun, which happened fairly often. I didn't always understand what she was even talking about when she made these pronouncements, but I'm not sure that it mattered. "What's fascinating," she said, "is that you've developed this pattern of stealing these material fragments that, more often than not, remind you of some sin that you've committed. The act of stealing these items is a sin in and of itself, of course, but often these are tokens from the various reckless things you've done. They're trophies of your sins."

"Not the lights," I said.

And Lydia said, "Please do not interrupt." And then she was silent for a moment or two, as if I might not be able to resist an additional outburst. Then she took a breath and said, "As I was saying, while not all these items are directly related to your sinful behavior, many of them are, or at the very least, they come from your experiences with individuals with whom you have troubled relationships. First you collect these items, and then you display them as a way of attempting, I think, to control your guilt and discomfort regarding both these relationships and your behavior." She consulted her notes before continuing, running her hand across the top of her hair again. Her voice was sort of lofty and speechified, as though she was talking into a handheld tape recorder for all of posterity and not to the person sitting across a picnic table from her, the person about whom the claims were being made. "These many sinful experiences are ultimately not sitting well with you, and you've been struggling in vain to put them to rest by attempting to glue them to a fixed surface as a means of controlling them, and thereby controlling your guilt. Of course this method is failing, which you already know. Choosing to hide the cottage-cheese containers when you knew that they would be easily found was one thing, but then continuing to hide them even after you had decoration privileges and they were no longer contraband was a blatant cry for help. You could have had those containers sitting plainly on your desk. You chose to try to imbue them with significance by hiding them. I'm not at all surprised that as you've made progress in your support sessions, you've felt less and less inclined to work on them."

"I hadn't thought of that," I said. I hadn't, and it worried me that maybe she was right, even though I'd never been into the cottage-cheese containers the way I'd been into working on the dollhouse.

"In fact," she said, a rare and genuine Lydia smile on her face, "I think it's time for you to throw them away. Today. First thing."

"I will," I said. And I did, as soon as I got back to my room. Just after I took off my fucking sweater.

. . .

Since Jane's mandate there had been no smoking sessions with what was left of the nonconfiscated pot, no trail running with Adam, and the three of us weren't even sitting together during meals anymore unless there were other people at the table with us. Lydia told me that this was a very good thing, because she'd noticed that there had been *negative bonding* among the three of us for too long.

We continued to communicate mostly through notes and shared moments in a hallway, as we loaded into the van, wherever we could grab them. Explaining the necessity of visiting Quake Lake as a condition of our escape route was difficult this way, but after a series of much-longer-than-usual notes passed back and forth, Jane and Adam were willing to let my everyday miracle run its miraculous course. I snuck the pull-out map from my Bethany book to Jane during our second visit to the Bozeman library, and while there I looked up and even photocopied "for my independent study" more recent maps of hiking trails around the Quake Lake area. I did this with the help of a dykey librarian: spiky hair, multiple piercings all the way up her earlobe, Birkenstock clogs. I think she thought I was just gonna go camping there with my friends or something. I guess I kind of was. I looked up a couple of articles about my parents' accident, too. It was difficult to gauge just where their car had broken through the guard-rail based on summary reporting and a map of the lake, but I had a general idea.

I managed to slip the photocopies to Jane as we shared the far backseat in the van on the drive to Promise. She was our Meriwether Lewis, after all. She slipped me a note about the supplies she wanted me to gather and be in charge of: three candles from the box of extras in the chapel; a book of matches, also from that box; the crappy can opener from the kitchen—there were several, but one was rusted and wouldn't be missed like the others; various nonperishable food items, the storage of which would prove tricky given Lydia's apparent love of room inspections. Adam had a list as well. Gathering these things in secret and hiding them (in my most Boo Radley of moves, I ended up using the rotted-out portion of a tree trunk that wasn't too far off the path to the lake) made me feel important and useful and just really good. It was kind of incredible, the little thrill I'd get from stuffing something else into the plastic bag I'd wedged into that tree trunk. Those small acts made our escape seem real in a way that it hadn't before.

The days ticked closer to June. I was allowed to call Grandma and Ruth again, just before exams. They were back in Miles City. Ruth's radiation was complete, but it had badly burned her skin and she had to have that area washed and bandaged twice a day, so she wasn't able to return to work, "At least not yet," she told me in that fake-bright voice she was still using to cover how very tired she must have been. "But it's nice to have a break."

"She's got places on her body that look like raw chuck steak," Grandma said when she got on the line. "I know it's more painful than she's lettin' on." Her voice was hushed, especially for Grandma, and I could tell she had stretched the long kitchen phone cord, the one usually tangled in chunky knots, so that she could walk somewhere away from Ruth, somewhere she could tell it like it was. "They're not even sure the radiation did what it was supposed to do. They don't know yet, they keep telling us. 'We just don't know. We'll have to wait and see.'"

"I bet Aunt Ruth's glad that you're there, Grandma," I said.

"Oh, it's Ray who's been waiting on her hand and foot. I just keep her company and feed her candy. You know, I still can't quite get used to the idea of summer vacation without you."

"Me neither," I said.

Then we talked a little about how all of them, she and

Ruth and even Ray, were planning to come and visit me at Promise (it had been cleared), over the weekend of July Fourth, partly because it was so close to the day Mom and Dad had died.

"So long as Ruth feels up to it," Grandma said. "But even if she doesn't, I might just take the Greyhound over myself and see what's what out there at your school."

I didn't trust myself to manage whatever lie I might have responded with, so I said, "Mmm-hmmm."

Grandma sort of coughed into the receiver. "Now I don't know how you'll feel about this, Spunky, and you've got time to think on it, but Ruth and I were talking about maybe all of us driving over to Quake Lake and having a picnic. She said it's practically right there and it's supposed to be a pretty spot, all things considered."

"It is really close to here," I said.

"You think you might want to do something like that? You and me won't be able to go to the cemetery together this summer."

"Will you still go for me?" I asked. "And bring flowers, but not lilies."

"I will surely do that," Grandma said. "You go on and think on the other thing I asked. You have all kinds of time to make up your mind before we get there."

After we'd said I love you and good-bye, I listened to Grandma jostling the phone as she walked back into the kitchen to hang it up. She said something, to Ruth, probably, something that I couldn't make out, something like *she sounds fine* or *everything's fine* or *it'll be fine*. I wondered when I'd get to call her again, and from just where I'd be doing it. And what I would say.

• • •

The week of final exams I had some version of the same dream almost every night. In it, Bethany Kimbles-Erickson and I eventually wind up alone in the study room and she's showing me some new book she's *miraculously* found that's also all about Quake Lake. And she sort of leans down next to me to fan the pages and her hair brushes alongside my face and our heads are so, so close, bent together over this drawing of the mountain tumbling, damming the rush of the water. And when she turns to ask me something, her mouth is so close to the side of my face that her words steam my cheek and how can we not kiss, which we do, and then Bethany takes the lead and pulls me up out of my chair and pushes me onto my back on top of the study table, and we're wound together on top of the book, it's pressing hard into my back, and I don't care, we don't care, and we can't stop. . . .

Every night I managed to wake myself at that point. I thought that I was doing so by sheer force of will, and I'd open my eyes to the dark, sweaty and gripping my sheet and wanting not to have woken up, my body buzzing and alive and all of me working to fight it just to see if I could, if Lydia was right, if I could just withstand these sinful urges until they passed. I would lie there still, keeping my muscles tense and my hands above the covers and concentrating every bit of me to keep from falling right back into that dream, from letting it pick up where it had left off. And it would work. She was right. When I fell back to sleep, it would be to a different dream, or none at all. But in the morning I wouldn't feel like I'd overcome sin, like I was closer to God or whatever, I would just feel inwardly proud of the discipline I'd shown, sort of in the same way that I felt proud and disciplined when I pushed myself running or swimming. I could see how you might let yourself get addicted to that kind of discipline, or denial; how it might seem like, if you kept doing it, over and over, that you were somehow living more cleanly or more *righteously* than other people. It was the same thing as following all those rules Lydia stuck to, and when that got old, making up even more rules to follow and then justifying them with some passage from the Bible.

I didn't tell Lydia about the dreams. I thought the first night would be the only night, and when it came back the next night, it seemed like I should have already told her about the night before, and then I decided that I could do this on my own; it was just a dream and I could handle it, and my feelings about it, without her.

But then came the night that I didn't wake up until dream-Bethany was just working her hand beneath my flannel skirt, and I'm not sure that I would have even woken then, but I heard my name, in nondream form, and then I heard it again.

"Cameron?"

When I opened my eyes the Viking Erin was right there, her face next to mine, hazy in the dark but her wide eyes so close to my own that I yelped a startled yelp and she whispered, "Shhh-shhh, no, I'm sorry. I'm sorry. It's just me."

"What the fuck?" I said, my voice sounding too loud and bright so soon after sleep, in the darkness of the room. Erin was kneeling on the floor next to my bed, and because I'd just woken from that world of X-rated Bethany, her closeness felt like more than just an intrusion of my personal space; it felt somehow like she'd seen the dream, too.

"You were making lots of noise," she said, sort of petting my chest, over the blanket. "I tried to wake you up from my bed but you wouldn't stop."

"What?" I know I blushed, even in the dark, even still

half asleep and unable to get over how she was right there, inches from me. I could smell the Scope she'd gargled with before bed, the pink Johnson & Johnson baby lotion she put on her feet and elbows every night.

"Last night and before—you were dreaming and I woke you up. I said your name."

"I didn't know you had," I said, turning away from her, toward the wall, but not all the way. "I'm fine now." I wasn't fine: I was buzzing and turned on and this conversation was getting in the way of the concentration it took to make that go away.

"What was it about?" she asked, not moving, not going back to her bed, following the rules, pretending to be perfect, but staying right where she was, not even moving her hand from on top of me, though she stopped petting me with it and let it rest.

"I don't remember," I said to the wall, to my iceberg. "It was scary."

For a little while she didn't say anything, but then she said, quietly but with purpose, "No it wasn't."

"Yes it was," I said, wanting her just to leave, to go back to her own twin mattress. "Were you dreaming it with me?"

"I was listening to you dream it," she said. "And those weren't scared noises."

"Oh my God," I said, turning onto my stomach in an angry flop, one that I hoped showed my annoyance. I mashed my face into my pillow and from there said, "Go back to bed. You're not the dream police. Seriously."

She didn't move. Instead she said, "I heard you say Bethany—I heard it more than once."

"I don't care," I said, my words still smooshed by the pillow.

"You said it like—"

"I don't care," I said, turning back toward her and talking right in her face, and also more loudly than was wise for that time of night. "I don't care. I don't care. Just stop."

"No," she said. And then she leaned in and kissed me. She didn't have to go far, there in the dark—our faces were close already—but it was still a big move, a grand gesture, and awkward because of it: She half missed my mouth, got some of my lower lip and the hollow before my chin. I didn't kiss her back right away; it was too startling. I flinched and turned my face some. But God bless the Viking Erin, that didn't stop her. She put her hand on my cheek, her thick, soft fingers, the scent of pink baby lotion even stronger, and turned my head back to her, my lips to her lips, and tried again, and this time was much better, partly because she found my mouth right away, but also because I knew that it was coming. We let that kiss turn into another one, and then one where she maneuvered herself up from her crouch and on top of me.

She wasn't a Coley Taylor; she'd done this before, with a girl, I could tell. I had on an old Firepower T-shirt and flannel sleep pants. The T-shirt was huge, one of the leftover XXLs, and it was stuck around me like a sack I'd climbed into, but she got it off in a couple of tugs. When she had her hand at the drawstring of my pants, I lifted the hem of her own T-shirt and she kind of pushed my hand away, just a small nudge.

I tried again, pulled her shirt up her back, to the middle, but she reached around, actually took my hand and put it alongside me, pinned it there with hers, and said, "Don't. Just let me do this."

I did let her. Her fingers were both soft enough and hard enough, and after the dream foreplay with Bethany

Kimbles-Erickson, it didn't take much.

The Viking Erin and I had been rooming together for nearly a year. We had seen each other in various states of undress countless times, and I knew well her pillowy shoulders, freckled and often pinkish, her surprisingly muscled, if thick, legs, her round, pale belly, her small (size six) feet, the twine color of her hair when wet and smelling of Pert Plus shampoo, and its half-gone-to-seed-dandelion color when dry. But in all this knowing I hadn't considered what it might be like to be with her, she was so, I don't know, so the Viking Erin, my roommate. Now, in the dark, in the aftermath of my dream, the Erin in my bed, her hand in me, was somehow a different Erin entirely.

After my muscles loosened and my breath came back to normal, my body filled up with that satisfied and dense kind of feeling. She let me kiss her, maneuver myself out from under to on top; but when I moved my hand below her stomach she stopped it, just like before with her shirt, and said, "No, it's okay. I'm good."

"Let me," I said, trying to work my hand away from hers, but she held it firm.

"I already did," she said.

"Did what?"

"While you were dreaming—" She stopped, turned her head to the side. "I don't want to say it, it's embarrassing."

"No, it's awesome," I said.

She laughed. "No it's not."

"It is," I said. "It's completely awesome." I meant it. I tried to kiss the part of her neck she had turned toward me, but she pulled it away.

I moved against her in little circles and I could feel her give beneath me, press back with her own small moves, but then she said, "Stop. Get off."

"Are you serious?"

"I should go back to my bed," she said.

"Right now?"

"They could do a pop-in any minute."

I kept moving against her, working at the hem of her shirt again. "They don't even do those anymore."

"Yes they do," she said, pushing me off her, toward the wall, which I let her do. "Lydia did a pop-in on Tuesday at like one in the morning." She got both feet on the floor. Then she was standing, pulling and rubbing at her shoulder, like she'd just pitched an inning.

"How do you even know?" I asked. "Don't you sleep?"

"Not like you do," she said. She didn't lean down and kiss me again, or some formal maneuver like that to say good-bye, or thanks, or to give an ending to what had just happened. Now that she was out of the bed, things were awkward, the communion of our closeness undone.

"Well, your dreams probably aren't as entertaining," I said. "So you have to stay awake to experience mine secondhand."

She half laughed, not her Erin giggle but something else. She got into her bed. The strangeness now between us, in the maybe eight feet between our beds, was as deep as the Scanlan diving wells. We lay in that strangeness for minutes and minutes, the furnace kicking on, turning off, kicking on, the way it does in the spring when the temperature is fickle.

At some point Erin said, "You can't tell anyone, Cam."

"I won't," I said.

"I really do want to get past this," she said. She said it like she might have been talking to me or just talking to remind herself. "I want a husband and two little girls. I want them for real and not just because I'm supposed to want them."

"I know," I said. "I believe you."

"I don't care if you believe me or not. It doesn't make it more true just because you do. It's true because it's the way I feel."

I didn't say anything.

We were quiet for a while longer. I thought she might have actually fallen asleep until she said, "I knew this would happen at some point."

"I didn't," I said.

"Because you don't think of me like that," she said. Her voice was very sad. In less than thirty minutes this thing that we'd just done together had gone from spur-of-the-moment (I thought) and sexy and exactly what I needed to ugly and bulky and very messy.

I thought maybe I could make her laugh, or at least lighten up, so I said, "I've been wondering something. Is part of the reason you like the Tandy Campbell videos so much because she's a turn-on? I think she's sort of hot."

"I'm not gonna talk about that," Erin said. "We shouldn't encourage each other's homosexual attractions."

"Are you kidding?" I asked. I really wasn't sure.

"I don't want to talk anymore at all," she said. "I want to go to sleep."

"That's fucked up," I said. "I *was* sleeping. You woke me up."

She didn't say anything. I did a couple of those obnoxious, heavy sighs you do when you want someone to know that you're pissed at them. She still didn't say anything. I waited some more and she was still quiet. Eventually I was pretty sure that she really had fallen asleep this time, and I was close, too.

But then she said, just barely loudly enough for me to hear

her, "Tandy Campbell's not even my type."

And I smiled, but I just let what she'd said hang there, no response from me, so that she couldn't be sure if I'd heard her or not.

• • •

Those of us who had completed independent studies did presentations about our topics for all the disciples. I made a big, dorky collage of photos and maps for the occasion, and I was thorough, I knew my dates and facts. I told a story about seventysomething widow Mrs. Grace Miller who had to be boated to her house postquake because it was now floating in Hebgen Lake, and once there she found her "teeth still on the kitchen counter, right next to the sink." People chuckled. Lydia, even. I described the way an earthquake that was 7.3 on the Richter scale could slosh a thirty-foot wall of water from Hebgen Lake and then sweep it through Madison Canyon, and just as that water reached Rock Creek Campground, literally half of a mountain—eighty million tons of rock—crashed down into the valley, one hundred miles an hour, and dammed it. There you go, presto, chango: a campground becomes Quake Lake. I knew my stuff. I earned my applause, but I didn't look at Jane or Adam once the whole presentation.

A couple of days later we took our finals at Lifegate Christian. They were exactly what we'd prepared for, no surprises. Afterward we went for pie at Perkins. I had fresh strawberry with whipped cream. I thought of Grandma. It was midafternoon and the place wasn't very full, a smattering of old people playing bridge, those ugly brown coffee mugs ubiquitous to these kinds of restaurants sitting in front of each of them; a lone businessman in a booth eating soup, his tie flopped over his shoulder; the mother of a family that looked travel rumpled ordering a grasshopper pie and a cherry pie to go. I had a hard time concentrating on my slice, on what Helen, who sat next to me, was saying. It was Thursday. We planned to leave Saturday morning after breakfast. With finals just finished, there were no study hours scheduled for the weekend, no mandatory group activities at all other than meals, duties, and church at Word of Life on Sunday, which we wouldn't be around for. Hopefully. None of us had been able to get into the locked file cabinet to claim our IDs, but we didn't care—we were going.

"If we used them, they'd have an easier time of tracking us down, anyway," Jane had reasoned. "So we won't be doing any air travel for a while, who cares?" We'd rounded up all the other supplies Jane had mandated; my Boo Radley hole was stuffed full. We had maps. What's more, we had a plan. It was time.

Lydia had already approved an excursion for the three of us: a hike and then a picnic at the farthest edge of a neighboring ranch, in a grove of western paper birch where there was a "table" made of part of the trunk of some giant tree, laid lengthwise over two stones, with four more large stones for seats. It was a place Reverend Rick had led several of us to before. Lydia told Jane that her pot-smoking punishment had not been revoked, but that she was granting her a weekend reprieve to celebrate the completion of her finals and the progress she'd been making in her one-on-ones. "Whatever gets us out the door," Jane had whispered to me that morning on our way into Lifegate Christian. "It's not like the law of Lydia will affect me for much longer."

While waiting outside the Perkins ladies' room for Erin to be finished, I, completely on a whim, scanned through the directory that was hanging from a cable off the pay phone. I was looking for Mona but doing so without expecting to find anything, until I did. There was a Mona Harris listed as living on Willow Way. I thought she'd said something about living in the dorms, but who knew for sure? Maybe she'd moved. I ripped the page with her number from the phonebook. It didn't make very much noise, the paper itself tissue thin and that hallway also housing the entrance to the kitchen, so the wait staff kept bustling by with trays of starchy foods, with trays of dirty dishes and wadded-up napkins. Nobody noticed. I folded the page into a tiny rectangle and slipped it inside the waistband of my skirt.

When Erin came out of the bathroom, we were weird with each other. She held the door open for me but stared out into the restaurant, avoiding my face, and I just sort of nodded at her as I went in. We hadn't spoken about what had happened between us. Not one word from either of us. We hadn't spoken very much at all about anything the past couple of days. We'd both been busy studying, and I'd been working on my presentation; but our silence wasn't due to our schedules, it was an agreed-upon thing, the easier route to take.

Once in the bathroom I had to soap and rinse twice to get all the cheap black telephone-book ink off my fingers. I noticed that my hands were shaky as I did this, and I wasn't surprised. I'd been the electrified, all-buzzing-energy version of me the whole week.

On my way back to the table, again passing the pay phone, I thought of Reverend Rick, away on a Free from the Weight speaking engagement. I'd been thinking a lot about the phone call he would be getting sometime Saturday night, wherever he was, Cleveland or Atlanta or

Tallahassee. I pictured that moment in a bunch of different ways. Sometimes he was in front of a big group of dressed-up, smiling Exodus International fans in a church or rented meeting room. There he was in his fancy suit, the one he'd worn when he'd come to Gates of Praise and had spoken to our congregation, the suit that made him seem even younger than he was, not older, like a little boy playing dress-up. In that version he was interrupted as he talked in that genuine, Reverend Rick way about coming out of the darkness of sexual sin and into the light of Christ; a woman off to the side of the room would motion to him, or a man wearing shoes that *click*ed and *clack*ed would walk right over to him and whisper something behind his hand, or maybe pass a note that Rick would read quickly before making his apologies and explaining that there was an urgent phone call he needed to attend to. His conversation with Lydia, the police, whoever was on the other line, was watched by the church officials who had invited him to come and speak, by some of his fellow Exodus–sanctioned ex-gays, all of them wearing faces of worry, glancing at one another and then studying Rick's responses to whatever was being said, waiting to hear, from him, after he'd cradled the phone, the complete story of just what had gone wrong out at Promise.

I also imagined him alone in his hotel room when the call came. Sometimes it wasn't a hotel at all, but instead a seedy motel sandwiched between a truck stop and an all-night diner, something out of the crappy crime movies I'd seen, a place with drug dealers and prostitutes holed up in it, the requisite neon sign blinking in through the dirty curtains at his window, everything dingy, a water stain on the ceiling, rust around the fixtures in the bathroom, the carpet something you wouldn't want to walk on in bare feet. In this version the phone that rang was that creepy skin color that some phones are, not quite beige but not tan either, and it had a tinny, clangy ring that was too loud for the room, something he couldn't ignore. I knew that his staying in such a hotel room wasn't likely. This wasn't some shoestring operation. Free from the Weight had backers with deep pockets, but sometimes I put him there, in my mind, anyway.

Most frequently I pictured him in a nondescript hotel by the airport, one with a small lobby, a breakfast bar, free newspapers, and maybe a snack when you checked in. He'd have the TV on but the volume low, maybe tuned to something surprising, MTV or HBO, and there'd be an open bottle of water on the nightstand. Maybe he'd already be in his small white boxers and T-shirt when the phone, this time something black and more modern, with a red message light, would ring its quiet electronic ring, undemanding. He'd be ironing his shirt for the next day and he'd take his time, put it back on the hanger, before walking over to pick up the receiver, say his hello. He'd sit down on the edge of the bed as the facts were told to him: Jane Fonda, Adam Red Eagle, and Cameron Post had not returned to Promise from their hike in time for dinner duties. At a little after six, Lydia March and a neighboring rancher had taken a four-wheeler most of the way to the spot where the three were to have been picnicking. The rancher parked about a mile from their destination, the trail too steep and full of obstacles to carry them, so they walked. The disciples were not at the picnic area, and there were no signs of them. The police had been notified by seven thirty p.m. They called the forest service. They also called the families of the disciples, who had yet to be found.

I didn't imagine an ending to Rick's phone conversation,

nor did I even really fill in his responses to what he was being told. I did imagine his handsome face move from surprise to fear and worry, and that part, especially in the version where he was alone in his hotel room, made me feel sorry for him and what our escape would do to him, would mean for him. But not sorry enough not to do it.

• • •

On Friday I had my very last one-on-one with Lydia. It was held in the same cramped meeting room off of Rick's office where, in August, I had first been introduced to my personal iceberg. The stinky gardenia on the windowsill had been replaced by an unwieldy air fern. Otherwise the room was unchanged.

We'd ended my previous one-on-one talking about my *addiction to the voyeurism of sinful acts through my obsession with rented movies,* another *coping mechanism* I had developed to help me, unsuccessfully, *ignore the trauma of my parents' death and the guilt that I felt over it.* We picked up there. I tried to be the open book that I'd been for weeks, but I had this strange urge to tell Lydia about the Viking Erin and me, what we'd done, what Erin had done to me. I pushed that confession away and told Lydia what she wanted to know, stuff about all the sex I'd seen in R-rated movies, the way that I'd watched them again and again, losing myself to those images and sounds, one frame after another; the way that I'd educated myself about *perverse homosexual acts* all alone in the quiet of my bedroom. But the urge to share the Erin experience came back: *Tell her, tell her, tell her.* I knew that I couldn't say anything, that if I did, Lydia would never allow me to go hiking the next day, no fucking way, and then our escape would be postponed, for a long time, maybe so long that we'd never get all the pieces in place again. But knowing the consequences didn't stop my desire to say it. I wanted to sit there so calmly and say, "You know what—there's actually something that happened recently that I think I should mention. The Viking Erin, you know, my roommate, she woke me up from this awesome sex dream I was having about Bethany Kimbles-Erickson so that she could climb into my bed and finish the job. I tell you what: She knew what she was doing, that one. Very professional; perfect timing."

Of course I didn't. We kept on with the session as usual, but at some point—and I can't even tell you what line of questioning led to this, exactly—Lydia said, "As we go forward, you'll need to work harder to acknowledge and uncover the role your parents played in shaping your current sinful identity. You've made some progress in exploring the ways in which their death contributed to your confusion about appropriate and Godly gender and sexuality, but that's simply not enough. Your gender troubles began much earlier than that, at the hands of your parents, and focusing on your most recent sinful behaviors is only part of a complicated picture."

She wasn't finished, I could tell, but I said, "My choices are my own, not my parents'."

A small look of surprise registered on her face, but not much. "Yes, and I'm glad that you're acknowledging that," she said. "But the conditions under which you made those choices, the treatment and expectations given to you as a child under their care, significantly contributed to the reasons you now make the choices that you make." She paused, made a tepee with her hands atop the table, and said, "You had already started down this path while your parents were alive. You can't move forward without acknowledging that."

"I have acknowledged that," I said, making my own hand

tepee, doing it deliberately enough that she had to know I was mimicking her. "I kissed Irene Klauson the day *before* my parents' accident. I wanted to kiss her again the entire day *of* their accident, and I did, that night. You think I don't know the kinds of choices I was making before they died?" These were all things we'd spoken about before, but I'd never said them in quite this way, laying out the sequence of events that made me cringe with shame when I thought of them.

Lydia smiled at me—a real smile, not her disapproving smile, which was more a kind of grimace, I guess. But this was an actual smile, genuine, and then she said, "I think that you let your guilt over their deaths keep your memories of them swaddled in a kind of protective covering. You've so convinced yourself that God was punishing you for your sins with Irene that you're blind to any other assessment, and because of that your parents are no longer people to you; they're simply figures that were manipulated by God for his great plan to teach you a lesson." She paused here, made sure I was looking right at her all-angles face, into her eyes couched beneath those severe eyebrows. She waited until I was, and then she said, "You need to stop making yourself such an important figure, Cameron Post. You have sinned, you continue to sin, you have sin in your heart, just like each and every one of God's children; you are no better and no worse. Your parents did not die for your sins. They didn't need to: Jesus already did so. If you can't accept this and remember them for who they were, and not who you've made them to be, then you won't heal."

"I'm trying," I said.

"I know, but you'll have to try harder. It is now time to try harder." She looked at her watch. "We're done for the day," she said. "How do you feel?"

"I feel ready to move on," I said. That was an honest answer.

Lydia didn't ask for clarification. She just said, "Good. That's promising. I hope your actions convince me of that."

• • •

That night Adam, Jane, and I packed our lunch for our approved "hike" the next day. We didn't have much to say to each other, knowing what we did about our plans, what we were gonna try to pull off. Plus, we were in the kitchen, so anyone could wander in at any time. Steve did, in fact, twice, taking a bag of baby carrots the first time and then coming back for peanut butter.

"I was thinking maybe I'd come with you tomorrow," he said, dipping carrots and chewing thick chews around his words. "How far is it to the rock thing?"

"It's far," Jane said, completely cool, sliding the plastic grips on a sandwich bag. "It'll take all morning, and we're heading out early if you're coming."

I hoped that I looked as calm as she did but worried that my signature blush was creeping. Adam had his back to Steve but was making big, freak-out eyes at Jane and me.

"Yeah, I don't know," Steve said. "I heard Lydia might take some of us into Bozeman in the afternoon. Maybe. You think you'll be back in time for that?"

"No way," Adam said. "Not even close."

"I figured." Steve twisted the lid back on the peanut butter. "You'll go back again this summer anyway. Right?"

"Sure," Jane said. "Rick always takes people out there."

"I think I'll wait and go then," he said, and nabbed a handful of grapes off the bunch I was washing before walking out.

Nobody said anything until we were sure he was down the hallway.

"He could change his mind, easy as that," Adam said. "Show up outside ready to go."

"He won't," Jane said.

"He could," Adam said. "You don't know. And then we're fucked."

I shook my head and said, "I say if he does, we just don't tell him what's going on, just go with the plan. He doesn't know where the rock is. He won't know we're not going that way."

Adam rolled his eyes. "I think he might figure it out when we don't ever arrive at a table-shaped rock."

But Jane was grinning. "He will, but not until we've already covered lots of ground, and then we tell him what we're doing, and if he wants to head back, he'll have to do it alone, and we'll be gone in the opposite direction."

"It won't be that easy as we're standing there in the woods telling him 'Surprise! We're running away.'"

"I guess we find out if it happens," Jane said. "He's not gonna show, anyway."

"He could," Adam said.

Jane threw up her hands. "Anything *could* happen," she said. "He *could* show up. Lydia *could* decide that we're not allowed to go. You *could* break your leg on the way out the door."

"That wouldn't stop you," I said. And that made Adam laugh, Jane too.

"We made a good plan," she said. "Now we just have to go through with it."

After that we walked back to our rooms. Said good night. Tried to act normal. Erin was reading, so I pretended to read too. A couple of times I'd thought about leaving her a note,

but I had decided against it. None of us was leaving anything behind that explained what we'd done. Eventually Erin
turned out her light, so I turned out mine, too. I slept just
fine, actually. And it didn't take me that long to fall asleep,
either. I don't really know what that means.

• • •

Steve wasn't even in the dining hall when we ate breakfast
the next morning. We had our eggs and washed our dishes.
Grabbed our lunches and our backpacks. It was cool, but
sunny and bright and a good day for hiking. Each step in
the plan clicked forth, like winding film on a camera: *click,
click, click, click, click.* And then we were on the trail and on
our way.

CHAPTER TWENTY-ONE

Quake Lake is six miles long. It bends and curves around outcroppings of stone and forest, in some sections wide, blue, and full of waves; in others narrow and dark, always in shadow. We weren't following the main road, US 287, which wraps up and around parts of the lake before dipping into the trees and then out again to climb along slopes overlooking the water, fallible guardrail here and there, when those slopes get steep and the turns get narrow and sharp. However, we could see some of that road and rail as we made our way down through thick tree growth to the shore. We couldn't see the other side of the canyon very well; it was a ways off in the distance, across the water, but the reflective posts on the guardrail popped like flashbulbs every so often, depending on the angle from which we were situated and the glint of the sun.

"You think this is anywhere close to where it happened?" Jane asked from just behind my shoulder. She was out of breath. Her leg bind had been bothering her for the last couple of miles (we'd hiked fourteen thus far), but she trudged on, didn't complain much, and didn't let us stop very often to rest.

"I don't know," I said. "It seems right when we check it with the map. However far off we are, it's still closer than I've ever been before."

"But you've waited forever," Jane said. "It should be the right place."

"You wanna stop and check it again?" Adam asked from behind her.

"No—it's gonna be right," I said, to convince myself as much as the two of them.

We hiked on, the slope a steep decline in some places, the ground thick and slippery with pine needles. More than once I lost my footing and my feet surfed the needles until a rock or a fern or my hand on a tree trunk stopped the motion. Partly because of Jane's leg, and partly because of the terrain itself, we'd done much of the hike, once entering the canyon area, in wide switchbacks, choosing the routes of least resistance down to the lake, even when those routes were anything but direct. Now that we could finally see the water, I just wanted to get down to it as quickly as possible, which meant looking at the ground and choosing my footing rather than focusing on the lake itself.

But at some point Adam asked, "Are those trees actually in the water or is it an optical illusion?"

The three of us stopped and we all looked out toward the lake. There were these trees, mostly trunks, just a few thick branches left at the top of a couple of them, stuck out in the water, a tiny grove left behind from before the quake and flood.

"They're like the ghosts of trees," Jane said.

"They're skeleton trees," I said. "They're the remains of trees."

"It's eerie," Adam said.

Jane nodded and said, "It is that."

"There was a picture of something like them in one of the newspaper articles on my parents," I said. The shot I was thinking of was mostly of the broken guardrail, smashed through, bent and hanging over the lake, the metal looking almost wilted; but part of the lake was in the foreground of that shot, and there were strange stick trees there.

"Then this is the place," Jane said.

"I don't know," I said. "I guess there could be lots of trees like that since the entire lake used to be a forest."

"I think it's right," Adam said. "I think this is the place."

As deep in the canyon as we were, it was practically night, at least it felt that way. The dipping sun was only a suggestion of light from beyond those high walls, brightening the sky far above us but less and less of the ground around us. It was the kind of place where I might be tempted to mistake the breath of wind fluttering the trees for some cheesy scary movie ghost whisper that somehow wasn't cheesy at all.

The closer we got, the stranger those skeleton trees looked too—there, just past the center of that section of the lake, many of them twisted or bent, their wood bleached and weathered, but in all these years since the earthquake, since the water had come and come and settled around them, soaked their roots beyond their capacity to grow, they hadn't toppled. Still they rose up out of the water, like gnarled walking sticks left behind by a race of giants. Or worse, the bones of the giants themselves, picked over by even more gigantic giants.

"What's the name of the invisible giant?" I asked over my shoulder. We weren't far at all now, and I wanted to fill up the silence, to talk away my nervousness.

"The BFG?" Jane said. "I don't think he was invisible."

"No, I meant Adam," I said, and turned around to look at him. "Who was that Lakota giant—the one who was supposed to be like visible to man forever ago, but isn't now, and lives on a mountain surrounded by water?"

"Yata," Adam said. "Why, did you see him?" He pretended to scan the forest around us, feigning anxiousness.

I stumbled because I wasn't looking where I was going. I lurched forward, but Jane somehow got a grip on my backpack and held me up. We stopped again so that I could find my balance.

"And which one of us has a Barbie leg?" she asked, smiling.

"Thanks for using your catlike reflexes," I said, shifting my backpack to resettle it and unbunch the straps that she'd pulled on.

Adam asked again, "So why'd you wanna know about Yata?"

I nodded toward the lake. "Those trees make me think of walking sticks for giants," I said.

"Cool," Jane said, and then she took a Polaroid. I was actually glad that she'd brought her camera; it was somehow calming to see her with it, this thing she always had. We continued on.

"That actually sort of works," Adam said. "This could be Yata territory. Yata is way into ceremonies. That's kind of what you're doing here, right?"

"I don't know," I said. "Don't pile the additional pressure of a mystic giant on me."

"No pressure," he said.

The lake didn't offer much of a shoreline, at least not the section we had worked our way down to: just tumbled rocks and a thin rim of gray-white pebbles worn smooth right at the place where water met land. I stopped a few feet before it and stood still, silent. Jane and Adam pulled up beside me. They looked at me, looked away, looked back, maybe waiting for me to pull some kind of memento from my backpack, let them in on some important funeral-type ceremony they thought I had all planned out. I went on staring at the water; they went on staring at me.

"It's pretty, but it's—" Jane started without finishing.

"It's creepy, right?" I said.

"Sort of," she said. She took my hand. "It's just those trees, I think."

"It's more than the trees," Adam said. "There's all kinds of powerful energy here. It's unsettled or something."

"Like unfinished business," Jane said, squeezing her fingers.

I studied the skeleton trees, wondered at the strength and depth of their roots to have kept them upright in the lake for all these years. I felt like everyone was waiting on me, including me. "I don't know what I'm gonna do yet, okay?" I said. "Just give me a minute or two."

"We three now own a seemingly endless supply of minutes," Jane said. "Feel free to use them at will."

Adam raised his eyebrows but controlled his expression of surprise, I guess for my benefit. "Don't you think they're looking for us by now?" he asked her quietly.

Jane shook her head. "No. I really don't. But even if they are, they won't start here. They'll branch out from where we were supposed to be picnicking, and that's almost thirty miles of Gallatin National Forest from where we are now." She snapped a Polaroid and then sat down on a big, black hunk of silver-flecked rock to unstrap her leg.

Adam stooped over the ground, hunting for smooth stones, skipping stones, I could tell, the way he connoisseured what he plucked: flat rocks, most about palm size. His hands full, he drew back his arm so as to send one hopping along the smooth surface, and right as he should have released, he stopped, arm frozen there.

He looked at me. "Is it okay to skip this? I don't want to

trivialize the situation or whatever."

"No, it's fine," I told him, watching the rock in his hand, wondering if I should have said no—waiting, almost frightened, to hear the stone bounce off the surface of the lake.

So he drew his arm back again, and this time, after another moment hovering there, he dropped all the stones back onto the ground, a swift trickle of clicks and clacks.

"I'll just do it later," he said. "It doesn't seem like the time to be skipping rocks." He sat on the ground near Jane, both of them waiting for me to do what it was I'd come here to do, but trying not to act like that's what they were doing.

It was then that I decided I needed to go into the lake. I hadn't been sure before that moment. Anytime I might have thought about visiting this place, daydreamed about it, I'd only seen myself on the shoreline. And in those daydreams it was a hazy shoreline, a smoky-swirly-dream version in which the main thing was that I'd made the journey, and what I'd do upon arriving was somehow both obvious and not as important as the fact that I'd arrived. But now, as I let the lake splash against the toes of my sneakers while an audience of two somehow crowded me, even in all this empty wilderness, I knew that I needed to be in that water, deep within it.

"I'm going in," I said, and I shrugged off my backpack and dropped it near Jane, then unzipped my sweatshirt right after, flung it on the ground, worked my long-sleeved T-shirt up over my head and flung that too, just so that we'd all be sure that I meant my words, that there was no going back on them. I stood there in my bra and jeans, the air on my skin cold and good.

"It'll be freezing," Jane said, and then she rummaged through her backpack. "I did bring a towel, though, a precautionary measure." She pulled it out and handed it to me. "Are you putting on your suit?"

"I left them," I said. "I don't know why; I could have had room for both."

Not wanting to look conspicuous as we'd headed off on our hike, we'd each brought only one school-size backpack of belongings and supplies. We also thought that it would be better if, when our rooms were inspected, even if that wasn't right away, it seemed like everything was basically there. But who would have noticed that my swimsuits were missing? Or what if I'd just taken one? Just one. I'd considered them—they were both in the top right corner of my dresser drawer—while packing my bag on Friday, after my one-on-one, the Viking Erin off on evangelical duty and our room empty. I'd looked for a lingering moment at my old swim-team version and my red guard suit, and then I'd left them. It seemed a stupid, stupid decision now that I stood in front of Jane without them. They were light and squishable and I would surely want them again at some point: like right now. I got that churned-up-stomach feeling you get when you wonder, upon recognizing one stupid decision you've made about something important, if it's possibly only the first of many, many stupid decisions you've made about this impor-tant thing, and maybe is just the first clue that the whole thing will crack apart under the weight of all of those stupid decisions once they've piled up. "So stupid," I said.

Jane reached for my backpack. "You don't need one," she said, removing the candles she'd told me to gather. "Don't get hung up on it." She dug in her leg compartment for a lighter.

"Thank you guys for this," I said, the cold air now mak-ing my words come out shaky. "I mean for getting me here."

"We'll start a fire," Adam said. "For when you get out." For a moment he put his hand on my bare shoulder, and then he walked past me back into the forest to gather sticks. Jane set out our pilfered food supplies, both of them busy with their little jobs.

"I'm just gonna take off everything, I guess," I told Jane, stepping with one foot onto the heel of the other foot's sneaker to work it off, the exact way Ruth had repeatedly told me would *just ruin* my shoes.

Jane nodded toward my feet in my used-to-be-white-but-now-dingy cotton socks. I kept stripping, unbuttoning my jeans, pulling them down and stepping out of them, somehow freed from my usual self-consciousness by the weight of the task at hand.

She sparked the lighter, lit a candle. "Makes sense, you'd just have to dry your underwear when you got out anyway, and that might take a while. You don't want to chafe." She twisted and pushed the candle into the rocky ground until it stayed put, and then lit the next. "*Chafe* is such a fantastic word, though."

"Can I have one of those?" I asked, tilting my head toward the candles, watching the orange flames bounce and sway but stay lit. They reminded me of this scene in one of the *Karate Kid* movies, the second one maybe, when Mr. Miagi takes Daniel-san to his homeland of Okinawa, and the villagers perform this sacred ceremony where they send lanterns out to drift along the water of a fishing harbor, their tiny, bobbing lights reflected in the surface: that scene still beautiful even with a Peter Cetera song playing in the background.

"Are you taking it in with you? Because I have a pen-light somewhere if you'd rather," she said, searching the front pocket of her backpack.

"No, I want the candle," I said. "Even though it'll no doubt go out."

"Probably," she said, but she lit the third candle, held it out to me anyway.

I stepped out of my underwear before taking it from her, the length of my body prickling from the cold even as my fingers clenched the smooth wax. I pulled the candle in to me, held it up in front of my chest, a choir girl on Christmas Eve. The tiny flame provided one small point of warmth, and I wanted it right next to my skin.

Jane didn't pretend not to look at me, naked and pale in the dark of that canyon, shivering, my face uplit and flickering with the flame of my candle, as afraid of messing things up as I'd ever been in my life. I loved her for that. She met my eyes and said, "You can do this. We'll be here waiting for you."

"What is it that I'm doing, again?"

"You know that already," she said. "You just think that you don't, but you do. It's what you came all this way for."

I nodded but wasn't as confident in what I knew as Jane seemed to be.

I did, however, know better than to feel the cold water with only my toes, then my feet, and to try to slowly, slowly adjust, inch by inch. There wouldn't be any adjusting to this lake on this night: there would be, at best, tolerating it. I stepped in, one foot after another, and just kept walking, the lake floor rocky in some places, gooey and thick in others. It was like walking on coals, maybe, if the coals and ash grew thicker and thicker with each step, burning with each stride a bit farther up your leg. By ten long steps out the water was at my hipbones, the cold sucking all the breath from my body. I concentrated on my candle flame, counted to three as I inhaled, and again to three as I blew out. And again. And again. My blood pounded in my ears, and something like an ice-cream headache pulsed along my temples. If I wanted to make it to that skeleton forest, I was going to have to swim.

I held the candle in my right hand, up and out from my body, away from the surface. I bent at the knees and let myself ease onto my back, so as not to jostle and splash the water any more than necessary. I let the burning water cradle me until I was all the way in a back float, face up to the sky, feet facing the bank where Jane and Adam were starting the fire, the candle still lit, above me in my hand. The wax poured along my thumb and wrist as I drew it back to me. It hardened almost instantly. I planted the candle's base just above my belly button and held it there with both hands clenched around it as if it was something solid, something grounded: a sail mast, a flagpole. My heartbeat drummed in my stomach, and the candle shifted with my shivering, my strained breathing, but it flickered on.

My body wanted to be tense, that's how it planned to keep me alive, by letting me know how serious the cold of this water was, how I needed to get out of it, by refusing to let me get used to it. The muscles in my neck strained like cables hauling something heavy, a piano or a tractor. I couldn't unclench my jaw. My feet, out of the water except for the heels, were curled and stretched in strange positions, like the feet of really old people I'd seen when caroling with Firepower at the nursing home. I concentrated on my candle flame and tried to let those muscles ease, to let the water control me, to own me in this moment.

Once I got my breathing under control, I dropped my right hand from the candle and sculled the water, propelling myself forward, gnarled feet toward the gnarled trees and the arching cliffside and road my parents had toppled from behind those trees. It probably took no more than a minute and a half to reach the little grove, but my arm and shoulder were aching by then. I regripped the candle base with both hands and again concentrated on my breathing. From somewhere beyond the canyon, from the knuckles of the mountains looming in the distance, wind came, and I lifted my neck to watch it tumble its ways through the pines and down the slopes, out across the water to me. The wind made the skeleton trees creak and crack, those sounds harsh. The wind also blew out my candle, or it seemed to: it went out completely, the black wick naked, but then it was clothed in flame again. And it stayed lit.

My headache was making everything hurt, even my teeth. I opened my eyes and then shifted my body, dropped my hips, did all the things necessary to ruin a back float, and let first my legs, then my trunk, then my face, slip just beneath the surface, a thin sheet of water on top of my skin, all except for my hands, clenched around the candle, those remained above. I could still hear the crack of the trees but I liked the layer of padding that the water glued over the noises. I made myself remember my parents, first my mom, then my dad, not together but separate, their faces, their bodies, the way they walked into a room, held the newspaper, stirred their coffee. It was hard to do, but I did it the best I could, lifting my head and pointing my lips to suck air when I needed to, before slipping just below again, back to my parents. My mother puzzling over the placement of something at the museum. My father using the blue hankie he kept in his back pocket to wipe his forehead. My mother teaching me how to hold a paring knife to cut vegetables.

My father driving the way he always did, with just one hand sort of lolled on the steering wheel.

I felt like I was fucking up this whole thing, this thing that I'd waited to do, and now here I was and I didn't know what to do, or how to do it, or how to feel. None of my standbys would work: no quoting the movies, no making a joke. It had to be now. I wanted it to be. I lifted my head back out of the water.

"Mom and Dad," I said, my voice sounding strange, like it belonged to the lake and not to me. Or maybe it was what I was saying with it. I hadn't said Mom and Dad like that, as a form of address, in forever. It was somehow embarrassing to be talking to them, even all alone, with no one to hear but them, but I decided that embarrassment was okay, it was maybe even right, so I kept on. "I can remember lots of stupid stuff I watched in movies and whatever, but not things about the two of you that I think I should remember."

I thought for a little while before I spoke again. "I used to want to come here to tell you how sorry I was." I took a breath in and then I just said it. "Not for kissing Irene, but for being relieved that you weren't gonna find out, that I wasn't going to be found out, because you were dead. That doesn't make any sense, I know, because you know everything when you're dead anyway, right? But even still."

On the side of one of the mountains there were suddenly four perfect rectangles of yellow: windows in a cabin I hadn't even distinguished from the dark of the trees until a light switch was flicked. I imagined people at those windows, looking out, down the mountainside to the lake, wondering about my single candle—or would it seem like there were two of them, with the flame's reflection on the lake viewed at so great a distance? For some reason I really wanted there to be people at those windows.

I kept on with what I was saying. "I don't think that I made your accident happen; I don't anymore, so I didn't come here for that. What I guess I wish for now is that I had figured out that you were people and not just my parents before you died. Like figured it out for real, and not like Lydia said, so I could blame you for the way I am. But even though I know that I would have wanted to know you as those people, I didn't, and I'm not sure you knew me either, not beyond me being your daughter, I mean. Maybe while you were alive I hadn't even become me yet. Maybe I still haven't become me. I don't know how you tell for sure when you finally have." I tilted the candle just so and let all the melted wax pooled around the wick spill free and cascade down my knuckles, the trail at first translucent, then quickly hardening into a river of white on top of my skin. Lots of wax cascaded all the way down my hand, off the edge, and into the lake, and once there became magical, tiny floating polka dots, like wax versions of the droppings of a paper punch.

I watched one of the dots float beyond the glow of my candle, and then I kept talking. "I don't know if you would have sent me to Promise, or to a place like it, or if you'd have wanted to even if you didn't actually do it. But you weren't around to and Ruth was, and I can't believe her when she says that it's what you'd have wanted for me. Even if it's true, I don't think it's something I have to spend my life believing. Does that make sense? Like that it might have been true, if you'd known me now, but because you didn't get the chance, I can just erase whatever might have been true about it? I hope that makes some sort of sense. The thing is, pretty much everything that's happened since you died has convinced me that I was lucky to have had you as my parents, even for only twelve years, and even if I didn't really know it when you were alive. And I guess I just wanted to come here and say that I know it now, and I loved you, even though all of that probably sounds a little late in the coming, or not enough or whatever. But that's something I've been able to figure out for sure." I let myself spin some there in the water, circles, not fast or slow, but movement, one hand sculling me around. "I don't know what will happen after I reach the shore," I said. "Maybe you do—I don't know how it works from where you are, what you can see. I like to think that you can see it all, and that whatever's waiting won't manage to trip me up. At least not too much." I stopped talking. I had nothing left to say, nothing left I could put words to. But I kept spinning. I'd finally come to this place to which it seemed like everything in my life thus far had somehow been tied, somehow, even things that shouldn't have been, and I wanted to soak in it. So I did. I kept spinning until I was dizzy. Probably I was dizzy from more than just that. I was frozen. Then I was done.

I didn't know how to end, to feel like I was finished, so I did the one big thing I could think to do, the one movie trick, and I blew out the candle. And even though it was so sort of, I don't know, sort of predictable, I guess, it still felt good and it felt like this act of closure or something. And then I swam toward the shore. I swam like I didn't even think my body would let me swim, hard and fast, my muscles tight and unwilling, and I made them do it anyway. I kept the candle in my right hand. It thunked into the water with each downward pull, but I wasn't letting go of it and I wasn't slowing down. I swam as close to the shore as I could before my knees, scraping lake bottom, forced me to stop.

Adam sloshed into the water, soaking his shoes before grabbing me by the elbow, pulling me up fast and perfect as if he'd done it so many times before. Jane came around from behind him, her arms stretched wide with the bright striped beach towel strung between. She wrapped it around me. Then, one on either side, they walked me to the shore, which was black and endless. But there was a fire waiting. And there was a little meal laid out on a blanket. And there was a whole world beyond that shoreline, beyond the forest, beyond the knuckle mountains, beyond, beyond, beyond, not beneath the surface at all, but beyond and waiting.

ACKNOWLEDGMENTS

These are unforgiveably long: please forgive me. Somehow, my phenomenal agent (before she was actually my agent), Jessica Regel, came to believe in this book while I drove her from Lincoln to Omaha, the day muggy and stifling, the air-conditioning whirring without much effect, and me doing a very ham-fisted job of summarizing Cameron Post's world to her. Though we very nearly ran out of gas, and I managed to get us a little lost on a back road trying to find some, Jessica's encouragement started during that short trip, and her guidance and dedication to the book have immeasurably helped me, and it, ever since. I am likewise indebted to my editor, Alessandra Balzer, for her great enthusiasm and kindness, and for not only knowing, at every stage, what's best for this novel, but for helping me to see why. Thanks, also, to the fantastic Sara Sargent—in fact, there is a whole car on my love train reserved for the entire team at Balzer & Bray.

I am endlessly grateful to the teachers and mentors who have offered me their insight, patience, and time: Eric Brogger, Julia Markus, and Paul Zimmerman at Hofstra University—thanks, Paul, for your early encouragement, your continued support all these years later, and your wit along the way. Thanks also to Gina Crance Gutmann, who made a small-town Montanan feel instantly welcome in the wilds of Long Island—without your support I'd never have survived freshman year, RA training, or poison oak. Though she wasn't yet named, I developed Cameron's voice during Danzy Senna's fiction workshop at the University of Montana MFA program, and it was Danzy who first encouraged me to continue with the piece, originally written as a short story. In Missoula I was also privileged to study with Jill Bergman (all those "scribbling women"); Judy Blunt; Casey Charles; Deirdre McNamer; Brady Udall, who was a fantastic adviser; and Debra Magpie Earling, who has always been so generous to me. Most recently, at the PhD in Creative Writing Program at the University of Nebraska—Lincoln, I was honored to work with and learn from Amelia M. L. Montes; Gwendolyn Foster; Jonis Agee; Barbara DiBernard, who taught me so much about teaching and who is, without question, one of the all-around coolest people I have ever known; Judith Slater, who rooted for this novel early on and who is endlessly calm and wise; Gerald Shapiro, who has near-perfect comic timing, knows a thing or two about falafel, and made me want to come to UNL in the first place; and the effortlessly brilliant Timothy Schaffert, who always has the best answers to even my stupidest questions (of which there have been many), and whose catalog of 1970s pop-culture references never ceases to delight me.

I am so grateful to my talented and funny friends, many of them writers, all of them inspiring: Rose Bunch, who once put shiny dinosaur stickers on one of my story drafts, which is maybe the best positive feedback ever; Kelly Grey Carlisle, who let me use the time pre and post our swims to go on and on about the book and who is a phenomenal giver of pep talks; Carrie Shipers, who read and edited some of the earliest drafts and who said such smart things, asked such smart questions, and remembered the kinds of details, weeks and months later, that made me proud to have her as a reader; Mike Kelly, who is my nineties-music kindred spirit and who read the first half of the book when that's all I had finished and asked where the rest of it was already; Adam Parkening, who tells me everything I need to know about films I'll probably never watch; Rebecca Rotert, who is my favorite reason to visit Omaha and who needs to finish her own novel already (ahem); Marcus Tegtmeier, artist and website designer extraordinaire; and Ben Chevrette, who is absurdly stylish and charming, who was one of the two best things to happen to me in college, and who will always, always be my favorite gay.

Love and thanks to my family, the Danforths, the Loendorfs, the Finnemans, and the Edsells. Thanks especially to my brother, William, and sister, Rachel: that *Thriller*-related torture experiment of yours probably ultimately did me more good than harm. (Probably, though it's still too early to say for certain.) I am also deeply grateful to my parents, for raising me to be curious about the world and everything in it and for their love and support as I've made my way.

Finally, and most of all, my love and thanks to Erica: for reasons too many to list. I know you tell people that you had nothing to do with the writing of this novel, and while that might technically be true, you had *absolutely everything* to do with my being able to write it at all.

• • •

In memory of Catherine Havilland Anne Elizabeth Mary Victoria Bailey Woods, who not only had the best and longest name of any friend I've ever had, but who was also the truest friend, the most honest friend, and the one with the greatest imagination.